THE
BLAZING
AIR

Author of

THE GINGER TREE

THE BLAZING AIR

Oswald Wynd

TICKNOR & FIELDS
New Haven and
New York
1981

Copyright © 1981 by Oswald Wynd

All rights reserved. No part of this work may be reproduced or transmitted in any form or by any means, electronic or mechanical, including photocopying and recording, or by any information storage or retrieval system, except as may be expressly permitted by the 1976 Copyright Act or in writing by the publisher. Requests for permission should be addressed in writing to Ticknor & Fields, 383 Orange Street, New Haven, Connecticut 06511.

Designed by Charlotte Staub

Library of Congress Cataloging in Publication Data

Wynd, Oswald, 1913-
   The blazing air.

   "A Joan Kahn book."
   1. World War, 1939-1945 — Fiction. I. Title.
PR6073.Y65B59   823'.914   81-5671
ISBN 0-89919-047-2   AACR2

Printed in the United States of America
P 10 9 8 7 6 5 4 3 2 1

For
EUGENE C. POMMEROY, JR.
*the only American citizen ever to be
commissioned into the British Army
of India, who saw much of what
happens early on in this story,
but who didn't live to see
what came after.*

Later, victims of Time and Loss,
We will return and gaze there—

And marvel at such heights
Conquered, such blazing air.

—from "Marriage a Mountain Ridge,"
Stewart Conn

PART ONE
ONE

Fay

ONE

There were sometimes snakes on Ruth's lawns at night, out from the pushed-back jungle edging the estate to the short grass still holding the sun's warmth. Fay, Ruth's daughter-in-law, had once seen a python curled ahead of her, glistening in moonlight, thigh thick, but somehow not really sinister, somnolent from just having fed. She had taken a wide detour, watching for the lifting of the flat, broad head, but if it saw her it issued no challenge. She had been frightened, but not with that blood-pumping fear that would once have hit her, as though part of ceasing to be an alien in this place was a deliberate acceptance of the idea that you were only sharing it.

Walking up to the Estate House after dark was always a calculated risk: Sungei Dema black panther country, some of the big cats bold, attacking man without apparent reason, perhaps wanting a diet change from village dog. Fay, scented with mosquito repellent, was haloed by insect whining, but not under actual attack; the heat lay like a shawl over her shoulders and down bare arms. There was no moon and she used a torch sometimes, though starshine gave the sky a burnished glow, making enough light to give shape to a big area of hibiscus, placed like an outpost to guard the intimate gardens immediately around the house.

The piano concerto coming from the verandah was as good as an announcement that Ruth's husband wasn't yet back from the mine. Ruth hadn't been able to tug Big John's feeling for music past his favourites, "Tea for Two" and "Tiptoe through the Tulips," which meant that Mozart never had a look-in when he was home.

"Come on up, honey," Ruth called from a lampless cave. "I'm over to the left of the steps. Mind those ferns. The lights are off to keep us relatively bug free for our local god's visit. When we hear the car, on go the illuminations."

Fay groped her way to a chair.

"Where are the men?"

"I guess still at the mine office. Probably now drinking. I fixed you a highball. It's right there by the Victrola."

When the record ended Fay asked:

"Did you have the Army for lunch as well?"

"Not really. It seems it's immoral for soldiers on duty to sit down at a table in the middle of the day. I gave them chicken sandwiches out here and stayed in the living room while they fought the war in Europe with John."

"This afternoon they've been fighting the war in Sungei Dema?"

"Something like that," Ruth said. "On paper. After visiting the defensive strong points we haven't got. Is your drink all right?"

"Lovely. Ruth, why did John let Hamish just go off that way?"

"What do you mean by 'that way'?"

"Well, so suddenly. And into the Army. At his age!"

"The war's beginning to suck up the middle-aged like a vacuum cleaner," Ruth said.

"Not in Malaya. And surely Hamish is vital to the mine? As our only real engineer?"

"I might have argued that, but John didn't try to. Hamish wanted to go, and that was it."

"But can you see him in these special operations, whatever they are?" Ruth asked.

"No. But then I can't see anyone I know in uniform. The Brigadier you'll be meeting soon was born wearing his, which is different. I couldn't see *him* in anything else. Why are you worried about Hamish?"

It was a moment before Fay answered.

"I don't know. I suppose that he could have a heart attack leaping around in a hot jungle wearing full kit."

Ruth laughed. "I never suspected you were fond of him,

Fay. And Hamish won't have a heart attack. He's used to climbing huge hardwoods looking for his orchids. He's the kind of man who lets leeches stay on his legs until they fall off gorged. I think he'll love Special Operations. And it could be a natural break from Lali."

Fay was surprised. "He wants that?"

"Well, she's been with him for at least a year and a half longer than any of the others. It makes Hamish restive when his women start feeling too secure."

Fay lit a cigarette. The lighter's flame showed Ruth looking small in a high-backed chair. Her blonde hair was in the style she wore most often, drawn back to a bun. Four babies had left her abdomen stretch-scarred, but it was still flat. If she carried five pounds more than she had twenty years ago, you wouldn't notice it.

"Hamish came up to give his stamp collection to Angus," Fay said. "He must have known then he was leaving. He didn't say anything about it. Just told me the Japs aren't going to attack."

"Amen to that. Has Roy called you in the last day or two?"

"This morning. He said he was ringing you right after."

"He didn't. He can never think of anything to say to me. We haven't shared an experience since he was six. If there's any news that isn't personal, would you mind passing it on?"

Fay smiled into the dark. "There was nothing personal. He told me that the jungle training they were doing was pretty silly since most of it was wading through mangrove swamp and the Japs don't like getting their feet wet."

The noise Ruth made wasn't quite a laugh. "Would you believe it? I suppose you could say my son has a logical mind. An invading army won't come through mangrove because they don't like getting their feet wet. Fay, I hope when you're older you won't have my problem. Which is feeling responsible for your adult offspring. I look at any one of ours and the thought comes that John and I really deserved something quite different. I said this to him once and he said, 'Hell, don't blame me, blame my Portuguese ancestress or that slave-running New England sea captain in your crowd.' I guess he has something there. Can you hear a car engine?"

"Yes."

"On with the lights!" Wicker creaked as Ruth got up. "The Brigade Major has that kind of pink skin you only find in Englishmen. Specially produced to be martyred to a tropical climate. You can have him while I have the Brigadier saying, 'What, what?' at me. It sounds like machine-gun practice."

The living room was huge, but made no bid for dignity, merely the result of partitions moved back as new additions were added to the bungalow. It was furnished with years of family accretions, including a memorial to the Portuguese ancestress, Josephina, that was vast and dark and carved, its original function hard to imagine, now converted to an outsize drinks cabinet. Ruth had contrived to give coherence to a scatter of chairs and sofas — some rattan, some wood with cushions — by two devices: the first, half a dozen table lamps made from big vases of dubious Chinese porcelain, and silk shaded; then, in the centre of the room, an octagonal teak table eight feet across with carved elephant legs. On this there was always a platter of fruit, magazines, the *Straits Times* of yesterday or the day before, depending on postal deliveries, at least three books Ruth was reading, and usually a frame holding a half-completed tapestry chair cover, one of a set of six being worked for daughter Anne. In the nearest thing to a corner the room had, and with a lamp of its own, was Ruth's desk and just along from it, a tallboy imported from Boston, now a battleground in a war against boring insects, but with its top still relatively intact. On this was the family altar, with photographs of all the contemporary Gourlays, Fay and Roy and each of the children in their own frames, a special honour. Bruce, the second son, who had turned his back on the mine and Malaya to become a stockbroker in London, had been made to share one frame with his wife. Their picture had been taken on the steps of Caxton Hall Registry Office after what Ruth called their Godless marriage and just before Bruce went into the Army. There was another wedding photo, this time

decently outside an English village church with the wind
blowing the bride's veil, of eldest daughter Anne Gourlay
and Bruce's friend she had met on what had been intended
as a three-month trip to the old country. Mary Jane, who
was in Melbourne studying economics, had tried to make a
Gourlay face look intellectual by the addition of horn-
rimmed glasses, but she had failed. Next to the tallboy a
bookcase featured Ruth's taste in history and biography,
her books bullied by Big John's standing order in Singapore
for every new Edgar Wallace published, plus his complete
collection of all that had been written about Dr. Fu Manchu.

Out in the hall Ruth was putting on more lights. Whenever there was the slightest excuse for it there was a sense of
occasion at Estate House, this whipped up as a counter to
the basic isolation of their lives. Tonight, for soldiers back
from a defence survey, there would be something like pomp:
Ruth wearing a long green dress, which she claimed kept
the mosquitoes from her legs; and on the dining table the
silver candelabra Big John said his grandfather must have
looted from somewhere. Already the aged Lister engine providing the illumination was thumping away in a back
courtyard, every now and then missing a beat like a diseased
heart.

Fay stood at the elephant table turning over the pages of
a magazine from the States that ignored the European war
with high-colour illustrations of lush living. She was envying
the Americans their total security from all external threats
when Ruth came back.

"What do you bet there's no ice?" she said, opening Josephina's cupboard. "Yes, no ice. You know, I wish to hell I
wasn't so slack."

"About Lim, you mean?"

"About everything. I'm not one of those women who run
their houses with a firm hand."

"You run this place. *And* the village."

"But not well. I'm not tidy. Here or down there. At the
clinic I ought to be giving the Tamil dresser firm guidance
on Western hygiene. And do I? Just look at this room. It
could be a hotel lounge after an Elks convention."

The military vehicle had brakes that squealed. Fay sensed Ruth's indecision about whether or not to go out into the hall to greet her guests; then, remembering that the men would be sweaty, needing clean shirts, Ruth only moved to put herself out of vision. There was the sound in the house of leather clattering on teak floors, then Big John's voice, surprisingly modulated as though, in spite of a firm intention not to let it happen, he had been impressed by the visitors.

"Lim will show you the way, Brigadier. And there's no hurry. I'll send you a dressing whisky."

"Civilized idea. Got my valise there, Archie?"

"Yes, sir."

"See you in fifteen minutes then, Gourlay."

Fay was sure it would be exactly fifteen minutes. It was. Brigadier Winton-MacGillivray appeared under the open arch to the hall with the Brigade Major just slightly behind one shoulder. Both were wearing sharply creased khaki trousers and starched bush shirts, the Brigadier with the extra of red tabs.

"Ah, Mrs. Gourlay. We meet again. What a splendid house this is. I like those dipper baths."

Fay was introduced. The Brigadier took her hand and held it, rank and touches of white at the temples giving him this privilege. He said it was quite marvellous to have feminine company again, that they got so tired of all male faces in the Mess. Especially at breakfast. He then asked where Fay came from and she said a village called Fleckney, south of Leicester.

"I know it! My wife and I have friends at Market Harborough. Quite near. We live in Dorset."

"With divided loyalties, I hope?" she suggested.

He stared at her. His face seemed to lack something, as though it needed finishing off, perhaps by a monocle he had abandoned because monocles had no place in modern warfare. Then he took her point.

"Oh, I *see!* The Scotch thing, the MacGillivray bit? Warrior tribesmen, what? Actually, I'm afraid we betrayed national heritage. Made an alliance with the English. Kitchen towels. The Wintons made millions. Still do. Most lucrative. Grandfather's doing. Moved us south. I'm grateful. Always loathed porridge. Morrison here's straight from the Highlands. Poor as a church mouse. Terrible handicap in the Army, what? It's a miracle you've got on as well as you have, eh, Archie?"

"Yes, sir."

Big John made entrances or, when he wasn't doing that, noised off. His absences left Estate House in the grip of an indefinable melancholy, as though the place resented not being properly used. Fay couldn't remember her father-in-law's ever having just appeared in the arch to the hall without a fanfare of his footfalls on creaking boards announcing his approach. But he was there now, materialized, looking a bit like an outsize ghost who has suddenly been deprived of a chain to clank. Even Ruth didn't seem to see him.

"Now that you've made your inspection, Brigadier," Ruth said, "are we defensible at Sungei Dema?"

"My dear Mrs. Gourlay, that's a leading question. We're trained not to answer them."

"By which you mean you can't do anything for us?"

"I didn't say that."

Big John said, "They're sending us a company. If anything happens."

Everyone turned to look at him except Fay, who was already doing it.

"Ah, Gourlay, you've showed up just in time to save me from your wife's interrogation."

"Could a company defend Sungei Dema?" Ruth asked.

"It could try. Which is what we'll all be doing if the balloon goes up. Singapore chooses to call my command a brigade. A brigade has three battalions. I have two. With them I have to defend eighty miles of coastline, most of it beaches. Quite a proposition, what? You could say I'm thinly spread. Which really doesn't answer your question."

"Yes, I think it does."

Big John had moved to Josephina's cabinet and was standing at it with his back turned, pouring the drinks he thought everyone ought to want. The Brigade Major detached him-

self from his commander to walk around and offer Fay a
light for her cigarette. He was perhaps in his middle thirties,
the untannable pink skin featuring white eyelashes and eye-
brows.

"Is that your house halfway down the hill, Mrs. Gourlay?
With the swimming pool?"

"Yes."

"Splendid-looking place."

"We have our doubts about it. I wish now we'd built in
wood. But the fashion then was poured concrete, so we let
them pour it. After which the architect painted it all pink.
My husband let him do what he wanted. I was too new to
the country to protest."

After a pause Morrison made an announcement. "Sungei
Dema is most attractive. I've never seen a mine that had
done so little damage to its surroundings."

"You must tell Ruth that. She's the landscape artist."

There was another pause. They probably ran a course
during the final year at Sandhurst on how to talk to odd
females at official parties, but the Major needed to be sent
on a refresher. Big John brought over two glasses, whisky
and water with no ice, setting these down and then going
back to stand with Ruth and the Brigadier on the other
side of the vast table. Morrison handed up Fay's glass.

"Did you have any difficulty in adjusting when you first
came out here, Mrs. Gourlay?"

"Yes, I did."

"Oh? In what way?"

It was a tidy, safe lead; he had to be encouraged to stay
with it.

"I was frightened a lot of the time. Especially after dark."

"Really? Why?"

"Well, at home you just pull the curtains and that's the
night kept out. Here there aren't any curtains to pull and
the night keeps coming in at you, with sounds. And things
like that big moth flying over your Brigadier's head."

A smile improved the man.

"I think I understand. Yes. You're exposed. Isn't that it?
I've felt it, too."

A Brigade Major really had no right to share a woman's fears.

"You like it now?" he asked.

"Yes. I sometimes wonder if I could live anywhere else."

"Not even Britain?"

"Perhaps especially not Britain."

He frowned.

"Dinner," Ruth said.

There was no war talk while they ate, and under that veto, enforced by the hostess, came any mention of the Japs. Ruth expected too much of her cook, and each course was a comment on this, not a total failure, but unmemorable. There were chips of ice through the ice pudding, which was probably why none had been available to put in the drinks. Throughout, Morrison remained a determined conversationalist, nearly all of this directed towards Fay, his assigned task for the evening. She admitted to a total disinterest in mountaineering, but it was his great enthusiasm and he ignored the silence that was her comment on what he felt about the lower slopes of the Himalayas. Under a verbal overlay of pitons and ice axes, Fay tried to listen to the Brigadier, who was being interesting about Army careerism during the twenty-year lull between the two wars.

"Mine wasn't a cavalry regiment. Tradition you rode with the local hunt whenever possible, what? Meant you had a real chance of seeing the chap senior to you take a fence wrong and break his neck. In my lot you could stay a captain until your hair went grey. Especially with a damn socialist government cutting us back right and left, what? Not that the Tories did much better when they got in. I was never a Stanley Baldwin man, were you, Gourlay?"

Ruth waited for John's reaction, but when this didn't come she said, "My husband's politics have always been determined by the price of tin," and added, "Has this war really pushed you fast up the ladder, Brigadier?"

Fay expected a half minute's silence during which allowances were made for the fact that their hostess was American, but the Brigadier's answer came at once.

"Absolutely! Jumped up from Major to half Colonel,

then full Colonel with an amputated brigade. As you see me now. New posting's in India. Get a division. Take over in a couple months as Major General. Wife's in Darjeeling. Soon be putting her knees under the best tables. All this without my ever hearing a shot fired in anger, what? Same goes for Morrison here. They nearly sent him to the fighting in Ethiopia, but thought better of it at the last moment. Gave him to me instead."

Big John was usually a vigorous host, believing that to keep a party going you needed noise, and willing to give a firm lead in this, which pointed up his quietness now. Lim, the houseboy, dropped what must have been at least three plates on the cement floor of the pantry.

Ruth said, "Now you see why we have this horrible dinner service. Every time we're in Kuala Lumpur I can get replacements. My Aunt in Boston wanted to give us imported English Crown Derby as a wedding present, but John said better not. I hadn't been here two weeks before I understood why."

Lim came in carrying the coffee tray. If he was in any way troubled by what had just happened, his long, solemn face gave no hint of it. John got up to fetch a decanter from the sideboard and start the port circulating. When it reached the Major, he was generous to himself, soon inspired to launch out on a new topic: his two weeks on a houseboat up at Sprinagar, a holiday on which he hinted he had been quite a naughty boy with one of the flower-boat girls. Fay saw the Brigadier looking at Morrison as though he was considering returning him to base H.Q.

The phone rang. Ruth went out into the hall without excusing herself. In seconds she was back at the dining room arch.

"It's for you, Brigadier."

A chair scraped.

"Sorry about this. Had to leave a number. Probably some nonsense."

The Brigadier's boots were noisy.

"Nopi One here. Eh? What's that? Why the bloody hell aren't you using our code on the phone? All right! Give me the message!"

"More coffee?" Ruth asked.

No one wanted any. Big John stared at the table as though all he had heard was the Brigadier's voice.

"Now give me that report again. Take it slowly. Yes. I've got that." A long pause. "I see. I'll be coming down at once. Codes to be used for all contacts. Got that?"

The Brigadier appeared under the arch. John turned his head, then stood.

"I could ask you to come out with me, Gourlay, for a word in private. To spare the ladies, what? But that would be damn silly. I've had a signal from Singapore. Our Hudsons and Catalinas have been shadowing a Jap fleet moving along the southern coast of Indochina. Cruisers and merchant ships. The ships almost certainly troop carriers. Direction seemed towards Siam. Looked like an invasion attack on Bangkok. Now the fleet's turned south. Heading either for Singora or northern Malaya. Perhaps both. We're on war alert."

Fay felt that this moment had been in her mind for a long time, held there ready for issue. There was no surprise, just an awareness that all the flimsy fictions used as an antidote to the inevitable had been ripped away. A cold calm lasted for seconds, then was followed by a surge of hysteria she recognized as idiocy even as it hit her. God shouldn't have let this happen! He could have kept the Japanese from doing this if He had wanted to! She saw Ruth's hand crumpling a napkin.

TWO

This is how people survive wars, Fay thought, by carrying on with routine. Until it starts happening to you directly, it isn't happening. In the bathrooms the taps still run; you check the kitchen in the morning to see that cook continues to steep the salad vegetables in permanganate solution. The dog needs walking. The sun shines. We heard the bombing of Kuantan airfield yesterday, the sound loud enough but no louder than thunder often is. There were three dead and an unknown number wounded, but they were nameless, almost as remote and unreal as the casualties in North Africa.

We can't stretch ourselves to take on a duty for the world, and those who pretend to are liars to themselves. All that happens is that some have larger areas of personal involvement than others. My area has scarcely been more than a small patch. It's almost as though I stand where I have been placed, unable from a kind of lethargy ever really to move myself. I care for what I cannot escape from because it is all around me — these hills, the long vistas from our height here, the clanking cars to the mine and, perhaps most, the jungle, which frightened me so much at first. I'm still afraid of it, as one fears the sea for what could come from it, but having it near becomes an addiction, like living at the ocean's edge.

The syrup of figs for Liza's constipation has worked too well. She says her behind hurts. She didn't even want to go in the pool. I wonder about those lead and opium pills Roy uses to stopper himself up sometimes, but I'm sure they're too strong for a child. Liza spat out the minced hard-boiled egg.

I can't get away from the feeling that Angus's lessons are somehow irrelevant. It's as though what I am trying to teach him from set books and set questions has no real usefulness for what he may now have to face. At his age, even in a war, we ought to be able to contrive something like a norm for him. He would be perfectly safe with Mary Jane in Australia if we decide to send him there, so there is no point in this shapeless worry. Why don't I have it over Liza? For I don't.

The phone shrieked. Its demands for attention had seemed to grow louder and harsher recently. Chow would reach the monster first, to silence it, then discourage any caller with the total indifference of a flat monotone. Fay heard him say, "She no here."

He avoided Cantonese on the phone, as a less serviceable instrument of his incomprehension. Ruth's shout was audible from ten feet.

"Well, *call* her!"

"I *am* here, Ruth."

The shouting went on. "We've had the most wonderful news! John got it from Nopi One direct. A few minutes ago. At dawn the *Prince of Wales* and the *Repulse* went past Kuantan. They were right out on the horizon but the haze lifted and they were quite clear. Nopi One said it was about the most glorious sight he has ever seen."

Nopi One? Oh God, yes, the Brigadier.

"But where are they going?"

As the question slipped away from her she knew it was stupid.

"Fay! What's the matter with you? To intercept the invasion, of course! All those barges coming down from Singora and the supply ships lying off Kota Bahru. They'll all be blown to pieces!"

"The radio didn't say anything about battleships coming up here."

Ruth could be heard sucking in her breath. "Honey, it's a *secret* mission! For a surprise attack! The news will be *after* the battle. And that's sure to happen soon at the speed those ships were going. John says, though, that we won't hear the big guns from here. Too far. Something like two hundred miles. Oh, I don't know! It's as though I've just been waiting ever since Pearl Harbour to hear of the Japs getting their first real wallop. And now it's going to happen. Those battleships! The Japs won't know what's hit them. You should see John as a result of this. It's as if he'd got his old self back. I've been worried sick."

"I know."

"Would you like to come up for lunch?" Ruth asked.

"I don't think I'd better. Liza has diarrhea. On the run all the time. And she needs someone to blame. Amah isn't enough."

"Then could I come down for a swim? I can't seem to settle to anything."

"Of course. Now?"

"In about an hour. I've got to take the dogs out first. I think we had panther around again last night. The dogs started howling with that funny note they reserve for the big cats. It doesn't sound as if they wanted to be brave at all."

"I'll have coffee ready," Fay said.

*

The Hamlett Home Teaching Institute, operating worldwide by post from Chicago, was basically designed for expatriate American children, to take them, if necessary, right up to college board examinations without their ever having seen the inside of a classroom. Sensibly it put almost as much emphasis on the teacher as the pupil, with key manuals as fat as the textbooks, these to be kept locked away when not helping to maintain parental prestige. It was suggested that the subjects dealt with could be supplemented by the parent-teacher's special knowledge, if any, but Dr. Judson P. Hamlett, B.A., M.A., Ph.D., stressed, in an introductory letter, that supplementary instruction, while allowable, should nonetheless be carefully rationed, the institute's courses having been designed by teachers and psychiatrists to provide a balanced and nutritious educational diet.

The advice was a considerable relief to Fay, whose only claim to special knowledge came from a wide early reading in Anglo-Catholic theology, this not really from natural inclination but simply because the books were there in her father's library and from the age of four she had been a compulsive reader of any print available. One and a half times through Josephus's *Antiquities of the Jews* had left her with sizeable chunks of this particular history still quite vividly in mind, but she didn't feel this was a subject likely to spark much reaction from a Gourlay, so hadn't tried to use it in her role as Angus's teacher.

The Hamlett Institute's beginner's geography seemed to put a disproportionate emphasis on North America, but they were catering to potential U.S. citizens and it was certainly a big continent. Fay put a prescribed question to her son.

"What is the capital of Idaho?"

Angus stared at the floor. "Alberta," he said.

Fay took a furtive look at the map.

"Alberta is a province in *Canada*. The capital of Idaho is Boise."

"Why do I have to know this stuff? And why do I have to know French, too?"

Fay cleared her throat. "Because, fluent as you may be in Cantonese and Malay, as well as speaking a little English from time to time, there's another half to this world in which a lot of people live who don't speak Malay or Cantonese or even Pidgin English."

She was rather pleased with the speech, considerably better than she usually managed, but Angus remained unimpressed. Fay weakened her point by adding to it.

"Besides, you'll go to America one day."

"I wouldn't go to a place called Boise. Anyway, the Yanks have got all their ships sunk. And we've got the biggest battleship in the world."

"Angus! You will *not* talk about Yanks! Would you call your grandmother a Yank?"

"Grandfa does."

"That's not the point!"

"Anyway, she's a lady. That's not a Yank. Can I go swimming when she gets here?"

"How did you know she was coming down? Did you listen on the extension?"

"I didn't mean to. I was just passing the bedroom."

It was Ruth who said that the Gourlays tended to get away with their lies by making them sound more than slightly ridiculous.

Fay frowned. "You were supposed to be in here doing French verbs. Not passing the bedroom or anywhere else in this house."

She had been going to say that he couldn't join them by the pool, then thought that if she died tomorrow all he would remember were her prohibitions.

"You can come swimming when you've learned the capitals of the states in America."

"But I couldn't! There's thousands."

"There are only forty-eight, Angus. But if that's too many, then all the states west of the Mississippi."

On her way out she thought that she should never have to teach anyone.

Under the arch to the living room she paused, in spite of war back for a moment into the domestic habit of years, wondering what she could do to make the place look less like a Spanish hotel lobby. The first time she'd seen the centrepiece to what was to be their new home she had wanted to ask the architect if he had been looking at a postcard picture of the Alhambra as he designed it. At the south end you went through a double colonnade to a terrace no one ever used offering a long vista of a section of Ruth's grass no one ever walked on except Tamil gardeners trailing behind a noisy power mower. At the north end was another set of pillars giving access to a large area of paving around the swimming pool. The living room's very high ceiling offered a lofty, contemptuous rejection of every piece of furniture Fay had put under it until finally she had said to hell with it and filled arrogant space with Hong Kong wicker.

The houseboy, Chow, was out between the northern columns polishing tiles, on all fours, his head a great deal lower than his behind. Beyond him, framed by an arch, was a backdrop of mountains, some going up to six or seven thousand feet, the viciousness of near precipice and jagged peak masked under a covering of jungle. All the way north to Kelantan there was nothing but this, no cultivated valleys to break up that rise and fall of heavy rain forest, not a stretch of rice paddy anywhere, nor a village. Primitive nomadic tribes, the Sakai moved about under the almost unbroken leaf roof, but their way of life left so few traces they were little more than a rumour. From where she stood the mine itself looked as though it wouldn't take the jungle long to erase it. All that was needed was a dismantling of the hoist tower over the shaft entrance and in a year or two the secondary forest would cover the scar. Even now, with the little cars motionless on the aerial line carrying the ore to the washing sheds, there was a suggestion of dereliction, and she realized that she was missing the distant clanking that formed part of days and nights at Sungei Dema — a sound that added a kind of guilty luxury to living, the assurance of others at work while you were not. Big John must have ordered a production shutdown for his flooding survey.

There was no suggestion of dereliction up on Estate House hill. Over the years the summit had been smoothed into gardens by Ruth in command of three Tamils. An American dislike of dividing walls and hedges had led to an almost completely open design: long stretches of disciplined grass broken only by occasional clumps of bougainvillea, or scrub palm, or irregular beds of multi-coloured cannas. None of the original jungle trees had been allowed to stay; the ones now given room to root had to guarantee a regular display of flowers. It was only after it had been built that Fay really began to understand just how much Ruth must have hated the intrusion into her gardens of the new house — and not even a house natural to the scene, of wood that would mellow to become part of it, but concrete that was going to age about as attractively as an abandoned fort.

As though suddenly made aware of someone behind him, Chow, still on all fours, spun himself around, then looked up. At least a couple of times a day he put on a performance of total martyrdom to his duties, with tile polishing most often providing the occasion.

Fay used Cantonese to tell him that Ruth was coming and they would want coffee by the pool. Chow sent his own adaptations of English down the phone, but he never quite understood Fay's English, forcing her into wild-bid southern Chinese. In spite of some years of semi-serious application, she hadn't even begun to master the subtle tone alterations that change meaning, making you ask for an obscenity when you actually want a spoon. The thought of nightly sessions of howled merriment in the servants' quarters over her idiocies, these compered by Chow, had bothered her until Ruth explained that Hailam servants will never stay with people who don't entertain them, and that if you can't accept the fact that you are doing this the only alternative is to take on highly volatile Malays.

Fay was in her room getting into a swimsuit when she heard a car arrive, and by the time she came out to the pool Liza and her grandmother were in conference at its edge. The child was appropriately dressed, for someone in her condition, in a pink romper suit with non-tropical bunnies appliquéd on it, plus a cummerbund of towelling wrapped about her middle. Amah squatted a few feet away. Part of the group, though slightly aloof from it, was Mick the Labrador, sitting, not lying, his tongue lolling, his legs spread out in a way Fay couldn't remember seeing before, a dog-of-the-world pose announcing that his puppy days were now over. Since his discovery of two bitches in heat in the mine village, Mick had certainly undergone a personality change. He was no longer the carefree innocent, content with Australian dog biscuits and walks with young master. Now a slight restiveness said he knew there was a lot more to life than that. He still offered the overall amiability of the well-bred, but had started to ration his tailwagging devotion to the human race.

Liza, more or less prone on two fat cushions set back against the stone retaining wall, was clearly enjoying her monologue, but Ruth seemed suddenly to tire of it, straightening and starting to unbutton the printed overall she wore over her swimsuit. The child yelled after an audience turning away; Ruth paying no attention, adopting the pose that announced one of her dives was imminent. These were unique, unhurried: first, arms raised over her head, then brought down with hands pointing towards the water, after which there was a slow swaying out of the body to the point of overbalance followed by a half–belly flop, half–seal slide. When Ruth surfaced, her swimming was ladylike, no attempt at the crawl, but a sound, conservative breast stroke that kept her head well out of the water and let her see where she was going.

Fay, coached by her husband, was a little uneasy in Ruth's company about displaying her own fair turn of water speed and quite creditable diving for which she had discovered an aptitude. To have entered the pool that way now would have been exhibitionist and also have splashed her approaching mother-in-law. She lowered herself in by the steps and began treading water.

"I've never seen you in that cap," Ruth said.

"Roy's choice for the little woman. Brought back from Singapore."

"It would be. Liza is delighted to find herself really interesting. I hope she isn't going to grow up into one of those females with a symptom for every occasion."

"It's possible. I have them."

Ruth ignored that. "What started it all?"

"I think a chill topped off with syrup of figs."

"She probably liked the taste and had another go at the bottle. I was a great believer in castor oil. With further treatment imminent. It wipes out any child's tendency towards hypochondria. You don't think Amah has been giving Liza something?"

"I forbade her to."

"That won't stop her. I caught the woman I had for Roy spooning something into him that looked like wet cigarette ash. I was so horrified I sent the package to K.L. to be analyzed. Word came back that it seemed to be dried lizard dropping, plus some powdered snake skin, plus a mystery ingredient. John just laughed. He said if you give them a chance babies will eat dirt and survive."

"Hello," Angus said from above. He was in swimming trunks.

Ruth looked up, one hand out to hold onto the ladder. "Ladies' hour at the pool," she said.

"Oh, Gran! . . . Could you name all the capitals in America?"

"Washington."

"No! Its *states*."

Ruth shook her head. "No, I couldn't do that. I only went to Vassar. And only got to the middle of my junior year. Your Grandfa refused to wait for a fully qualified intellectual. Come on in if you like, but if you're going to dive do it over on the other side."

It might have been a bid to re-establish herself as the point of interest that had Liza suddenly travelling down the paving by the pool at some speed, followed by Amah. The child glared at her relatives as she went, then disappeared into the house.

"I'd better go to her," Fay said.

"I wouldn't. One of the few compensations in our lonely life is that there is always someone else to wipe their little bottoms."

Liza didn't return until Ruth and Fay were sitting in wicker chairs drinking coffee, and this time she walked very slowly, ignoring the world, eyes down to paving. Amah, in attendance, was carrying a cushion.

Ruth said, "What do you bet that cushion's not for herself?"

It went under Liza, putting another layer between the child and cement. Amah then squatted. A low mumble came across the water, which could be the woman's talking, or even singing, to her charge, with Liza looking about as attentive as Cleopatra in her barge to the musicians following in another boat. Mick was now asleep at Ruth's feet, and from his twitching, really enjoying his subconscious.

They had said nothing about the war. Fay lit her second cigarette since coming out of the pool. Her smoking had doubled in the last few days, as though the drug did at least have the power to push back a continuous, churning speculation about the uncertainties surrounding them. For Fay these were somehow made worse by the surface norm at Sungei Dema, work at the mine stubbornly continuing, the ore cars again clanking out their steady, twenty-four–hour reassurance. Whatever the Chinese workers down in the village might be saying about the war, the servants, sensitive barometers of trouble, didn't seem under any kind of stress. The company of soldiers who were to have been sent up from Brigade hadn't arrived and this seemed almost part of a conspiracy to keep up a front that everything was under control. With the appearance of those battleships, Big John's forecasts would now be massively optimistic.

Angus was putting on a performance for his grandmother, a crawl from which the foot feathering left only a creaming on the water.

"Don't you need sunglasses?" Fay asked.

Ruth shook her head.

Fay's glasses hadn't been in the Alhambra room. When Chow, manic about tidiness, found anything away from its formally assigned place, he whipped it off to where it ought to be. Fay didn't find them on her dressing table, either, but neatly cornered in a drawer. It had taken her some time to get used to the idea of the man's regularly going through her more personal possessions — ostensibly to correct an out-of-place fold or put a lid on a box — and, beyond this, she'd had to accept that Roy and she really had no private life, that on any given morning Chow would only need a couple of minutes in their room to assess in highly accurate detail what had gone on there the night before. In a way it was like living as royalty, with ladies of the bedchamber and gentlemen of the robes having access to every cupboard and forever popping in and out.

Fay was turning to cross the room when there was a thud as though someone had slammed a heavy door. The sound was repeated. It could be Liza in a tantrum. Then there were three more booms, clearly from outside the house. The air seemed to vibrate as it had done during the Kuantan airfield bombing. There was a feeling of change in atmospheric pressure.

Ruth was on her feet, staring towards the mountains beyond the mine village. Angus came dripping from the pool, standing to shake water first out of one ear, then the other, his too long, straight black hair hanging in front of his face. The boy's body already had an adult compactness, filled out and muscled.

He was looking at Ruth now, having pushed the hair away from his eyes with a thumb. She turned her head to Fay and said, "They must be blowing up the iron ore mine at Dungun."

There was a row of four booms.

"Would we hear anything here from Dungun?"

Ruth was positive. "Anything big enough, yes. We ought to have stopped the Japs getting ore from that mine months ago. John heard only last week that another of their ships sailed laden for Yokohama. Days, almost hours, before they attack us. Do you find yourself wanting to pray horrible prayers?"

"About what?"

"Asking that those battleships will blast the Japs off the map. I remember a tough old Far Eastern hand at a dinner in Singapore saying that every mission school we built in Japan saved them that much money for their cruiser-building programme."

They walked together to the house. In the living room Ruth stopped, looking back towards the boy still standing by the pool.

"I shouldn't have talked like that in front of Angus."

"We can't screen him from what's happening."

"I suppose not."

The Austin had been left in the sun and even with its windows lowered was like a tin oven waiting for the cake. Ruth opened the driver's door and stood leaning on the frame.

"Fay, have you heard planes from the Kuantan airfield since the bombing?"

"No. But I thought the runways were unuseable?"

"John says they started filling in the holes the day after the attack. He thinks it must have been to have the field operational when the *Prince of Wales* and the *Repulse* came up this coast. It's the only one south of Kelantan that could be used to give the ships air support. Which is why I've been listening for planes. Wondering if I'd missed them. We always used to hear those Buffalos."

"I can't say I've heard anything. But hasn't the wind been mostly from the north?"

"Maybe that's it."

Ruth got into the car as Chow came out of the house. He was carrying something on a tray, neatly folded, the button-through dress left by the pool. Ruth thanked him and put the dress on the seat beside her. Chow gave a little parody of a bow and went back to the house.

"I don't know how I used to rate with your houseboy," Ruth said, "but as a woman who drives around the estate half-naked I've lost a lot of marks. I'll ring if John knows anything about the noise from Dungun."

The Austin groaned away in low gear just as the booming came again, this time louder than before, reaching an unbroken crescendo that seemed to go on for minutes. The vibrations said bombing. Fay went through the house to dive into the pool, swimming the length fast, then turning to swim back to the deep end. She pulled herself up the ladder. Liza was slumped on cushions and appeared to be asleep. Amah, surprisingly, had deserted her charge. There was no sign of Angus.

A midday buildup of heat seemed to roll down across Ruth's open spaces as if propelled by a breeze, though there was none. Fay took a towel from a chair to pat away dampness that was more sweat than pool water, her swimsuit feeling like wool underwear. She walked around the concrete to where Liza, apparently tucked down in sleep, opened her eyes without moving her head, as a dog does, to see if there was anything developing in her interest. She shut them again.

"Where's Amah?"

"Dunno."

"What you *do* know, Liza, is that you're not allowed to be out here alone until you can swim."

"Can swim."

Fay sat down on the paving, leaning back against the stone wall, and thought: If I begin to tell Liza a story now, it would probably embarrass her more than anything else; she is used to her stories in Cantonese. And I'm out of practice. I tried with Angus. A parental duty. Was he as bored with me by the age of four as Liza probably is? I seem to be always finding out what the children are doing and ordering Amah not to let them. It makes her their source of support, the face they want to see when they wake from a nightmare. Only there are no hints that either Johnny or Liza have ever had nightmares. Maybe you don't if you're brought up in surroundings where you become conscious very early of your own status. The deference to their little identities doesn't diminish with the years, either; it swells. At eight and a half Angus is the unquestioned leader of the local secret society where the rest of the boys are all older. He goes down the hill like a young god experimenting with the world on an excursion from Olympus.

Not at all like growing up in the Vicarage, a cold house, a cold stair, huge rooms, the only morning fire in Papa's study, which smelled of old pipes, cat, and the decaying leather bindings around theology. I escaped to the sun, which allowed me ten minutes of itself daily, followed there by the accusing eyes of an old priest who had only had a daughter in order to have someone to keep house for him in his old age.

And the flow of gentle accusations hadn't diminished when Roy and I visited him in a home for retired clerics. Papa's eyes did the talking while his words offered a text in Christian acceptance: "It makes me a *little* sad that I will never see my grandchildren. Still, you young ones have your own lives to lead." I didn't even try to offer any excuses for having left Angus in Malaya with Ruth. Papa wouldn't have listened if I had. The matron hated me on sight. She said my father was a saint. I really must write him again. It's more than a month since I got that postcard showing Winchester Cathedral.

A shuffling along the terrace was Amah returning, with apologies. She hadn't meant to be away for so long over a call of nature but *she* was also suffering from an uncertainty of the bowels. Fay felt dismissed.

*

Fay was thinking about another swim in the full afternoon when the phone by her bed rang.

"Were you asleep?" Hamish roared. "You sound as if you might have been."

"I was lying down," Fay said. "I usually do after lunch."

"Sorry I woke you."

"You didn't wake me. I was reading. And the connection isn't so bad you need to shout."

"Sorry."

"Hamish, will you stop apologizing? What is it you want?"

"You think I wouldn't ring you if I didn't want something?"

She had no answer to that.

"Actually, you're right this time. I do want you to do something for me. It's personal in a way. I thought about it a long time before I decided to ask. . . ."

The call was interrupted by what sounded like a military voice shouting at someone. Hamish's words were reduced to an insect whining in the background.

". . . You damn fool!" the military voice said, then slammed down a receiver. Hamish came back like volume turned up.

". . . You scarcely know her. Except probably by sight in the village."

"Who? I missed some of what you were saying."

"Lali."

"Oh." Fay stared at the wall opposite. A chicha lizard had moved off the ceiling onto it. "You want me to go down and see her about something?"

"No. It's not that. . . ."

His doubts about the course he had embarked on came over the line from two hundred miles away. He had found Fay unsympathetic.

"Hamish, go on, tell me!"

"Well . . . actually, I was wondering whether you could

bring Lali as far as K.L. with you? That is, when you come out."

"Come *out?*"

"Fay... you must realize by now that Sungei Dema... well.... I shouldn't say this on the phone. But developments might... in fact they almost certainly will.... Hell, I'm no good at this guarded stuff!"

"You mean we'll have to evacuate?"

"Well, yes."

"But there are no signs of anything happening near us?"

"Good God! Perhaps you wouldn't..."

"Hamish, is the line fading again, or is it you?"

"I can't talk about military matters on this phone."

"Well, don't. What about Lali?"

"You sound almost angry?"

"I'm sorry. My turn to apologize. Maybe I was just remembering what you said. When you came to give Angus your stamps. I wasn't to worry because the Japs weren't going to attack. Did you believe that then? Or was it just soothing syrup for the woman left at home while her man was away at the wars?"

"Fay, you *are* angry with me!"

"I'm not. I'm just being stupid. I'll help you in any way I can. Yes, if we have to leave I'll find room in the car for Lali. Or Ruth will, in the big Siddeley."

"I'd rather Ruth wasn't in on this. I mean, that you'll do it. You'd probably be leaving sooner. With Angus and Liza. Naturally. Fay, this would be an enormous load off my mind. Lali won't have much stuff, probably just a bundle. When I left I took most of her things with me to K.L. and sent them on from there."

"Where to?"

"Telok Anson. That's where her people are. She can get there easily enough if you leave her in K.L. She'll have time to get back to her family and... well... sort of cover things up."

"Her association with you?"

"Yes."

"For when the Japs come?"

"Yes."

"Hamish, if you know something we don't, will you *please* tell me?"

"I can't talk on the phone. I shouldn't be ringing you at all. Can I count on you for Lali?"

"I've said you could."

"Then bless you."

"I don't feel blessed. You'll be in touch with Lali direct about this?"

"Yes. Thanks. *So* much."

He hung up. Fay put the receiver on its hooks and lay back, feeling the pillow's cold damp from earlier perspiration. After saying that the Japs weren't coming, Hamish had gone straight back to his orchid-hung bungalow to order Lali to start packing.

In his room Angus was trying out once again the ukelele Ruth had got him from the States by mail order and on which he could now plunk out a just recognizable "Valencia." He knew the words, too, and sometimes sang them, though he wasn't doing that now.

The phone rang. Hamish had forgotten something.

"Yes?"

For a moment she didn't recognize the husky voice.

"Fay? John. I've just heard from the Brigadier. The *Prince of Wales* and the *Repulse....* They're sunk! Those goddamned bastards have sunk our ships! Both of them! And we heard it happening!

THREE

Ruth had given her two sleeping tablets and Fay had taken one. The three of them had drunk a good deal in the Alhambra room, trying to put a haze screen between themselves and a reality too sharp-edged to be dealt with in any other way, at least for the time being. They used words for sedation as well, mostly Ruth and Fay talking, John only sometimes, as though whisky wasn't helping him as much as it did the women, and when he spoke it was almost like a condensation of their joint longer article, the points they had been trying to make emasculated by the stone-ground knife of his economy. He had got up sometimes to walk around the room, down to the arches by the terrace, then up to the other set with the pool beyond, as if impatient of marking time, of waiting for some inkling of the consequences to them of what had happened: two ships sunk whose names, when Fay heard them, had for seconds meant absolutely nothing.

Ruth and John left about midnight, driving off in the lumbering Armstrong-Siddeley as though they had been down for dinner and a normal evening, Ruth looking back to wave. The moon was rising, the jungle pushing out arthritic black fingers to clutch at the shining grass. Fay had stood listening to the sound of the car on the long curve of the drive, then to its gear changing for the final sharp climb. When engine noise ended, the reassurance of clanking ore cars took over.

Whisky let her go to bed with what felt like the solid conviction that life had a reliable pattern, that what had been established by hard work over the years endured, history somehow accommodating itself to this endurance. She woke feeling sick, shivering slightly, as though from terror in a dream she couldn't remember. There was sweat on her face but she didn't reach out for a handkerchief, feeling that if she didn't move, even slightly, the sickness would pass. Moonlight in the room had isolated the bed and its framed mosquito net, the cube of white mesh a dazzling screen between her and the furniture beyond. Anyone standing out there could be watching her while she could see nothing. She listened. The sound that had woken her must have pushed through the dream. She became certain there had been a sound.

It couldn't be the servants back in the house. Even if Amah had come to check up on Liza, her wooden-soled sandals chattered about where she was going, and she always wore them, too terrified of hookworm to risk bare feet, even on tiles. Chow could be quiet enough in his movement, but his signing off from the main house after supper was as final as a written resignation.

It was only after Roy had left for training with the Volunteers that she had really become conscious of her home as something like a huge concrete tent with flaps raised to catch the breeze; you could walk in anywhere through openings with shutters that were never shut, and, though there were doors that had keys in them (not many), the keys were never turned. At Sungei Dema the Chinese miners fought amongst themselves only rarely, conflicts usually just noise, with theft almost unknown. A thief would have little chance of getting out of the valley with anything of value before nemesis, disguised as Big John's foreman, caught up with him, and the houses on the hill had always been immune even from prowlers, as though ringed by an invisible, protective fire.

Fay knew that the fire had now been switched off. She heard a faint, shuffling noise, then a whisper

"Mum?"

Sitting up drained the blood from her head. "Angus! What? . . ."

"Ssh!"

Then the whisper again.

"They've come!"

"Who?"

"The Japs."

He *did* have nightmares. Talk in the house had reached him in spite of precautions that it shouldn't. If he had stood by the railing of the upper hall he could have heard what was said in the living room. Whisky had put them off guard. John, walking up and down, had sometimes been quite loud.

"They're out there," he said. "By the pool."

"Angus, please! . . ."

"Ssh!"

Fay swung her legs clear of the covering sheet, toes tangling with the foot of the net. She paused to let nausea settle into giddiness. She pushed aside flaps of cotton mesh, standing out in a room blanched into near strangeness by moonlight. Angus had moved away, almost flat against the wall near the open window.

There was a cough. It came from outside.

Her heart became a hammer knocking against the thin partition of her control. Angus signalled with a hand, the gesture authoritative. He was wearing shorts, nothing else. He always slept naked. He must have got up to put them on, carefully, before he faced up to whatever had disturbed him. He wanted her to come in beside him, along the wall.

She slid along it, leaning, listening to the hammer, not wanting to look where he was looking. He turned his head back to her, the rest of his body rigid. He would see her fear. In moonlight it must be stark in her face. He might even hear her heart.

She saw the bicycles first, laid out in a half-arc on Ruth's grass, as though at a rendezvous point for a Victorian picnic. The chromium shone. She began to count the picnickers down their straggling row at the edge of the pool: nine men, six sitting tailor fashion on concrete, the other three sprawled in wicker chairs. One was half-hidden by a sun umbrella.

They were eating what seemed to be thick slices of bread. Cook had baked yesterday, as if preparing for this. Fay counted the bicycles: eleven. Two of the men must be inside the house. Drinks were left out in the living room, an invitation. There was an almost full bottle of whisky, brought in and opened just before Ruth and John went home.

The Japs had raped their way through China.

Rifles were stacked against an empty chair. The men were in open-necked shirts and breeches caught below the knee by puttees. The puttees ended in canvas rubber-soled shoes. All were bareheaded. One soldier finished his bread and rubbed his fingers over a clipped scalp, then picked up a cap and put it on. There was a badge above the peak. The man sat hunched, arms around his knees, as though concentrating on rest before an action signal that could come at any moment. There was no whispering amongst them, not even much turning of heads to look about, as if they had no fear of being disturbed, certain they were under no threat themselves; instead they were the carriers of threat, their Trappist silence purposeful. The single cough had been muffled.

The hunched man straightened, stood, taking a couple of steps forward. His right hand went down to the front of his breeches. He began urinating into the pool, the sound of this quite loud. The man under the umbrella got up, stepped over to the soldier making water, jerked him around, then hit him across the face with the back of a closed fist. The soldier, his breeches still open, came to attention in front of his superior, arms thrust down hard at his sides, head back as though to accept another blow. Not a word had been spoken.

Fay wanted to close her eyes, shutting out what she saw, freezing reality into a dream that could be dismissed. Experience couldn't come like this, everything known not just under threat but wiped out, and with no conceivable alternative available. Invaders, come in silence, were in possession, and she had nothing with which to challenge them. She was left only with this craven impulse to hide. Fear was a personal revelation that shocked even as it held her.

Angus turned his head again. It was only then that she remembered her daughter. She whispered, "Liza?"

His lips formed the words: "Asleep."

Her son had given her the excuse to stay where she was, to do nothing. He had been in his sister's room before he came here. He might have listened and watched from the railing of the upper hall while soldiers moved about in the rooms below. He hadn't come to her for protection. He had never been one to ask for what he wouldn't get.

She must go to Liza. The child would have to be woken carefully, Angus helping her to do that. The window of Liza's room also faced the pool, and even a smothered cry might be heard. Then the three of them must hide. There had to be some place in this house searching soldiers wouldn't find. She thought of cupboards, of the back stairs closed off by one of the few doors, but a concrete building doesn't provide places to conceal refugees from men with guns, the rooms high ceilinged for coolness and with no access that she could remember to attics. They might use the back stairs in a wild bid to get clear of the house, then run in moonlight across Ruth's grass for shelter in the jungle.

She stared at the white-curtained frame around the bed in which she had slept for ten safe years, waking sometimes to the double reassurance of the ore cars' clanking and Roy's snores. A southerly breeze was softening away sounds from the mine but she could still hear the cars moving on their cables. Less than a mile and a half from this room the norm blundered on while under her window a silent picnic pronounced sentence on all yesterdays.

She felt nausea coming back, a wave of it to which she was going to surrender. She went to a chair on the opposite wall, sitting, bending forward to push her head down between her thighs in the way she had been taught to do as an adolescent subject to fainting spells, those blackouts a protest against the changes of growth. If she started to retch, the soldiers would hear. She was certain that this sound, more than any other, would bring them. She could hear a planned and careful silence ruptured first by shouting, then crashing from below, then voices on the stairs. It was their laughter she dreaded most.

The nausea eased. She raised her head a little to rest it on one leg. The idiot thought came that she must look like a non-conformist at one of her father's High Church masses, refusing to go on her knees but ready to bend herself double nonetheless, the supplication only different in kind. The God who had let this war start wouldn't notice her now. She ought to pray for the children, that they be spared somehow. The words wouldn't form in her mind.

"Mother?"

The formality of that jerked her attention. She looked up. Angus was standing in front of her, legs slightly apart, braced. He looked like a man determined not to be thrown off his feet by an earthquake. That thought could not be qualified; he looked a man, not a child of eight going on nine. He didn't in any way suggest Roy, or Big John, or any of the tribe, but an identity determinedly separate from heritage, and owing no allegiance. Certainly no allegiance to her.

"What?..."

"They've gone."

"What?" she said again.

"Pushing their bikes."

She stared. "Which way?"

" 'Round the front of the house. Maybe to the drive."

She stood, walking to the window. The poolside was empty. It looked as though it had never been occupied by aliens, not a hint of them left behind, the whole area now waiting in moonlight for dawn and a new day of use by the family. She had the feeling that it would never be used that way again. Or not by her. Though she wasn't aware of it, she must have swayed, turning away from the window.

"Mum? You all right?"

"Yes."

"We got to phone Grandfa!"

She thought about that; then her reaction was almost violent. "No!"

"But — "

"Not now, Angus!"

Her voice was too loud. She went back to a whisper: "We can see from the guest room if they're out front."

She went to the door he had closed coming to her, and

turned down the handle to find that he had locked it. What had been in his mind when he did that? She turned back to look at him but he had gone out of sight beyond the square of the mosquito frame, gone around to the telephone table. She caught him as he was lifting the handset, wrenching it from his fingers.

"Didn't you hear me? I said not yet! They can't have gone far! Anything could bring them back!"

She couldn't see his eyes. She didn't want to. An explanation of fear only exposed it.

"Come with me!" She made it an order, out of a half-anger. She would have pushed him in front of her if that had been necessary. They went into a hall walled off from moonlight, lit only by a glow from the well over the entrance area below, secondhand moonlight from flanking rooms. They stood listening for sound, Fay holding Angus by one arm.

"They're not in the house." His voice was almost loud.

While they moved she kept him back from the railing along the upper hall, as though the well beyond contained a geyser that might at any moment explode. Down there, all over Chow's tiles, would be the prints of rubber-soled shoes, easily polished away, but the other imprints of the use of her house couldn't be got rid of; the place was now subject to inescapable hauntings, images of jungle-stained soldiers going to and fro under those doubled arches.

The opening of the guest room door released a sealed-in heat from yesterday's sun. The place smelled of disuse and mildew. A closed window was a screen to sound but it gave a clear view of a drive unshadowed for a hundred yards until flanked by two of Ruth's flame-of-the-forest trees, planted like gateposts and now huge, in the flower season strewing their blood blossoms on dark asphalt. The drive was empty.

It was bright in the room. The lack of a shelter porch or roof overhang had made the glazing of these windows necessary. Angus pulled her arm.

"Down there!" He pointed.

She could only see one man, unmoving, his shadow projected out beyond the sharply defined shadow of the house.

He stood as a disciplinarian teacher might stand, very straight, waiting for his class to settle, perhaps listening for any hint that an alarm had been raised either here on the hill or down in the village, but what he heard could only have been what Fay could faintly hear: the clanking of ore cars, proof that Sungei Dema was still aloof from war, minding its own business. While she watched, the man out in the moonlight lifted high and quite close to his face what seemed to be a folded map, but he was apparently unable to make out what he wanted. He produced a small torch from a pocket in his sagging breeches, cupping it in one hand to confine the beam. After his unhurried study of the map the paper was folded carefully and slid into a haversack hanging from his belt. Using the light again, he consulted a watch on one wrist, then what must be a compass on the other, then put the torch away and gave a hand signal before stepping back into the deep shadow.

His men began to emerge, one by one and in no hurry, pushing their bikes out onto the asphalt that Big John had laid only a year ago on the sloping estate drives to counter an erosion of the natural orange laterite soil. There was nothing disciplined in the way the men assembled; they seemed almost as casual as a party of youth hostelers setting out on a day's run, their bodies hung about with impedimenta — rifles slung across backs, two or three with bayonets attached to muzzles, narrow mirrors reflecting light. Each man had two compartmented-cloth belts hung from one shoulder, one belt fat with bumps that might be grenades. The carriers on the bikes had nothing strapped to them, as though transport could be abandoned at any time without diminishing the unit's effectiveness.

It was minutes before their leader appeared from around the corner of the house, the man distinguished from the others only by one extra haversack. He pushed his bike over grass to the head of a straggle column without looking back or giving any signal, at once starting to pedal up the drive. His men followed, irregularly spaced but keeping distances, as though obeying rules that could only be understood by themselves. When the last cyclist had gone through the flame-of-the-forest arch, Fay waited for their leader to appear higher up against the hillside, moving along the road, which stayed level for a time, then dropped for a fork that led either back to the mine village or to Kuantan.

The leader, pedaling hard, appeared far sooner than she would have thought possible. She turned from the window. Angus wasn't in the room. He had gone to the phone downstairs. In the hall she stood listening. There was no sound of anyone moving down below, or of Angus's voice kept low. She went to her bedroom, 'round the net, and lifted the handset. The line was alive and hummed, but no one was using it. She knew she had to.

The ringing went on for half a minute. Then came Ruth's voice, heavy from sleep.

"Who? ..."

"Fay. Listen to me! The Japs have been here! You've got to wake John!"

"What? Japs? What are you talking — "

"Ruth! They've been here! By our pool! Eating!"

"Eating? Fay, are you all right?"

"Angus was with me. We've been watching them. They raided our pantry. Ate our bread. By the pool. Now they've gone off on their bikes."

"You're sure ... Japanese?"

"Yes! With slung rifles. And, I think, grenades."

"John's here."

Big John's voice was alert.

"Tell me, Fay."

She told him.

He said, "They've come down those jungle tracks the way I thought they might. I warned the Army. Stay where you are. We'll be with you soon. Now get off this line. I'm calling the Brigadier."

She hung up, closing her eyes, opening them again to that brightness in the room through which she had walked to look down on the impossible. She went out into the hall. This time she called her son's name from the upper landing. There was a sound below, not his voice answering, something else. She ran down the stairs.

He came towards her from under an arch, the moonlight behind him. He had his hand curled into a fist held tight in against his mouth. He stood still. He didn't take his hand away.

"What is it?"

He seemed to be staring at the tiles. He let his hand drop. "Mick."

She didn't say anything, was frightened to.

"I guess he barked. I guess I heard that. They heard it. There was a kind of growling, too. I was sure when I woke up. That was when they went in."

"The Japs?"

He nodded.

"They killed Mick. With their bayonets. To stop him making — "

He broke off, then finished the sentence. He wasn't crying.

" — a noise."

"I'm sorry," she said. "Oh, I'm sorry."

"I guess they had to."

"What?"

"Kill him. In a war. Not to make a noise."

Oh, God protect him, Fay thought. I can't! She said, "I phoned your grandfather."

He nodded.

FOUR

It would have been better if they had run away, like Cook, dissociating themselves as quickly as possible from the about-to-be-defeated. Instead they had stayed while she packed the car, Chow in particular hanging around as though waiting to be told what to do, but actually resenting seeing the things she was taking removed from their proper appointed places. Amah had been with Liza until the moment of getting into the Armstrong-Siddeley, emerging from the house with the child when exactly the right time had come. A back door opened into a small nest amongst the heaped luggage, this flanking a larger hole for Angus into which the boy was already settled. Amah's face had shown nothing — except once, briefly, when she saw Lali, cloth-wrapped bundle on her knees, sitting in the front seat very erect and staring steadily up the drive, ignoring the act of departure as though her thoughts were already totally concentrated on the idea of her escape. The look Amah sent towards Lali couldn't have been personal; it came from a deep-rooted antipathy between the races plus something Amah had seen all her life: the Malay contriving a tidy sidestepping of impending troubles while the Chinese were left to endure them.

As *I* am sidestepping them, Fay thought, driving this lumbering car down a road with a camber that keeps trying to put us into one of the drainage ditches. Thank God they didn't wave, standing on the steps of the cement house. I couldn't have endured it if either of them had so much as lifted a hand. But they didn't. They just stood side by side with those huge empty rooms behind them that are going to be a lot emptier before they are ever used again. If they ever are. There is bound to be looting when Ruth and Big John leave.

I should have let Ruth take our silver to put along with hers in that hole John is digging back in the jungle. How am I going to cart a case full of silver around with me? Did I think it would be useful for barter? I don't know what I thought. It was a crazy packing. Like taking that small Bokhara from beside our bed. Symbolic of what? The thousands of times Roy's bare feet and mine have stepped on the thing? Where am I going to put that now? Spread it by the next bed I share with my husband?

I should have tried to talk to Lali while she was with us, Fay thought. Hamish is supposed to have taught her a good deal of English. And she was being uprooted, too, though she didn't look it. All the way to K.L. she looked like someone who has everything planned. If she hadn't been sitting beside me she would have been contentedly chewing betel and spitting red. We automatically dislike the women of the race our men choose when straying from us. Ruth feels this. She may pretend not to, but she does. Hamish probably picked Lali up at a Ronggeng dance. A knobby-kneed, middle-aged Scotch lecher eying the girl from below, then getting up on the wooden platform to sway his broad hips opposite her slim ones. Though not so slim now. Lali got out of the car with her bundle, smiling, glad to be rid of us. She didn't wave.

I took my Bokhara. Angus took the stamps Hamish had given him. He left the ukelele from Ruth behind. I wonder why? I wouldn't have told him not to bring it. He has been almost as silent as Lali. Liza sleeps most of the time. It may have something to do with the stomach upset. She took New Teddy, and Old Teddy, and that Chinese doll she calls Wango. Amah packed for her, I hope sensibly. But it will be.

*

Fay dreaded passing the convoys of troops going north as the Siddeley went south. Since Kuala Lumpur there had been three of these: long processionals of unhooded lorries; soldiers packed in the back, some standing; not British troops from Indian regiments, but dark-faced men with black eyes, many of them staring down at a refugee car moving cautiously along the edge of a drainage ditch as though in fear of having its escape cut off. It was a real fear, too, of a puncture, of the engine's coughing to a stop, leaving them blocking a down lane while the convoys rumbled by only a few feet away. As she waited for help, the men in the lorries might spit on her, or want to. Two children, her passport for being on the way south, wouldn't seem valid to them.

While they were in Kuala Lumpur she had gone into Gian Singh's; the store remained as usual, the Eurasian girl still smiling behind the lingerie counter. There was nothing Fay really wanted or needed, but she picked things up, looked at them, then dropped them again. A loud contralto voice brayed from a distance, like a loudspeaker: "Arthur says we've got a sort of Maginot Line at Kangar. We're reinforcing it. And the Argylls are moving up. The horrible little monkeys won't get past *them*. No, *of course* I'm not leaving. We'd never get Cook back if I did."

A white-painted stone beyond the drainage ditch said eleven miles to Tampin. Less than one mile before Tampin was the minor road she would be taking, and then off that onto the laterite track through rubber trees to the Musgan Tapan Estate House and the Cowans. Jessie Cowan would have high tea waiting. Her high teas had endured all assaults on them from established tropic practice. One hour before sunset, when the rest of the country was beginning to think whisky-soda with ice, you sat down at Jessie's to a steaming pot and an intensive course in starch heaviness from a vast assortment of home bakings. Jessie's bakings they were, too, all of them — her verdict being that no Chinese really knows how to use an oven. Willie Cowan, wanting his whiskey like everyone else, had to endure, under his wife's eye, the building up of a huge, floury padding in his stomach against even a hint of insobriety later.

Fay longed for the side turning. You assisted your endurance of a war by finding in it little sheltered oases of apparent norm, either of your own manufacture or somebody else's. At Musgan Tapan the shade would be provided by Jessie, her welcome setting up a vibration even out on the open verandah, with dogs barking and Willie in the background, his smile lifting a moustache stained by an almost unbroken succession of Java cheroots. Jessie's body looked as though it had been designed to deliver eleven children without really noticing, but not one had arrived. Even on a first meeting years ago Fay had felt that somehow this was the domestic cross that Willie was made to bear, rising early for the morning muster of Tamil estate workers, leaving behind a heavily sleeping wife whom he had certainly failed yet once again. Only the dogs multiplied at Musgan Tapan.

Angus never seemed to talk merely for the sake of doing it, but his silence since leaving K.L. might have been something deliberately imposed on himself, probably with an element of contempt: the certainty that she would have no answer for any of the questions in his mind. How long would he remember seeing her in a terror that had frozen her will to do anything? Probably always. Just as she remembered her father on the day of her mother's funeral: a man word-perfect for grief, as he had never been in his sermons, suddenly offered the opportunity really to exploit his talents as an actor, and seizing it. Frozen into herself on that day, too, but with desolation, not fear, she had walked beside him as a necessary prop to the performance.

There was no sign on the main road pointing the way to Musgan Tapan. The turning could easily be missed and, even if spotted, issue no invitation; moon craters in broken asphalt threatened the car's springing. After the turn-off there was no indication of a rubber estate either, only a good quarter of a mile of secondary jungle on both sides of the road. The forest had at one time been cleared, probably for more rubber plantings, but the market price must have slumped and the expansion abandoned. Now undisciplined growth was up to twenty feet, its green walls already seeming poised to suffocate the track between them.

The lurching woke Liza. There was a wail from the back seat.

"I want to go poo-poo!"

Fay avoided a pothole filled with water from last night's rain.

"We'll soon be at Aunt Jessie's."

"I want to go poo-poo *now!*

"Shut up!" Angus said.

Surprisingly, Liza did. Fay wondered if there would be an arrival disaster.

The laterite surface was smoother, funnelled in places by the rains but without the cavities, and beyond was now the tidiness of rubber forest, all undergrowth cut down and carted away. The road climbed and the trees climbed with it in almost measured rows, as though planted by a precise mind dedicated to symmetry. The sun that got through the leaves reached the ground in patches, spotlighting the struggling grass. In this area the trees were young, not much thicker than an elephant's leg but already tapped, the bark cut away in slanting circles down the trunks, white latex dripping into a cup fastened just below the lowest cut. It was too late in the day for the Tamil estate workers to be about, and the long, empty, darkening aisles seemed to stretch away into unthinkable distances, up and down over the swelling and falling ground offering a formal setting for the kind of unbroken loneliness featured only in dreams.

Then, as the car came up over a rise sharp enough to demand a lower gear, the rubber to the left was tenanted. Fay's reaction to what she saw was to brake, making the Siddeley skid about, coming to a halt beside heavy planks laid over a ditch. She put the car in neutral and sat staring, not really able to believe that this had happened to tree-proud Willie Cowan. For almost a hundred yards back from the road, what had been carefully raked, almost swept, ground was churned into a wheel-patterned bog of mud, as though all these vehicles had arrived during heavy rain and, simply ignoring their effect on laterite soil, driven at once onto the chosen site to get quick cover from the air. The leaf roof hadn't been thought sufficient to hide the mobile guns and these were under camouflage nets. Most of the tents were decorated with branches torn from the trees. A huge lorry seemed to be a workshop; the loud whine of a powered tool was coming from it. An outsize mess tent had its side flaps raised and alongside it, in the open, cauldrons steamed.

Fay's first sense of outrage at this desecration of what was sacred for Willie faded. She was able to accept that these men were taking exactly what she needed herself — time out from tension. They were, as she hoped to be, temporary escapists absorbed in the chores of making camp, of brewing up, of almost luxuriating in the slow cooking of a meal within a rationed space of what could be only hours. They were human again, identifying themselves and those around them with laughter, looking forward to unbroken sleep.

"Are those ours?" Angus asked.

"Oh, yes."

That was one question she *could* answer. And if there had been any doubt, that would have been wiped away by the appearance from behind canvas of a shortish man wearing a British Army officer's peaked cap and khaki shorts. He stared at the Siddeley for a moment, then swung around to pull a shirt off a tent pole. As he started across the mud towards them, buttoning the shirt, Fay put the car in gear and the engine, which had begun to sound tired, hauled them up another slope. She drove beyond a drop that completely hid the encampment behind them; the rubber forest was once again tidy.

The estate bungalow was on top of a conical hill, with the rows of Tamil workers' cement houses hidden in a gully at the back. For twenty-eight years Willie Cowan had been getting up just after dawn to drink a cup of tea and eat half a papaya, then go down the verandah steps to an area of combed gravel between the house and a garden that did its best to imitate the tidy, railing-encased front gardens of suburban Glasgow. More than once Fay, sleepless as she often was in other people's houses, had joined him for the papaya and after it to stand beside Willie while he took five minutes off to look out over his kingdom at those green sea waves of his trees rolling from three directions towards the raised island of the command post. To the west were the jungle-covered peaks of the main range, but they were too far away to offer any threat of a ravenous return of the rain forest, which was firmly under orders, either Jessie's or Willie's. Even the roses, with British names and in two octagonal beds, put up a creditable fight to survive a heat for which they were not intended.

The car crunched over gravel; then Fay switched off the engine, expecting to hear at once the first salvos of a guaranteed welcome, a huge barking of dogs, and Jessie's roaring at the animals to be quiet. But there was no sound at all. It was so still that when the first wave of mosquitoes moved down on the car their mass whining seemed to fill space, like the drone of attacking planes.

Angus was out of the car first, Lisa yelling at him to let her out, which he did, having to tug at the heavy door on her side. While Fay was finding her bag and pulling the handbrake another notch tighter, Liza took off for the house on her own, plodding purposefully past an area decorated with whitewashed stones and up the steps, apparently without interest in whether or not she was being followed. Fay got out of the car and stood for a moment to look towards the bungalow into which Liza had now disappeared, wondering whether Amah had started the kind of toilet training that meant the child could manage on her own. It didn't seem likely. She began to walk towards the steps. Angus, looking out over the rubber trees, turned to her.

"Have they gone away?"

Fay shook her head. "Tampin to shop, I expect. Your Aunt Jessie will have run out of flour or something. And they always take all the dogs."

"But Grandma was going to phone we were coming?"

"She couldn't give times. They probably thought we'd be much longer in K.L."

Staying longer in K.L. would have meant driving with blackout headlights down night roads, something everyone was avoiding if they possibly could. She went up the steps and across the verandah into a living room where the corners had already lost definition and the furniture had a shrouded look. There was a wail.

"Mama! I can't find it!"

Fay went across to an arch where she remembered the

light switches were assembled, trying one, then another. No
light came on. She went down a passage, locating her daughter by sound.

"I want *Amah!*"

"It's all right, Liza. It's in here."

The Musgan Tapan water closet had been installed before World War I, when these devices were sybaritic luxury
in Malaya, and it was raised up not one step but two. When
reached, particularly in semi-darkness, it seemed to challenge
you to use it, and in its earlier years the weak-willed may
have taken to the woods rather than face up to the ordeal.
Fay, first working with buttons, then lifting Liza and continuing to keep hold of her, realized that this was only about
the third time — aside from family picnics — she had ren-
dered her daughter this service, and that she had never even
once done so with Angus. There hadn't been much nappy
changing either.

Her drill must have skipped something Amah always in-
cluded, for during the buttoning up Liza began to whimper,
words working their way through the sound, but not really
intelligibly. While Fay washed her hands in the cement-
floored bathroom next door, Liza stood in the passage, no
longer half-tearful but indulging in a low, muttered monologue against a world in which things weren't going her way.
The child needed to be in bed, after having something to
eat. Where on earth were the servants? Surely one of them
would know how to switch on the Lister engine for the
lighting?

On their way back to the living room, Fay offered her
hand to Liza, but this was rejected. Angus was waiting for
them with news.

"The engine's bust."

"That'll be why they've gone off to Tampin. To get an
engineer."

"It's not bust that way. It's smashed with a hammer. The
hammer's still there. The servants aren't in their house."

Fay's defense of the norm was a clinging to it. "They may
just be taking time off."

He shook his head. "No. They packed. One of those big

baskets is half-full of stuff. Like they had to go before they could fill it up."

"Stop inventing things, Angus!"

"I'm hungry," Liza said.

They were all hungry. And tired. Ever since K.L. Fay had known she had been driving the Siddeley towards one of Jessie's high teas, the mere sight of her laden table a nourishment to morale, but beyond an only dimly visible arch, the huge circle of polished mahogany was bare, not even a centrepiece of one of those non-Malaysian pot plants that Jessie cultivated so doggedly — a scented geranium or a Busy Lizzie.

Fay neded to get out of rooms that already seemed to smell of disuse, but even the verandah was airless, the day finishing without a hint of the usually flamboyant tropical sunset, as though change was also climatic. An eerie light now hung over Willie's forests, a greenish yellow that could have been a by-product of a dying sun. The children followed her out onto creaking boards, as Liza lapsed back into the muttering that mightn't be a monologue after all, but instead two parts of a split personality talking things over.

Oddly for him, Angus seemed out to make conversation. "Grandfa says Liza's a girner."

Fay didn't feel like encouraging him. "Well?"

"Is girner a Scotch word?"

"Yes."

"I'd rather be Scotch than English."

"All *right!*"

She nearly shouted that, then added, "Actually, you're a quarter American." And we've all lost our battleships, she told herself.

"There's a motorbike coming," Angus said.

It took her another three seconds to pick up the sound; then it was loud, from a surge up the last steep rise. She thought the man riding it was the one who had turned to put on his shirt but, when he stopped his machine and got off to pull it up on its stand, she saw that this man was much taller. As he straightened to look at her, she had the feeling he would never be seen without his shirt in front of "other

ranks." He was wearing a webbing belt but the revolver
hanging from it was in a highly polished holster, as though
a protected heirloom. When he was on the steps, she saw the
crowns on his shoulder tabs. His thinness was more skinny
than lean and he hadn't the legs for shorts.

"My name's Haxton. They told me at the gunner site
you'd come up here. Anything I can do for you?"

That was polite enough, but the way it was said seemed
to place Fay in her category, a civilian nuisance. Her voice
sounded stiffer than she had meant it to. "We came to stay
overnight with the Cowans. Do you know where they are?"

"Yes. Singapore. They left yesterday."

"You mean . . . for good?"

"That's right."

"But they can't have just. . . . What's happened to the
servants?"

"Gone to Tampin. I arranged that. Army transport and so
on. Fact is I've had to requisition this place."

She stared at him. "Are you saying that you've put the
Cowans out of their home?"

He straightened. She had the feeling he was going to tell
her there was a war on, but he didn't.

"It wasn't quite like that, Mrs. . . . ah. . . ."

"Gourlay. Why does the Army need this place? The Japs
are hundreds of miles away."

"Can't give you reasons, I'm afraid."

"You didn't give the Cowans any reason either?"

He had no answer to that. Fay went to the railing and
leaned on it. The light had almost gone but the bumps of
mountains to the east were still drawn against the sky, and
for the first time they seemed sinister, looming, covered with
jungle that could come flowing back with the annihilating
ruthlessness of lava.

Without looking at Haxton she said, "We'll have to stay.
For one night. There's nowhere else we can go."

"I'm afraid you're not in the picture. I've taken over here.
My gear is in one of the bedrooms."

She turned. "You're not staying with your men?"

"Good Lord! I'm not a gunner!"

"What are you?"

He ignored the question. "I'm sorry about your disappointment, Mrs. Gourlay, but the resthouse at Tampin isn't far. If they can't take you in I'm sure they'll find you something else in town. I could come along to see that you're fixed up all right."

Liza was now sitting on a swing seat suspended by ropes from the rafters, making it creak into movement by one toe just touching the boards. Angus had gone back to the door of the living room, almost merged into the shadow behind. Fay was conscious of her son as, for once, an interested audience.

"That's very kind of you, Major Haxton. But we're not going to the Tampin resthouse tonight. We're staying here, as the Cowans would have wanted us to. There is no reason why you should be disturbed. We'll be off in the morning."

His back went even straighter. The tone of his voice implied his patience was now under considerable strain.

"I see you still don't understand, Mrs. Gourlay. I'm on my own here at the moment, but that could end at any time. Without notice. Because of this I can't allow you to stay."

"This house is now out of bounds to civilians?"

"If you choose to put it like that."

"What if I refuse to budge? Will you call in those gunners to throw us out?"

"I can't believe you'll be unreasonable."

"Then start believing it now. Because we're staying. I'm going to find a meal. There are bound to be tins left. Unless the Army has requisitioned them, too?"

"No need to be unpleasant!"

"Sorry. Put it down to travel fatigue. Angus, there must be candles somewhere. See if you can find them."

"Sure, Mum."

Fay went down to the car to haul out an overnight bag packed with essentials for the three of them. It was heavy, and she came up the steps lopsided. The Major had disappeared. Liza was still sitting on the swing seat, still making it creak, but now as an accompaniment to a low, tuneless humming that might be a bid to reproduce one of the

Hailam songs Amah had taught her. She seemed quite content once again, as though she knew for a certainty that, despite minor inconveniences, her life was always going to be surrounded by others charged with a mission to keep her at least reasonably comfortable.

There was no sign or sound of the Major for over an hour, during which Fay got Jessie Cowan's paraffin cooker going, serving a hot meal of tinned stewing steak, tinned potatoes, tinned peas, and tinned creamed rice, all washed down with milk made from powder whipped up in water from a tap trickling out the last gallons in the reservoir tank. They ate at a scrubbed table on which for a quarter of a century Jessie had rolled out her dough, now desecrated by four candles bedded into their own wax. Liza was hungry but Angus, uncharacteristically, was not. Fay kept wanting to ask him what was the matter, but said nothing. There wasn't much said at all. The kitchen was hot from a closed back door, with huge moths battering against the copper screens on two windows — assault troops trying to make a breach for an army of the night's insects.

The Major didn't knock, but there was a certain diffidence about the way he came into the room, standing just inside it, bringing with him an unlit storm lantern.

"I thought you'd better have this. The gunners lent it to me. I won't be needing it. Though you'd better watch where you put it. The blackout's pretty sketchy in this house. The Japs don't do much night flying, but you never know."

Fay got up. "I never thought of offering you a meal?"

"That's all right. The gunners will feed me. I've left my gear. I'm just taking a sleeping bag. You said you'd be off in the morning?"

"Yes."

"Oh, the water's getting pretty low. We'll be fixing up an emergency pump, but tonight — "

"Don't flush the loo?"

He nodded. Then, putting the lamp on a kitchen chest, he withdrew slowly into the shadows of the passage without shutting the door. Fay sat down. She was conscious of unkindness on her part but couldn't feel any shame from it.

Angus was staring at her. She nearly told him to look at something else.

The displaced really have no time for others, she thought. We need a fixed base from which to operate the charity of feeling.

FIVE

S he knew the sound well enough: the scream of a dog taken by one of the big cats, always horrible, near the ultimate in pain and terror, but now it seemed to make contact with naked nerve endings. She wanted to cover those cries with her own. She put her hands to her face and then slid them around to her ears. It wasn't from a distant village this time, but much nearer, the Tamil workers' houses in the gulley, a mongrel left behind from a mass exodus, wandering about amongst those emptied concrete cubicles looking for food. Yesterday it would have been a childrens' pet.

The screams stopped. The hand she pushed out along the seat cushions for cigarettes was shaking. She took one out, lit it, then threw the match onto the boards of the verandah. In the still air it continued to burn, a small torch. What had Jessie done with her dogs? Taken the four to Singapore, pampered evacuees? Big John meant to shoot his two at Estate House before Ruth and he drove away. She knew that, so did Angus. At least a big cat wouldn't get them. They had buried Mick, almost with ceremony, the first martyr at Sungei Dema.

Liza had slept through the dog's agony; she would be yelling now if she hadn't. Angus could be awake, lying in the dark with his thoughts, possibly of Mick. If he came out here to find her she would have nothing, really, to say to him, words between them not much more than signals in living's routine ceremonials. He was being completely non-provocative, coupling this with a new attentiveness to Liza that Fay felt was less a sudden crisis upsurge of affection for his sister, more a matter of considered policy. He might, of course, be trying to help his mother, though there was no way she could know his intention and he wasn't likely to indicate it.

Clouds were in a conspiracy to keep the night as dark as it could be, a thick wadding blocking out moon and stars, with not even the slightest stirring to hint that a wind was coming, perhaps with thunder, to bring relief. The air she breathed felt used, as though jungle beyond the rubber plantations had sent up tentacles to suck in what it needed, leaving a residue that was almost a waste product, tainted with the smell of rotting leaves.

Only a week ago the *Straits Times* had carried an article on the revival of faith in England. Not a filling of the churches so much as a return to the belief in the basic simplicities of good and evil, with Adolf Hitler as the embodiment of evil, and therefore the good, with God, on our side and Mr. Churchill functioning as the Almighty's current chief agent. It sounded almost like one of her father's worst sermons, and yet perhaps you had to have a faith like that to survive as a person or a people in times of terror. But the tropics were the wrong climate for it. Here, where the black panther seizes the deserted dog, you were ten thousand years away from village evensong. You could, though, see Kali easily enough, goddess of life and death, the many-armed, with blood on some of her hands.

Fay did what she never had allowed herself to do: she lit a new cigarette from the butt of the old. The light she saw in the distance didn't give her a stab of panic; it was too bold to be threatening. Its glow, first like a mini moon rising behind a bump in the road just before it fell away down to rubber, suddenly became a straight, bright beam directed towards the bungalow, lingering on it with a slight bouncing from the carrier's walk, before swinging to the Siddeley, asking questions there, too, checking the number plate, lifting to note that the car was packed to well above window level. The light went out. There was a crunching of boots on gravel, getting louder and louder towards the steps. It stopped. Fay could hear breathing.

"You're not Major Haxton. Who are you?"

"God! You frightened me! I didn't see your cigarette."
He had a smoker's cough. "Actually, I was just coming up to
leave this. Sort of moral obligation."

"What?"

"Loot. One of my chaps found it. In the room behind you.
The old boy got rid of all the others. Smashed them out the
back. Would you believe it? On the cement."

"What are you talking about?"

"Whisky, as a matter of fact. Felt I ought to return it.
Crazy idea in the circs, I suppose. This place'll be stripped
when the Army leaves. Look, I'll just put it here. At the top
of the steps. And push off. Hope I didn't give you a fright?"

"No. Why bring back the whisky?"

"Ah. Put it down to Welsh ancestry. Methodist chapel.
Interested in theology?"

"Not any more. Wouldn't you like to stay for a drink? I'm
a friend of the owners."

"Well, of course, that creates a different situation.
Thanks."

He came up the steps. Fay thought that the sound of boots
on boards might wake Liza, or Angus, if he wasn't awake
already. Her guest blundered about, awkward at finding a
seat, politely not switching on the torch to have a look at his
hostess.

"You're the officer in charge of the gunners?"

"Makes me sound like a nursemaid. But yes. I see the
Major has briefed you. My name's Bennett. Temporary Captain Royal Artillery. Bank clerk practically by birth and
certainly by breeding, which means that nobody had much
hope for me from about year six."

He paused, as if for a reaction. It was difficult to send encouraging signals in the dark; she couldn't find the words
that would do it. He went on, committed to a performance.

"My career, a branch office in East Grinstead. Know the
place?"

"No, I don't," Fay said, trying to make the negative sound
alert and interested.

"Stuffed with old ladies seeking out their last days before
heaven on eighty thousand in conservative investments

yielding a safe three and a half percent. Maybe safer without the half. Used to give my Manager sleepless nights when he had to recommend that one of his ladies risk four percent in order to keep up living standards. But not my problem. No one ever asked my financial advice. My temptation was to keep from putting on my best through-the-grille smile, then to say: 'Madam, Christians, including Anglicans, are under a strict injunction to give all they have to the poor.' It would have been one way to leave banking."

He seemed pleased that Fay laughed, and set up a grateful rustling of the wicker in his chair.

"This bottle had been opened by one of my splendid lads just before I got to him. But I think we ought to drink out of glasses, don't you? Enough of this camping."

Fay stood. "Lend me your torch and I'll get them."

Willie Cowan might have smashed all his whisky tumblers along with the bottles. She could only find a sink glass and a cup. Perhaps he had buried cut crystal somewhere under his rubber, along with the family silver, as Ruth might be doing now. She gave Bennett the glass and cup without switching on the torch. Their contact so far had been completely non-visual. She liked his voice, she mightn't like his face. There was the sound of pouring.

"Take yours neat?" he asked.

"Yes. It works faster."

He gave her the glass. She took it back to the swing seat. There was silence until he broke it.

"You're making for Singapore? From where?"

"Sungei Dema."

"Never heard of it."

"It's near Kuantan. On the east coast."

"Don't know that side at all. All my hard driving to get away from the enemy has been down the west."

"You're a long way behind them now."

"You think? The slant eyes are everywhere. I've got so I look at every bush with suspicion. We've been nearly overrun twice. Had to hold them off with rifle fire while we got the engines started. So far I've been spared leading a bayonet charge. No training for that. No stomach for it, either. Us gunners aren't supposed to be exposed to the close-quarters stuff. Somebody has boobed when it happens. Our role is to send over shells from a comfortable distance behind the infantry. The twenty-five pounders I'm nursing these days haven't got nearly the operational range I'd like. Still, you can move them quick in an emergency. I reckon it would take us seven minutes from the first alarm to be out of that wood down there and on the road again. That's one drill we've really practiced. You seen anything of the Japs?"

"Yes."

"When? How?"

It was easy to tell him. She wanted a cigarette, but didn't want the flame from a match, a revelation of faces, of appraising eyes, their contact suddenly on a totally new plane. He must feel the same; for all his smoker's cough, he hadn't offered a pack. You could confess fear to someone on easy nodding terms with his own.

"The worst thing about it was no trace in the morning," Fay said. "Absolutely none. Not even bicycle tyre marks. If my son hadn't been with me I might have been down to looking for traces of bread crumbs on the terracing by the pool, for proof. And as the day went on nothing happened. The Japs didn't attack the ferry; they didn't even have a brush with any of our men out hunting for them. And that was practically all of two battalions. The Brigadier came up to Sungei Dema himself to question me. It was weird. I mean, sitting there in my own house, with everything normal, even the mine still working. You could hear the ore cars. Then he questioned Angus, that's my son. Without me there. I felt guilty."

"What the hell for?"

"I don't know. I suppose for upsetting what had been just as usual up until then. Of course it had to come, but I didn't have to be the instrument of its coming, if you see what I mean?"

"Sounds like you've got a farm of ostriches up there, all hiding their heads. They'll have to pull them out of the sand damn quick if they want to get clear of the Japs. You were sent ahead with the kids?"

"Yes."

"Maybe your Brigadier found it hard to believe in that patrol, but I don't. Already there have been dozens of them. Soon there'll be hundreds."

"But why didn't anything happen around Kuantan?"

"Easy. The job assigned those men was to get as far south as possible as fast as possible. Without attracting attention. They took a risk coming to your house. But they live off the land and needed food. Whatever defense position we set up, there are now always going to be sizable bodies of Japs tucked in behind them. Task: to spread panic and alarm. It's good strategy and it's working. Too bloody true it's working."

"You don't think the Kangar Line is going to hold?"

"The *what* line? Kangar? I must have missed it when I was up there a couple of days ago. Where did you hear about this?"

"K.L."

"A handout from the local sub office for propaganda. Won't be long before it puts up the shutters for good."

"You sound defeatist."

"Oh, lady! Got a white feather for me?"

"I didn't mean it like that!"

He laughed.

"More whisky?"

"Yes."

His chair creaked. He loomed over her. He took her glass and from the sound almost half-filled it. He was as generous to himself before wicker protested at his weight.

"If it were possible to weep for red tabs I'd be doing it for the ones up on command hill in Singapore. They've got real problems. A big one they invented themselves. Deciding years ago that the jungle was impenetrable. It made things a lot easier for the paper work. Now the Japs are just walking through the impenetrable. In some places, as you know, pushing bicycles through it. That's bad. But the really big worry has to be that ninety percent of the men brought into this country to do the fighting couldn't care less whether it's taken over by Japs or Eskimos. And why the hell should they? Two years ago most of them hadn't heard of the place.

That goes for the British as well as the Indians. There's also the fact that the country hasn't been too sweet to them since they arrived. You ask any of my men down under the rubber what they think of Malaya and they'll tell you that the cities stink, and the jungle stinks, and the mangrove swamp stinks worst of all. As for the rubber forest, for the rest of what I hope will be a long life I'm going to have my nightmares set under rows of those damn trees to which there is no visible end. They even plant their oil palms the same way. Forty-seven different kinds of insects drop on you from oil palms if you're camped under them. Did you know that?"

"I've never camped under oil palm."

She heard him gulp from the cup. He lowered his voice.

"Sorry. A slug of whisky and I start sounding like a Welsh revivalist preacher on hellfire. God knows what I'll be saying when I finish this cup. I'm a frustrated singer, really. I love the sound of my own voice making as little sense as a Handel recitative. I didn't mean to upset you."

"You haven't. I quite like not being protected."

"Is that what they did at the ostrich farm? Protect you?"

"It's what I asked for when I went there."

"You got what you asked for? It's never happened to me. Not once. Enough to make a man lose faith."

"What did you mean about this country not being too sweet to the soldiers come to defend it?" she asked.

"In general? Or the personal?"

"The personal."

"Right. As an officer, with the elevated rank of Captain, I rate temporary membership in any of your clubs. And what happens when I go into one? Room is made for me at the bar by Scotch estate managers who probably wouldn't rate driving a bus in their native Glasgow, but out here are *Tuans* in command of whole companies of black Tamil rubber tappers. My label with these *Tuans* is temporary gent. Coming from that source I don't like the label. I punched one of the *Tuans* in the nose at the Taiping Club. Terrible. I was in my cups at the time. He made a remark I found offensive about the fighting qualities of the troops in this country. Probably true, but still offensive. The matter was hushed up. I didn't even lose my temporary membership.

But I don't expect ever to be in Taiping again. The Japs will soon be using the club without the privilege of honorary membership."

There was the sound of his drinking. He seemed to be concentrating on it.

Fay asked, "Planters' wives haven't been kind to you either?"

"Oh, I wouldn't say that. Some of you ladies have a very gracious way of handing over a cup of tea at a mobile canteen. And we all love you for it. Makes up for home and mother. Though not really for girlfriend, if you know what I mean? For that we have to substitute the Kuala Lumpur whore shop. Not always satisfactory."

He went into a silence deep enough and lasting long enough to be remorse over what he had already said coupled with a whisky-fumed determination to say no more. The only sound was from behind them, a couple of chicha lizards conducting phase one of their complicated sex life on the living room ceiling. She was certain he had now emptied his cup, while she had only sipped from her re-fill. She had a slight feeling of power, like a mesmerist over the about-to-be mesmerized, but it was Bennett who suddenly took the initiative again.

"I've always had big feet," he announced, speaking slowly, almost putting a full stop between each word. "Even as a schoolboy. Do you realize that if your feet are out of proportion to the rest of you, you don't make a good footballer? You might think you would, but you don't. This is a handicap at the start of life. Now I don't mind so much, except when I look at them. Some women like big feet in their men, I've been told, but I never met one who claimed to."

Again silence. The chicha lizards had decided that the whole thing was far too much bother and had given up. Fay allowed the whisky more time to work, then used a quite loud, firm tone.

"Captain, why has Major Haxton requisitioned this house?"

"What?"

She repeated the question.

"Oh. God's adjutant. Intelligence Corps. Enough to make

you suicidal in this show. Had some terrible times recently. Like when he was sent back to fix up a new divisional H.Q. Found the right house and everything. Splendid view. Decent plumbing. Mosquito nets up. Cook working on the cucumber salad. Signals section functioning. Slit trenches dug."

He paused for a smoker's cough that turned into a bark of a laugh.

"Staff car comes swirling up the drive. General steps out and is about to mount to the front verandah when Japs come in the back door, firing from the hip. Like a Hollywood horse opera. Maybe that's why everyone got away. Including signals and the cook. Don't know what happened to the cucumber salad. But it nearly broke poor old Haxy's spirit. Almost cost him his crowns as well. Which is why he's being so careful now. Wouldn't you?"

"You're talking about the Major's fixing up a new H.Q. for his general."

"What?" A pause. "My lips are sealed."

Fay laughed. He wasn't drunk, or not very.

"Lips unsealed," he said. "I like the clever way you come to a conclusion from facts served you on a tray. Refusing to be sidetracked by small talk about big feet. Sure, this'll be an H.Q. if top brass approves. And I can't see any Major General declining to use a water closet that has a couple of steps up to it."

"Isn't this bungalow too exposed?"

"Oh, well, they'll throw a couple of camouflage nets over the roof and keep vehicles from messing up the gravel out in front. The Japs aren't doing all that much bombing these days. Economising for their next invasion. They're sure they can drive us off this peninsula with second class mortars. If our generals didn't have that worry about enemy patrols sneaking up on them in the dark, they could sleep as easy in estate managers' houses as they used to in those French castles. You know this, we could now be sitting on what will become a historic verandah. Site where big chief flown in from India issues famous order to stand and fight to the last man and the last round."

"What happens then?"

"We all move seventy miles farther south to a new impregnable line across Johore."

Wicker creaked.

"I must be getting back to my nest under the rubber. Otherwise I'll be breaking Army Regulation three-four-seven-two-A."

"What's that?"

"An officer will not be seen by other ranks rolling back to his tent dead drunk. Especially when he's requisitioned the bottle from one of his men. I thank you for your hospitality. And envy your arrival in Singapore tomorrow."

She heard his feet on the steps. Then his voice again.

"Speaking of arrival in Singapore, how are you off for petrol?"

"I'll have to get some. I thought maybe Tampin or perhaps Gemas."

"You haven't a hope in hell of finding a civilian pump operating around here. As you leave you'll see just below tree line a regulation five-gallon can of service fuel apparently abandoned by the road. It will be full. Empty the contents in your tank and put the can back where you found it. And without tying on the note of heartfelt thanks that could get me court-martialed."

"I don't know what to say?"

"You could say I'm a lovely fellow."

"You're a lovely fellow."

"I do agree. If I survive this unique shambles some lucky girl is going to find that out one day. I hope she has money of her own."

Fay listened to his feet crunching away on the gravel. Then they came crunching back again.

"One thing more. When you get to Singapore don't be tempted to hang around. Go to the nearest travel agency and book yourself out on a ship to Australia. And when you get to Australia don't settle in Sydney. Move on down to Hobart. I've got a feeling that the white man may *just* be able to hang on to Tasmania. 'Night."

SIX

The can was where Bennett had said it would be, beyond the bump in the road thrown up like an earthwork to hide the bungalow. Fay braked the car on a steep gradient and Angus got out. He had to be ordered to do this, the boy walking slowly over to the rubber, then half-dragging the can back across laterite as though it was too heavy for him to lift. Sturdy muscles would have let him carry the thing if he had wanted to, but this was a demonstration of protest that didn't stop when he reached the car but went on, with gruntings, as he unscrewed the tank cap and started to pour. He was spilling a good deal; she could smell it, but didn't get out of the car to supervise.

Angus had been listening from the living room the night before. She hadn't accused him of this, there was no point. He might have denied it, which would have put another brick on the barrier of falsehoods between them. During a breakfast from more tins, his manner had been a declaration of anger, a private rage for which Fay could find no adequate explanation, as though something said in the dark out on that verandah, perhaps something said by her, had jarred against the compact dogmatisms that kept a boy's living neat and tidy.

She heard the tank cap being screwed back on, turning her head just as he began to shove the can, using one foot, towards the side of the road.

"No, Angus! Back in the rubber where you found it."

He looked at her, then picked up the can, strolling towards the trees, taking his time to find the exact spot from which it had been lifted, pretending to search the cropped lalang grass above the drainage ditch to discover where it had been flattened. Then he came back to the car, getting into the seat beside her, slamming the door shut.

Fay started the engine. For no reason she could credit, her heart was beating faster, almost palpitating, as though issuing a warning that under prolonged stress it could run amok, destroying itself and taking her with it. A sense of parts of her body as leading their own existences, these only linked to hers in a potentially fatal Siamese twin hook-up, was something left over from childhood, absurd fantasies that were the by-products of loneliness, but clinging, more limpet-like than any memories. She had often lain in a wide, cold bed monitoring the thumpings of her heart, admonishing it, telling it that the creakings in an old house on a night of wind were not from footfalls at all, nothing more than the complaints of aged timbers as they shrivelled.

The road went down into a hollow, then lifted itself over another wave of ground beyond which was the gunner camp. The mess tent still had its flaps raised and the cauldrons alongside were steaming again. A man without a shirt was shaving at a mirror hung on a tent pole. Even from a distance it seemed to Fay that his booted feet were outsize. There was no engine running in the camp to cover the sound of the Siddeley's heavy descent of yet another slope, and the man turned. Lather covered the lower half of his face like a cut-down Santa Claus beard. She put a hand out of the driving window to wave. He lifted a safety razor in return salute. She accelerated, eyes back on the road again for a surge up, wondering if she would need to change gear.

"That man's a coward," Angus said.

Fay put her foot on the brake, then took it off again. She didn't turn her head to look at her son. In the back seat, tucked down into her nest, Liza was humming to herself. Against Angus's aggressive certainty there wasn't much that could be said. A homily came into her mind, a nicely tied parcel, that a coward was not someone who felt fear, but someone who let it take over. The cliché seemed to have taken on a shining patina from a long and successful use in suppressing further enquiry into the subject. She would have needed more authority than she had to use it on her son.

After the last of Willie Cowan's rubber trees, the road became a straight line sliced through secondary jungle. For minutes before they reached it the main highway loomed as a U-shaped gap, swelling steadily, repeatedly filled and then emptied by cars and heavy lorries. There seemed now to be a steady two-way flow, both north and south. Fay, always a slightly uneasy driver, was suddenly dreading being caught in a processional of vehicles, especially Army ones, where her speed would be dictated, subject to what she suspected would now be a half-angry military discipline accompanied by honking horns, with huge engines panting on the Siddeley's tail.

At the end of the side road, she had to wait for a wide enough break in the traffic to let her get the car up an incline in low gear before accelerating away as part of the traffic stream. She was over-cautious, missing a couple of chances, conscious of her son's difficulty in suppressing comment, squirming in his seat. A serious bid to get going was brought to a sharp, braked stop on the cover over a drainage ditch by the fast approach from the north of a big, khaki-coloured Ford with a pennant fluttering from a rod mounted behind the radiator cap. The staff car had its sunshine roof pushed full back. Thrust up through the opening was more than half of a burly, turbanned Sikh standing on a front seat. In spite of springs underfoot, he put up a fair imitation of a soldier on sentry duty, rifle held straight up at the present. Angus shouted, "Get behind them!"

The khaki car had been given the dignity of considerable space to itself. Fay, jerking the Siddeley up onto the road, caught a glimpse of a man with a red band around his cap staring at her through an open back window. On the tarmac she used the accelerator too heavily and the engine coughed a protest, then recovered. They went in pursuit of the big Ford.

"That man's watching for planes," Angus told her. "If we stick with their car we can pass everything when they do. See?"

She saw all right, but thought it could be tricky, with a long convoy coming at them in the up lane: canvas-hooded lorries open at the back, identified in her driving mirror as a supply column.

Angus said, "The man in that car's got red on his hat. Like the Brigadier at home. Does that mean he's a general?"

"Probably."

"Why is he going away from the war, then?"

"Generals have conferences they have to go to."

"Away from the war, you mean?"

"Sometimes."

"How do you know?"

It was a direct challenge. She couldn't take it up properly and drive the car at the same time.

"I don't really," she admitted.

Angus celebrated victory with another shout. "Their driver's signalling. He going to pass something! Mum, you're not close enough! You've got to follow *close!*"

Fay pressed down the accelerator. The staff car swung out into the up lane, revealing the vehicle it was passing: a Mercedes with a mattress on its roof and on top of the mattress a trunk and suitcases, all crisscrossed with clothes line in an hysteria of roping. She recognized something she had seen from her seat in an air-conditioned K.L. picture house: a *Movietone News* of refugees fleeing from Paris after the fall of France.

She put out a hand. The staff car was sliding back into its own lane, revealing a lorry coming around a bend towards them not more than a hundred yards away. She jammed her foot to the floor, conscious of the size of the car they were passing, its length, and the time they were taking. As she swung in she saw the face of the lorry driver. He blared his horn, swearing at her, his mouth wide to do it. They had been in their own lane for at least a minute before she said: "Angus, don't you ever try to tell me what to do when I'm driving! Do you hear?"

Rage against him was pointless, flaring from that other rage she had caused. He didn't even seem interested.

"What? Did you see that car? The Mercedes? There must

have been twelve Chinese in it. I guess they're rich, with
that car. But I don't know how they all got in. I mean, those
ropes went through the tops of the windows. I don't see how
they could open the doors. Maybe they all crawled in
through the driver's door. There was a dog, too. A big
Alsatian."

"Angus, will you *please* be quiet."

The General was alone in the back of the khaki Ford, his
red banded cap centred in the rear window. The road
ahead, a division between rubber trees to the left and oil
palm to the right, was suddenly clear of traffic, with the staff
car accelerating. The Siddeley's speedometer needle pushed
up from the top forties into the fifties, then moved towards
sixty. Fay began to get the feel of wheel wobble through her
hands, but didn't ease off on the pedal, as though a com-
mitment to keep up with the car in front had become a com-
pulsion.

"You're doing sixty-one," Angus said. "I don't think
Granfa ever drove this car so fast. Last time we went to
K.L. he never went over forty-five. And that was only two
times. One of them was that long straight bit before the
Jerantut ferry. Why does it have a hundred miles an hour
on the speedometer? I bet this car couldn't do seventy-five.
I bet it couldn't do it even when it was new."

Why was he talking so much? Could it be he felt himself
already such a long distance from any comprehensible norm
and travelling farther from it every minute? He might be
offering this chat as a kindness, in a bid to distract her from
tensions, but in these circumstances she preferred the standard monosyllabic commentary.

Angus reached up to the handle for the sliding sunshine
roof.

"What are you doing?" Fay asked.

"Opening it."

"You know I don't like it open. It blows my hair and it
just makes the car hotter."

"But I was going to stand on the seat and watch. For
planes. Like that Sikh."

"No!"

"We can't see a plane coming if I don't!"

"There isn't going to be a plane coming. We're hundreds of miles from the war."

"Why is that General waving at you?"

Angus pointed. There was certainly a face looking back at them from under the peak of the red-banded cap. There was also a hand waggling. The General began shaking his head from side to side.

"Why doesn't he want us to follow him?"

"I don't know. But we've as much right on this road as he has!"

She caught the tightness in her own voice but didn't ease off on the pedal. It was as though they were in some way coupled to the Ford, and if they broke the coupling they might be left powerless, suddenly thrown off a conveyor belt taking them all to safety.

The road went into a double S-bend, the corners sharp, needing brakes, and when it straightened again, rubber had gone leaving jungle on both sides — primary jungle unchallenged by man, putting them in a darkened tunnel between hundred-foot-high walls of almost solid leaf screens. Even above engine noise Fay could hear the screeching of a colony of monkeys, their wild, exercise-period leaps agitating areas of branches that no wind touched. In the green gloom she felt suddenly protected and the driver of the car in front must have felt the same, slowing down by at least ten miles an hour, as if to linger in shelter. The Siddeley's wheel wobble stopped. The General had given up his signals.

Light exploded at them from around another bend, the blast of it much more than hard sun, as though the cleared ground ahead functioned as a giant reflector. The road came out into the open in an arc around a vast, undulating acreage stripped of all traces of the forest; even the stumps of the huge hardwoods had been pulled out, and pineapples now supplanted the jungle. The long, nearly interlocking rows of the shining, spiked plants provided no cover at all from a dominance of sky, the glare pitiless even to eyes protected by dark glasses. To the left of the road, curving with it, was young rubber not yet in production, the upper branches of the trees still thin and tentative, leaf cover patchy and in places yellowing, as though scorched.

The staff car put on speed suddenly. Fay pushed the Siddeley over sixty in a bid to catch up. She was almost back in position again when the white-turbanned Sikh turned around from his sentry duty. He held his rifle in one hand, using the other to make sweeping gestures that were more than a signal, instead suggesting anger. He might have been shooing a stray dog away from a porch. The General was back to his hand waggling.

"They don't like us," Angus said.

His own wit pleased him, and he giggled. Fay didn't laugh. She had an impulse, just controlled, to put a finger on the horn button and hold it there. She might even show them by passing, even if this did mean going up to at least sixty-five, maybe more. The wheel wobble was noticeable again, and she gave up the idea.

"I'm hungry!" Liza called.

"You should have eaten your beans," Angus told her.

"I *hate* beans!"

On a piece of swelling ground, set amongst the pineapples and seeming to proclaim their triumph, was a big sign almost the size of an advertising billboard, hard black lettering on shining white:

LIM TAHANG ESTATE
DE LARCHE FRERES.

Fay heard Big John's voice, loud from the top of his own dinner table: "That bloody De Larche Company! Working right now with the Japs in Indochina. They're pro-Vichy. Damn collaborators. I don't know why the hell Singapore allows them to carry on here. They should have been chucked out of the country. All their estates confiscated!"

This one looked well tended still and, even in a quick glance away from the road, Fay could make out huge numbers of swelling fruit already turning from their growth green to the gleaming red-brown of ripeness. Less than a year ago Roy and she had stopped the car at the edge of an estate like this. They had been coming home from a holiday weekend in Singapore, the afternoon cooling towards sunset, and both had the impulse to do something almost never done in Malaya — take a walk. Those pineapples, too, had been planted over rising and falling ground, and the challenge to explore came from an almost ridiculous curiosity about whether such an impeccable tidiness could possibly continue beyond the rise they were looking at, and on down into the gulley beyond, then up again. They had walked in a straight line along one row until seeming to find themselves lost in a rolling sea of pineapples, with jungle just visible from crests, like a distant, dark, looming of land.

Suddenly they'd been as tired as two over-ambitious swimmers, dropping to rest in a hollow. It was minutes before Roy had moved. She remembered the line of his bare, brown back as he'd sat up, pulling a knife from the pocket of his shorts, and then, kneeling as though hiding from some enemy creeping up on them along other rows, he had begun testing pineapples, taking his time to find one that was ready. He'd cut through the stalk, peeled away the ridged skin, and handed her a wedge from which finger pressure alone made the juice spurt.

Lying in that hollow they didn't speak, but she was ready for him when he came over on her body. His hands had still been sticky from the fruit. The well of heat into which they sank left them both gasping even after they had separated. She remembered shutting her eyes against stinging perspiration. She remembered something else, that walking back to the car she had wanted to laugh at the carefully planned weekend just behind them: a sea-view room in Raffles with a breeze from the Dutch Islands blowing the curtains; dinner in a courtyard under the stars; wine; a planned revival for love with everything scheduled, the moment for getting between the sheets practically timed; a nightcap poured. And it hadn't really worked. But in a pineapple field it had. She couldn't say this to Roy for fear he wouldn't find it funny. He thought her self-conscious about sex, she knew that, though she hadn't been aware of performance, or lack of it, lying on her back on that bare ground baked hard by sun.

"Mum! They're getting away from us!"

What had felt like an elasticized belt between two cars was now stretched to the maximum. Distracted by pineapples, she had allowed the staff car to be nearing the end of a long, slow bend just as the Siddeley went into it. The speedometer needle seemed sluggish, refusing to climb.

Angus shouted, "There's a plane! A Jap!"

Fay didn't see it. Her eyes searched the drainage ditch for an escape route. She saw planks over the gap and a track under rubber leading from it. Automatic fire was a metallic coughing. There were bangs, growing louder, then all other sound was suffocated by the roar. She wrenched the wheel around, aiming the car towards the planks. A huge shadow travelled up the road.

"Angus! Keep down!"

The Siddeley seemed to leap the ditch, into an opening between piled-up embankments on which the lalang grass was tall. The car skidded, missed a tree, then settled into gouged ruts masked under leaves; these ruts controlled the car's progress as though it were on rails until the drive wheels hit bare laterite softened by damp, and started to excavate the ground, losing all traction. Orange mud sprayed out behind them. As the noise of the plane's engines faded, the car's whine of protest mounted. Fay switched off.

For a moment she just sat there, accepting the sudden blessing of silence. There was no rumble of traffic from the road, no hint of a wind ruffling the tops of the rubber trees. The still morning heat, ruptured by a projectile ripping through it, appeared to sew up the tear at once, restoring the norm. A sharp crack was only a dead branch, loosened by vibration. Angus pushed down the handle of his door and got out, walking off around the front of the car to a polite distance before stopping to relieve himself against a tree, just as he might have done after arrival at a chosen picnic site.

Fay turned to look at Liza. The child was holding Wango in both hands in against her body, staring over the doll's head towards the back of the seat in which Angus had been sitting. If she was frightened, it didn't show now; she was in one of those moments of total withdrawal from what was happening around her, indulgences of intense privacy that Fay had more than once envied, as though the daughter had learned some trick of escape that had evaded the mother.

"You all right?"

For a moment there was no reaction to the automatic parental question; then Liza said, "I want to get out."

Wango came with her, both of them sinking into a camouflaged pothole, a happening that should have produced wails of fury but didn't, as Liza continued in total self-absorption. At some distance a car engine started up against a stillness that made the altering noise levels of its gear changes distinct. There would soon be the rumble of heavy convoys again. Fay helped Liza to firmer ground, then turned to look for Angus. He was running towards them, heavy-footed on the deep layered leaves.

"Mum! Plane! Coming back!"

Branches above were no more protection than a skylight. The pilot had spotted them, a big green car travelling in company with a flagged Army vehicle! He had seen them escaping from the highway into a wood of thin trees.

"Angus! Away from the road! Away!"

But Angus came on. As Fay was reaching down to lift Liza, she saw him stumble, go his full length, then push himself up on his arms. The roar of the plane, baffled by some rising contour of ground, became a Niagara pouring over the rubber forest. Fay went down flat on leaves, feeling Liza trying to squirm away. She held onto the child's ankle. Above them branches flailed each other. The earth jerked from explosions. There was unbearable white light, darkness, then white light again. Fay moved a hand up Liza's leg, meaning to pull the small body under her own for protection. Liza's mouth was opened wide to let out screams that couldn't be heard.

The roaring eased. There were three bangs from somewhere down the highway, followed by a loud hissing that didn't seem to come from the air. Around them the wounded trees quietened. Liza, nested in leaves, with Wango abandoned well beyond her reach, was sobbing. Fay stood, the movement awkward, with an almost arthritic creaking of bones. Angus was again coming towards them, slowly this time, his feet lost in leaves, as though he was wading through a shallow edge of sea with a strong undertow.

Fay looked back towards the car. It was spotlighted from a huge hole in the forest roof, a wide shaft of sunlight slanting down. It seemed undamaged.

The plane noise had gone completely. Liza's sobs swelled into something like a howl.

"She's messed her pants," Angus said.

SEVEN

Somewhere Fay had read that it was called a brownout. It was meant to be more, an order intended to achieve the effect of London's main defence against the Blitz, not a chink of light showing anywhere, or at least not enough for it to be seen from the air. Here civic duty, or fear, had totally blacked out some of the houses, these like huge, dark rocks at the centres of their gardens, while others were relying on verandah roofs as shutters against the sky, and beneath that shelter the glow of life in rooms continued. There was music from radios, and while the car stood by a kerb, with Angus out of it to read a street sign by flashlight, Fay clearly heard the words of a song that had its own absurd pathos, an import from England, but now in a way applicable here as well, offering a kind of stubborn denial of the takeover by misery.

> "... There were angels dining
> At the Ritz,
> And a nightingale sang
> In Berkeley Square ..."

From across the street came laughter, a man's and a woman's, though there was no sign of movement in the shadow of the trees drooping over the pavement.

Angus called, "It's Kelawang Avenue."

There was exhaustion in his voice. He hadn't been able to sleep in the car.

"I think that should be right," Fay answered. "If it is, Sembang Road is somewhere off this."

"Want me to walk along and read signs?"

"No, get in. I ought to recognize the turning. We'll be there in a few minutes. Then food and bed. You must be tired out."

He went around the front of the car, climbing into his seat and slamming the door before he said, "I'm all right."

She pressed down the self-change pedal. The Siddeley jerked a protest at being asked to move off in second gear. Another car was coming towards them, shape invisible, identified only by glimmerings through the slats of its hooded headlamps. It seemed near the crown of the road. She had a moment of fatigue panic that the driver hadn't seen the Siddeley's lights, but the cars passed safely enough, two shapes groping through a near-total dark, their speeds held well below a reckless fifteen miles an hour.

"There's a side road," Angus said.

Fay braked to a stop. She hadn't seen it and still didn't, as though her eyes had gone into spasm. She sat without moving, again with the feeling that nature had changed to accommodate itself to the times, night issuing a thick overcast of cloud cutting out moon and starshine. Without asking whether he should, Angus left the car.

I ought to have talked to him after we passed the Ford, Fay thought. Instead of just driving on, not even turning my head. I should have had something to say then. But what, in God's name? There are no fairy stories for a near-nine year old driving through a war. Or for a three year old, either. Only I'm sure Liza didn't see anything. She was slumped down back there holding Wango. It was just Angus looking out. He saw it just when I did. I shouldn't have tried to hide my horror, pretending that what was in that ditch had nothing to do with us. He knew that it did.

The narrow beam from a torch with adhesive tape covering half its glass shone up a pole and then a street sign Angus shouted, "Sembang Road!"

The house was one of the black rocks surrounded by silent garden, with no light cracking through the masked windows. Fay couldn't see much as they turned into a drive beyond the stone gateposts, but remembered the place well enough: poured concrete like the Pink House, no old-fashioned nonsense of wide verandahs, but colonnades in mock Spanish rancho style, the local architects in recent years all seeming to suffer from a design virus picked up in Southern California. Trees made the garden even darker than the road; the drive was laid with fine gravel to give householders a last-minute warning of visitors and to slow down their approach. The Siddeley's tyres seemed unhappy on that surface; the car wobbled.

"Look out!" Angus yelled.

Fay braked. "What is it?"

"That car in front! You nearly bashed it!"

She still wasn't certain that she saw another car.

"It's a fifteen-horsepower Daimler," Angus said.

Fay took a deep breath. She spoke her thought out loud: "Edward never drives himself. Always has his syce do it. Why has the man left the car out here?"

"Maybe they're going somewhere," Angus suggested. "Or maybe the house is empty like — "

"Stop it!"

"Sorry. Are we getting out?"

"Yes."

"Liza's asleep again."

Lucky, Fay thought. On the gravel their feet seemed to make a lot of noise but there was no reaction to this from the back seat.

"We'll leave her for a moment," Fay said.

Angus's voice came from some distance. "Want me to ring the bell?"

"If you can find it."

"I have already."

There was a faint sound of chimes. In Singapore you had solid front doors, and the long windows were fitted with burglar-proof locks. Even upstairs in the bedrooms a proper caution meant inadequate ventilation, never that sense of the 3:00 A.M. breeze coming into the house from below to sweep away all pockets of yesterday's heat. In this dark, the Lallard place was like a fortress, determined to keep them out, but Fay had no sense of its being untenanted. She went up two steps.

"Ring again. Longer."

The distant chimes seemed to play a little tune on a theme of contempt. She saw the glow of the radial dial on Angus's raised wrist.

"What time is it?"

"Twenty past nine. Maybe they went out to dinner. And the syce brought the car back here to wait until they phoned up for him. Or something."

"The door would still be answered."

"Granfa says that in Singapore the servants do what they like."

There was a distinct, sharp clicking of heels on tiles in the hall beyond the solid slab of teak. The door opened. The light that shone over the terrace and gravel beyond it broke all the War Emergency regulations. Edna Lallard was wearing a long red evening gown, which hid her legs but left exposed thin bare arms and bony shoulders.

"Oh, my *God!*" she said.

Fay, subject to shock herself from unexpected visitors, still couldn't press back a rising resentment.

"You weren't expecting us?"

"Well, yes, but. . . . When we didn't hear from you we thought . . . I mean, that you wouldn't be coming tonight. Driving in the dark is so impossible now."

"Unless you have to," Fay said.

"Oh, my dear, I'm sorry! It's just that we have guests to dinner. A departmental thing, not friends. Rather important to Edward. Though, of course, we *are* ready for you. As much as we can be with everything in *chaos*. The houseboy has left. Not a word that he was going, none of the usual excuses. And he took Number Two Boy with him, as well as his wife. And she used to help in the house. There's just no hope of getting anyone else. The war is upsetting them. Even though Edward had them all in only last week to say that Singapore is absolutely secure, even if there are *some* bombings. I'm just praying that Cook won't go, too. His wife is helping a little but really she is quite useless.

Oh, I do feel awful about this, not seeming ready. And don't just stand out there. Come in. Where's Liza?"

"Still in the car."

"But I never thought! You'll have brought your Amah with you. How marvellous! She could be an *enormous* help!"

"We haven't got Amah."

"Oh. Well, we'll all work it out somehow, I suppose. Now, bags and things. I'll try to get hold of Syce, though I haven't a clue where he is at the moment."

"Angus and I can manage."

"Can you really? Well, look, may I just nip back for *one* minute to the drawing room? Tonight's been an absolute shambles, as you can imagine. We had to turn dinner into a sort of buffet. Just when Edward was *so* wanting to impress Señor Caldera that things are going normally in Singapore and that we *will* be buying those Chilean nitrates. Put your things down there and we'll have them taken up later."

The heels clicked, then stopped.

"Have you eaten?"

"No."

"Oh. Well, maybe we'll be lucky and Cook's wife won't have cleared away in the dining room yet. She's so slow, I expect she hasn't done a thing. Back in *seconds*."

The heels clicked again.

*

The knock on the door was tentative.

"Come in," Fay called out.

She was at the dressing table brushing her hair and saw Edna first in the mirror, wondering why she seemed so hesitant about coming into a room in her own house.

"Getting ready for bed were you, dear?"

"Yes. I'm semi-conscious. Nearly dropped off bathing Liza."

"I know. I simply loathe long drives myself. They absolutely exhaust me."

Even with a syce doing the driving? Fay put down the brush and turned around on the stool.

"Edna, I think I ought to try ringing Sungei Dema just once more. Can I use the phone in your room again?"

"But of course. And afterwards I wonder if you could give Edward just a tiny bit of help? You see, these South Americans are being dreadfully *odd* about this war. It's as though they expected the Germans to win. Especially now the beastly Japs are in on their side. Señor Caldera as good as said that at dinner. Edward pooh-poohed the idea, of course. Especially now the Americans are in with us. But apparently South Americans think that the Germans will win in Europe before the Americans have time to build up their navy again. And all that sort of thing. Really, I can't imagine why the Señor has to drag his wife around with him at a time like this. It's so frightful to have to entertain people you can't care about even in ordinary conditions. But just *now!* The talk got rather tense. I did my best to get on with the Señora, but her English is awful and all she would talk about was what she had been eating for the last six weeks. Javanese curries upset her. And, of course, we *would* have a *Malay* curry. I think she's got indigestion now, which could mean that they go back to Raffles before Edward has got anywhere. And it's going to be quite *grim* for him if the nitrates deal doesn't go through. Caldera seems frightened of a Jap takeover, which would mean that he wouldn't get the money for his shipments. It's all so *frantically* difficult."

"What could I do?" Fay asked.

Edna took a deep breath. "Well, I know you don't feel like meeting these people. God knows, I wish I hadn't to. But it could be an enormous help if you came down to the drawing room for just a little while. Half an hour would do. Time for a drinkie. You see what I mean?"

"No?"

"The thing is you've just arrived from the north in Malaya. A woman driving on her own and all that. Even at night. And everything quite normal."

"*What?*"

"Well, I'm sure it wasn't easy, Fay. But if you could just pretend a little that it was ... you know, everything absolutely all right and all that, it would help back up what Edward is saying to Caldera. About the war."

"What's that?"

"Let me think. Something about the attacker always having the advantage at the start. But that soon we'll be hearing the old British lion roaring. And then it was horrid, really. I mean, Caldera's reaction. He seems to have no sense of being a guest in our house. He said a lot of people these days were thinking that the British lion has rheumatism. Wasn't that a beastly thing to say at someone's dinner table? It really is *too* much that with all his other problems Edward should have to be dealing with South Americans as well."

"I'm sorry, Edna, but I can't come down tonight."

"It's only for a little, darling. Not half an hour even. Fifteen minutes."

"I couldn't do a good job of convincing them all is well up country."

"But you *got* here, didn't you? Nobody stopped you. And you said the shops were open in Kuala Lumpur. You didn't have any trouble on the roads?"

"A Jap fighter attacked. We'd been following a military car. Quite close. When we saw the plane we were lucky. There was a crossing over a ditch into rubber. I took it. The Army car was hit by cannon fire. Burned out. When we passed we could see the bodies."

"Oh, my God!"

"They'd been signalling us not to follow them. And like a fool I kept speeding up to do it."

"I think I have to sit down."

There was a straight-backed chair near the door. Using it, Edna, for all the red evening dress, looked like someone waiting to be interviewed for a job she knows she isn't going to get.

"I'm sorry," Fay said. "I didn't mean to tell you."

Edna raised her head. "Why? Because you think I'm the kind of fool who prattles on about having been on a War Emergency committee with Lady Duff Cooper? Well, I suppose I am. But I still get sick of Edward's confidence that everything is under control." She paused, as though taking time to reject totally her project in coming to this room.

"Of course you're not going down to meet the Calderas. To hell with South Americans. We'll go through to the phone. Maybe you'll get Sungei Dema this time."

In Edna's room the twin beds were caged in a glass-panelled air-conditioned box that looked like a tomb for the embalmed. The phone was inside, where an artificial coolness was maintained at sixty-five, the air clammy. Fay thought of her father's chronic bronchial complaints in a damp rectory. They sat on one of the beds. Edna asked, "You don't mind if I stay?"

"Of course not."

The switch from Edward's interests had been total, as though she was incapable of dedication to two causes at the same time, especially when these conflicted. Edna was waiting now to be a moral support when the phone call didn't get through. It didn't, the operator half-singing her message: "Sor-ree. From Kuala Lumpur to north no calls. You wish get Kuala Lumpur one half hour, maybe."

The voice had been loud enough for Edna to hear.

"Ruth and John probably left very soon after you."

Fay was certain they had not, but she didn't want to talk about it. They were still sitting side by side in the box for refrigerated sleep when the sirens started up, first from a distance that could be the harbour area, then from subsidiary units all over the city. The sound became so loud that it seemed to penetrate to nerves through skin as well as the ears.

"There isn't any place to go in this house," Edna said. "Edward just won't allow us to do anything about a shelter, not even a cupboard under the stairs. He says it would look bad for us to have anything like that up in these suburbs when the Chinese downtown can't do a thing to protect themselves. I suppose he's right. Though all our friends who have stayed do have something. There's one house with a reinforced-concrete cellar. They've got a drinks cabinet in it. Oh, my God! The Calderas! We can't drive them back to Raffles through this! The harbour area just gets sprayed with hot metal. They say it's from the Ack-Ack guns. Fay, would you like to take the children downstairs?"

"I don't think so. I'll go and see how they are."

The heat outside was an embracing comfort, even with that wailing pushing through it. At the top of the stairs Edna hesitated, as if dreading the descent of an Alp.

"What does one do with people one can't send home?"

She started down slowly, not expecting an answer. Fay crossed the hall. Angus was at a window, blackout curtains separated by his hand, the strip showing a pattern of searchlight beams loosely woven against the sky. Feeling no real alarm for herself or the children, she closed the door as though, despite the servants leaving, the big solid house was almost guaranteed inviolable. Even under the controlled discipline that Ruth and John had established, with its ordered routine, Sungei Dema had never felt like this; it was a small island in that immense sea of jungle, vulnerable in isolation. Here the island was huge, bristling with guns turned towards the enemy, as well as being packed with defenders of the fortress. While Fay stood by Liza's bed, peering down for any sign that the child was awake, the sirens gave up their warnings, but with reluctance, although one of them, at some far point, stubbornly carried on for another minute.

Angus had heard her come in. "I've never seen them before," he said, "except in pictures."

"What?"

"Searchlights. They must have about a million."

"Liza hasn't woken at all?"

"No. She's only just stopped snoring. I don't see why I have to be in a room with her? There are plenty of other rooms."

"Not ready. You heard about the servants."

"I could make a bed myself. I don't like being in a room with a girl. Even if she is my sister. That's all."

"Maybe we can do something about it tomorrow."

"When's Dad coming?"

"I don't know."

"Well, he can't be so far away. We knew he was in Johore."

"Yes."

"That's a long way from the Japs. Do you think he'll be in any fighting?"

"I hope not."

"I wish I was. I could kill Japs."

"Don't say that!"

"Why not? It's a war, isn't it? They started it, didn't they?"

"Keep your voice down!"

"Liza doesn't wake up. You could drop bricks and she wouldn't."

The first thump was not unlike a brick being dropped, not a big sound at all, but the noises that followed were a much louder sequence of bumps.

"Angus, come back from the window!"

"Mum, look! There's planes! You can *see* them!"

She went over to stand beside him as he began to count out loud. Fay echoed the count in her mind, getting up to ten as he reached eleven, but the aircraft were in broken formation and it was hard to be sure of numbers. The sky around them became flecked with small explosions, colour against the ghost white of searchlights.

"They're bombing the ships," Angus told her.

The window frame formed the edging to a screen on which she watched a film of something happening to others. She remembered a recent letter from a friend in Leicester, now married and moved to a house high up in the Chilterns from which the girl and her husband watched the blitz on London as immune eyewitnesses. The husband was in a reserved occupation and behind the words on the letter card there had seemed to be an undertone of something near complacence, as if the Fates or God had seen fit to keep secure two slightly more important than ordinary people. Fay could identify something very near that complacence in herself, a woman sitting under a sun umbrella by a pool reading about the fighting in North Africa or, only a few days ago, not permitting a raid on Kuantan airfield to disrupt the usual ritual of her morning swim.

Now it was fatigue and nothing else that put the screen between her and a bombing of Singapore harbour. The guarantees of security that had seemed to be issued along with her marriage to Roy dissolved in a circumstance as far outside all forseeable norms as a huge earthquake.

The Ack-Ack guns became very noisy, one suddenly opening up at what seemed only streets away. Liza woke and cried out. Fay went over to the bed, tucked against an inside wall, and pushed aside the mosquito net to bend over the child.

It was Cantonese she heard behind Liza's whimpering — a steady flow of words that came too fast to have any translatable meaning. Fay reached down to lift the child, but was resisted violently, arms and legs flailing.

"Mum, slap her!" Angus said. "Go on!"

*

Edna opened the door to the air-conditioned box.

"Oh, Lord! The beds aren't made! I forgot. It's so weird not having the servants."

"I'll help you," Fay said.

"You'll do no such thing." She yanked up a sheet, then a coverlet. "Sit here. I'll go down and get some coffee and bring it up. Roy said he'd ring back at ten-thirty sharp, but you never know, do you? I'll bring some toast, too. Are you starving? Would you like more than that?"

"No thanks."

Edna bent down to pick up a pale green sarong from the passage between two beds.

"Edward's," she said. "When he first came out here he had curly black hair and someone said he looked cute in a sarong. It wasn't me. Whoever it was, he's worn them to bed ever since. I can't imagine what they'd say if they knew at the Department. But I've kept it dark, as much for my own sake as his. I'll be back in a jiffy."

"I'm sorry you had to breakfast the children."

"Why darling? It was a pleasure. I hope you don't mind Angus's going off like that with Edward in the Daimler? The syce has strict instructions to bring him straight back, and no stopping anywhere. As for Liza, she's been an absolute angel."

"Really?"

"Telling me her whole life story. You'd think she'd lived for a hundred years. All I did was listen. And I wasn't pretending to. I was fascinated. Did you know that she has a pet snake at Sungei Dema called Boom Slang?"

"No, I didn't."

"It seems Boom Slang gets a cup of milk a day. It comes from the jungle through the grass to meet Liza as she goes out carrying a cup. It's a girl snake, not a boy snake. I wanted to ask how she could be sure of that. I gather she doesn't like boys of any kind."

Maybe my trouble as a parent, Fay thought, has been that I haven't listened often enough to my daughter's creative lying.

At the door to the box Edna turned. "I did put one question: how Boom Slang drank her milk out of a cup. Liza needed no time to think up an answer: The snake puts out its tongue and then makes a noise like Amah drinking soup."

The door clicked shut. With just a kimono over a short nightdress, Fay felt the cold at once and was reminded of frosty mornings at the Rectory. She badly wanted a cigarette, but no sign of an ashtray on the phone table probably meant that Roy's prohibition on all smoking inside mosquito nets was also operative in freeze cages. There were two blankets at the foot of the bed on which she sat and she pulled one around her shoulders, thinking that the world really was going mad when you paid more to get cold in a hot climate than you did to get warm in a cold one.

The phone rang. The challenge was so loud and direct that she stared at the instrument for a moment in half-panic. She put out a hand as a first step towards resuming, after a two-month break, the most intimate relation in her life, but all that came out of her mouth was a little croak that sounded as though she had laryngitis.

"Fay? Is that you? Are you all right? You sound strange?"

"Something in my throat."

"But you're well?"

"Oh, yes. Fine. The Lallards are really looking after us.

It's quite a descent on them really. I've got the feeling that I should start looking for something else right away."

"Why? They've got that huge house. Do them good to have some life in it. You know what I've noticed about Edward? Even the Singapore climate never melts the starch out of his shirts."

"But they're not used to children, Roy."

"Who is? I've never got used to mine. How are they?"

"Fine. Missing you, of course."

"You surprise me."

"And I'm missing you. And don't you dare say that surprises you."

"I won't."

"No use asking where you are, I suppose."

"No."

"What's the news from Ruth and John?"

"They're fine."

"What? Does that mean you've been in touch by phone?"

"Not direct, no."

"Then how? . . . Have they left the mine?"

It was a moment before he answered. "Yes."

"You don't sound very certain?"

"Yes, I am. They've left the mine."

"So they're on their way south?"

"Well . . . yes."

"Roy, what is it? You're sounding strange now. About your parents. If you know where they are why can't you tell me? Are they in K.L.? I know it's hard enough to phone anywhere just now — "

"Look, I can't talk about this. We shouldn't be mentioning places at all. I'll explain everything when we meet. In the meantime you're not to worry."

"But if they're coming to Singapore I must know where to!"

"If they go to Singapore they know where *you* are."

"If? Does that mean you think they may not come down to the island?"

"Fay, I'm just *not* going to talk about this, do you understand? So drop it. They're safe. That's all that matters, isn't it? And that's all I can tell you at the moment. Give my love to the children. Tell them I'll see them soon. Now I've got to go. 'Bye."

"Roy, wait! I — "

The line crackled as though overloaded wires immediately took over the space left by a signing off.

EIGHT

The leader of the Philippino orchestra was trying to make his two violins sound like the Glenn Miller strings. He was a dark-skinned, serious little man conducting a team of serious musicians, all with personal identities eclipsed by what they were wearing; bright floral shirts and scarlet cummerbunds strapping in their stomachs. Out on the floor three couples danced, defying the lonely stretches of parquet and the empty tables around them, some of which were half-screened by potted palms the waiters had pulled forward.

They hadn't canceled this dinner dance the night Penang fell, Fay thought, when the radio from up there had announced in Japanese-English that the place was to be rechristened Tojo-to after one of their damn generals. The Japs would have another name ready for Singapore, too, when the time came.

Hamish is sitting there wondering whether he ought to ask me to dance. I hope he doesn't. But if I don't say something soon he will. "I wonder why the orchestra has stayed on in this country?" she asked.

The orange-shaded lamp made his sunburned, battered face look almost purple.

"They can't go home," he said.

"No, of course not. How stupid of me."

She wished he wouldn't stare at her. He had done this sometimes at Sungei Dema, at dinner in the Estate House, or when she was playing hostess, the kind of stare that indicates a processional of assessments going on in the mind be-

hind the eyes. He didn't like Western women. He could
have had one easily enough and probably had, when
younger, from the annual fishing fleet of girls out from
home. Maybe it was early experience that had made him
go for the Malay easy-transfer system he had operated for
long enough, a basically commercial arrangement. It was
difficult to imagine any of those women, and particularly
the hard-mouthed Lali, wanting Hamish for his own sake
rather than for what was in his wallet. Though, who knows,
he may be a sexual giant. All I know is that I don't want to
dance with him, now or ever.

The Philippinos stopped work. Six people left the floor,
the girls with clicking heels, to occupy three tables on which
the orange lamps shone out like spaced lighthouses set by
a desolate sea. In the shadowy background hovered an excess of waiters. The men of the orchestra, leaving their instruments on chairs, filed out towards a door with a dimly
illumined exit sign, one of the saxophonists rubbing the
back of his hand across his lips.

"You haven't told me what you think of Roy's letter,"
Fay said.

"Am I supposed to think anything?"

"You know what I mean. What he says about Ruth and
John. It's as though I had to be told *something*. To keep me
quiet."

He stared at her again. "I don't read that into it."

"You think it is all likely? The mysterious Chinese Towkay friend at Morib who has a junk that will get them over
to Sumatra? Why on earth would they want to go to
Sumatra?"

"Well, they have connections with the island. All the
children went to that school at Medan. And John was interested in tin exploration over there. He even had a minority
interest in a Dutch-controlled mining company at one time."

"But Sumatra *now*, Hamish? John's a realist. Don't tell
me he thinks that if we can't hang on to Malaya the Dutch
will be able to keep the Japs out of Sumatra and Java?"

"Our war here is a holding operation. To buy time for
Allied reinforcements to arrive."

"Don't quote Malaya command at *me!*"

He grinned, then said, "Sorry," adding, "Getting to Sumatra first is one way of reaching Australia."

Fay felt then that she was returning the Hamish stare, the processional of *her* thoughts containing a lot of material that she mustn't allow herself to put into words.

"You got this letter yesterday?" he asked.

She nodded. "Delivered by hand. A brother officer, the man said. I didn't even know that Roy had been commissioned. The three times he's phoned me since I got down here he has said nothing about it. I thought he was still a sergeant and would stay that way. He used to say that only shits became officers in the Volunteers."

Hamish laughed, but said nothing.

"Would he get a commission for some special duty?" she asked. "Is that why he has never been able to get off to come here? Could they have been using him as a scout to get behind the Japanese lines? And now he's way up north somewhere? *You're* in a special service, but *you* get down to Singapore."

"Aye, but I'm not commissioned. They didn't think I was worth it. Other ranks get special leave facilities. At least in our lot. Don't let your imagination run away with you about what Roy is up to. I know it must be pretty grim just sitting around down here waiting."

She checked a comment on that "sitting around." The orchestra was returning with a singer, a Eurasian girl in an even brighter floral print than her colleagues' shirts, her shoulder-length black hair in corrugated waves. A waiter approached carrying a huge, double menu card, followed by two youths who could have been accolytes.

"Considering that Cold Storage is supposed to be packed out with stuff," Hamish said. "I don't see why the food here has to be so damn awful. Even though there's a war on. What would you like next?"

"Coffee, please."

"Sure?"

She nodded. Someone had told the Eurasian girl that her voice was like Vera Lynn's, and she had worked on this, the result a far miss.

> *Don't know where, don't know when,*
> *But I know we'll meet again,*
> *Some sunny day . . .*

"Like to dance?" Hamish asked.

"No, thanks. I can't bear being the first couple out on an empty floor."

He looked at the other tables. Fay willed those at them not to move and no one did. He didn't want to dance with her; it was just one way of passing the time with a woman made slightly neurotic by waiting for a man who stubbornly refused to show up. When the waiter and his attendants had gone, as soft-footed as cats, she said, "Ruth told me she thought you'd quite like the jungle work you're doing."

"I don't know about that. But I've sweated off twenty-seven pounds."

"At Sungei Dema you did carry a little extra."

"It's gone now."

"Lali wouldn't know you." She paused. "Do you hear from her?"

"No."

"You think of her?"

"No."

"Having arranged her travel to Telok Anson and a redundancy payment, you've been able to put her right out of your mind?"

"Yes."

"Hamish, you've really had a marvellously satisfactory life in this country, haven't you?"

"In some ways."

"Is that what you're fighting for? To get it back?"

"I haven't done any fighting yet, but when I do it'll be for that."

"After all these years we seem to be really getting to know each other."

"Wonderful for us both," he said, without a smile. "Clap!"

"What?"

"The girl. She's finished."

Fay clapped. Hamish was making a sizeable noise, cheerleader for the other tables, at which the men began to show considerable enthusiasm, but their partners did not. The Eurasian girl was pretty. She wouldn't stay a singer for long. Still clapping, Hamish asked Fay if she had thought about taking the children to Australia.

"You mean leaving Malaya without seeing Roy again?"

"It might be a relief to him to know you were safe."

"I'm not a Lali."

"Shut up!"

It was as though he had slapped her. She sat straight in the chair, pushed back in it, suddenly having to fight tears, determined that he wouldn't see the feebleness of that.

They always present a united front, Fay thought. Hamish knows a lot about what Roy is doing. They may have met. They could even be meeting quite often. And if that has happened Roy has given him strict instructions that I'm not to be told anything that might keep me awake at night. Knowing nothing can keep you awake, too. But if I said that to Hamish he'd probably suggest a double whisky before going to bed.

"Did Roy tell you to take me out when you got back to Singapore?"

He smiled. "Handing me twenty dollars to cover the bill? Along with my instructions?"

"Well?" she asked.

"This was entirely my own idea. A little return for what you did for Lali."

"And you haven't seen Roy up-country?"

"No."

"Or heard what he is doing?"

"No."

"It must be something quite important, if they gave him a commission for it."

"In this war all kinds of people are being commissioned. *I* might even be in the end. When things get desperate enough."

The bill arrived with the coffee. Hamish looked at it, then, smiling at her again, put down two ten-dollar bills, telling the waiter to keep the change.

"It's been a lovely evening," Fay said, picking up her bag. "But I'd better go. I like to be home if there's a raid."

"Are the children upset by them?"

"No. Not in the slightest."

"Isn't Liza missing Amah?"

"She did at first. Then set about training Edna Lallard as a replacement."

"Successfully?"

"So far, very. Not a hint of a tantrum since we arrived. And Angus has got Edward where he wants him. Both my children seem to have a highly developed instinct for self-preservation. I don't know why I still worry. Angus calls Edward "sir." No surer way to the heart of a top civil servant. I can't remember his calling anyone else "sir." Roy doesn't expect that kind of deference. Were you "sirred" at Sungei Dema?"

"No. I'm just an engineer with dirty fingernails."

"Their talents must have come from Roy."

"A convenient thought for you to carry around. I once saw Liza kicking Amah. Did you know that happened?"

She nodded. "But I never had any real evidence. By the time I'd arrived, only denials from both parties that there had been any violence."

After a moment she asked, "You've never liked Liza?"

He emptied his glass, put it back on the cloth and stared at it. "Before she could walk it looked as though she had all the markings for growing up into a proper bitch."

The blunt, outsider's view was a shock. It was a moment before Fay put another question. "And Angus?"

"I wish he was my son."

*

Fay had used the kneeling cushion twice before she realized that Angus was completely clueless about the ups and downs of High Anglican ritual. While they were coming into the cathedral he hadn't asked any questions to remind her that he had grown up as innocent of church experience as his father and, pretty certainly, his grandfather before him. The Hamlett Home Teaching Institute made a firm point about leaving religious instruction to the discretion of parents, which meant that when Angus hadn't raised the matter of God she hadn't either. There was a certain escapism in this, an escape from knowing that her own convictions, if they could be called that, were too wobbly to be put over to the boy as effective simplicities. In fact, all her early reading in theology had made such simplicities totally impossible for herself. One of the things she had found so surprising in her mother-in-law was the way in which Ruth had been able to hang onto hers, apparently resorting to prayer at the drop of a hat, claiming that, if you were married to a Gourlay and living in the jungle, you had to.

It was to Edward, not to his mother, that Angus was looking for a lead through the unknown, and Fay could appreciate the wisdom of this. Edward was as purposeful in his religious observance as he was in all his other spheres of activity. He was the leader who contrives to slide down on his knees in a gesture to the Almighty just slightly in advance of the rest of a congregation. In prayer, he seemed to continue to issue a challenge to competitors, the near-hawk profile still lifted, though with the eyes now shut. Angus couldn't risk shutting *his* eyes, but in everything else was a remarkable understudy, going down and coming back again only a fraction of a second behind his mentor. For the hymns, it was Edward who found the place and handed Angus his own book to hold.

It could have been for the hymns that they had all crowded into the cathedral on this Sunday immediately after the Japanese occupation of Kuala Lumpur, surrendered without a battle. They had come not for words, not for the Bishop's re-arrangement of platitudes, but for the singing, for the sound of massed voices backed by an organ still able, in spite of the tropical damp, to send out the tonic of its heavy, confident reverberations.

> *O God, our help in ages past,*
> *Our hope for years to come,*
> *Our shelter from the stormy blast,*
> *And our eternal home.*

Edward's was a firm baritone, adding to the massed effect, and in the second stanza Angus suddenly launched out with confidence, in a clear, near-choir-boy treble last heard singing "Valencia."

> *Under the shadow of Thy throne*
> *Thy saints have dwelt secure;*
> *Sufficient is Thine arm alone,*
> *And our defence is sure.*

Fay, feeling the fool she had long suspected she was, had to fight tears, abandoning the singing herself, standing to stare straight towards the high altar on which the candles flickered and dipped, as though from a wind that would soon be reaching to all corners. By the last verse, she felt rigid, frozen into this immobility, her spirit at some kind of end, a wall it couldn't climb.

> *O God, our help in ages past,*
> *Our hope for years to come*
> *Be Thou our guard while troubles last*
> *And our eternal home.*

The organ made a bold attempt to pipe them, newborn, into the downtown heat of the city. From a brazen sky came a hum of planes and with it, since there had been no sirens, talk about "ours," a sudden flare-up of secular hope that this could be deliverance sent on the heels of matins in a cathedral: the long-awaited squadron of bombers with its supporting fighters come at last to halt the upstart Japs.

The pavements stayed crowded; there was no general movement towards cars run on rationed petrol or to the rows of waiting rickshas using unrationed manpower. The churchgoers were standing to look up, women holding onto broad-brimmed hats against a brisk breeze from the Straits. Fay had an impression of white gloves everywhere, an added courtesy during worship. She had forgotten hers, as she had also forgotten to ask Edward for a prayer book before they left the house.

"Sir," Angus said. "Do you think they're ours?"

Edward looked down. Fay was becoming aware of just

how much he enjoyed playing the role assigned him ... a surrogate for Big John. In a way he was more effective than John had ever been, putting into this child-adult relationship a kind of intensity that no Gourlay would ever attempt. Edward, appealed to, gave his complete attention to the supplicant, and with an apparently total concentration that both flattered and comforted.

"I'm not sure," he said, deliberate over this honesty. "It could be a Jap force using the Straits as their route to another target."

"Oh."

The boy's disappointment demanded more detail on the assessment.

"They're keeping well over to the Dutch Islands," Edward said. "See that glinting? I can't see them turning north now to come in over us."

"Maybe they're making for some of our ships somewhere?"

"You could be right. I hope you're not. Anyway, best get to the car. I wonder where the syce has parked it?"

There wasn't going to be the glorious spectacle of Allied planes coming in low over the city en route to landings on the island's empty airfields. In the Daimler, Angus sat between Edward and the Tamil chauffeur, three heads half-blocking a screen on which there was a speeded-up documentary of Singapore's streets, rickshas, carts, cyclists, dogs, children, lorries, all in a pictorial flow that seemed to divide to let the car through, then fold together again, permitting only the briefest close-ups of pedestrian faces. Fat Chinese women don't walk, Fay thought, they waddle — a display of extra weight, evidence of rich living.

Edna blew her nose. "I got quite weepy in church," she said. "I think it must have been the hymns. And all the Eurasians. During the raid last night I lay thinking about them. I mean, the ones in K.L. Maybe it had something to do with the ships taking people away from here. There are no ships for them." She dabbed at one eye with a handkerchief. "It could have been what my hairdresser said. About England. As though it was some kind of heaven. She's never been there, of course. I wonder if they've all been to church

today, up in K.L.? They nearly all stayed behind, you know.
There was just no place for them to run unless they had
relatives down here. And they're half us, aren't they, after
all? It's what I feel anyway. It seems so awful that they have
to be the ones to face up to the Japs. Learning to bow low.
That's what the Japs make everyone do. Alice was telling
me. She saw it in Shanghai. Everyone had to learn to bow
low to every Jap wherever one met them. Even the most
ordinary soldier in the street. The new gods of Asia!"

Edward turned his head.

"Edna!"

*

White's had banners pasted along the tops of show windows that had been strapped against blast damage: "Winter
Sale Ends January 25th." Fay went into the store feeling
that Edward would certainly approve of this business-as-
usual approach, but what she saw beyond the swinging
doors wasn't reassuring: shelves half-empty, and most of
the display cases holding nothing. This was no clearance for
re-stocking, but a clearance, full-stop. The only thing in
unlimited supply was staff, Eurasian and Chinese girls, plus
some men, all in movement, as though the alternative to
standing apathetically behind stripped counters was this
pantomime of bustle. The word must have gone out that
there was nothing left worth buying, for there were few
customers in the aisles. Fay was reminded suddenly of crossing the Pacific with Roy in the Depression-blighted early
thirties. They had travelled on the huge *Empress of Japan,*
flagship of the Canadian Pacific fleet, with first-class accom-
modation for more than six hundred. But on that voyage only
thirty were using it, the dining room had been a wilderness
of unset tables manned by a small army of stewards whose
function seemed to be to maintain just this fiction of perpetual movement, while the ship's sad orchestra of three
sent down Strauss from an overhanging balcony.

Not ten paces from the door, Fay was taken over by a
portly middle-aged man who looked important enough to
be normally almost unapproachable, almost certainly Ma-

lacca Portuguese. He was now offering the welcome smile that he hadn't been obliged to put on for at least ten years. What was Madam's pleasure? She said it was boys' shirts. Immediately, he admitted that there was a problem. He would conduct Madam to the department but he couldn't offer much hope. Madam would appreciate that, until the war situation stabilized, re-stocking was an impossibility.

"The shirts I used to get here for my son," Fay said, "were almost always Japanese."

"Ah," the man was reluctant to admit this. "This way, please."

The commercial desolation seemed to get bleaker the farther they penetrated to the back of the ground floor. Two women came downstairs without parcels, obviously from the still functioning restaurant, each trying to tell the other a bombing story. Both stopped talking to stare at another European but there was no exchange of acknowledged recognition and a moment later Fay heard one of them say, "Wasn't she Taiping? I'm sure I've seen her at the club when we've been up there staying with the Hendersons."

Men's Wear could be said to be still functioning. There was even a dressing gown on a dummy. Perhaps the reason no one had snatched it off during the first days of the sale was the all-wool problem of overheating it offered. There sseemed to be men's shirts as well. A large woman at one of the mahogany counters was looking through a selection of at least half a dozen scattered in front of her, all heavy-weights meant for departees on home leave about to face up to freezing Britain.

"That's an awful price," the large woman said, then turned.

Fay was engulged by her almost before she had time to recognize Jessie Cowan. The only thing lacking in their reunion was the sound of yapping dogs.

"My dear, I knew you had to be down here! But where? We tried all the hotels and half the boardinghouses. But it's hopeless finding people. You just run into them like this. These last days I've been feeling that I was running into everyone I'd known all my life in Malaya. Ruth and John with you?"

"No."

Jessie stepped back to stare. "But . . . where are they? Where else is there to go?"

"They're supposed to be in Sumatra."

"*What?* That's nonsense!"

"Jessie, please don't say that!"

"Eh? Lassie, there's something. . . . We'll away upstairs to have a cup of tea. I'll just take these two shirts first."

They seemed to know Jessie in the restaurant. She ordered French cakes and got them, shot questions at Fay and got the answers, pouring tea before she said, "We'll ask Willie about John's connections with Sumatra. They may be there, right enough."

"Just now you didn't think they could be."

"I was surprised, that's all."

"I think they didn't get out in time."

"Oh, don't be silly! Ruth would never let them stay too long. If ever a woman had sense, that one does. But God knows how she's put up with a Gourlay all these years. If Willie had tried. . . ."

She broke off.

"Jessie, there had already been one patrol through Sungei Dema before I left. Of Japs. They may now be using it as a route south. I know something of John's plans. He had to flood the mine, for one thing. Another, he wanted to do what he could for the Chinese in the village. Helping any of them who wanted to evacuate. It would all have taken time. Too much time. John just would't go off and leave his workers."

"We've all had to!" Jessie's voice was loud. "Whether we liked it or not. It's just about been the death of Willie. Thank God I'm getting him to Australia away from all this. Not before time, either."

"You're sailing?"

"Aye. Day after tomorrow. You haven't told me how Roy was when you saw him?"

Fay stared at cakes that looked as though they had been coated with varnish to preserve them under rationing.

"I haven't seen him. He hasn't been able to get to Singapore since we came. I think he must be on some kind of secret work. He's phoned me three times. The last one was just after the New Year. Still that same story about Ruth and John making for Sumatra. Nothing new."

Jessie reached out for the teapot. "What's in your mind then?"

"Oh, a lot of things. The other night I woke up with the idea that the Gourlays had worked out some scheme for what they were going to do at Sungei Dema if there was a war. I was to be packed off out of the way, with the children. The less I knew the better."

"Oh, you're just letting your imagination take over. Ruth and John couldn't stay on at Estate House. Are you saying they wouldn't have the sense to see that?"

"There's always the jungle."

"Eh? You mean hide in it?"

"I mean a prepared camp. To sit out a war if it came."

"I don't believe it. Whatever ideas John might get, Ruth would never be so daft."

Fay considered that, then said, "She might make a noise about John's idea. but in the end she'd do what he wanted. It's always been the way with them."

"So they stayed? For what? John was going to flood the mine. The Japs won't try to start it up again. They've got twice the tin they'll need already. So what would be the point of John's staying?"

"To keep a watch over Gourlay territory," Fay said.

*

The Balmoral reminded Fay of the boardinghouse to which Roy had taken her on a Singapore holiday when a falling price for tin had made him accutely economy-minded. Her reaction to four days in the place had been a firm statement that the next time he felt in need of a low-budget break, he could take it alone. The air of gloom started on the verandah; even out there the light was already half-excluded by screens of climbing vines, with ferns suspended at various levels from the roof rafters. Though Jessie said the place was packed to the walls with refugees from up-country, an hour before sunset there didn't seem to be anyone about, as if all the guests — including the children, whose toys made walking dangerous — had fled from this mortuary melancholy while the sun was still out.

The only sound as they crossed a large lounge hall was Jessie's quick, shallow breathing. On the stairs it became an almost desperate panting, and halfway up she stopped for a rest.

"Can't get Willie out of our room. Comes down for meals, that's all. Won't go out for a walk. At home walked miles every day. Sold our car soon after we got down. Good thing. Wouldn't get anything for it now. Hundreds of cars nobody wants."

It seemed a long stair, with a long passage beyond taking an erratic course through a mysteriously shadowy annex, windows shrouded by dropped bamboo screens to hide peeling grey paint. Sounds emerged here: a heavy baritone snoring that turned out not to belong to Willie Cowan, who was sitting in a chair in reflected sunshine almost bright enough to be stage lighting. A newspaper was spread on his knees. He didn't look up at once. A wiry, slight man, he now seemed to have shrunk into his boardinghouse chair, supported by its straight back and uncompromising arms.

Jessie shouted at him: "Willie! Don't you see who this is?"

His return from wherever he had been didn't seem reluctant so much as deliberate, his eyes having no mechanical difficulty in focussing. Willie saw her perfectly well; he was simply taking his time about walking through the door from yesterday into today.

"Fay!"

It was when he stood that she really became acutely aware of the physical change. He rose like a patient in a convalescent ward for surgical cases, moving with great caution, deeply conscious of a still-raw wound. Fay wanted to urge him to sit down again but he did this soon enough without being told, releasing her hands when she had kissed his cheek. The room provided one other chair and she was made to sit in it while Jessie took the bed and beamed towards her husband a loud summary of Fay's recent history, how with the children she had used Musgan Tapan on the way south, hadn't seen Roy since he left Sungei Dema, and was now working in the central library to let some of the permanent staff off for war jobs.

"She's staying with people called Lallard," Jessie said. "We wouldn't know them. They're Crown Colony Civil Service."

She stopped for breath. Willie stared at Fay. "So you're working in the library?"

Fay nodded. "Back to my old job. It's not much to do for the defence of Singapore but I thought I'd be better at it than trying to drive something."

"What about the children?"

"Edna Lallard looks after Liza when I'm at work. And Angus is at a temporary school. I must say I'm enjoying not having to be teacher."

"What school?" Jessie asked.

"St. Joseph's."

"The Papists? You're letting him be exposed to *that?*"

Willie leaned forward, as though rejecting the need for back support. "It'll be all right if it's only temporary," he said. There was a pause before he went on. "We had to put the dogs down. They wouldn't have them here or anywhere else. It was hard enough for me. Much worse for Jessie."

Jessie was staring out of the window, her hands clasped in her lap. "Better than what *could* happen," she said. "I just hate people who think of their dogs last. Fay, you should come with us to Australia. I could get you on our ship all right. I'm sure of that. And you've got a sister-in-law out there."

Fay was very conscious of Willie's eyes on her. She shook her head. "I've got to stay here, at least until I see Roy. I couldn't take the children and go without a word to him. And there's no way I can get in touch."

"Letters?" Jessie asked.

"I write. He doesn't answer. I don't think he can."

"She's got the idea Roy's behind the Jap lines," Jessie said. "And that Ruth and John are still at Sungei Dema. I tell her she's havering. Willie, you tell her the same. John would never be so daft as to go on staying."

For a good half-minute Willie was silent; then he said: "It's what I wanted to do."

On the walk down the path to the pavement Jessie said, "You're not to mind Willie. He's not himself. Maybe things will be all right in Australia. We'll get a little house somewhere."

She stopped and turned to face Fay. "We meant to end our days at Musgan Tapan. There wasn't to be any going home for retirement. We had it all worked out. I was going first. I'm older. I've had a heart condition for years. And Willie would have managed fine without me. He's that kind. It was all we wanted, Fay. Just to be left. All Willie wanted was that place and his trees."

*

NINE

Angus didn't actually ask what she had come for, but she could see how near he was to doing it, looking up from two sets of pages open in front of him, one his own notes, the other some kind of text. As a student he had been given his own room down at the end of the passage, a distance both from Liza and his mother. Fay closed the door with the acute feeling of being a parent on a visit to her offspring in whom she took only a sporadic interest. If they had been Victorians, Angus would have stood to attention behind the table, his face invisible in light masked by a thick shade. It was a big room, almost chilly, as though behind the concrete walls and blackout curtains it manufactured its own temperature. She felt that the movements of her body were gauche as she walked towards her son, imagining that his eyes held comment on this. She stopped in front of the table, cancelling sharply a brain signal that said she was to put out both hands to support herself.

"That looks really serious," she said. "What is it?"

"Algebra."

Angus had the Gourlay stare, inherited from his grandfather.

"They start you awfully early on things like that these days. How are you managing?"

"All right."

"I don't mind admitting that I was dreading algebra. As teacher."

He grinned suddenly. Tension eased.

"I hated algebra at school," she said, the confidence permissible from the seemingly certain knowledge that she would never have to teach him again. "And geometry, too. I could never get the hang of it."

"Mum, your French accent's terrible!"

"Yes. I suppose so."

"We've got a Frenchman teaching us at St. Joseph's. He escaped from Indochina after the Japs took it. They say he's pro-Vichy and hates the British."

"Oh. But his accent's the real thing?"

Angus giggled. "Yes, it's got to be."

"What's his name?"

"Father Rompier. I think it's silly calling everyone Father. There's one new Father who's only been that for two months."

"It's just a title. Do you have religious instruction?"

"Well, sort of."

"What's sort of?"

"Well, the Virgin Mary and all that."

"But you're not expected to pray in chapel?"

"Not us temporaries."

"Do you ever pray?"

"I haven't yet."

Fay felt she wasn't up to probing that statement. On the table was the new stamp album bought in Kuala Lumpur, but no sign of Hamish's old one. She put out a hand towards the cover, then remembered that for these things you ask permission.

"May I?"

He nodded. She turned over a few pages.

"You've got all of Hamish's stamps here?"

"He must have been collecting for about a hundred years. They're all in. It was a lot of work. There's whole sets, some of them. They'll be valuable. If there wasn't a war I could find out how much. There are some people who make a living collecting stamps forever."

"It doesn't sound too safe a way to make a living." Her words seemed to underline a dominant theme in her life. She added, "I'm going down to hear the news. Coming?"

He shook his head. Even the fighting near Johore didn't

seem to interest him. If he thought about his father at all, it didn't emerge from anything he said; his own quotations from his past experience now tended to involve Big John or, more frequently, Ruth. Fay went down the corridor envying her childrens' fluid acceptance of changed circumstances even if the background to it was violent.

We're always trying to screen them from the brutal realities, she thought, and all that does is earn their contempt, like Angus's for me that night with the Japs by the pool. Or when I never said one word to him about the bodies in that burned-out car. I should have said this is happening to me *and* you. Both times he was the adult, something I've never even attempted to acknowledge.

In the drawing room the radio was already switched on, and Edna and Edward in chairs from which they could stare at the fabric-covered disc of the speaker, as though it was a screen. During a tail-off of Chinese percussion music, she sat down as well, also looking at the box. From it would come news of yet another planned withdrawal successfully accomplished, the broadcaster's English too careful to betray any feeling. Contrary to what Fay expected however, he sounded elated, disciplines thrown aside.

It has just been announced from Malaya Command that Australian forces, under the command of Major General Gordon Bennett, have achieved a series of highly effective counterattacks against the advancing Japanese, the first of these being on January 15th when, after a column of the enemy troops had crossed a bridge a few miles north of Gemas, the bridge was blown by our sappers, killing all the soldiers still on it. Those who had crossed were then set upon from ambush and annihilated. It is estimated that well over a thousand of the enemy were killed, while the Australians had less than a hundred casualties.

Following this, on January 17th, the Australians once again made contact with the enemy on the west coast road south of Muar, attacking in a cutting from ambush a column of Japanese tanks, destroying ten of these, killing all the crews except in the last tank, from which men were seen escaping. It is reported that one of the escaped had blonde hair, almost certainly a German military advisor.

From the Russian front it is reported that the Germans are falling back along a huge sector of the battle. . . .

Edward, on his feet, had switched off the set. His voice was loud.

"I knew it had to come! We're stopping them! Not just slowing them down. *Stopping* them!"

Edna was on her feet, too. "But Muar's not very far, is it? We used that beach just south of it for picnics. It only took us about two hours to get there."

"Nearer three, Edna! And don't you see? The Australians will now be falling back on the Johore Line. Where we are really dug in to hold. Where our troops and artillery are massed solid. It is from that line that the counterattack will begin. Reinforced by fresh troops and supplies from home."

He began to walk up and down. Edna sat again, in deference to her husband, listening to his explanation of strategy, how this had been Wavell's plan all along: the necessary withdrawals from indefensible territory; up-country fighting merely a series of delaying actions to allow time for the firm establishment of the Johore Line. It might be a matter of a month or two, or even three, but when we were ready for the counterattack, the Jap's wouldn't know what had hit them. Edward stopped at a side table.

"Anyone like a drink? I'm having a whisky. I'll sleep tonight."

"Make mine a gin, dear. Plenty of tonic. Fay?"

"Whisky, please."

The lecture on strategy didn't continue when they had their drinks, though Edward appeared completely satisfied with what he had said, as though all that they had to do now was wait, with reasonable patience, for his assessment of the local war to be confirmed by developments. He didn't linger with them, but took a half-full glass into the hall without saying that he had paperwork to get through in his study. The sound of his feet on the expanse of tiling was almost like a tap dancer's. Edna had found one of the pieces of sewing that she scattered throughout the house as part of a campaign to convince herself she was never idle.

"Edward isn't very often wrong, Fay. At least about things like that."

"I'm sure not."

There was silence. In the tropics, one often longs for a fire to poke, Fay thought, the cosy symbolism of keeping up the flame in the hearth whatever happens.

"I'm perfectly certain that Mr. Churchill is going to send us those planes we need," Edna said. "It's Roy you're thinking about all the time, isn't it?"

Fay looked at her friend. "No. And I don't believe Angus is thinking about his father, either."

"But . . . what on *earth* do you mean?"

"Perhaps we're both getting used to the idea that we won't see him again."

"Fay! That's nonsense! He could be here tomorrow, and you know it."

"No, I don't."

"Oh . . . you're numb with worry, that's what it is. People do get that way. I don't think you ought to be going to that job. You know I like looking after Eliza, but she needs her own mother."

Fay said nothing. Edna pulled open a drawer in a small chairside table, shoved the sewing into it, then slammed the drawer shut.

"We're all living on the ends of our nerves, that's what's the matter." After a moment she added: "So you don't believe Edward?"

"No."

"Oh, God! Neither does he!"

*

The daylight raid put all the library staff down into the cellars where a shelter of sorts had been constructed, with a gesture of putting in place some wooden uprights as props to the roof. Fay had never been down into the place before and, as soon as she was seated on a bench against a dank wall, wished she hadn't come. For one thing, the smell suggested some process of fermentation going on just down the passage outside; for another, the ceiling above was lumpy concrete with cracks. The Head Librarian, deliberately jokey as the bumps from the bombing became jolts, said that it was almost a satisfaction to him to find some use for these cellars since books stored down here were heavy with mildew after twenty-four hours.

A little Eurasian girl, who shared with Fay the administration of the now much neglected reference section, suggested that in the London Blitz everyone sang in the shelters. There were one or two murmurs of assent to this, but when the proposer of the idea started off with the first two lines of "Run, Rabbit, Run," no one backed her up. The thin voice stopped abruptly and the poor child, who somehow reminded Fay of a marmoset, seemed to cringe into herself, only her eyes staying frantically active.

As the bombs fell nearer to them, the massive Victorian building, its foundations sunk in swampy ground, began to react with jerks that had the light bulb bouncing on its cord. The lady who had her desk upstairs placed where she could keep her eye on Modern Fiction, which tended to get stolen, now had a handkerchief pressed against her mouth to keep sound from escaping, but every now and then it did, a quite loud, "Eek!" It was very hot, which gave them all an excuse for the way they were sweating, that smell almost replacing the one that had been waiting for them. Fay was reminded of the cramped changing-room at her school immediately after the arduous winter hockey she had loathed.

She sat waiting for panic to claim her, for it hadn't yet. She felt almost outside of her physical body — as, some say, the dead are conscious of being, immediately after dying; able to look back with something like pity at what they are leaving behind. The clawing terror would come when the light went out. Already the Head Librarian, looking for something to do, was fumbling with the mechanics of an oil lamp he had obviously never before tried to light.

She remembered what she had said the other night about not thinking of Roy. Edna had reacted with the surface shock she seemed to keep always available as a gesture to her husband — what Edward would expect from her — after which, as a kind of trailer, came her own feeling, often in direct opposition to the official one.

Most wives do this, Fay thought, and I lived it with Roy, faithful to a model that was practically set up and waiting for me when I arrived in Sungei Dema. Now the obligation is removed — probably for him, too — and we're both not thinking of the other, our separate lives too crowded with the unsharable. I wonder if he played as hard at being a Gourlay husband as I did a Gourlay wife? There must have been a pattern for him, too, one available from childhood. Two of the Gourlay children had torn theirs up and stayed in England. Mary Jane in Australia might be doing the same thing.

A crash bounded the light on its cord. The bulb flickered but stayed on. She was thinking about Roy now, but from a distance and with no sense of contact. When apart, there had never been anything like psychic communication between them; the mental separation was always as total as the physical. She had never lain alone in the bed they usually shared longing to be able to reach out to touch him, though when he held her and was on her body she had usually enjoyed it. She was certain she had known when Angus had been conceived, though not Liza. If, away from her, he had slept with Malaysian or Chinese girls, part of the Gourlay pattern, she had received no intuitive warning that this was about to happen or been aware, when he came back to her, that it had. Yet Ruth always knew with Big John, or said she did.

The all-clear was almost anti-climax, reprieve when least expected. Fay saw the Head Librarian glance up towards the concrete roof, inspecting it for new cracks; then he stood, sliding back into a carapace of dignity. He was once again the supremo of an important institution; the time for little jokes to keep up morale was over. Like a headmaster announcing a surprise half-holiday, he told them that the library would not re-open that afternoon and that they could all leave as soon as they had tidied up in their departments — adding the human note that he was sure the ladies were worried about how things were at home.

Fay was one of the last to leave the building, closed out of it by an irritated janitor who thought she had taken far too long over her tidy-up. She went down steps of heavy, cracked stone that looked like enduring monuments to the stability of the society that had put them there, back into what felt like a guaranteed immunity from what was happening around her. The raid seemed not really to be part of her experience at all, though she could see the smoke from its fires rising straight up in the still air, one column black and solid as a giant's leg. The broad street, too, was somehow protective, the pavement on her side almost empty of people, though on the other was panic: scurrying, shouting, old women with bundles; young men carrying nothing, but nearly running; rickshas going in the direction Fay wanted, but already loaded with cases and sacks, now and again with a child's frightened face peering from amongst them. Orchestrated into the din, a background to it, was the clanging from hand-rung bells on fire engines and the whining of ambulance sirens.

The ricksha might have been sent for her, coming down as it did on her side of the road, pulled by a man big enough to be a Manchu, who was only half-jogging, indifferent to the yells for his services from the crowded pavement. Fay wasn't surprised when he stopped by her and put down the shafts. His left forearm was wrapped from wrist to elbow in a dirty brown carrying cloth, and there were stains that could have been blood.

"You're hurt?" she asked.

He shook his head, stepping clear of the shafts to help her up into the seat. Ricksha coolies didn't often touch you, but this one took a grip on her elbow, giving her a half-lift, close enough for her to smell his sweat. It seemed almost unnecessary to tell him where she wanted to go; he was already turning the ricksha in the right direction, swinging over to join the stream of refugees, getting behind a handcart, shouting at its puller, then jerking out to pass. They were travelling faster than the column, passing load after load by grunting men. Then there was a break in traffic by the opening into a side street, giving Fay a clear view to the left, a frame lasting just long enough to be a piece of censored film: a row of two-storied Chinese houses as tightly packed together as teeth in a crowded mouth, but now with one gap — a hole in which there was fire beneath smoke, like new, raw pain.

The suburbs revived her feeling of immunity; they accepted her back into an apparent safety that came from the disappearance of frightened faces. The traffic thinned out and became almost decorous. The few people on pavements were not running from anything but were walking, shaded by jungle trees disciplined to become part of gardens surrounding the almost invisible houses. An amah was with two small European children — a boy and a girl, both very fair — their routine apparently undisturbed by what had happened downtown. The woman was swaying on feet that weren't bound but might almost have been, as though there existed a racial heritage from a hundred generations of her sex who had struggled to walk on artificially crushed and mangled bones.

The ricksha man took her straight to the Lallard gates without hesitating or looking for numbers, as certain of what he was doing as if there had been a long history of his giving her this service, though she was sure she had never seen him before. Not even attempting to pull his ricksha up over the gravel to the house, he set down the shafts at the pavement's edge and stood clear of them, his eyes on her. Still seated, Fay opened her bag, leaving loose change untouched and taking out instead two dollars, which she handed to him as she stepped down. It was absurdly more than the usual charge but he accepted the money as a reasonable fee, tucking the notes into his belt, unsmilingly watching her, giving her the feeling that the payment hadn't completed the transaction between them.

"Your arm?" she asked. "Still bleeding?"

He looked down at the brown cloth. The stains on it were larger.

"It must hurt."

He shook his head. Then he grinned. She had never in Malaya been frightened of a Chinese, and thus didn't at once recognize her fear in reaction to this man. He seemed huge as he stood there, legs slightly spread, his face half-shaded by the trees. His grin might almost have been a statement that he saw himself as central to a coming chaos in which she would also have a part. She had meant to thank him, but turned away without doing it, wanting to get beyond those gateposts. Her feet slithered on deep gravel; her walk slowed down. She was certain that the man was standing to stare after her. She didn't look back.

The big green Siddeley, immobilized because there was no petrol for it, was parked in front of the house, screening another car that had been driven into shadow under the portico. She didn't recognize the tapering, streamlined rear end of the Jowett Javelin until she was a few feet from it. She stopped.

Roy's folly, Big John had called it. The car had been specially imported, then found underpowered for Malaya, but Roy had hung onto it as something unique in the country. In K.L. streets, people had stared at it. Roy and she sometimes came out from the club on the Padang to find a little crowd around the Javelin. Once there had been initials scratched on it — three big letters marring the paintwork — and Roy had been furious, finding it almost as shocking as taking a penknife to the deep lacquer on a Rolls. That had happened to the High Commissioner's car in spite of a syce's being on constant guard.

The Javelin's paintwork wasn't shining now; mud covered most of it, but even the mud could not mask huge dents on the body. On the steps to the house Fay paused, hearing the thumping of a heart that had the habit of threatening loss of control when its owner was still perfectly calm. She turned to look back at the car, trying to identify something on one of the seats that would serve as a kind of preface to their meeting, but there was just a general untidiness of army gear and papers, as unlike him as was the mud on the black paintwork.

There were no mirrors in the hall. She couldn't go up to her room to see to her hair. She must go at once to where there were voices. She stood listening, hearing nothing clearly. The big house had the feel of emptiness that Edna said had infected it from the moment the servants started to leave. The sound of Fay's feet on the tiles as she went towards the drawing room announced her return home. Then she stepped onto felt-backed Persian rugs and was a ghost with a loud heart.

They were out on the lawn in one of those arrangements of chairs that said Edwardian England: fan-backed wicker from Hong Kong merely playing at being in the Orient; a laden tea table, covered in white lace that tended to snag the feet of a silver teapot; the whole a set for a game Edna played when she had a reasonable excuse. There should have been a white-capped maid in discreet attendance, perhaps waiting out of earshot on the terrace, but Cook must have done the carrying out of the tray, with Edna setting the table herself. There was no war. There had been no daylight raid on the city. Even the huge trees looked Anglicized, like limes gone limp on one of the three days of British summer heat.

Children were allowed to tea in the garden, Liza on a tartan rug, sitting up and facing the house but not noticing her mother, absorbed as she was in a performance for an apparently attentive audience of two. Edna reached out to offer the child a biscuit from what Fay knew to be the last Cross and Blackwell tin, and this was accepted with no break in the flow of chatter. Edna put the plate on the table and settled back in her chair as though content to be only a bystander, casually listening to an exchange between father and daughter. If Roy said anything, Fay didn't hear it. Still standing just beyond the doors to the drawing room, she had a sense of impending ordeal, of having now to stake her claim to the man whose one arm in a long-sleeved khaki shirt she could just see, together with two booted legs beyond the chair. She was doing it with eyes watching Edna, who was clumsy about concealing curiosity, and Liza, who resented a scene stealer. It was almost like being back in one of those dreadful command appearances of childhood, standing behind a door that would open onto a roomful of eyes all suddenly focussing on a girl wearing a school uniform a couple of sizes too small for her.

Edna suddenly turned her head back towards the house. She got up. "Fay! *See* who's here!"

That could have been from an actress who had said her lines so often she had suddenly started to shriek them. Fay went down onto the grass as the wicker of the fan-back vibrated from Roy's rising. He turned to face her. It was Hamish!

She stopped. He began to walk towards her.

"The car," she said. Then much louder. "Roy's car!"

She felt a pain across her chest, not sharp but more like the sensation of wearing a too tight blouse that constricted her breasts.

"Oh, God," he said. "I never thought — "

"How did you get Roy's car! Hamish! Tell me!"

"He gave it to me."

"Gave it?"

"To use while he was away. . . ."

Liza was coming towards them, while Edna, finding a role for herself, came in hot pursuit.

"We've got to talk somewhere," Hamish said.

Edna took charge, assuming the suddenly forceful role of the nanny who tolerates no nonsense. Liza had promised to help cut flowers for the house and they were going to do that now. *Right* now. Liza didn't even protest. Hamish stared after them, as though the solution to his problem had come too quickly.

"Roy's been hurt," Fay said.

He shook his head. There was some kind of jungle sore or boil on one side of his neck, healing now but still with marks of the adhesive dressing that had covered it.

"He's not hurt. Not that we've heard."

"Tell me!"

"He's a prisoner of the Japs."

The pain was tighter, threatening her breathing. She wanted to call out Roy's name, very loud, claiming him back from wherever he was.

"I shouldn't have come in his car. I'm a fool! I'm sorry."

"The Japs don't take prisoners," she said.

He answered quickly. "They are doing so in this country. We know that. They're using Pudu Jail in Kuala Lumpur as a sort of collection point."

"Roy's *there?* In that jail?"

Hamish nodded. "He was seen being taken in."

She remembered the jail: yellow walls; a Moorish-styled gatehouse that might have been designed to mask the place's real function.

"Who saw Roy being taken in?"

"A Eurasian working for us. He got the message out by radio. He knows Roy well. Was working with him earlier."

"Working with him? Doing what?"

"Reporting on Jap movements mostly. But some demolitions. Bridge blowing."

"Roy blew up a bridge?"

"Well . . . not quite. The charges weren't big enough. Fay, come and sit down. Want me to get you a drink?"

"Just some tea. Is it still warm?"

He felt the pot. "Yes."

She took the fan-back. Edna and Liza were down by a clump of bourgainvillea breaking off sprays. The first afternoon breeze from the Straits was bringing with it a smell of smoke. Hamish handed her a cup. "Roy will be all right."

"*Please* don't say that!"

"Sorry."

He sat on the chair Edna had been using, leaning forward, staring at his two hands clasped between spread thighs. He might be thinking what she was, thinking that the Japs could be taking prisoners now for interrogation, not for keeping alive. Only months ago a man had been hung in Pudu Jail: a Malay gone amok who had killed eight people with a parang. British justice, that was. The Japs would be operating another kind now.

She remembered standing behind her stall at the annual village fête in Fleckney in aid of the church fabric fund, the Vicar's daughter given the home baking, with Roy looking at what was on offer, not buying anything, then going away. He had come back again after she had sold the last of the cream cakes and introduced himself, telling her where he was staying and suggesting a Saturday car run across country to Shrewsbury, if she had nothing better to do. She had said that all there was on her schedule was the weeding of a herbaceous walk. They had both laughed. He had been conspicuous at the fête because of his tropics tan, dark on a cloudy day. He had never lost the tan. She had never seen him without it.

She put down her cup. "Hamish, you knew that Ruth and John were staying behind at Sungei Dema?"

He didn't look up. "Yes."

"Who else knew? Besides Roy and you?"

"Only Hang, the mine foreman."

The mine foreman had been allowed into the secret that it had been decided to keep from Fay.

"Where are they? Captured and taken to Pudu, too?"

"They're free."

"How can you know that?"

"Because I know where they were going."

"To a jungle hide?"

"Yes."

"Did you help them get it ready?"

"Yes."

"How long had they been preparing this place?"

"More than six months."

"All that time and I never suspected. You covered up well."

"Fay, don't! They were thinking of the children."

"No. They were thinking of *me*. What Fay could stand. They didn't want my howled protests when the time came."

She put up her hands to her face and, behind them, made a sound like someone going to be sick. Then she took her hands away. Hamish was sitting up straight, staring at her. She thought: he's waiting for me to start howling now.

"Give me a cigarette," she said.

TEN

The whirring from the sewing machine set up in a corner of the drawing room stopped. Edna picked up scissors, snipped threads, then added another square of backing for an emergency field dressing to the pile of these on a second table beside her.

"There's something I've been meaning to ask you, Fay. It's been a little awkward. There was no way I could know if you'd told Angus about Roy. I mean, he doesn't mention his father."

"I told him. As soon as Hamish left."

"What did Angus say?"

"Nothing much. If anything he's ashamed."

"*What?*"

"That his father is a prisoner."

"Oh, no!"

"A boy wants a hero. Not a man behind a prison wall." She saw the wall again, the Moorish gate, yellow-orange.

"I don't know how you can say that!"

"I was speaking for Angus, not myself."

The machine whirred. It went on for a minute; then the scissors came into action and another square went on the pile.

"You said . . . before you knew . . . that you didn't think about Roy much. That isn't the way things are now, is it?"

"No."

"Fay, he's going to be all right."

When Edna got no reaction to that, she started the machine again but stopped it before another square was finished.

"Does Angus know about Ruth and John?"

"Yes, I told him that, too. I'm not keeping anything from him now. It doesn't do either of us any good. Besides, I couldn't have kept up the pretence."

"I suppose not. What about Liza?"

"Angus is in the conspiracy with us there. With any luck she won't remember this war. Or not much of it. Or her father."

"Fay, stop!"

Fay stood. "Yes, I must."

"You're not getting much sleep are you?"

"Not as much as usual."

She began to walk up towards windows shrouded with blackout curtains, as though she was going through them into the garden. She stopped and turned, staring down the long room to Edna, still behind her sewing machine.

"It wouldn't be so bad, somehow, if I didn't know the place. I mean that jail. We drove past it often. You look at a jail — it makes you look — the high walls. You wonder about what sort of living is going on in there. I can remember doing that. Now, I. . . ." Fay began walking back to her chair.

"You've never cried, have you?" Edna asked.

"No. Neither has Angus, I'm sure. Instead he's angry. He told me once he wanted to kill Japs."

"You let him say that?"

"If you'd had children, Edna, you'd know that when they reach his age it isn't a question of what we let them say." Fay sat down.

"Why don't you have a drink?" Edna suggested.

"No thanks. I'll be all right in a minute. You caught me unawares, that's all. I'm managing, Edna, so leave it, will you? Oh, I didn't mean it to sound like that! The main reason I'm managing is because of you and Edward. I was thinking last night, supposing I had been in one of those damn boardinghouses? With Liza and Angus? And meals in a crowded dining room. And the latest stories about how Churchill is going to save us at the last minute with a vast air armada from six carriers out in the Indian Ocean."

"You're not fair on Mr. Churchill!"

"Perhaps not."

"He's doing what he can," Edna said.

"Maybe those of us out here can be allowed to wish it was a little more."

"You think he's written us off, don't you? That he did that when the *Prince of Wales* was sunk?"

"Yes."

"Well, please don't say that in front of Edward."

"I wouldn't. Isn't he terribly late tonight?"

"Yes. Perhaps we should have the wireless on for the news? It will have started."

Fay went over to the domed set, which sat like a mastodon's egg on its own special table. She turned a knob. The valves took their time about warming up and she was seated before the reader's voice came through.

> ... The last of the British troops to leave the mainland were the Argyll and Sutherland Highlanders — two hundred men, all that remained of the regiment — who marched onto the Causeway from Johore led by their piper playing the Scottish lament for the dead, "The Flowers of the Forest." After they had crossed, the Causeway was blown up. Singapore is now an island, and the enemy has complete control of Malaya.

"Oh, my God!" Edna said. "Those *were* guns we heard. Not thunder!"

Another radio voice said:

> We are now going over to G.H.Q. Malaya for a special message from the Commander in Chief, General Percival.

While the speaker gave out nothing but static, Fay lit two cigarettes and took one over to Edna, who was still sitting behind the sewing machine, both her hands on a rumple of white linen. She took the cigarette, put it in her mouth, inhaled, then seemed to forget to take it out again. The voice from the speaker might have been disinfected against all emotion:

> The battle of Malaya has come to an end and the battle for Singapore has started. For more than two months our

troops have fought the enemy on the mainland. The enemy
has had the advantage of great air superiority and considerable freedom of movement by sea.

Our task has been to impose losses on the enemy and to
gain time to enable forces of the Allies to be concentrated
for this struggle in the Far East.

Today we stand beleaguered in our island fortress until
help can come, as assuredly it will come. This we are determined to do. In carrying out this task we want the active
help of every man and woman in the fortress.

There is work for all to do. Any enemy who sets foot in
the fortress must be dealt with immediately. The enemy
within our gates must be ruthlessly weeded out. There must
be no more loose talk and rumour-mongering. Our duty is
clear. With firm resolve and fixed determination we shall
win through.

Fay went to switch off the set. Edna had taken the cigarette out of her mouth. She was holding it well away from
her body and the crumpled sheeting in her lap.

"I'm shaking," she said. "Just as though I was coming
down with an attack of dengue." A moment later she asked,
"I wonder what Edward will say now?"

"Won't he agree with the General?"

"No! He never has. Edward was one of the few in government who wanted to give the Chinese military training.
Forming regiments with their own officers. And the Chinese
wanted it. God knows, they have plenty to hate the Japs for.
This is their country, too. They would have known what
they were fighting for, not like those Indians we've brought
in."

And British, Fay thought. Edna pushed aside the sheet
and stood, going over to the drinks tray, standing with her
back turned. Her voice was more bitter than Fay had ever
heard it.

"Now the General wants the active help of everyone on
the island. What sort of active help? They trained a few
Chinese air wardens and fire fighters. That's all. Command
here decided that the Chinese weren't to be trusted with
guns. Edward has been angry about it. His Chinese friends
kept asking if Command thought they would turn the guns

they were given on the British? Edward says that if we had started to train them even as late as a year ago there could have been a hundred thousand Chinese in Malaya ready to fight it out with the Japs."

Edna came over to Fay with glasses in her hands, holding one out. "You ought to leave. Right away. For the children's sake. Go to Australia."

"With Roy in Pudu?"

"What good can you do him by staying on here?"

"I can at least be near. Two hundred miles."

"That's crazy and you know it!"

"Would you leave Edward?"

"Fay, I'm here *with* him. In this house when he comes home. I'm not just doing my splendid duty as a bandage roller and making these pads. I believe he needs me, whatever he may say about that."

"Edward wanted you to go?"

"Ever since the Japs landed at Kota Bahru. He even tried ordering me. It was a surprise to him, after all my dutiful years, when I told him what he could do with his order. But there's something else as well as Edward. You mayn't have faith in Mr. Churchill, but I do. He's going to see to it that this island is saved from the Japs."

*

The cat looked very Chinese, fat-faced, as though years of rice-eating had puffed out its cheeks. Its eyes, instead of being slanted, were straight slits that somehow seemed to put the whiskers in the wrong place. All cats humped down are a series of circles, but this one seemed much more ovoid than any of the felines Fay had lived with at the Vicarage, the only pets her father would tolerate. The cat's name was Lao-hu, Old Tiger, and it had both stripes and many years behind it. It was now the pampered substitute for Cook's wife's grandchildren, who had either strayed from her ken or had never happened.

Though Fay had seen her working at it, Liza had made no impression at all on Cook and his wife, the pair's racial susceptibility to children not stretching to European chil-

dren. She had, however, managed to seduce their cat. Lao-
hu was intrigued by Liza, possibly because her egotism was
in some way a challenge to his own. She could do what she
wanted with the old tom, more or less stealing him from under the usually watchful eyes of Cook's wife to hump the
beast about the garden under one arm. When she wanted to
use that arm she put the cat down and he sat where she had
placed him, a motionless fur lump half-hidden by the long
grass of a now unmown lawn, though he always faced in her
direction, apparently watching intently what she was up to.

Liza was quite often worth watching, especially when suddenly she took the notion to act out some passage in her in-
tensely private life. Fay straightened from her attempt to
convert a failed bed of roses into a successful sweet potato
patch, resting a sore back while her daughter executed a for-
malized dance in and out amongst the overhanging branches
of a free-standing bourgainvillea, the child's arms lifted
above her head as if for a Scottish fling, while her feet
worked out a complicated hop and skip. Fay was too far
away to hear whether Liza was singing any accompanying
music, but a ballet without sound had its own fascination,
the child's feet following a pattern so precise it might have
been clearly stamped on the bare ground under the shrub.

Fay got to work with the chunkle again, using the local
tool with a new understanding of why the spade is not much
help in breaking up laterite clay, a peculiar substance that
refuses to be dug in the normal way but has to be sliced,
much as a carpenter might take an adze to a beam. Since
the slicing has to do down for several layers to aerate the
soil for seed growth, one soon gave up the idea of preparing
new ground fast. All the Tamil gardeners she had seen working had seemed outstandingly inefficient in output, but she
now knew why: The tools they worked with, the substance
worked in, and the heat, imposed this slow to dead-slow
tempo.

The grass had been abandoned completely and the whole
two acres would have been allowed to return to nature in
any way it liked if Edna hadn't come home from bandage-
rolling with the news that the seven hundred thousand peo-

ple on Singapore Island were going to starve to death unless vegetables were grown on every scrap of ground available. Fay, redundant from the library due to daylight bombing, volunteered to dig for survival. It gave her something to do and released Edna from minding Liza to free her for a secret life: driving a small van converted into an ambulance, something Edward would have stopped if he had known about it.

In spite of the fact that General Percival had forbidden rumours, Edna usually came home with a few, some of them lurid. Departed servants were said to be organizing break-ins at houses where they had worked; luxury housing in the suburbs was being carefully preserved from bombing for Jap use when they took the island; and a really sinister one — with Edna saying she didn't believe a word of it — was that certain Chinese tongs, or secret societies, were in alliance with the enemy and were just waiting for a signal before sweeping up from the crowded downtown streets to pillage and kill in the European quarter. Edna said that if Edward even got a hint of this wild talk it would make him absolutely furious. Everyone knew that the Chinese were utterly loyal; why, there was that millionaire Wang something-or-other, who had offered a bottle of champagne to every British pilot who shot down a Jap, though she didn't suppose he'd had to give out many bottles before the R.A.F. left the island.

Fay carried on with her chunkling. When she straightened to wipe sweat from her eyes Liza had disappeared, together with Old Tiger. Both were probably off on some secret mission into the area Edna called her wild garden, which had grown a lot wilder recently. It was only when the air-raid warning sounded that Fay became concerned, calling out, then turning to see Liza disappear into the house through the long windows of the drawing room, and carrying the cat.

Old Tiger was forbidden to enter the house, Edna declaring that in the tropics all cats were mobile flea incubators and, in addition, clawed the upholstery. So far none of the fleas had been passed on to Liza, or at least she hadn't been seen scratching, but this was Edna's home and guests, particularly refugees, had to abide by house rules. While the siren wailed, Fay went after a daughter who knew perfectly well that she had taken the cat into forbidden territory.

Liza was trying to settle her friend into a chair. "You stay there, Lao-hu. Stay!"

"Let him go," Fay said from just inside the windows.

Liza turned. "What?"

"You heard me. You know he's not supposed to be in here. And so does the cat."

Liza let him go. Lao-hu came half-skidding at great speed across bare sections of tiles, past Fay's legs and out into the garden.

"He's *my* cat!" Liza shouted.

"No, he's not. He belongs to Cook's wife. You only get him on loan."

"I'll take him to bed tonight!"

While the warning sirens died away and before the Ack-Ack started up, Fay was faced with one of those recurring situations in which she either threatened to paddle Liza's bottom, which her child-guidance manual said would be the easy way out as well as being sheer sadism, or alternatively took the manual's suggestion of training by a replacement attraction. She stood there trying to think of a replacement attraction for Old Tiger but didn't come up with anything until the first anti-aircraft shell exploded somewhere over downtown Singapore.

"Wango would be awfully jealous," Fay said.

Liza stared. "What?"

"If you took the cat to bed. She'd be terribly unhappy."

For a moment Fay thought she might have guessed wrong about Wango's sex, the matter never really having come up before, but Liza was consistent about liking few things male, unless they were grown men, and a moment later mother and daughter were off up the stairs to find out what had happened to Wango in the last week or so. The doll was discovered under the cot bed, at the very back against the wall, covered with fluff, having been pushed there by Cook's wife with a speeding mop.

"She *is* looking sad," Fay said, dusting the doll. "I don't think you've been kind to her recently."

Liza looked sullen but she took Wango. Fay thought: I sound like one of those dreadful organizing women at a tiny-tots party.

The Ack-Ack was noisier than it had been recently, covering the drone of approaching bombers. Fay went to a window to watch distant pyrotechnics that held the red of fire, not just the usual white puffs; the sky to the south offered a backdrop haze screen. She couldn't see the planes and the gunners didn't seem to be getting their range, though they were certainly trying — a display that might have been put up to counter another rumour that the island was running out of Ack-Ack ammo.

She ought to take Liza downstairs, but the child was now sitting on the bed making a ceremony out of her reunion with Wango and, with the raids continuing to seek targets mostly in the harbour area, it had seemed wrong to create an atmosphere of something like panic every time the sirens went. Liza herself seemed to accept the din as part of her new pattern in Singapore, apparently making no link at all between it and what had happened in a wood on the way south.

Fay was watching the sky above the trees in the garden when a heavy roaring pushed through the din of Ack-Ack. She looked east. A bomber had come over the suburb. It was low. Its wingspread looked huge. It had been hit, trailing smoke and fire from one engine. It seemed to be making a wide circle to avoid the anti-aircraft fire. It might be aiming for one of the mainland airfields the Japs had captured.

She was looking at the spire of the chapel at St. Joseph's when the plane's underbelly opened. The air sparkled with the silver of dropping bombs. They fell in a family constellation. She couldn't move back from the window. She was staring at the spire.

If the window hadn't been open, blast-shredded glass would have torn into her body. She understood that as panes shattered and fell, shards about her feet. The air had been sucked out of her lungs, but she could see. She could see the spire still there. The bomber was tossed in the updraught from explosions, then, lightened, was able to start the climb away. It came over the house, bellowing. As the noise eased, Fay heard Liza's screams.

*

Cook's wife shook her head. Fay shouted at her: "Why won't you do this?"

She stared past Fay, as though half-expecting her husband to emerge from the big house's kitchen, coming to support her neutrality.

They hate us, Fay thought, that's the truth of it. All servants hate the people they have to serve. It was true with Chow if I had only seen it.

She opened the handbag she had brought down from the bedroom, pulling out a five-dollar note and dropping it at the woman's feet.

"Look after my daughter! She's crying. I must go."

The wild Cantonese seemed to make no impression. "My son! At the school. . . ."

Fay turned and ran, around the house to the drive where the Siddeley sat useless. The gravel beyond the car sucked at her feet like soft sand at the sea's edge. On the pavement she could really run. She did that until she had no breath left and had to stop. Her handbag, hanging from her wrist on one strap, was open. It was a moment before she could reach down to close it. She ran on.

The spire kept showing itself through the trees, but was slow to swell in size. She came into the street over which it claimed sovereignty, but she had a long way to go down it. The houses on both sides were closer together and smaller than the Lallards, but still with tree screens around a carefully protected privacy. She saw fire. It was a tree burning, high up, flames coming out of the charred stumps of its top branches as if fed by an oily sap.

She had to stop again and get her breath back, close her eyes. Opening them, she saw in the distance an openness where houses should have been. She saw strong light, an invader that seemed to be completing the destruction, a hard

sun from above, a red glow below. In tree shade were two
fire engines, small and feeble-looking, and a converted van
with a red cross painted on its side. Fay didn't see people
until she got closer. There was a crowd, but all under the
cover of trees. She was the only one running out in the middle of the road. She remembered that the raid was still on.

There were four intact houses between the ones destroyed
and the brick wall enclosing the St. Joseph's compound. Fay
couldn't see over the wall but as she ran again towards the
gate a priest in a tropic soutane came through it, leading a
party of boys. They turned the other way along the pavement, unhurried, almost like a choir's processional. At first
all she saw from the gate was a wide stretch of empty concrete; then there were more boys, a huddle this time, some
of them under the shelter of a gallery along the front of a
two-story building. The others were spilling out from that
shadow, and she saw two more priests with them, one of
them shouting something.

Fay ran across the concrete. Angus came out to meet her.
"Mum!"

She felt then, standing, looking at her son, that she must
explain why she was here. All around were the buildings of
the school intact, their bulk completely concealing other
bomb damage. There was smoke rising beyond the chapel
spire, but that was all.

"Are you all right?" Angus asked. He had come quite
close. He was carrying his books and a pencil case.

She nodded. "I tried to phone. I couldn't get through."

"You thought we got bombed? We nearly did. I was in
French class. Boy, you could hear it. The plane. Roaring.
There's cellars under the chapel but there wasn't any time.
We just sat. Father Rompier was praying, you could see
that."

Fay didn't say anything.

"Mum? Does God save Catholics specially?"

She took a deep breath. "I don't think so."

ELEVEN

The gunfire to the north had become too heavy and too continuous to be accepted as background noise even to the routines of living on an island under siege. Inside the house the booming seemed to bounce from floor tiles to be echoed off concrete ceilings, and out in the garden the rumbling was like the preface to the shock waves of an earthquake. There were some recesses, but these reprieves into silence remained under threat, the air heavy, prophetic of a renewed pounding. When that started again it was almost a relief, better than the waiting for it.

Edna came back from a morning spent at her ambulance depot three streets away, in which she had been drinking tea and waiting for a raid, the inaction filled by talk that was mainly more rumours. The one that appealed to her most was that the huge naval guns had at last been turned around from pointing out over the Straits and were now directed at the enemy in Johore. The Japs, she said, were taking a pasting; huge fifteen-inch shells exploding all over their attempts to assemble a fleet of small boats for an amphibious landing on the island.

"You mean those shells are being fired right across the city? To land in Johore?"

Edna nodded, bright-eyed with faith. "Yes. They have a range of fifteen miles. Which puts them right on the Jap positions. Half the noise we're hearing is them exploding."

"What's the other half?"

"Fay, you're being skeptical again!"

"Sorry."

"I wish you could get out. It's not good for you to be here the whole time, doing nothing, meeting no one."

"You're forgetting my war work. I've started on the third rose bed. Whatever happens to Singapore, we're going to have sweet potatoes. That is, if a Jap General doesn't decide to take over this house."

"Fay!"

"I'll get back to my digging. Cook made chicken sandwiches. I left half."

"What did Liza have?"

"Soup made from the bones. Nourishing."

"There shouldn't be a shortage of food. Mabel's still getting meat from Cold Storage. There's plenty there, she says. I'm just never near Cold Storage and I can't ask Edward to go. I *did* have a big stock of tins; I can't think what happened to them."

Fay thought of Cook's wife but said nothing, Edna already had enough on her mind. The Gourlays had outstayed their welcome, but Edna would still hate it if they left. For Fay the family evening dinner, still somewhat formal, was the hardest to endure. Liza was already in bed after an egg and dried-milk pudding, and the four of them sat at the polished table, Angus on the other side of a diminished fruit bowl. The talk was rarely about the war, Ruth's Sungei Dema mealtime regulation half-enforced here, too, by Edward. Edna kept all the day's rumours out of the dining room, probably because under her husband's critical analysis they would fall to pieces.

When she was back in the garden again, with the chunkle in her hands, Fay was conscious of this digging as a form of daytime escape. If you worked hard enough the blood pounding in your ears overlaid the sound of guns. At first the chunkling had really been a device to let her keep an eye on Liza without actually trailing the child about as Amah had done. Fay had the feeling that what Liza found acceptable from an amah, and what was indeed a servant's duty, would not be pleasing coming from her mother. And, much as the child loved an audience, when the potential for this was limited to Old Tiger or her parent, she seemed to prefer the cat.

It let you get on with the digging. She had stopped to look at a hardened blister at the base of one of her fingers when Edward called her to attention in a voice pitched to carry well above the gunfire.

"Fay! Can I have a word?"

He was standing only a couple of yards away, his feet hidden by unmown grass.

"You're home early."

"Yes. Where's Liza?"

"In the bushes somewhere. Why?"

"Perhaps she shouldn't hear this."

"Well, she won't. What is it?"

"You're sailing tomorrow. With the children. And Edna."

He was wearing his official face that a smile could relax away.

"What are you talking about, Edward?"

"I'm talking about your leaving Singapore. Fast."

"But why this . . . suddenly?"

"Because the Japs have landed. On the island. In force. It happened twenty-four hours ago."

She stared at him. "Twenty-four hours? . . . But the radio said nothing?"

"No. And it isn't going to. Not until after a new counterattack. To see if it works."

"I just don't understand?"

"Fay, there have been two counterattacks already, designed to push the Japs back into the sea. They didn't do it. The enemy has got artillery over and there's talk of tanks, too."

Any talk Edward repeated, he believed.

"Surely they can't keep news like this from the people of Singapore."

"No! And they're damn fools to try!"

She remembered her reaction to hearing of a Jap fleet turning towards Malaya. This fear wasn't quite that. She said.

"We'll never get on a ship. Not now."

"I've arranged it. An old China coaster. She's slow, but she'll get you there."

"Where?"

"Java first. After that, Australia. The ship's been reserved mainly for wives who stayed on doing some job and a few people who mustn't be caught if the Japs get to the city."

"I don't see how I qualify under that?"

"You don't. But I've squeezed you in. I'm entitled to do that. And to hell with anyone who doesn't like it."

"Edna has said she'll go?"

"I've just told her to start packing. If she won't do it, I'll do it for her. As for you . . . do you want your children prisoners of the Japs? For that's what it will amount to."

"No, I don't."

"Then pack. You won't be able to take a quarter of the stuff you brought down. Two or three suitcases. No more. You'll have to carry everything yourself."

"Edward, what about you?"

"I'm staying."

"To become a prisoner?"

"Probably."

"What's the good of that?"

"This is my city. I can be useful until it happens."

"I'm thinking of Edna. Leaving you?"

"Edna will manage. Perhaps you can help her in Australia. Get settled and all that."

Fay was standing with the chunkle handle leaning against her waist, like a flying buttress propping her up.

"Roy would have sent you away long before this," Edward said. "I should have done. I wouldn't see what was happening. Wouldn't let myself believe it when I did see. The boat sails tomorrow at about eleven. To get out to sea before the afternoon raid. She's called the *Ming Kai*. Small, only about three thousand. And packed. It won't be a comfortable voyage. How are you off for money?"

After a moment Fay said, "I haven't much. Roy didn't manage to add anything to our joint account here. Perhaps he forgot. We really just kept it open for shopping when we were down."

"But surely your K.L. account would be transferred south?"

"I asked about that. There was no record of it."

"You should have told me, Fay! Is there any Gourlay money outside this country?"

"I don't know. But I remember that John kept sending banker's drafts to Mary Jane in Australia. Ruth said something once about John's not trusting Europe, about his investing any capital they had outside Sungei Dema in mines and rubber. That would mean Malaya or Sumatra."

"Just what he would do. He reminded me of those fifth- and sixth-generation Dutch over in Java. Stubborn mules about being Easterners who had cut most ties with the West. Up at Sungei Dema I used to feel I was visiting the local Sultan."

Fay smiled. "Did you ever tell him that?"

"Once. He bellowed with laughter. Flattered, I expect."

"Edward, you believe they're still up there?"

He nodded. "They'll come out, too. We'll all come out. The Jap visit to southern regions will be a short one. You'll see. I'm going to cable a thousand-pound credit for you to the Chartered Bank in Sydney. A loan to the Gourlays is safe enough."

"You can't! It's far too much! And Edna will need any money she can get in Australia."

"She won't, you know. She can have some of her own sent out from England. Edna came to me rich and grew richer holding onto what was hers, just using what was mine. I'll charge the Gourlays five-percent interest."

He smiled at her. "Put down that chunkle," he said. "There isn't going to be time to grow your sweet potatoes. Come in the house and we'll all have a drink."

*

The Siddeley's engine was rough, racing every time it was held in neutral. Twice it had coughed, threatening a stop. Edward said that the last one-gallon ration must have stirred up sediment in the tank. To prevent this blocking the carburetor, Fay was to keep revving hard whenever they were held up in traffic.

The long processional of empty army lorries moved forward in jerks as one vehicle after another was signalled across the road to the dock gates and halted for a check by soldiers who looked under the hooded back covers, then waved it on. For each lorry the inspection seemed to take minutes. Fay had the feeling she was revving away whatever was left of that gallon after the intricate pattern of back streets through which Edward had navigated them. She didn't really see the soldier with the slung rifle coming from the pavement until he was within a few feet of the other side of the car. Then she couldn't see his face, just a sweat-stained shirt, brown arms with black hairs on them, the thumb of one hand thrust behind the webbing of the rifle strap.

"Are you checking our clearance papers here?" Edward said, through the open window.

"Nope," the man said.

There were more soldiers on the pavement, all with slung rifles, all staring at the Siddeley.

"Then what are you doing, Corporal?"

"Having a look." A pause. "So you're leaving us, mister? I hope your fuckin' ship sinks!"

The man turned and went back to the pavement. His companions were laughing.

"Edward!" It was a wail from Edna. "Why didn't you tell him? He thinks — "

"I know what he thinks."

"But it's not fair! It's — "

"Edna!"

"Oh, God!"

The lorry in front moved. Fay pushed a foot down. The Siddeley gave a jerk in pursuit. She could feel the soldiers on the pavement watching them. She had to brake again and rev the engine. Edward had turned his head to the back seat.

"Angus, I think those are the masts and the funnel of the *Ming Kai*. Can you see . . . beyond that godown?"

"Yes, sir."

"You're going to have double duty as porter. You won't get any help. At least a couple of trips up the gangway."

"I know."

"Edward," Edna said, "I'm sure if you tell them at the gates who you are they'll let you through."

"They have orders to let no one into the dock area except those with clearance for the ship. I explained all this last night."

"So what do you do? Just get out and leave us when we reach the head of the queue?"

"Yes."

Fay had to brake again. She used the throttle to keep up engine revs. She felt an intruder on what should have been private moments between the two.

Edward's voice was loud: "Edna, for God's sake! Don't you think I'd see you onto the ship if I could?"

"Yes, of course."

"Don't start weeping *now*."

"I'm not, Edward."

The lorry in front moved. Fay let back the change pedal; the movement was too sudden. The car jumped, needing restraint from the brake.

"I'm sure they'll stay," Edna said. "Cook and his wife, I mean. They'll stay and look after you. I had a talk with him in the kitchen just before — "

"I'll manage fine. Don't worry."

"At least you'll be starting off with a stack of clean shirts. I saw to that."

Above the noise of the engine the rumble of gunfire seemed suddenly overbearing, louder than they had heard it in the suburbs nearer to the action. The processional of lorries began to move faster, as if under this stimulus; the checking at the dock gates became almost perfunctory. In the back seat Liza had lost Wango in the heaped luggage about her small ration of seat and Edna was helping in the search, making small, pointless noises as she did it. Edward touched Fay's arm. She looked at him. He nodded, then reached around to open his door. He was out of the car before Edna had lifted her head. His goodbye was a signal from the pavement, one hand raised, then dropped. He began to walk away fast.

Fay didn't look at Edna in the driving mirror.

"I suppose that was best," Edna said. "If I cry a little it doesn't mean I am going to be silly and useless. I promise. Angus, why don't you climb over in front? You seem to be in charge now."

"All right," Angus said.

Edna was very controlled about her crying. Fay revved the engine. To Angus she said: "The clearance papers are in the parcel shelf. Have them ready."

"Yes, Mum."

*

From the dock the *Ming Kai* had looked as though she felt herself too old for wars, a starboard list sagging her against concrete, and when they got into the C deck reception area in front of the Purser's office, Fay could see how narrow the ship was, built for working her way up muddy Chinese rivers. She would be shallow draft, too, which meant heavy rolling with any kind of sea running. The children had never been on a ship before and might turn out to be as bad sailors as their mother.

"Mum, you watch this stuff," Angus said. "I've got to go back for those other bags."

"Not on your own Angus. Wait until your Aunt Edna gets back. Then I'll come with you."

"But she could be away for hours looking for our rooms. Every place is full of people. Just look at those stairs. And you'd never get down that gangway. There's mobs coming up it."

The mob was almost entirely women, a few towing children, all hauling huge suitcases they had never before been obliged to move themselves. A girl in a loose, flowered dress, heavily pregnant, stepped carefully over the sill of the watertight doors. She was carrying only a small suitcase. Her head came up when she was safely on the coconut matting laid over linoleum. She was Eurasian, pretty, eyes heavy from recent tears, given a pass to leave because of marriage lines to a man in uniform, and the burden she was carrying. She stood for a moment staring at a world in which she had no friends. She was pushed from behind.

"For God's sake move yourself!"

Fay caught the girl's arm and pulled her in towards a bulkhead. "Here, sit on one of these cases."

"I'm all right, thank you." The voice was sing-song. "It's just that . . . what do I do?"

"Wait," Fay said, smiling at her. "We're supposed to be having our cabins assigned. I don't think the Purser knows what's happening."

The girl turned her head, identifying one thing in her new environment. "That fat man is the Purser?"

Fay nodded.

"Mum," Angus said. "I'm off. I won't be long."

"Angus, wait! . . ."

"I won't be long! Liza's going to want to wee-wee soon! You can tell."

He grinned at her, then disappeared towards the gangway, hidden by bodies.

"Your son?" the girl asked.

"Yes. There are still some bags in the car. I don't think — "

"My name is Anita. I am Mrs. Johnson."

"I'm Fay Gourlay."

"May I stay with you now, please?"

"Of course. But. . . ."

It was Edna, pushing her way from the foot of the stairs. "We've got a cabin! Or rather a girl called Susan has got it for us. She's some kind of army wife. They'd put her in a cabin with us. Down on D deck. Absolute bowels of the ship."

"Angus has gone ashore for the things we left, Edna. I must go and help him."

"But you can't! Don't you see, we've got to get all this stuff up to the new cabin? Susan is defending it. She says it's going to be war soon. With the wives of top brass. They've been reserving B deck for themselves. We're going to have to fight for that cabin and the sooner it's full of our things the better."

"This is Anita," Fay said. "She's coming with us."

"What?" Edna stared. Fay knew what she was thinking

. . . costume jewelry counter in White's or typist in a bank.

"I don't know if there's going to be room," Edna said.

"We'll make room."

"All right. Come on. Get hold of these bags. Ready, Liza?"

Liza stood up from a suitcase. A new world was being organized for her. She looked up at Anita, assessing the stranger's place in it. They moved off towards the stairs, up, the traffic on these much thinner than on the ones down, as though the occupation of B deck had proceeded in an orderly manner, remote from the squabbles below. It became quieter as they climbed. At a bend in the stairs, Edna rested for a moment, leaning against the railing.

"There are only eight passenger cabins on B deck," she said. "We couldn't get one of the two with its own W.C. Would you believe it, most of the doors are locked, but you can hear voices inside."

Until they entered a narrow passage with mahogany grip rails, it was as silent as a corridor leading to penthouse suites in a luxury hotel; then suddenly the security of privilege might have been under attack from a menacing rabble. Fay, with arm muscles giving out, half-dragged a huge suitcase along linoleum while Edna struggled, panting, behind a holdall her husband had once used on inspection tours in colonial Africa. Liza, her impression of the new environment unfavorable, began to complain.

They were ambushed from behind a door under a sign which said LADIES. The woman who emerged was not in uniform but still looked as if she were in her grey alpaca skirt and matching tailored shirt with long sleeves. At least twenty years of tropical sun had calloused what was perhaps once a peaches-and-cream English complexion into grey parchment almost matching her skirt. Bobbed hair stuck out as if under perpetual stimulus from an excess of electrical impulses to her brain. She stared at the intruders, especially at Liza. Her own children, if she had any, had long since been despatched to school in England or evacuated to a private institution in one of the more civilized parts of Canada.

"I'm afraid you've got the wrong deck," the lady said. "These cabins are reserved for field rank and above."

Edna peered around the holdall. "My husband is a senior in the Administrative Secretariat. We take precedence over field rank below Major General. Do you mind getting out of the way?"

The cabin was down a short side passage with two doors facing each other. Edna knocked on one of them.

"It's me," she called.

The woman who opened had red hair, a pink skin, and very white teeth.

"Reinforcements just in time," she said. "There were a couple of attacks while you were away. Frenzied knob rattlings and shouts. I think they're massing against us. United under a female with a voice like a foghorn."

"We met her," Edna said.

"What in heaven's name is that you're lugging?"

"A holdall. No gentleman went on safari without one."

"Could it be converted into a bedroll? We're going to need something. There are only two bunks."

"This is Anita Johnson," Fay said.

The redhead looked at the Eurasian. "Pregnancies get the lower berth. Come in, all of you. And your gear. Then we'll run a test to see if we can shut the door."

"There's more luggage. My son's bringing it. I'm going down to help him. Edna, see to Liza, will you?"

Fay was in the main passage when a heavy drumming swamped the hum of the ship's dynamos. The bombers had come early. Sirens, caught napping, sounded hysterical.

She began to run towards the stairs. She was in the vestibule that crossed the ship when the first bombs hit the water. Storm doors giving onto the portside covered deck were closed, but light came through their small portholes like tongues of white flame. A mini tidal wave from the explosion lifted the *Ming Kai*. Fay was knocked off her feet, still sprawled when the ship sank down again, hullplates scraping a concrete dock.

Ack-Ack guns in the dockyard area almost covered the sound of more explosions but she could feel the thump of bombs hitting solid targets. She was getting to her feet when a ship's officer, young and fair-haired, came running down the stairs from the deck above. He looked at her but didn't stop.

The ship's siren gave a long blast. Before it stopped, Fay had reached the half-landing to C deck. On it, at the very edge of more stairs, a woman was locked onto the ship's officer's arms. She was yelling up into his face, "... Jesus Christ in heaven, I didn't have to come on this damn ship! Don't you understand that? I'd have been all right in my house. I don't care about the Japs. They can't be so bad. I'm not scared of them. Look, help me! Please! Just get me a taxi. I know you can. I'll pay you. A hundred dollars. Right here, I've got it. I don't need my things. I'll leave them. A ricksha would do, even. There are bound to be some about. I'll go home. Two hundred dollars! Help me to get off! Away from the docks!"

"It's too late to get off, madam."

He shook himself free. The woman went back against the stair partition, clutching at a roll bar, just saving herself from falling. The ship's officer had gone. Fay stopped. The woman lifted her head. She yelled. "What are you staring at, you whore? Get to hell away from me!"

In the entrance area someone was banging on the closed shutter of the Purser's office. Half the watertight doors where the gangway had been were shut, and two Chinese sailors were about to close the other, to seal it with clamps. The young officer turned to face a small crowd of women and one old man.

"I can't help it if there's anyone left!" he shouted. "We've sailed! We've got to get away from the docks before more bombers come!"

The pain across Fay's chest was tight. She stood alone in the middle of an empty space of floor, feeling through her feet the vibration of the ship's engines. Then she saw two suitcases and a bundle she had tied herself, a refugee's bundle with big knots on the top. Angus had stacked the luggage there because he hadn't known where to take it. He had gone to look for them. He would have been directed to D deck. She turned and ran for the stairs down.

PART
TWO

Roy

ONE

The hour of the bitch was always strictly on schedule: three in the afternoon, before the heat had begun to ease. She didn't appear every day, only two or three times a week on average, coming to work in a quietly patterned Japanese summer kimono, the obi tied with formal correctness. She carried a European-type green silk parasol with a tasselled cord hanging from just below a silver knobbed handle. She wasn't young and was plump, with heavy breasts bulging up from the constriction of the tight, high sash. Two gold-trimmed teeth sometimes glistened and even when the interrogation sessions were reaching their peak her voice never lost a genteel sibilant quality. She bowed frequently towards the captain of the military police, in modest apology for the necessity of her presence as interpreter, and only when the screaming became very loud did she sometimes reach into the sleeve pocket of her kimono for a piece of folded tissue to press against her lips.

The rope thongs striking bare flesh made a sound like a carpet being beaten, and this was amplified by the vaulted cement roof. If the bitch was in any way disturbed when strips of blood appeared across the victim's spine, she never showed it, though sometimes she stepped back a pace or two as though to give the soldier using the whip more room for his work, or perhaps because the smell of his sweat was offensive.

There were three things you could do during the bitch's visits: stay in your cell; go out into the three-story centre aisle to shout protests up to the Kempetai Captain; or escape into the sunshine of the exercise court. The protests had been loud at first, once even approaching a riot, and the Kempetai Captain's reaction to that had been to send in a posse of prison guards to carry out selective beatings. After that, the protesting died away, the setting up of the torture rack encouraging a general exodus into the open air. If you went to the far side of the fountain in the court, its splashing meant that you were spared the bitch's voice, though you still heard the screams.

Roy stayed in his cell. The wound in his thigh was suppurating again, and essential visits to the open air latrines left him exhausted. He lay on a concrete slab and looked at a concrete roof. Today's victim was very young. Though the Chinese men tied to the rack screamed, Roy had never heard any of them whimpering. The boy was doing it. Between the carpet-beating sounds he let out whipped-puppy noises and words, always the same ones: "I'm thirteen! I'm thirteen!"

As though there was some kind of age exemption from torture, Roy thought. Christ!

The thick walls of the cell didn't keep out the bitch's voice; the door was open, must never be shut, by order of the Imperial Japanese Army. Her Cantonese was smooth, due perhaps to long residence in China, or maybe here in K.L., as the bowing wife of one of their shopkeepers, offering green tea on a lacquer tray.

"You carried messages for your brother! He is a Communist bandit!"

The Kempetai Captain muttered something in Japanese. There was the carpet-beating sound. The boy shrieked: "I'm thirteen!"

*

It was impossible to sleep through one of George's returns from a working party, or even to pretend to sleep through it. He was still a massive man, wasting certainly, layers of folded skin on his stomach a reminder of what he had once been, but there was plenty to lose yet, the lard remaining in his tissues as good as a guarantee of at least another six months' survival. His voice still boomed. It filled the cell with migraine-inducing reverberations.

"Well then," he said at the door, like a husband returning to suburbia after a hard day being a good provider for his loved ones. Roy waited for him to add "I'm back" but he didn't. Instead he was mysterious: "I've got something for you."

Roy opened his eyes. Whatever it was had been hidden in one of the bits of impedimenta hanging from the webbing belt George always wore out on working parties on the principle that the time the Japs spent searching him improved the chances of one of his men getting back into the jail with his loot undiscovered.

"How's the squitters?" George asked.

"All right."

"How many times to the latrines?"

"I don't know. Eight, nine."

"That's *not* all right."

He must love me, Roy thought. After all I was his choice to share a cell with; he wasn't mine. I was too weak to care. Maybe the sight of a wound with seeping pus brought out the maternal in him. He's a good man. The presence of a good man within feet of you for at least half of every day and all of every night makes you realize what a bastard you are yourself.

"I am a bastard," Roy said. He thought he had said it under his breath but George asked, "What?"

"Nothing. I'm twitching to be surprised."

It was an egg. George held it up between two fingers.

"An old Chinese woman gave it to me. She waited until the guard was looking the other way, then was out of her stall and in again before I could really say anything. How do you say God Bless in Cantonese?"

"You don't."

"An egg's what you need. Binding."

"I'll have half and be half-bound."

"The egg is for you."

"George, when you go Christian on me I can't take it. So just cut it out, see?"

"You're a funny chap, Roy."

"Weird."

"I wonder where we could get an egg boiled? I don't like giving it to the cooks."

"Don't tell me you don't trust our prisoner cooks?"

"Well...."

"We could eat it raw. Though I admit a raw egg is hard to divide in two. Doesn't Henderson sometimes cook? On that little fire he makes behind the shit boxes?"

"The fire's for welding things for his wireless."

"It could still cook an egg. We'd offer a commission. A slice off the bottom. The white only."

"I'll ask him after roll call."

George sat down on a corner of the cement bed slab. There was only one in the cell. At night he slept on the floor, snoring. The invalid was raised up out of dangerous circulating draughts. "I hear you had the Bitch again," he said.

"Yup."

"Bad?"

"I don't want to talk about it."

"No, of course not."

"Anything happen with you?"

"Well, yes. Something funny, really."

"I've been dying for a laugh all day."

"Not that kind of funny. I didn't see it myself. Our squad was split up. Half of them went to the Cold Storage plant to clean out the rotting meat. Three of them saw it."

"What?"

"A big Jap car."

"Exciting."

"It was flying the General's flag."

"You've got me on the edge of this slab."

"With a white woman inside," George said.

"Eurasian."

"No. This one had red hair."

"Some Eurasians do. As you'd have seen if you'd been a wild boy and gone to dance halls. Instead of spending your time writing home."

"This was a *white* woman. And there's been a rumour about her."

"I don't want another of those. We've had six today."

"This one was confirmed by that Tamil dresser who comes into the hospital. He gave our doctor the woman's name. It's odd. Addington? No, that's not it. But she used to live here."

After a moment Roy said, "Adminton?"

"Yes."

"I don't believe it."

"You *knew* her?"

"I knew a Louise Adminton, yes. She was pissed a lot of the time. Didn't get on with her old man. No wonder, when you saw him."

"What was he?"

"Some kind of civil servant. Look, George, Louise would have been evacuated long ago."

"The story is she went and came back."

"*What?*"

"That's it. Went down to Singapore long before K.L. fell and then came back to her house just before the Japs arrived. Without her husband. He's supposed to have left for India."

The good are not above enlivening a dull P.O.W. day with a little juicy gossip, Roy thought. "The story is that she's now a Jap General's girlfriend?"

"Yes."

"Pissed or not, I don't believe she'd do that. Besides, I can't see any Jap General fancying her. The years were wearing her out fast."

"They say she's still living in her old house. With him."

"Maybe he just wanted a gracious hostess to help him with the social side of being C.O. an occupying force."

"Well, it could be, couldn't it?"

"No. That dresser's got hold of half a story and then added his own three quarters."

George got up from the slab, holding the egg very carefully, conscious that if he dropped it that would be a disaster they'd have to live with for weeks. He found a safe place for the egg inside an empty cardboard box near the roll of old blackout curtain he used as a pillow.

"I wish I knew what to say to them," he said.

"Who?"

"The Chinese outside. When they give me things. It's always the Chinese. The Tamils never come near us. Nor the Malays."

"The Tamils are scared and the Malays are minding their own business."

"There was that girl who gave me a piece of pineapple last week. I thanked her but I don't think she knew any English."

"She got your message. All Chinese know some English. Are you angling for Cantonese lessons?"

"Well, if I even had a few phrases — "

"No! If you had a few phrases you'd add them to your faith in God and try to escape. I don't want your chopped-off head on my conscience."

Roy stared at the cement ceiling. There were cracks in it with mould growing out of them. Pineapples. He thought about Fay. That didn't happen every day. The field. You forgot how it felt to want to screw anyone. Your wife or anyone else.

George had taken off his shirt. Looking at the man, Roy wondered how his wife could see him every night getting into pajamas and still want to bear his children. They had five. She must have wanted it. George would never rape anyone. Quite good-looking, too, from the three snapshots in his wallet.

The cry "grub up" echoed down the lofty nave of a correctional cathedral built by British colonialists.

"Where's your mess tin?" George asked. "I'll wash it out."

"I did it after our midday snack."

"Roy, I've told you to leave things like that to me. You need to conserve your strength!"

"Yes, dear. Before you go, hide that egg. Hopkins is coming to do my leg after supper. He'll think I pinched it from the hospital."

"He'll think nothing of the sort!" George sounded outraged. When you upset him his whole body winced.

I must watch it, Roy thought. Try to be a nice chap, not just a funny one. Why doesn't he just walk out on me and find a cellmate who would appreciate loving kindness? God, these awful wartime marriages!

One of Fay's great charms was that, when I was suffering from morning sickness after a heavy night, she never wanted to put a cool hand on my fevered brow. I'm starting to think of her again. Is she thinking of me? No. Too busy organizing the kids in Australia or wherever. And with no servants. It's really hard on these girls, forced to get dishpan hands after the easy life we gifted them with.

George came back with the food, boiled rice congealed into lumps and in a bowl something steaming that smelled of death.

"I'm not having any of that rotten mummy soup," Roy said. "And don't tell me that the doctor says we need the protein."

"Well, he does say that."

"I don't think eight-times-boiled decayed pig from a broken-down Cold Store is doing anybody any good. I know what it does to my guts. I don't know how you can get that stuff into you."

George had been about to sit in his corner of the cell. He turned. The light was fading, but he seemed to have flushed up.

"I can get it into me because I need it! I'm out working every day. And I *work*. I don't just stand around playing the officer."

"You're supposed to. According to King's Regulations."

"There are no King's Regulations for a damned Japanese prison camp."

"George! It's lovely to have you showing strong feeling."

"Oh, shut up!"

Roy lay with the untouched soup and rice beside him, trying to control another surge of the promptings threatening disaster at the lower end of his digestive tubing. He sat up carefully, expecting and getting the usual dizziness, more troublesome than the hot pulse in his leg. His bare feet fumbled for clogs and then he decide to go without them. George had stopped eating and was watching, probably contrite about having administered a rebuke to a dying man. Carefully, Roy stood. The jail reeled about him, then steadied a little. He went to the open door.

"Want me to come with you?"

"No. You can have my soup. I'll eat the rice later."

"You haven't any paper. Here."

The newspaper they used was strictly rationed. George, as usual, had been generous. Roy walked down the empty nave, past the cells where mess tins clanked and were scraped. Cauldrons of rotting-pig soup had been poured into alimentary canals slightly less sensitive than his, at least at the moment. A few men were belching, but he was solitary on the road to the latrines, alone under a sky beginning to go purple, with big tropical stars fighting for precedence. The path to the bogs had once been loose gravel, now rolled into a hard surface by shuffling feet. When you were seated on the boards you had to be careful not to squirm around too much or you got splinters in your buttocks.

If I had concentrated on meditation during all the hours I've sat here, Roy thought, I could be a good few miles along the road to karma or the eternal nothingness. The trouble is I can't focus the mind. Malnutrition leaves you a mental grasshopper. Though even that can be harnessed to the creative. There is our gunner who sits in his cell writing poetry. *French* poetry. "Les papillons qui flip-flappent." I told him that was one of the most moving lines I had ever heard. It was, too. My tubes don't stand up well to any kind of emotional extreme, including belly laughter.

I wish those stars weren't so bloody bright. It reminds me of Sungei Dema, bowled by mountains, the sky above us a lid to the bowl. God's in his Heaven and Big John up on high ground just under Him.

I wonder if Fay ever wanted to escape? She never gave any sign of it if she did. Perhaps when you've escaped once you haven't the energy to do it again, especially when you've complicated your living with children. Also, she loved Ruth. There was an alliance between those two; you felt it when they were together. I didn't get any credit for the success of my wife hunt; Ma regarded it as a fortunate accident. Yet almost the moment I saw Fay, or, well, when I came back

and had another look across those tea cakes, I knew she
would suit Sungei Dema and it would suit her. The "us"
was secondary, as in a royal marriage.

I have looked at her sleeping and felt pity. Maybe there
was no need for that. When you haven't been stung by a
violent love, it could mean that the gods favour you, are
ready to go on tucking the sheet up under your chin every
night in your sheltered backwater. She'll have got to Australia all right. Mary Jane will look after her there, an
extension of the Gourlay influence.

The jumping grasshopper doesn't take me to a view of
Ruth and John in the jungle. Every now and then I make
a duty of thinking about it and the duty doesn't work. I
can't believe they are there. I can't see Sungei Dema shut
down, the mine flooded, the houses empty. It is one of those
things that must endure whole in the background, like
George's domesticity in England has to. His wife and kids
are safe inside the old picture; the bombing doesn't affect
them, he says, not allowing it to, because he, George, is out
here taking the nasties, buying their immunity. If God gives
you credit like that for being good, maybe I should have
tried it somewhere along the way.

I am still in the same town with Batu Road Maisie, the
three-customers-a-night girl who managed to welcome the
last of them as though he had been lovingly in her mind all
week. It's a great gift in a whore. The gift is probably still
functioning for the Japs.

The shuffling on the walk was George's bare feet. "Roy,
are you all right?"

"Fine."

"You've been so long. Hopkins is waiting to do your
wound."

Roy thought: If George has left him alone in the cell I
bet he's found the egg.

There was nothing to indicate this when they got back
into the block: Hopkins demure on the edge of the slab,
ever the neat hospital orderly in frequently laundered shorts
that there had been no point in leaving on the body of one
of the deceased.

"I think he has a fever," George said.

Was I talking out loud again on the bogs? I'll have to watch this. To Hopkins Roy said: "How are things in the hospital?"

"Oh, not good, sir. Funeral tomorrow."

"Who this time?"

"You probably wouldn't know him. An Aussie. Only been in with us three days. Out on a working party last week. Went down sudden. They do on this diet. It's all the meat they used to get at home. Can't get the good out of rice."

"So it's another bowl of fruit on a coffin?"

"At least we get the fruit for the hospital, sir. How's your leg tonight?"

"Much the same."

"The pus has come through again," George said.

Roy lay back on the slab, watching Hopkins unwind a dirty bandage. He looks sleek, he thought. The orderlies, like the cooks, get extra food, for all they swear it doesn't happen.

"I'm going to have to pull this off now, sir. It'll hurt."

"All right." A moment later he was sweating, breathing hard. "Christ, it did!"

"I could bring you some tea, sir? From the hospital. With sugar in it."

"No."

"Go on," George said. "You're a patient."

"No. Just get on with that bandage."

The boiled-up piece of old sheet, looted on a working party, smelled of its previous uses. You got accustomed to that smell, like many others.

"New man in today, sir," Hopkins said.

George was surprised. "I didn't hear about that?"

"It was this morning. When you were out. The Kempetai handed him over. He'd been with them for weeks. For questioning. They caught him way up north, near Alor Star. The Kempetai thought he had been working with the Chinese guerillas, but he says not. Just that he was walking."

"Walking where?"

"To India. He escaped from Singapore when it surrendered. Crossed the Straits by stealing one of the boats the Japs had used to land on the island."

"Alor Star! He got a long way on the road," Roy said.

"That's right, sir. He might have made it. It's something to think about."

"How was he caught?"

"He was down with malaria. A Chinese family nursed him for weeks. Then somebody squealed. The Japs shot the Chinese. They shot the whole family, including the kids. Made him watch while they did it. Then took him to Taiping."

Roy had shut his eyes.

George asked: "Is he all right?"

"No, sir, he's bad. Doc says he won't live."

"What's his name?"

"Eddie something. I forgot. I don't know his unit. We just call him Eddie. It hurts him to talk much. You only get a few words at a time."

The scream that probed into the cell could have been from a woman. Or a boy. It rose higher and higher, then was cut off.

"Good God!" George said. "The Chinese wing! We've never heard them at this hour before?"

"The carpentry shop, sir. We got the gen in the hospital from the cooks. There was to be an execution."

Hopkins knotted the bandage carefully.

TWO

He had been thinking of Fay again. The rain had just stopped, thunderous rain, drumming on the prison roof. He lay with his earlier conviction — that Fay had escaped to Australia — undermined, as though he should have been able to imagine her there, established in one of those bungalows with a huge spread of garden you had to look after yourself, and which would keep her busy. He could picture the place all right, had seen the prototype on two trips Down Under, but he couldn't see Fay in the setting. Or Angus. Or Liza.

He knew what it was: the four-in-the-morning horrors, worse in this circumstance. Much worse. You woke to a collection of the horrors all crouched in a circle around you, all patient in the knowledge that each of them, in turn, would receive your full attention. Death wasn't amongst them. In this place, death was most often merciful. You looked at the wasted corpse lying there and wondered why the hell you were hanging around yourself? Two or three times he had felt that, but only once so acutely that he came damn near saying the yes please which was all you needed, on this food intake, to slide away. That one time had been when Mike had sat up and said: "Christ, I feel better this morning," and had died.

Moonlight had been switched on. It lay, patterned by bars from the high window, over George's feet, big feet with big toes. Very slowly Roy sat up. His tubes behaved themselves and the dizziness didn't come. It was a surprise. The hot pulse in his thigh was perfectly endurable without its usually faithful attendants. He stood, his head all right, as

though the rain and the coolness that followed had cleared
it. George wasn't snoring, but this didn't mean he was
awake. He had moments of apparently total withdrawal into
sleep that brought you almost to the brink of a tenderness
for him, but not quite.

This time, Roy said to himself, I am not going to the bogs.
He went instead down the nave, to stairs leading to the two
upper tiers of cells, all of these empty and out of bounds
to P.O.W.'s, as were the stairs themselves. Not many climbed
them: only a few at night, as Roy was doing, to escape into
that ultimate luxury, a brief freedom from the pressing sense
of others continually pushing past the margins of what, in
any other life, would be a stubbornly defended privacy.
Climbing those stairs, you took the risk of a surprise nighttime roll call's finding you out of your cell, and then the
alarm's sounding, the clattering of booted feet on cement,
shouts that always seemed like hysteria put to a military use.
According to the Doc half the guards were convalescent
syphilitics, and not very convalescent at that.

On the first landing he had to lean back against a wall
to rest, his breathing an old man's, his lungs pumping in
and out. Still, the dizziness stayed away and the fist in his
abdomen remained passive. There was no point in waiting
here with no view and too near the sleepers. Someone had
a bad cough. He began to climb again, slowly, as though
each tread had been newly carved from ice on an Alp and
had to be tested. At the top, his heart was telling him to
panic. He slid down onto the floor, two hands grasping the
bars of the huge, arched grille; he was half-aware of assuming the almost classic pose of a prisoner, of feeling driven
by a need to get his face close enough to one of the gaps
that there would be nothing between his eyes and the roofs,
and lights, and houses climbing the hill behind the padang
on which colonial exiles had stubbornly played cricket
through the main heat to a sweaty tea break. He could see
the dome of the mosque on its nearby island in the river
and one of the turrets of the Moorish station hotel. A train
whistle hooted, but the streets were as quiet as they had been
under curfew. No rumble of carts came in from the surrounding vegetable gardens as there would have been a year

ago. It wasn't just his imagination that told him the city had turned sullen; even in daylight, men in from the working parties confirmed this. The Japs didn't appear to have much flair for establishing anything approaching a norm after conquest, almost as though they recognized the transient nature of their occupation and couldn't be bothered to. Their very presence in the streets somehow suggested impermanence: the thumping soldiers in boots that always seemed too large for their feet almost seemed aware that their time on these pavements was strictly limited.

His hands still holding the bars, Roy knew that the Japs would have to go. Already there were signs that the huge snake of their conquests would choke to death on a meal it couldn't swallow. Which didn't mean that Malaya would return to the norm that had meaning for him — and in the white moonlight after the night's rain he was already half-mourning a loss. This had been his town, his place, almost as much as Sungei Dema; K.L. had been the source of everything beyond the home-grown, including the experiments of adolescence. At eighteen, alone in Batu Road for the first time, he had been frightened by the four whores up in their box watching him as he drank beer. He had only taken a couple of sips of the beer before practically backing out into the safety of the street. In the third house there was a little Siamese girl who looked as scared as he felt. The house mother kept insisting that the girl was very clean. She had certainly been kind, losing her fear in his incompetence. A million years ago. Oddly, he heard Angus saying that.

It wasn't his childrens' voices, or Fay's, he heard very often now, but Mike's, as though everything from that first sentence in a Kempetai cell — "What have they got *you* for, Chum?" — had been put on a record and the smallest accidents of a day's circumstance could flick on a pickup needle, bringing not only the voice but a laughter that had once been the underpinning to Roy's flurries of courage, helping them last a little longer.

He could see Mike, too, not in a flow with a kind of continuity, like the voice, but in a series of fixed prints: Mike lying on the floor of the Kempetai cell at the first meeting; Mike still curled up from the pain of a torture session, but looking up, curious, interested, hoping for a companion who would be congenial through these distresses.

You could say that we were congenial, you could say that. I loved him from an empathy I had never known before. It wasn't that we didn't need to talk, we talked all right. Talk was the only indulgence available — hurling words at each other, making a competition of them until the guards would slide back the hatches to look at us and sometimes shout at us, for they were angered at what they could see was some kind of pleasure being enjoyed by those who should only be allowed to know pain.

I suppose he was really almost an ugly man, a head too small for the broad shoulders it sat on and with only a very short interruption of neck. His head had a streamlined look, his ears and nose somehow packed into it as though they weren't to be noticed. He said thinnish lips indicated an ascetic, un-sensuous nature, a dead cert at least for Beatification if not Sainthood, if he could contrive to get himself martyred for the Holy Church instead of — what looked much more likely — for the goddamned British Army. His laugh seemed to come from a spring, often released when you had no reason to expect it, as though something in his own running commentary on what was happening to himself had suddenly seemed sharply funny. When there was no obvious reason for private mirth, he didn't try to explain it but seemed half-apologetic at having to appear just faintly mysterious.

I think I knew before we were both moved to the Kempetai H.Q. at Kuala Pilah that the Japs were coming to believe my story, and it was then that Mike began to urge me to tell them everything. He said that when you were the prisoner of barbarians, King's Regulations were crap, and there was about as much point in just giving your name, rank, and number to the Japs as to Genghis Khan's storm troopers. Under torture you tried for one thing only: to hold onto facts that would destroy others if they were revealed. He didn't say it, but that was what he was trying to do. I didn't have to hold onto any of my facts because none of them could possibly destroy others.

At Kuala Pilah he was getting the burn torture and I

wasn't. He could never sleep after it, but he could talk, or more often listen to me talking. God Almighty, what did we talk about? I can hear my voice going on and on, then stopping, my thinking that he just might have dropped off, but Mike's saying, "Well?" to prod me. I do remember telling him about the legacy to all the Gourlays from Josephina, the Portuguese, her aristocratic Malacca family line infiltrated since about the seventeenth century by Chinese, Malay, and who knows what other blood streams.

I never talked to Fay about Josephina. She never asked any questions even after those first dinners up at Estate House with the alleged, very dark portrait of the old girl staring down at us from the dining room wall. Probably any curiosity she felt was early satisfied by Pa flaunting our ancestress and the dowry that had let the Gourlays set up those first coffee plantations. He was fond of saying that his grandfather had come to Malaya with one pair of trousers and something near to an Irishman's charm. Pa is totally confident that all the racial streams stemming from Josephina have long since been swamped by the strong Scotch central flow. And in my case it ought to be swamped by another strong flow, from New England.

I have never been so sure, not just because my skin doesn't quite lose its tan in a cold climate, more that I have no other country but this one, and never could have. It wouldn't be possible for me to do what Bruce and Anne, and now Mary Jane in Australia, have all done: turn my back on it. Not even after this war. Maybe especially not after this war. It's not, either, that I am heir to Sungei Dema, flooded or otherwise; I know for sure that, away from this spit of land pushing into the equator like a swollen penis, I would be a kind of ghost, as I am half a stranger to all those sleepers down below, but wasn't to Mike.

I suppose at Kuala Pilah I really understood what he was trying to do, working to make me dissociate myself in the eyes of the Japs from what he must have seen clearly enough as his own likely end, the usual ritual of digging his grave before being decapitated into it. While we were together there was a considerable risk that one grave would serve for two. So I was to do nothing and say nothing; that would reduce the chances of our being separated. I went along with this, wanting to live. When the time came I went out of that cell, leaving him. I don't really know why I jumped from that lorry as it slowed for a bend except that maybe by then I needed a new crime in my dossier, one that would take me back to Kuala Pilah. Instead I got the bullet that brought me here.

They brought Mike here, too, when he was dying. That was why the Kempetai handed him over. Doc took one look and said so. Yet if Mike had known this verdict, and perhaps he did, he would never have accepted it. I never saw the look in his eyes we've all grown used to, the look of a man on his way out, and who wants to be.

When Mike died the Japs said they had used up all the coffins. They put him naked in a barrel with his knees up to his chin and nailed down the round lid.

*

George was wearing his back-from-church expression, which meant he had been visiting the boys in hospital, bringing them the cheer of his natural optimism, often in the form of an announcement that the war would be over in six months. Roy was never quite sure whether this was a case of wishful thinking on George's part, or a serious conviction. Since this had been the cause of the nearest thing to a flaming row in their domestic life, the matter had never again been under discussion. Roy remembered asking who the hell George thought he was, Nostradamus? For a couple of days all talk had been savagely minimal. Then George had broken down to become caring again.

Now he sat on the edge of the slab, continuing to look like a man facing up seriously to the realities of the world all around him. "I had a talk with that new man."

"Oh, yes?"

"The one they caught at Alor Star."

"I remember. How is he?"

"Better than they were expecting."

"Good."

"A funny sort of chap."

"There are so many of us," Roy said

"He told me quite a bit about how he got away from Singapore. He says he would never have got off the island if it hadn't been for the boy."

"What boy?"

"Some sort of Eurasian. Eddie didn't say. But I think the boy must have been pretty black. The Japs kept taking him for a Tamil. Or a Malay. They were dressed that way."

"So what happened to the black boy?"

"Eddie's not sure. They were both at the house of some portrait painter. On the coast somewhere. A white man."

"British?"

"Yes. But the Japs hadn't taken him in. He seems to have ignored the war, staying in his house. Just letting it go past him. It was quite a lonely place. Eddie says the house was full of paintings of the man's servant. Mostly naked. Eddie didn't like him."

"But the painter liked the black boy?"

"It would look like it," George said judicially. "Anyway, he started painting him."

"You don't think Eddie is seeing himself as the Pudu teller of tales?"

"What do you mean?"

"He could be having you on."

"Why should he want to do that?"

"To pass the time in here. We all have to work out some way of doing it, or go nuts. Especially those who are bed down. Somehow I can't see this painter left alone by the Japs to carry on with his male nudes."

"But they arrested him while Eddie was there."

"Then what happened to the boy?"

"Eddie doesn't know. But he's sure it was the servant who called in the Japs. Soldiers took them all away, including the servant."

"Where was Eddie when all this happened?"

"In swimming. He saw the lorry coming along the shore road with the soldiers in it. He hid in mangrove at the end of the beach. Stayed there all night, scared the Japs would come back looking for him. But it wasn't the Japs who came, it was Malays. They looted the house and put all the paintings on a bonfire."

"Muslims," Roy said. "They never hang pornography in the living room. So we'll never know if we've lost another Gaugin. What did Eddie do then? Start walking north?"

"Yes." All he had was his shorts and a pocket knife. There wasn't a thing left in the house. He says it was a beautiful place, like something in a movie. But after that he never tried to stay with anyone until he got malaria and those Chinese found him. At night he hid and he stole his food. He had quite a bit of luck. Got an almost new pair of boots off a body on a rubber estate. Then there was a big car hidden down a jungle track, full of stuff. No bodies around it. He'd no idea what had happened to the car's owners. He stayed there for a couple of days, resting up, sleeping in the car. There was a case of tinned stewing steak and he emptied every tin. It blew him up like a balloon before he got the squitters."

"I'm beginning to believe Eddie's story. You must have asked all the right questions. A natural detective."

"I'm interested in people," George said.

*

The sound of "Jerusalem" sung in a sturdy baritone pushed its way into the cell, almost as total a takeover as screams from a flogging. Hopkins stared at Roy's thigh from which another dirty bandage had just been removed.

"I think you should let the Doc see this again, sir."

"Why? There's no pus coming out."

"It's the inflammation around the wound. If we just had a little sulfa powder. The Japs act as though they'd never heard of it. Funny the way the bullet exit hole's healed up. I was wondering about the possibility of another bullet's still being in there. Could it be?"

"Don't ask me."

"I mean, can you remember when it happened?"

"Too well. I was lying on the ground thinking I was dead."

"But you could have been hit more than once?"

"I could have been hit a few times. When you're dead you don't really notice."

"It's just that this entry wound is so big for one bullet."

"I must say you're getting highly professional, Hopkins."

"Well, I see a lot. You pick things up. Especially in this bloody place. What you need is an X-ray. Doc says it's like practicing medicine without medicine. Or instruments. Not much better than three hundred years ago. Except he *knows* why people are dying."

"He might try bleeding. The Japs ought to let us have leeches. They wouldn't cost anything."

They were interrupted by the baritone, producing astonishing volume for someone on a low-protein diet.

"Funny their letting us have a concert," Hopkins said, wrapping the bandage.

"My cellmate says it's because the war's nearly over."

"What do you say, sir?"

"I think it makes a change for the prison guards. From that whorehouse across the road."

"I meant about the war?"

"That has just begun. Only don't quote me. I'd be up before the Colonel for undermining prisoner morale."

"Why do you think they took the Chinks away?"

"There wasn't room enough in that wing for the numbers they're having to arrest."

"The Chinks are getting it a lot worse than us, aren't they?"

"Yes."

"Some blokes out on a working party by lorry went through a village with ten heads on bamboo spikes. All Chink heads. One of them was an old man with a beard. I think the Japs love cutting off heads."

"If you have an ancestral sword in the family, it's always a temptation."

"Ho-ho-hosanna," sang the baritone. "In the hi-hi-highest."

"God!" Hopkins said, still wrapping bandage.

"You're not musical?"

"That bloke does something to my back teeth. Or where they used to be before the army dentists got them. You know, sir, I went in for a filling at Pirbright when I was training and the dentist took out two molars. I guess because it was easier. Acting Major he was, too. I got a day off duty for it and went into London. But you miss your teeth."

The applause that reached them sounded like the end of Act One of *Tannhauser* at Covent Garden, Roy's single experience of grand opera. He hadn't stayed for Act Two, and only sat through Act One because his mother had told him it was his duty, while in Europe, to expose himself to Wagner. None of her children had inherited her intense reactions to music. This wasn't a grief to her; it just irritated her that flesh of her flesh could be so aesthetically insensitive.

"You remember that woman I told you about, sir? The white woman? The one living with the Jap General?"

"Yes.

"She's got a kid now."

"By the General?"

"The kid's about ten."

"That seems to rule the Japs out. What kind of a kid?"

"A boy. Eurasian, I guess. But he looks white, so the blokes say. He rides with her in the car. The one with the flag. Looks like she's adopted him."

"Lucky Eurasian. There can't be many of them having it so easy. I hope it lasts."

"What do you mean?"

"The General's wife might arrive from Japan. They tell me you're beginning to see a lot of Jap women around in K.L. Come down to bring Rising Sun culture to south regions. Flower arranging and the tea ceremony. The sort of thing we all need."

"Like shit I need their culture."

"That's taking a very narrow view, Hopkins. Maybe you ought to get out and about more. Join a working party and see the world."

"No, sir. Before I got this job I was beaten up three times outside. Real bad, too. I guess they didn't like my face. I notice it in hospital when the guards come in. I sort of keep out of their way. Leave it to Doc. They're scared of him. He roars at them."

"I've heard it."

"Not that it does any good. All we get is more aspirin."

THREE

"A funny thing happened today," George said. He waited so patiently for a reaction that Roy felt obliged to send one over.

"You got another egg?"

"No. I didn't get anything. You know those biggish houses up the hill behind the club? The ones in the woods with the jungle trees?"

"I've been to parties in most of them."

"Jap Army brass have them now. A detail of my blokes was there today tidying gardens that have gone wild. One chap was on his own with a Jap guard. Mason. He used to be a car salesman in Singapore. Not one of your Volunteers; he joined the gunners. Blue eyes. Lost most of his hair."

"I know who you mean."

"Well, Mason turned around from his hedge-cutting and there was this boy coming down the drive on a bicycle. As soon as the boy sees Mason he brakes and gets off his bike. He was about ten, well set up, black hair. Been eating well, too, nothing skinny about him. The boy didn't say anything, though he was quite close. Mason thought that was because he had just spotted the Jap guard asleep under a tree. Then it was pretty plain it wasn't the guard the boy was looking at, but the prisoner of war. As though he didn't like what he saw. It griped Mason the way the kid was staring, standing there well fed and in a clean white shirt. As though he didn't want to have anything to do with scum like us. The guard was the one they call Poface, with a hell of a temper, and Mason was scared to wake him up. He asked the boy's name in a pretty low voice but got no answer, and a moment later the kid was pushing the bike away up the drive."

"That'll be the Eurasian boy the General's lady is supposed to have adopted?"

"Right. Only Mason swears the kid isn't Eurasian. He says that down in Singapore he got so he could smell out the mixed blood in any room he walked into."

"We must have him along to our cell some evening."

"Why?"

"To see if he smells me out. I've inherited a Chinese streak. It could be, though, that the smell begins to wear off after the third generation."

George was staring at the floor. It was too shadowy in the cell to see whether he had gone into one of those sudden flushes that could deepen the pink of his sunburn.

"Roy ... I'm sorry."

"No need to be. I'm not cringing. Tell me, why are you so worked up about this boy?"

It was a moment before George answered. "I don't know. It may be the idea of the Japs adopting him as some kind of mascot. Like a regimental goat. Having him out on the lawn every morning before breakfast to bow towards the Emperor in Tokyo. That kind of thing. I keep thinking of my own son. He's eleven. If it had been him. You've got kids yourself. You must know what I mean?"

"I know this. Those of us who last to walk away from the Japs will do it because we've been able to drop a fire curtain between now and what we had yesterday. All that matters with that boy is that he survives the war."

In the dim light Roy could feel George staring at him. "Is that all that matters to you?"

"Yes."

"I think that's a helluva thing to say!"

"Is it? Most of us in here have had our chances to be heroes and muffed them. The heroes are all dead. The rest of us are working for survival. And damn all else!"

"I hate it when you talk like this!"

"Put it down to my mixed blood."

George got up and walked out of the cell. He was still

out of it when a Japanese guard started yelling "Tenko! Tenko!" The roll call shuffling sounded louder than usual. Coughing spread like an instant infection down the line of men forming up under the high roof of the nave. Roy started to push himself into the sitting-at-attention position demanded of the sick out of hospital. The dizziness could have been waiting for him up at the new head level, almost a takeover, the cell beginning to heave like a cabin on a liner fighting a typhoon. He heard the counting outside, an assortment of accents, none of them Japanese-sounding: "*Ichi, ni, san, shi, go, rokku, shichi, hachi, ku....*" The voices fuzzed, then fused together. As he toppled off the slab he saw a guard in the doorway, staring with his mouth open.

*

He was running over grass at Sungei Dema, the lawns no longer sloping down from Estate House towards the village and the valley bottom, but rolling like monster green waves, up and down, and when he reached the crest of one he could see the crests of others ahead, all smooth and beautifully mown, unencumbered by trees or shrubs. And always from those heights there was the sight of his brother, in a romper suit, toiling up the slope of the opposite mound, slowly but purposefully, a child halfway bent over, deeply intent on what he was doing...running away. Roy, able to run much faster, had to stop him. But somehow the distance between them never altered; the small figure seen from each crest was in exactly the same position, going up an opposite slope. Roy kept calling, but Bruce never turned his head. He seemed completely confident, as though he knew his exact destination and how he was going to reach it. Roy knew Bruce was leaving Sungei Dema forever. He had to be stopped. Somewhere ahead was the last of these huge green mounds and beyond lay the beginnings of jungle, a no-man's-land into which Bruce could escape. Then, as though released from checks operating against his own movement, Roy was catching up. He called out again. For the first time Bruce turned. He was laughing. Only it wasn't Bruce, it was Angus. Roy stumbled and fell on grass that was like a bank of penknife blades all sticking up to receive him.

A voice said, "I'm sure his eyelids flickered, sir."

Another voice, "It doesn't mean anything. Get that stuff into him. It's all we can do."

Roy tried to push himself up from the stabbing grass.

"Sir . . . his hands! . . ."

"I saw that. I'll get the tube out. Get a basin. He'll be sick."

Angus was still there on the crest, looking down. He had stopped laughing. Roy saw his face clearly, the expression serious, determined. He turned and began to disappear down the opposite slope of the mound. Roy tried to call out but couldn't. Something in his throat was moving, like a snake. It hurt. Then the pain seemed to come from those grass knives again, all over his body. A sound filled his ears. Slowly he recognized it. He was vomitting. When that was over the green mounds were gone. He wasn't at Sungei Dema but had been pushed down onto something after the sickness, and on his back. He opened his eyes to terrible light and had to close them again.

"Sir. . . ."

"I saw it. What's the matter with you, Hopkins?"

"I don't know what you mean, sir."

"Every time I come in here you're with this man."

"But he's — "

"You don't need to tell me how he is! There are twenty-four others in this room, six of them as bad as this one. Three worse."

"Yes, sir."

"Thinking about a job in Malaya after this war? That Gourlay could fix it for you? Listen to me! There's no intensive care in this pretence of a hospital. Or there shouldn't be. We've done too much for this man already. Everyone in here should have an equal chance to live. A bloody poor chance, but he should have it. Understand?"

"Yes, sir."

"You'd better. If you don't want to go back to outside working parties. Marston's messed himself again. Clean him up!"

"Sir!"

Roy lay with his eyes shut. If he hadn't recognized the doctor's voice, he would have recognized the smell permanently trapped under the low roof. Even the sumatras blowing in through the unglazed, barred windows never managed to clear it away. The mumble of voices never ended either, not even at night — the convalescents talking to each other, the dying to themselves.

So I'm back, Roy thought. He stretched out a hand, working the fingers, a test he had used before. He tried the other hand, then his good leg. He didn't test the one with the wound, he was too exhausted. He opened his eyes. Still too bright. He shut them again, but not before he had seen Hopkins three pads down cleaning up Marston. Roy's stomach sent a message welcoming his return to consciousness: the fist opening and closing; dizziness, too, the moment he tried to move his head. But there was sleep. Nearly always he had been able to reach out for that and get it, the only gentle mercy to be relied on in this place.

*

No one comes near me. Hopkins is scared to after that stripe torn off him by the Doc. I have a partition on one side and a non-talkative Aussie on the other. He lies staring at the ceiling. He didn't answer any of the three questions I put to him; he's deep in that self-hypnosis most of us get pretty good at. From the look of what's left of him I'd say he wasn't a city type, probably from the Outback, used to being on a horse and with a hundred miles of nothing but gum trees and snakes in every direction. The last thing he wants is a temporary cobber on a pad twelve inches from his pad. We share smells, but nothing else.

I can move all of me now, even the bad leg, which doesn't feel anything like as hot as I've been used to. Maybe if I sat up the dizziness wouldn't come. Mike sat up, sure his wouldn't. Christ, the thought of that puts fear in my swallow. Somebody come and talk to me . . . Hopkins!

From the way he's looking in this direction he might have heard the shout I didn't give. But he's not coming. It's not

Marston this time, but a moaner over on the other side. Maybe that's what you need to do in here to get attention.

Stare at the ceiling. Find a stain on it that you can convert into the perfect, pulsing circle, contracting and expanding, but finally wide enough to be your escape hatch, with yesterday's sun shining through. Sungei Dema. All right, I can see it, but I'm still here. The screen won't become the real thing. I can see my mother, more often called Ruth in my mind, an echo of my father's bellow. I can't see me. When I look for me it's Angus who comes in, with his closed face that only seemed to open for his grandmother. Maybe for Fay sometimes, though I can't remember that.

What I do remember is Fay with that look that came near to surprise, as though she had been a sleeper suddenly waking to a situation for which she could find no real explanation. The look said she was almost embarrassed that somehow, without quite knowing she was doing it, she had surrounded her life with an extraordinary collection of things that were hard to account for: a husband, two children, in-laws, a concrete house and a swimming pool, plus a set pattern governing almost every move she made.

I only half-saw this then and only understood a quarter of it. Probably because I wouldn't let myself. But it was the thing we had most in common. Both living according to a prescription, the ingredients ground and mixed for us by those two chemists up at Estate House. All we had to do was swallow the powder that would fix us up, like santonin for intestinal worms.

Fay and I never really talked. Talk would have betrayed us both. I was damned if I was going to let that happen. Maybe in Australia she is thinking of me. More likely, my imagination, on overtime after fever, seems to bring her close. Romantic to fall in love with your wife of more than ten years lying on a pad in a stinking prison camp hospital.

*

"Ought you to be talking to me?" Roy asked.

Hopkins looked around towards the open door into the

other ward. "It's all right, sir. The Doc's up at the camp office with the interpreter. Trying to get some sulfa powder."

"Any hope?"

"No. He'll get more of those bran tablets the Doc says would make a good laxative for cats. And the one thing we don't need in here is laxatives."

"I know I was fed by a tube," Roy said. "But how long was I out?"

"Five days. A record. I mean, for anyone talking afterwards."

"What was the matter with me?"

"Septicemia complicated by only half-treated malaria. From not enough quinine. Doc says you had most of the symptoms of blackwater fever. You kept getting rigors while unconscious."

"Must have been fascinating to watch."

"Yes, sir. Anything else? I can't hang around."

"What did you pour down that bicycle pump tube into my stomach? Rice gruel?"

"No. Raw eggs whipped up with glucose."

"Where did you get the glucose?"

"Jap presento. A couple of months ago. A working party was clearing out one of our old supply dumps. There was a sack of it. The Japs thought it was sugar at first but, when they tasted it, not the kind of sugar they like. So out of their big, generous hearts they give us back some of our own stuff. The Doc heard that sack was coming into camp and he was up meeting the evening dismissal parade. He requisitioned the glucose. One of the things for which he is hated by all the boys. Until they get sick."

"Did I get an egg a day?"

"Two."

"How the hell?"

"From your cellmate. Don't ask me how he did it. Organized his boys outside, I guess. They like him. A few times he's got himself beaten up, instead of one of them."

Roy stared at the ceiling.

"He's a good bloke," Hopkins said. "I never heard anyone say a word against him. In this place that's something. Those eggs came in marked for you."

Roy had a question for the orderly but, before he could get it out, Hopkins had pushed himself back on his heels and stood. He went into the other ward. Slowly Roy turned his head. The Aussie was lying on his back, but now his eyes were shut. From the piece of cloth over his middle his legs were thrust down the pad, long legs that seemed to have nothing but the bones left.

*

"Not so fast!" Roy said. I sound like a peevish old man, he thought. At one of those English seaside towns. Rich and nasty. Grudging the price of my male nurse's attic bedroom. Why do they all stay faithful? The Doc hates me, though.

"Where are we going?"

"To that grass bank, sir."

"My legs won't get me there."

"The Doc says it's time you used them."

"To hell with the Doc!"

"You don't really mean that."

"Don't tell me what I mean, Hopkins! Oh . . . sorry. It's just my legs, not solid at all. Liquid. I don't see why we have to be so far from the hospital?"

"It's not far. Doesn't it feel good to be out in the sun?"

"Nothing feels good. I've been a bloody convalescent, haven't I?"

"Yes, Mr. Gourlay."

"*Captain* Gourlay. One of the troubles in this place is the way rank is being allowed to slide away. I got my commission, Hopkins, from a Malaya command that didn't know what the hell it was doing. And if you'd be interested to hear whether I think I've fulfilled the trust they put in me, the answer is I do not."

"You mustn't talk so much, sir. You can't do that and walk, too."

"You are three quarters carrying me, Hopkins. I've had a great deal of that. Recently, and not so recently. Lying in there, you have all time on your hands for making assessments. Only alternative is trying to identify the assorted stinks."

"Talking's making your breathing come funny again."

"I'm delirious from fresh air. It's like fortified wine to a total abstainer."

"Just five more steps to the bank."

"Five steps but ten shuffles. And then you can lay me down and leave me to my assignation. I know that after all this time I should be excited. But I'm not."

"You'll be glad to see him again."

"Does a man freed from his conscience for some weeks rejoice at being reunited with it?"

"I don't know about conscience, sir. But he's a good bloke."

"So you've said before. And more than one."

"Here we are now. The grass is nice and dry. We should maybe have brought some kind of hat to shade your face. Though you haven't really lost your tan."

"Some day I may let you into the secret of my tan. Under oath."

This bank receives me as a grave might, Roy thought, accommodating itself to an alien object it will eventually absorb. My bones have no real resistance to the ground; they could easily start flowing into the red laterite beneath this grass. Under my hand the grass blades are positive to my negative. This is real weakness of body and mind. The mind keeps chirping away, but only from a top layer of its cells; a deeper exploration could explode it.

"Well, I'll go now, sir. If there's nothing you want?"

Roy looked up. "Nothing. Thanks, Hopkins. Don't mind my mutterings."

"I never have."

"Oh . . . just one thing. Will they be putting someone else on the Aussie's pad today?"

"I don't know. Maybe you'll be lucky."

"Why lucky?"

"I thought you'd be glad of the extra space?"

In a moment Roy said, "No. It's too empty."

He shut his eyes. There was no sound of Hopkins going away, just a whirring of traffic from the city. Some maniac in the road beyond the jail was driving on his horn. It would be a Malay teenager. Just like old times. The Japs must have plenty of car juice to have this build-up of noise in the town. Kuala Lumpur seemed to be recovering from its gloom, probably even the Chinese community nearing the end of its available martyr material. Everyone learning to be happy under Co-Prosperity. Asia for the Asiatics. The scrap heap for colonialist pigs like the Gourlay tribe.

He opened his eyes. George was standing there staring down. George, the walking wounded, looking like he wouldn't get far in any column, liable to fall into a ditch and stay there.

"Christ! . . ."

"I'm not as bad as I look," George said.

"What the hell happened?"

"A lorry. On a working party. Turned over. I seemed to get the worst of it."

"Your arm? . . ."

"My wrist's broken. But I'm. . . ."

He stopped. He's shaken, Roy thought. The unshakeable George whose war was going to be over in six months. He doesn't believe that now.

"Sit down!" Roy said.

In hospital you become expert at assessing the state of recovery, or lack of it, by the way patients sit down, all of them nursing themselves, but some beginning to be casual about it. George wasn't casual about the way he sat.

"What else?" Roy asked. "You've a black eye."

"Well, I must have landed on one side of my head. It was swollen up."

"What about the dysentery that kept you from coming to see me?"

George was staring towards a cell block. "I didn't have it."

"The idea was to protect me from seeing you? In case I died of shock?"

"The Doc thought it better you didn't."

"How long were you bed down?"

"About a week."

"In our cell?"

George nodded. He was still looking at a section of penitentiary architecture.

"I hope you slept on the slab?"

He was slow with his answers. "I tried it. But I didn't really like it. You get used to the floor."

"Who looked after you?"

"Oh, everyone 'round about. You know. Bringing me food. And all that."

He doesn't sound very convincing, Roy thought. "How did you get to the bogs?"

"What? Oh. Well, the fellows helped me there, too."

Under a Kempetai interrogation George's story would crumble away into the truth. And damn soon. If I had the strength to go on with this I'd be getting at the facts quickly enough. But they'll have to wait. He's stubbornly not looking at me. He knows those spaniel eyes would betray him.

The sun was bringing up sweat through the parched skin of Roy's arms. He looked at that waste of saline solution he could ill afford, then closed his eyes, lying back to stay quite still. He had a sense of George's being grateful for this, the man wanting to wrap himself in layers of silence, which wasn't like him at all. There was a kind of peace in the hospital yard, the Jap guards rarely coming into it. The Doc said they were scared of picking up assorted infections and were zoning the area for avoidance whenever possible, which would make it the perfect escape setting if anyone had the strength to climb a wall.

I should have spent my convalescence planning how I was going to get out of here, Roy thought. It might have kept my temper sweeter. There is something spaciously comic in the idea, too, my plotting to be faithful to that para in King's Regulations about your duty not to resign yourself to prisoner status. Who's afraid of all those third-class samurai just waiting for a good excuse to use their steel choppers? I am.

"Gourlay!"

You couldn't even be an outpatient at the hospital without recognizing that voice at once. It would bring me out of a deep sleep ten years after peace has been declared.

Roy opened his eyes. The Doc was holding one of the round aluminum mess tins that were hand-me-downs to the P.O.W.'s from those other unfortunates incarcerated under British justice. From a dent in the side of this one he knew that it was his.

"What's this?" the Doc asked.

"My rice."

"And why haven't you eaten it?"

"I wasn't hungry."

"What has that got to do with not eating your rice?"

"Not a lot, I suppose."

"Perhaps you were waiting for an egg?"

"Isn't that a bit rough? I haven't had an egg for more than two weeks."

"But before that you had every one that came into my hospital. At least some days."

"Did I ask you to pour them down my throat through that tube?"

"Roy, don't. . . ." It was George.

The Doc ignored him. "You wouldn't have been here, Gourlay, if I hadn't."

"Right! Now tell me that ten men in that hospital died because I got the eggs!"

"Doc, please leave him alone!"

George again, and George not noticed.

"No, I won't tell you that. But I'm going to tell you something else. How those eggs were paid for."

"Doc! You mustn't."

George should keep out of this. It wasn't his war.

"They were pricey, those eggs, Gourlay. Very. George here organized the men out on his working parties to buy them. They had to be paid for on the black market. You can't steal eggs easily. So your cellmate sold his watch to raise the necessary dollars. Nothing much wrong in that, you'll say. Prisoners sell things all the time to the Japs. However, the watch sold was a British make, available in the better Woolworths at home, price seventeen shillings and sixpence. Called the Reliable. But as a non-Swiss watch there wasn't a ready sale of Reliables to the Japs. George had never been able to get rid of his. That is, until he explained to the honcho in charge of his working party that the Reliable had Swiss works inside a British case, and was therefore worth a great deal of money. The honcho gave him twenty dollars for it."

The ground under Roy on the bank was warm. He was beginning to feel cold. The chill seemed to come seeping up his limbs from hands and feet. Beside him George made another noise. It might have been a protest; it never became a word.

"The honcho had a Jap friend who knows about watches. George's bad luck. The honcho came back to George really angry but still prepared to leave the matter with a couple of correctional socks on George's jaws. That is, if he got his money back. But George didn't have one note left in his pocket. It had all gone out to his men for your eggs. You've seen the Japs go beserk, Gourlay. That's what happened. They were working in a timber yard. The honcho didn't just pick up a stick, he used a plank. The first blow broke George's wrist when he was trying to ward it off. The second got him on the side of the head. Knocked him out cold. Our men thought he was dead. The Japs brought him back to Pudu later, after they'd had one of their own doctors set his wrist. If I didn't know them better I might think they were ashamed of what had happened. Anyway, they didn't let us see him. Or treat him. They put him in a cell up at the guardroom. All by himself. And that's where he's been, until yesterday."

From the entrance to the prison came the squawking of a supply truck horn, almost certainly bringing more rice but not much else. The Doc held the bowl out.

"You eat that," he said.

Roy took the bowl in both hands. He stared at the congealed mass in it. The Doc walked away. George's voice came high, almost shrill. "You're not to mind what he says, Roy! You didn't know! And it doesn't matter!"

Very slowly Roy turned his head. "Tell me you'd do it again, George. Tell me that. Maybe it'll stop me from blubbering."

PART THREE
Louise

ONE

Sometimes Louise was lucky, the General ordering the gin bottle put on the table, passing it to her, watching her eagerness. Then she would go up to her room, out onto the verandah beyond it, and everything in the moonlit garden beneath would seem exactly as it used to be. All the old props to the norm would be there, the sounds almost the same, the owl still hooting from the huge jungle tree that had stood sentinel over her life for so long. She hadn't known there were owls in Malaya when she first came to this house, and years ago that call in the night had seemed a link with England, almost like a formal introduction to this new place after which you were supposed to become established by your own efforts.

She hadn't been much good at that, for herself or for her husband; the house and garden had increasingly become a fortress from which to make sorties into the world, forced by Henry. He would insist on her occasional appearances at the club where she always felt herself to be the only stranger. Looking for Henry usually meant going through a huge room in which no one sent her any real recognition signals, her footfalls sounding elephantine on the polished teak as she crossed the dance floor. Finding Henry wasn't much of a reprieve from that sense of isolation; he was usually entrenched in a clump of males all holding beer glasses and he didn't seem to notice her either.

She found shopping in Batu Road equally unnerving; all along those pavements she was conscious of eyes flicking over her with brief, concentrated interest — brown eyes in

Chinese faces, or Tamil. Only the eyes of the Malays were incurious.

The garden was much more than the outer ramparts of her fortress; it was her kingdom, full of her shrub subjects whose lives she protected against a harsh sun. For one clump of tri-colour rhododendrons, their pale, untropical pastels an unbelievable contrast in this lush setting, she had even devised an artificial peat as an added nurture to their shade. Even in the old days before the Occupation, she had been the only one who ever looked at them. To guests who had come to the house as part of "duty entertaining," those flowers would only have seemed an idiotic eccentricity. Henry had believed in leaving gardens to the Tamil garden boys. So she had learned to keep private her triumphs over the red clay soil and predator insects, coming even to prefer things this way, each small success a mark to her credit in that personal score book that always seemed to be lying open in her mind, and with too many debit entries in the broad column reserved for them.

The rhoddies were still there, in fat bud now, preparing to bloom again in their artificially achieved season. They still had her attention. A couple of weeks ago, when the General had once again been generous with the gin at dinner, she had walked alone afterwards over bristle-stiff jungle grass to her Himalayan bushes and in the moonlight had discussed with them the matter of loyalty. It had been a monologue but hadn't really felt like one; she had had a distinct sense of her bushes' attention and their listening. Drunk she must have been, really quite drunk, but the recollection of a conversation remained, and its theme, too.

Loyalty, that's what they'd been discussing. It was a matter that still troubled her sometimes, more disturbing than any thoughts she had about what she had done to Henry. There was no need to worry about him. He would certainly have got to India, since he had left early enough to make sure of this; once there, he had no doubt found some key post, probably in New Delhi, his usefulness unchallengeable. People would think him well rid of an alcoholic wife. He wouldn't be weighed down by any worries about what had happened to her. It had been her choice. The wife who had occupied the bed next to his for nearly twenty years had picked up two packed suitcases in a Singapore hotel bedroom and had carried these down to the car herself, past a startled doorman who had never seen a European woman carrying anything heavy. She had driven away, heading north, in the car Henry had been prepared to abandon because he couldn't get his price for it. She hadn't even left a note for the man who had paid for her board and lodging for so long. She had thought about writing one, but couldn't find a thing to say. And in not saying anything, she left intact his own assessment of himself as a patient and considerate husband.

The night of her talk to the moonlit bushes, and under the influence of gin, she had suddenly begun to laugh. The really big choice in her life had been between Henry and her bushes, and she had chosen her bushes. Her laughter hadn't been in the least hysterical, but it had been quite loud, and the General had heard, coming across the grass to her, probably worried that his staff officers, billeted 'round about, would think the English woman had gone mad. The General had shouted: *"Nani? Nani?"* and then taken her arm above the elbow, steering her back to the house, up steps past the wisteria she was trying to grow in half-shade from a pot on the lower verandah.

In spite of the gin, she remembered the obeisance drill to the Lord of the House when they had reached the foot of the stairs. She had bowed and used one of the two Japanese phrases that seemed to be all she was expected to learn, managing the right one that time despite many earlier errors that had seen her wishing him an honourable good night when she was meant to be welcoming him home. More than once, as the General got out of his car under the porte cochere, she had used the wrong phrase and seen in his eyes that he was considering hitting her, but he never did. In that he might almost have been Henry.

Since the Occupation, no one had hit her, not even the soldiers who first came to the house. They had arrived in an open truck, a good dozen of them pouring through the rooms, their boots clattering on the floors. Three had found her out on the verandah of the bedroom she used to share with Henry. She had got to her feet in front of the wicker chair in which she had sat for hours listening to the sounds from the city and her heart's thumped comments on them. Getting up like that had been, in a sense, her first obeisance, and the three soldiers who had come out on a verandah they had expected to find deserted had dropped the butts of their rifles on the boards and had stood to stare.

Instinct must have prompted Louise's first bow, or it might have been something she had heard about what the conquerors expected. It wasn't much of a bow, not really more than a bending of the neck, nothing like the Japanese woman's deep bow in which she was to receive instruction later. But it had been a gesture in the right direction, a signal that she was accepting the new situation, not resisting it. The leader of the soldiers seemed to understand this. He came towards her and, with shouts, started her on a training course of what was expected from the vanquished. When she proved an awkward pupil he still didn't hit her.

She could remember a sense of unease coming from those soldiers. It was as though, only minutes after they had been bellowing in triumph through empty rooms, smashing things as they passed, the three had been winded to find her standing there where they had expected to see no one. Trained in violence though they might be, Louise had been sure even then that no thought of rape had been at the back of those narrow, staring eyes. They were boys still, in spite of their experience of war, and must have seen her as a grandmother, with wrinkles set on her face.

She knew now that this was how the General had seen her, with no thought of rape in his mind either, nor even of a bedding with consent after whatever rituals the Japanese male used to preface these occasions. From that first night after his takeover of the house, he had allowed her the continuing privacy of her room, never entering it. In a way this bolstered an illusion the gin helped her almost to believe in: the feeling that the norm of her life had never really been interrupted. Most of her dreams seemed to be set in the lost past, and she would wake from one of them to lie waiting for Henry's snoring to start up. When it didn't, she would turn her head with a throb of alarm towards that other bed, identifying time now by a bare mattress.

The charade of seemingly unbroken patterns was an essential part of the General's field study of Western customs, especially their domestic aspects. Except for the small, necessary concessions to Japanese civility and respect for the male — the bowing and the polite phrases — she was left unmolested in her performance as hostess in her own home. Even the new servants were instructed to support her in the role. They did this well enough when the General was about, only lapsing into near insolence when his car had driven off. But they were never quite openly rude, due to a deep respect for what could happen to them if the woman in his house was goaded into putting in a bad report to the General. She had power of a kind, enough to see that she wasn't interrupted in her plans for the day, though not enough really to give any orders. She had no say in the food that came from the kitchen and the arrangement of the elaborately set dinner tables on which glittered crystal that had never belonged to her or to Henry but was instead the result of the houseboy's experience under another roof. Louise had never found out where the servants had worked under the British, but she suspected that if it hadn't actually been Government House it had probably been one of the establishments just down the hill from it.

Her plans for the day were nearly always the same. After bowing away the General's be-flagged staff car in the morning, she turned back into the house to a first task of doing the flowers. The servants, their pretence at cleaning suddenly over, went back to the kitchen and their own quarters in a separate building. She came in from the garden to empty rooms, taking a long time to arrange the sprays in their vases. Unlike Henry, who had never noticed these displays, the General would sometimes stop in front of one of them, his hands clasped behind his back, his head pushed forward on a short neck as though he was studying what he saw. His face always stayed completely expressionless. She never knew whether or not an arrangement pleased him. He could well be thinking that a Japanese woman would put the same material to a much simpler and more effective use.

Once, an urge to provoke some comment from him had Louise on the very brink of asking whether he liked the flowers but, as if he had seen this and wanted to stave off the query, he had swung away and started to give what he called an instruction. That time it had been that she was not to wear sleeveless dresses. If she had many of these, he told her, she was to cut some of them up to make sleeves for the others. He always ended these instructions with two words: "You understand?" She always nodded and bowed as she had been taught to do.

After arranging the flowers, Louise gardened through rising heat, working in borders with her trowel and breaking up clay lumps with a rather silly looking small-bladed lady's spade that Henry had given her as a Christmas joke but had turned out to be highly useful. At noon, soaking with perspiration, she would come in for a shower and afterwards eat a salad the houseboy left for her in the dining room along with a jug of fresh lime juice. All the alcohol in the house was kept locked up, and the General had the key. Henry had tried this discipline, too, but it had always lapsed. The General's laws continued to be enforced.

She didn't mind, really, having nothing but soft drinks in the daytime; only towards sunset did the need for gin become really acute. She wasn't able to sit still for any time. She walked around through shadowed rooms at dusk, not putting on lights, not wanting to see herself in mirrors. One thought overtook her mind: a hope that the General wouldn't be late and that, as she straightened from her bow towards the arriving car, she would see him smiling. If he smiled it could mean that he was in the mood for what he called "English custom sundowner, *Ne?*" and would unlock the cupboard to give her a gin, perhaps even two.

There were other days when there was no smile. He would get out of the car with only a grunt for her and go straight to the room Henry had called the library, which the General used as an office. It still held the books that were never read, then or now, rows of them behind glass, their bindings bursting under pressure from green mould.

The General's bad days meant bad evenings for Louise. She went upstairs to wait for the dinner gong, keeping on the move — around her bedroom, out onto the verandah, in again. Sometimes she had to run to the bathroom to be sick, afterwards coming downstairs pale and with shaking hands. He never seemed to notice her state when he joined her. Quite often on bad nights he didn't come into the dining room at all but instead had some food sent into his office. When this happened she went upstairs without eating to lie sweating on her bed as the night deepened, wanting to cry out but, even in that twisting of mind and body, afraid to.

There was no way she could get gin without the General's knowing; she had no money. Now and then he sent her to the shops in his staff car, but always for some specific purchase. He seemed to have checked on prices beforehand, or had one of his underlings do it, so that at breakfast he gave her the exact sum she would need in the war script the shopkeepers were still accepting with obvious reluctance. She bought his shirts that way: white ones he wore with the collars opened back over the lapels of his uniform tunic. Once her mission had been to choose a length of Siamese silk for someone back in Japan, almost certainly his wife, though all he had said was, "Not young. Not bright colour. You understand?"

She wasn't given the money for that operation, merely chose the material to be set aside for payment later. Never once had the General suggested that she buy something for herself, though on one of the good days he brought her a present, a dwarf pine in a blue pot, insisting that her centrepiece in the dining room be demoted to the sideboard to give the place of honour to the little tree. "You rike?" he asked, "You rike?" She hadn't liked it at all; it looked deliberately stunted and gnarled, as though by torture, its miniature limbs a mass of rheumatic lumps, but she had smiled and nodded, and he had taken the key to the locked cupboard from his pocket.

There was a third kind of evening with the General, when

she was expected to play a more elaborate role. These usually happened without warning, the car swirling up the drive, its windows lowered, voices and laughter coming from it. The General would get out first, becoming slightly involved with his long sword in the process and, while he stood with a hint of a sway to acknowledge Louise's evening greeting, she was peered at from inside the car by faces on which recent laughter had been swamped by curiosity. The General's cheeks would be flushed from drink taken down in the officer's brothel housed in what had been the European Club, but he would wait politely for the end of her usual performance before shouting: "Engurish party!"

This was the signal for her to go up to change her dress. The General preferred her in something long, and, from camphor boxes, Louise had unearthed a selection of tea gowns dating from the early thirties when hemlines had suddenly dropped. Always thin, and much thinner now, the dresses hung on her like lengths of curtain material thrown over a rack, but the General seemed pleased enough with her clothes, for they were "English style," as she guessed he was informing his young officers.

He explained to her the reason for these dinners. They were a necessary part of training his men for their future roles as administrators of conquered territory. After the surrender of Australia and the raising of the Imperial flag over Canberra, the General was expecting to be made the military governor of one of the provinces, probably what was now called New South Wales but would soon be given its proper Japanese name. To rule successfully, the rulers must understand the customs and habits of the ruled, even on occasion adopting some of these customs in the spirit of Bushido, the warrior's way, the code whereby the conquering strong show great understanding towards the defeated weak.

"You understand?"

Louise had bowed, but only slightly. For the seated female this was all that was necessary to acknowledge an instruction. Much more was expected of the General's young officers. When he told them something, they had to stand to attention indicating comprehension by loudly repeating, *"hais!"* They bowed a great deal, too, but in a sharp military manner, and some, imitating their new German allies, clicked heels as they bent their backs. They couldn't be called very relaxed evenings, at least not in the early stages.

The English parties were held nearly every week, the General presiding with flushed cheeks and a slight unsteadiness on his feet when he moved about but, in spite of this, expecting from Louise a performance with all the disciplined perfection of lifeboat drill on a crack liner. She was to bow to each of the officers in turn as they came out of the staff car, some returning the courtesy, others not, after which she had to slip away to her room to dress, being particularly careful about the way she did her hair.

She had no proof of this but was certain that her hair was often the subject of their talk and sometimes of their jokes. One young officer, his nervousness dissipated by drink, had reached out across the table to touch her hair but had been stopped by a bellow from the General. The young man was then made to leave his place and walk down to where his commanding officer had risen from Henry's carved teak armchair and was waiting. There was first verbal instruction, followed by physical correction: The General hit the young man with a closed fist on one jaw, then on the other. After that the party continued, though with a slightly subdued tone, which lasted while Louise was in the room.

She was only expected to stay for the meal itself as instructress in Western table manners. There seemed always to be more courses than food, the servants setting down nearly empty plates and then taking them away again. Louise selected the cutlery for each round, the eyes of the officers on her fingers as she did it. The long, drawn-out performance finally came to an end with fruit knives and finger bowls on lace doilies, the General firmly suppressing all terminal belches as against English custom.

On party nights it wasn't easy to go on pretending that a norm continued in this house. When she looked down from the verandah beyond her bedroom: The garden still seemed unchanged; like symbols of permanence, the huge trees remained motionless in the hot stillness; and under a rising moon there was still the same shrinking back of shadows from the grass to leave it whitened. But, pushing out through open windows, the noise from the rooms beneath her was utterly alien: shouting sometimes, scraps of songs, then the thumping of boots, laughter, all this permitted relaxation once the lessons were over and the red-headed woman had left their company. The General had once told her that in Japan only devils had red hair. He told it as a joke, which meant that you were expected to laugh. Louise had laughed.

She always heard the officers going home. The General didn't keep his Tamil driver on duty for them, so they walked down the steep slope of the curving drive after many loud wishes that the great one would have a restful sleep, their voices respectful for a distance from the house, then — the drink taking over again — bellowed laughter and shouted songs. Lying in the dark and listening to that, Louise's awareness of their contempt seemed to stab her in a way it never did when she was facing them downstairs. She felt like weeping sometimes on those nights, but never actually did; instead she just stared up at a ceiling that became, with the loss of the moon, black enough to be a sky from which all the stars had been taken.

TWO

She hadn't wanted the boy in this house, certain that his coming to live here would mean an end to the privacy of hours alone in empty rooms and out in her garden. Even before she saw him for the first time, Louise had been certain that the boy's presence would undermine the little patches of authority she had managed to build up. And that had happened. The whole precarious balance between a fiction she had tucked around her living and the reality had been upset. Noise was the biggest threat, some of it without any understandable reason, sudden eruptions of it not just from his room but from anywhere in the house. He even penetrated to the kitchens, forbidden to her, and was apparently unchalleneged even out there. He didn't seem to be looking for company; he certainly showed no signs of wanting hers, though he watched her. She would straighten from digging and turn to find him on one of the verandahs staring at her. Once it had been from the upstairs verandah to which there was no access except through her bedroom.

The General had got a bicycle for him and the boy spent a lot of time on it, circling and circling on the gravel of the drive in front of the house, the crunching of tyres reaching a crescendo at a time when rising heat was damping down sounds from the city. Then he would tire of that game and go sweeping down the drive with the bike's bell clanging, the shrill hysteria of its ringing telegraphing her continuous reports of where he was in the limited area of hill suburb in which he was allowed to ride the machine.

Her solitary lunches were a thing of the past. She still had

her salad and jug of lime juice but the General, having decided that the boy needed building up, ordered special rations from some army catering service established in the city.
These meals consisted of Japanese food packed in boxes and
ready for eating: cold rice in one and a mixture of cold
vegetables and fish in another. Louise would sometimes ask
what he was eating, getting a reply condensed to a minimum
of words; but he always seemed well informed about what
was in those boxes, staring at one of the exotics held suspended between chopsticks before identifying it as octopus
or squid. Once he was surprisingly expansive, as though
with a piece of knowledge that couldn't be kept to himself.
It concerned a pickle, which he named, and some form of
radish root, which he claimed the Japanese couldn't live, or
fight, for long without. They imported it to Malaya in barrels, stinking barrels he said.

She hadn't known how to exploit that sudden opening,
wasn't even certain that she wanted to. She had no experience of children, had always avoided them — especially the
European ones, who seemed so aggressive and confident even
at an early age, even the youngest bullying their amahs.
European children were to be found in mass only at the
Golf Club, where they used the swimming pool. Louise had
rarely been there, Henry having decided that if she wasn't
going to use the place properly there was no point in keeping up her subscription. Children had never had a place in
their occasional entertaining, either; they'd always been left
at home. She wouldn't have known what to do with them if
they had come, no more than she knew what to do with
this boy who stared at her, though only from a distance.
When they were near each other their eyes seemed to go off
on elaborate private journeys that had no point of contact.

She rarely used his name, though the General did frequently, making of the simple John something that sounded
like a heavy bell, especially when he repeated it, as he did
often: "Jon, Jon." She had noticed something about the
boy's reaction to that name, something that wasn't just due
to the half-Japanese sound the General made of it, but applied to her use of the name as well: a fractional hesitation

before he acknowledged it, as though it took him that time
to fix himself in this identity. She became convinced that
John wasn't his real name. From this came the feeling that
the boy had some purpose behind his stay in this house that
was beyond and outside the General's purpose in having him
here.

What John thought of her she tried to keep from considering, but it was impossible not to be aware of him most of
the time. He even broke into her dreams. There had been a
certain innocence about her dreams before the boy came, as
though in sleep she had been allowed a straightforward
escape into an idealized yesterday, her garden and sometimes
her rooms blissfully without reminders of either the General
or Henry. Only John seemed able to move into what had
been a carefully margined privacy, and she woke to feel almost certain that in his room along the corridor the boy was
awake, on his bed in the dark, staring at nothing while he
willed an invasion of her mind. She had heard that lovers,
when separated, could sometimes waken to an almost physical consciousness of the loved's presence, but it had never
happened to her. And she found this parody of an alleged
experience half-frightening, the recollection of it never totally dispelled by daylight.

*

Louise was waiting for John to come up to his room, and
with a feeling she couldn't quite define. It was more than
just wanting to know why the General, at the end of another
dinner for his officers, had dismissed her but told the boy
to stay. She had come up the stairs slowly, remembering another night when she had been dismissed, but then a servant
had left the dining room door half-open and she had risked
watching from a darkened hall.

What she had seen was some kind of dance, four men
holding hands as though part of a psychic circle that went
completely around the long teak table — the invisible, perhaps dead, comrades. The steps were simple, not much more
than a heavy-booted shuffling, and every now and then the
linked hands were lifted high. They sang their own music,

a tune for drunken voices. One of the men produced a wavering falsetto to which the other voices became a chorus, the thin screeching perhaps an imitation of geisha. All the faces were solemn. She couldn't see the General, and thought he must be continuing to sit in Henry's carved chair as he watched his men at their glum ritual. She hadn't wanted to watch for long.

Tonight there didn't seem to be any dancing down in the dining room; the proceedings were almost noiseless. From the upper hall Louise had heard a kind of muttering, but that was all, and now, out on the verandah, there were no sounds coming from inside the house. The noises reaching her were from the city, human cries probably from street vendors but touched with fear by distance. A railway engine hooted about its intention to pull a train out of the mock Moorish station. Two cats shrieked and a dog complained about this — something of a surprise, for it had seemed to Louise that all the dogs had disappeared from the streets. With the price of meat what it was, they had probably been eaten.

The clank of a chain followed by a rush of water came to her via ventilation transoms. The plumbing fixtures in the house were antiques, noisy as if out of pride. She turned her head to look towards the window of the boy's room in the back wing. It stayed dark, but that could be because he had pulled the blackout curtain as a defense against mosquitoes. The General had ordered all these curtains taken down in the rooms he used, saying that with the Japanese about to invade India there was no danger of bombers from any quarter ever reaching Kuala Lumpur. He explained that the partial dimout of street lighting was not from any fear of attack, merely "war-belt-tighten-to-sure-victory."

Voices from under the porte cochere meant that the party was over and the officers on their way home. They didn't talk loudly going down the drive and there was no singing. They were also leaving much earlier than usual, which suggested some kind of conference after dinner, but there seemed no point in having John stay for this, listening to talk in Japanese that he couldn't possibly understand.

Louise crossed her bedroom and went out again into the upper hall to listen. She heard the General coming back from seeing his guests away. He went into the library and shut the door. There was the sound of the houseboy moving about in the dining room; then he shut that door, too.

Down the corridor to the back wing a dim light came from the transom above John's door. Louise went down to stand and listen under it. She heard nothing. She had never been in that room since the boy took it over. Her hand went out to the knob, slowly.

John was lying naked on the bed, on his back, one arm up over his face as if to shield his eyes from the glare of a light that had been lowered to only a few feet above the pillow. Louise had herself made that war emergency shade for the bulb from black paper, forming a cylinder that cast a spotlight on the upper part of his body. He had drawn up one leg and the groin beneath it was shadowed. The thrown-back arm showed his rib cage, the definition of bones pushing through a thin flesh covering.

The General had been right; the boy was almost emaciated. She hadn't noticed, only conscious of a repressed energy in him that seemed tireless and almost explosive. Now she remembered that he hadn't seemed to eat much of the rice from those special meals. From just inside the door she saw the way he had come to throw himself on that bed, his undressing a marked trail of dropped shirt and shorts and kicked-away sandals. His underpants were a white patch beneath the curtain he had pulled before switching on the light.

Louise was thinking about leaving the room when he said: "What do you want?"

He hadn't moved the arm that was shielding his eyes. She found it hard to make herself say anything. Before she did she closed the door. When she turned to face him he had pushed himself up against the pillow and tugged a sheet across the lower half of his body. His face was out of the glare of light. He seemed to be gazing at his own feet, waiting for her explantion.

"I wondered why they kept you? After dinner?"

He didn't turn his head towards her. "To pray," he said.
"What?" She couldn't believe that she had heard him
right.
"To the Emperor," John said. "In Tokyo. They were all
doing it. They made me."
Louise came halfway towards the bed. His face was still
protected from the hard light by the shade she had put over
the bulb.
"*Made* you?"
"Sort of." His voice was matter of fact. "If I want to go to
Australia."
"John . . . I don't understand?"
"The General's taking me to Australia. He's taking you,
too. Only you don't have to pray to the Emperor. Women
don't."
He turned his head, as though he wanted to see her face
in the shadowed room. She had the feeling he might reach
up to lift the light, beaming it at her.
"The General says you'll help him teach Australian
women. He said that before we prayed to Tokyo. You face
the sideboard."
"You do *what?*"
"You face the sideboard. Tokyo's that way. And the Emperor in his palace. He's their god."
"John, he's *not* a god."
"Sure he is. They pray to him. And it works, doesn't it?"
"What do you mean?"
"Well, look what they got. They'll get India next. Then
Australia. Then there'll be a peace for a while until they
start another war. Against Hitler. When they beat Hitler
there'll be another peace for a bit. Then they'll fight Amer-
ica again. That'll be the last big fight before Japan wins
forever."
There was an alarm clock on the table by the bed. Its
ticking was loud.
"The General told you all this?"
"Sure."
"You're not to believe it!"
"Why not? Don't you? You came back here. You didn't
have to."

"I . . . came back to my *house*."

John had no comment. The silence in the bedroom became an indictment. Louise stood with her hands by her side, unmoving, as though she had just heard a sentence passed on her that was quite unbelievable in its harshness. She might have been waiting for an escort to lead her away, taking her firmly by the arm. Then words came in a rush, as though sweeping past frozen thought, from some deeper level of her mind.

"John! You're not to believe what you heard down there tonight! Any of it! And what you did doesn't matter!"

"I didn't do anything. I just prayed like they showed me."

"Listen to me! What happened down there doesn't matter!"

"Okay," John said.

*

The driver of the General's care was a civilian, a Tamil who had no official uniform but who had done his best to provide himself with an imitation: khaki shirt and trousers, plus a white arm band on which Japanese characters in red presumably described his important function. John had tried to sit up front, but this had been firmly resisted by the driver. Louise understood why, even if the boy didn't. It was one thing to be friendly with a survivor of the old regime when they were both up at the house, quite another to be seen on familiar terms with him as they drove through the streets of the city.

The car was very grand and was kept highly polished, a Chrysler Imperial with twin wire wheels fitted beside the engine bonnet. Inside was a glass partition between front and back seat, which was always raised for the General, who liked to give his orders through the speaking tube. In the rear compartment the back and side windows had tasseled blinds that could be drawn to ensure almost complete privacy and John, still surly at being banished to the back, had half-drawn the one on his side and was slumped on the seat peering out from under it.

At lunch he had been almost unnervingly talkative, and about nothing much, which was most unlike him; his present habit of hugging himself in silence had become more natural to him. Louise was completely unprepared for another burst of talk.

"I don't see why we can't go out of Kuala Lumpur. In this car, I mean. I'm sick of being cooped up. Why can't we go places with the General? On one of his trips?"

"Those are official inspections," Louise said.

"The driver says the General doesn't inspect much. Just likes riding in this car. He never had a car like this when he was in China for the war there. This car belonged to a Chinese towkay. Did you know that?"

"No."

"Syce told me." John used the Malay word for chauffeur, not the man's name. "There used to be whisky and things in that cupboard down there. But the General doesn't keep anything in the car. That towkay was really rich. He had a lot of tin mines. Syce doesn't know whether he got away or not. But probably he did because he had junks as well as everything else. Maybe he got to India on one of them." There was a pause, then the boy added: "That's where your husband got to, isn't it?"

Louise stared at the road ahead. Two layers of glass seemed adequate protection against anything out there, but she was completely exposed to John.

"I don't know," she said.

"He probably did. But he may have to go somewhere else again. The Japs are already in India."

Louise made a bid to switch him off the theme of Henry. "You're not to say Japs. It makes the General angry."

"Sure. I forget. Did you know that the Japanese had got to India?"

"I don't hear much news."

"Doesn't the General tell you things about the war?"

"Not often."

"Well, there's an English news on the radio from Singapore. You could listen to that."

"I could, but I don't."

"Is that because you don't believe it's the truth? Is that why you don't listen?"

"I don't listen because I don't want to! Whatever's happening has nothing to do with me. I can't help it."

That seemed to silence him. He turned his head to peer out from under the half-lowered blind. Louise looked out from the window at her side. The Chrysler was curving its way down the steep roads of the suburbs, past houses half-hidden in their gardens and almost overhung by the surviving jungle trees. She wondered who lived in those houses now. The Japanese Army had only taken over a few for their officers; some might have been looted and just left, others occupied by invaders from the town. You couldn't tell from the road, though most of the gardens were still being tended in a casual way. There was no hint of the grooming she remembered, with the Tamil gardeners using powered mowers every day. You never heard the whirr of those motors anymore; they had been almost like time checks, starting up before the big heat of the day, or announcing that it was over.

The car overtook a solitary pedal trishaw with no fare in the double seat up front. The man in the saddle was holding his vehicle by the brakes on a steep down slope, going much more slowly than he needed to, as though in no hurry to get back into the city. He was a Malay, wearing a hard round hat with a tassel hanging from it. He didn't look at the Chrysler as it passed him. Louise glanced back to see if the man was still staring down at the road, and he was. The Malays were greatly skilled in the art of not noticing what did not concern them. She had been trying to copy them in this, but without much success.

John raised his blind. "Are you going to speak about it to the General?" he asked.

"What?"

"I told you. His taking us on one of his trips. Syce says he goes to Kuantan quite a lot. I'd like to go there. You have to go through the mountains. If you said you wanted to go, the General would take us."

"John, I don't want to go anywhere!"

"Are you scared?"

"Why should I be?"

"I mean, of the Reds. There's lots of them in the mountains. They blow up things on the roads. Trucks and that.

Syce is scared to go that way. But I'd like to. If we went to Kuantan you could teach the General all kinds of things on the way. Like you do in the house."

"I'm not going to talk about this!"

"Okay."

He started batting at the knob on the pull cord of the blind, back and forth. The movement of the car seemed to increase his interest in the game. But it only lasted for a couple of minutes.

"Syce says that all these handles and things back here are real silver," he told her. "He has to polish them. But he doesn't mind. He loves this car. I guess it's wonderful after that rattletrap he had in Morib for a taxi. It was a Dodge tourer. The open kind. I guess maybe about a hundred years old."

When Louise indicated no interest in silver handles he showed no signs of being discouraged. The car moved out of the area shaded by big trees into the hard sunlight on the wide road leading past the station and its adjoining hotel. She stared at the hotel's minarets, remembering a joke heard long ago at the club about the minarets' having been put there as a convenience to guests, so they could climb up to get nearer to Allah to make their complaints about the food and service. It was one of those jokes at which everyone else had laughed, but she hadn't been able to. She could never see the sense in most jokes. The people who kept telling them always seemed to have red faces.

The government buildings were decorated by domes instead of minarets, and under these were long, pillared galleries to keep the rooms behind them cool. Louise had always thought that the tall palms in front of these important offices had a haughty look, like camels. On John's side the club, with its wide grassy padang, looked as it always had except for a bright patch on the roof where a Japanese bomb had pierced through into the ballroom. It was one of the few bombs dropped on Kuala Lampur and it hadn't killed anyone.

When she saw the main shopping street, Louise was glad she had decided to take this expedition right after lunch, for the heat had almost cleared the pavements. It meant that she would be able to get out of the car and into the shop before a crowd gathered. She had been more than a little frightened by the crowds that had formed quite quickly to watch her get in or out of the General's car. They hadn't been noisy, not much talk, but just watched the red-haired woman about whom they had heard the stories. She could only remember Chinese faces watching.

*

The department store was almost empty, some of the counters unattended as though the girls hadn't felt the need to hurry back from lunch to deal with non-existent customers. There was just one man in the tailoring department, an Indian, his plump face made half-mysterious by dark glasses. Louise wondered how in that gloom he could manage to see the bolts of cloth, but perhaps it wasn't necessary that he should; there were so few of them that he had his stock memorized. The only length of material that seemed at all possible for the long trousered suit the General wanted made for John was blue and slightly shiny, like stuff for a raincoat. Her instructions were to order something to be worn on semi-formal occasions, their exact nature unspecified. The only alternative to the blue was khaki, with its suggestion of a uniform, which she knew wouldn't be right. John thought the blue was fine and submitted himself to be measured, but styles didn't interest him and he refused to look at a thumb-worn fashion book, wandering off instead and leaving Louise to do the choosing.

She had a long wait for some invisible cashier to approve an official Japanese Army promise to pay, but finally the Indian came back to say that the suit would be ready in ten days. Louise walked down the store expecting to pick up John by a counter. He was nowhere in sight. From behind glass doors, she saw a small crowd around the car. Someone moved on and she had a glimpse of the boy sitting on the back seat, his arms folded across his chest.

Two Chinese women with shopping baskets joined the watchers, and a youth pushed his bicycle up on the pavement to stand leaning on it behind them. Louise knew how quickly a small crowd could become a big one, even in this heat. She left the store and was halfway across a wide pavement when she noticed that the syce wasn't in his seat behind the wheel. John hadn't seen her coming. He might have locked the car door from the inside. Twice before, bigger crowds had made a passage for her, but there were no signs of this one's doing it; they were all watching the boy.

She stopped and said loudly, "Excuse me."

Faces turned to her. One of them seemed to swell out from the others. She saw pockmarked skin, a black bristle of hair. When the man spat, his spittle hit her cheek like a bird's dropping.

She didn't call out. Her handbag fell to the pavement. She was looking down when someone kicked it. It burst open, contents scattered, an accumulation she knew to be rubbish.

The car door opened. A man yelled as it struck him. She didn't really see John, even when he had her by the arm, pushing her. She fell against the back seat, and had to twist her body around.

The syce was back behind his glass screen, staring straight ahead. He had started the engine but the rear door was still open, John out on the pavement picking up everything that had fallen out of her bag. He was taking his time. She saw him pick up the stub of a pencil.

There didn't seem to be anything of hers left on the pavement when John straightened with her bag in his hand. He clipped it shut, holding out the bag to her as he got into the car. He pulled the door shut and humped his body past her legs to the corner he had been using. The syce took the Chrysler away from the pavement gently, as though he was carrying invalids. There was shouting from behind them.

"Your hanky's in your bag," John said.

She looked at him, not understanding. "Your cheek," he said.

He sounded impatient. She opened the bag and groped for the handkerchief. She rubbed her cheek with it, then folded the linen over and rubbed again.

"It doesn't matter," John told her.

She began to cry.

PART
FOUR

Hamish

ONE

Allowing that half my feelings about the Major are rooted in Scots working-class prejudice against English upper-class privilege, that still leaves the other half completely rational. And there is more than just intuition telling me that this snoring man isn't going to be able to do the job for which he has been sent into Malaya. His basic approach to our mission, if you can call four men with a radio and a hand-cranked dynamo a mission, is that all we have to do on reaching the guerillas is plant the Union Jack on a pole in the middle of their camp and then just wait for the Malayan Communist Party rough boys to be converted back to British imperialism. I think he is really looking forward to this as an emotional experience. God knows that before, during, and after our submarine voyage, I've tried hard enough to point out to him that the one thing the M.C.P. guerillas want less than a Jap occupation of their country is a British re-occupation of it. The Major didn't even half-listen to me. But then he never does, on principle.

The military brass in Ceylon didn't listen to me either. It was as if they considered me touched in the head as the result of that long hike across Sumatra with the Japs at my heels, not to mention the Indian Ocean junk voyage, or it could simply be that I was born in Glasgow, and not in one of the better suburbs. At any rate the information I had brought out of Japanese Malaya was suspect from the moment I handed in the written report that was such hell to get down on paper. They particularly disliked what I had to say about the vast difference between the Malayan jungle and the kind in Ceylon they were using to train the go-back units.

Then the age factor came into it. Anyone over forty is a military antique unless he has reached the rank of Brigadier or above. I'm pretty sure they called me Dad behind my back. My commission as a Lieutenant is really a survival award. The Major would have much preferred a Sergeant as his guide, or preferably a Corporal. Lieutenants, especially middle-aged ones, sometimes have a tendency to talk back, and it's irritating to have to pull seniority to shut them up.

If the Major ever marries, this snoring is going to be an awful shock to his bride, though maybe the girl he would choose would come from the kind of guaranteed background that includes a Mum who has told her daughter that snoring is another of those unpleasant things you have to take from a husband. Lali used to kick me. Come to think of it she was the only one of my girls who ever did. But then she was the only one who smoked cheroots in bed. I wonder if I'd ever have got rid of Lali if the war hadn't happened? The whole thing was getting a bit worn, including the three tricks she used in strict order of priority to get me worked up. Predictable, that's what Lali was. Nothing like as predictable as a wife, though.

I remember saying something of the kind to Ruth once during one of those open and frank exchanges between us that were part of the intellectual life in Sungei Dema. I didn't know at the time that Big John was just back from one of his excursions to re-discover his sexual identity in a kampong outside of Kuantan. I wasn't asked up to Estate House for a meal for two months, and when the ban was finally lifted I went into that huge living room to find John still at the mine with Roy. Unsupported, I had to face the eyes of two women who had just had my personality stretched out on the dissecting table. I don't know much about New England Puritans, but there must have been a strong line of them among Ruth's ancestors, along with that other line from the slave-ship captain. Yet in our own way the boss's wife and I love each other. Not a hint of sex in that, not even six layers down. She thought she had the local Caliban trained by kindness. Maybe she did. It could be she believed that on account of my vulnerability to boils no white woman could ever want me. Probably right there, too. Who the hell, including the non-whites, has ever really wanted me? It's a lonely life I've led with my orchids.

The Major seems to be toning down the volume. It must be moonlight on his face. His subconscious is telling him he's being kissed by the pale English sun. No . . . hope deferred. The tremolo was only a lead-in passage to all stops out. How much sleep have I lost to this man since war thrust us together? In that tiny mess cabin in the sub, I lay on the deck beneath the Major's hammock thinking that this couldn't go on. But it has. Maybe I should be taking more advantage of the chance the racket offers for a review of my past life, searching for threads of a pattern through my days. I'm damned if I can find any. I'm here. I have put up with the fact to the best of my ability, avoiding the more acute distresses whenever possible. And on the whole, except for one fantasy, keeping myself safe from emotional excess.

Even a Scots mining engineer who gets boils can be allowed one fantasy. I wonder what that Dago poet Roy would think if he knew that I kept seeing Angus as my son? Correction, Roy only *looks* like a Dago poet. If living had administered even a couple of hard kicks on that olive-tinted arse it might have helped him evolve a positive identity. When Roy was still a youth coming down to borrow my books, sometimes with our sitting out on the verandah at night getting bitten by mosquitoes — our talk solemn, like a couple of Free Presbyterians discussing predestination — there was visible in Roy a non-Gourlay personality in embryo. He certainly has brains when all a Gourlay really needs is instinct.

Angus will be at school in Australia. He's probably chucked collecting stamps, a kid's game.

*

The Major had cultivated a loathing for any form of inaction, totally rejecting the commonly held view that war means long periods of waiting punctuated — fortunately — by much shorter ones of extreme nastiness. In his war you kept moving unless you were on leave, and even then it was best to do things that kept you from getting slack, like a bit of winter climbing on an iced rock face.

"Hamish?"

He always uses my first name as though he was holding it with tongs, Hamish thought. "Yes, Major?" And I always call him Major, toadying to his unexpressed wish.

"This chap of yours. I'm beginning to wonder if he's coming back?"

He wasn't *beginning* to wonder at all; he'd been doing it ever since they had climbed out from under the Chinese cabbages on the vegetable lorry that had brought them here.

"What I mean is, we could be in a trap."

"Yes," Hamish said.

"Well, dammit! I don't sit in traps! Waiting!"

"You give the orders, Major. Where do we move to?"

"There's no need to take that line! You know perfectly well you're the guide."

It would be hard to decide which was worse, the Major asleep or the Major awake.

"I know I'm the guide," Hamish said meekly. "But I thought I'd explained my problem. I don't know where I'm guiding you to."

The Major inhaled deeply. "I can't accept that. We left Ceylon with certain specific information about the organization of the guerillas. We know that they are formed into area groups with a central command, probably somewhere in Johore. We're not trying to locate central command, which I admit might be damn difficult since it's probably mobile. What we're looking for is a local command area H.Q. We are in the area we want. And the local commander is an old friend of yours."

After that barrage the Major stared.

"Old acquaintance," Hamish said. "We met perhaps a dozen times. We once played golf. He was good, I wasn't. He didn't want a repeat."

"Half a dozen meetings should have given you a reasonable insight into the man's thinking?"

"Not with me. I'm slow on insight. It comes from having spent so much time down a mine."

"Oh, very funny! Unfortunately this is no time for comedy."

Any time is the time for any comedy you can scrape off living, Hamish thought. And especially on an expedition like this one.

From the next room came the mumble of non-commissioned voices — the two other members of the party — amplified by the emptiness of the place in which they sat. Neither was in the habit of looking with wide-eyed admiration at their leader. This could be a real problem with behind-the-enemy-lines penetration groups, the men who volunteer for them tending to be stubborn individualists who haven't taken too well to standard military disciplines.

"What about this resort place you were telling me of?" the Major asked. "The one up the steep road and easily defensible? Couldn't our man be using that? Mountain fastness? Ideal base and all that?"

The picture of Cheng Lee Kwa, the highly civilized lawyer, toasting his feet in front of the open log fire of the Frazer's Hill resthouse, with a bottle of claret from its cellars at his elbow, was attractive but not really to be entertained.

Hamish said, "At Selangor, Wa Ting told me that the hill station is being used as a Jap convalescent centre. But even if it weren't, it's too tricky to get up to and down from for sorties against the Japs. And Cheng has been active. Wa Ting said he's celebrated for the way he has been blowing up police stations. As well as operating a vengeance squad."

"Vengeance against Chinks working for the Japs?"

"Yes."

"Frankly," the Major said. "I don't trust any of them. I didn't much like the look of your friend Mr. Wa, and even less the look of your friend Mr. Ho. Which is why I don't care for sitting here on my backside waiting for the pair of them to do what they like with us."

As a gesture of protest the Major pushed himself up from the rotting frame of an unglazed window, standing in silhouette against the blaze of sunset it revealed, an end-of-day performance already beginning to be shot through with night purple. The six-foot-two length of him, now upright on a rigid spine, was vaguely symbolic of something, but Hamish couldn't quite think what.

The Major went to his pack and pulled out a map from one of the side pockets and unfolded it, laying it out on the uneven boards of the floor, then stabbing at it with one finger.

"There's your hill station, right? What's this thing called the Gap just below it?"

"A pass through the mountains into the state of Pahang. The main road west uses it."

"And south of that road? All this area?"

"Mountain jungle. The Japs may have maps marking Sakai tracks through it, but we don't. It's the stuff that Malaya Command used to call impenetrable. And between the Gap and the Pahang River there's nearly forty miles of it."

"Cheng could be anywhere in that?"

"I wouldn't think too far in. He'd want reasonable access to the Gap Road. But the fact remains, Major, that even if he's only a mile into that stuff we could spend a month looking for his camp and never find a trace of it. He's got a mighty good hide somewhere. Ho says the Japs have low-flying aircraft out almost every day searching for it. They're not using the Gap road at night; too many of their convoys have been shot up along it."

The Major picked up the map, folded it, slid it back into the pack's compartment, then began to walk up and down the room. Hamish continued to sit on his bedroll, which, unlike the Major's, had remained laid out all day. Near him, on the boards, was a pile of cigarette butts indicating to the eye of the trained observer that he had stayed put in one place for some considerable time. People marching up and down in an empty, mouldering Chinese estate house created a peculiar disturbance, not so much of noise as of dust raised, of insecure floorboards tested, and the ancient building seemed to grumble its protests. A family of rats was still active up amongst the roof rafters but the chicha lizards, deprived of an audience for their exhibitionism, had long since moved out. The previous night had been quite cold after sudden, heavy rain, and it was beginning to feel as though this one might be the same. A thousand feet up in the foothills of the main range, the central heating of the tropics suddenly switched off after sundown and, if rain plus the wind from Sumatra came with the dark, you shivered. Or at least Hamish shivered. The Major didn't allow himself to.

The pacing up and down stopped. "How long have you known this Ho?"

Hamish thought for a moment. "Ten years. Maybe eleven. We bought a lot of our mining gear through his agency. I saw him most times when I was in K.L. Used to have meals with the family quite often. If the Chinese went in for that kind of thing I might well have been asked to be godfather to one of his seven children."

"So you trust him? In spite of the fact that he seems to be doing pretty well under the Jap occupation?"

"I'd expect Ho to do pretty well under any occupation. The Chinese believe in survival. When they can't manage this as individuals, they contrive to do it as a race by making certain there are plenty of them around and plenty more coming."

"You haven't answered my question. Do you trust him?"

"We are forced to trust chosen people. The alternative is impossible," Hamish said.

"I'm not sure I've ever accepted that!"

"I know you haven't. But you've been spared the jungle. Because we've used my Chinese contacts. If we'd decided not to use them and had tried getting to where we are now on a compass bearing, it would have taken three weeks. Maybe a month."

"What?" The Major was staring. "For fifty miles?"

"Fifty miles avoiding all towns, villages, kampongs, even having to skirt rubber," Hamish said. "Because you wouldn't have been easily disguised as a Tamil by merely applying permanganate to your skin. I might have got away with it, and our other two, but not you. Anyone spotting our party

would have known what we were, and the Japs would have
been looking for us within days. Don't forget, either, our
load with that wireless. No porters to carry the stuff. Not to
mention the risk of losing it in a bog, and therefore losing
the whole point of our mission."

"I heard all these arguments in Ceylon. They convinced
our superiors. We are doing things your way. Committed to
that now. The only thing I am questioning is the reliability
of your contacts. And I question it more and more the
longer we have to wait here."

"Ho made it quite plain it was going to take time to contact Cheng."

"He's *had* time," the Major said. "Practically thirty-six
hours and damn all's happened. Except that Jap plane that
came over low. I didn't care for that."

"A routine patrol out looking for guerillas."

"So you say. It could also have been a tipoff out looking
for us."

"Yes, Major. It could have been. So what do we do about
the possibility? Pack up and make camp for the night in the
jungle beyond those overgrown rubber trees? Or start walking towards the Gap? It's only about eight miles as the crow
flies. I reckon we could make it in five days on a compass
bearing. And we have enough rations."

"You keep exaggerating about the Malayan jungle. The
Japs got through it all right."

"On tracks their spies had spent twenty years mapping.
They didn't just come dancing through the raw stuff. In
that kind of jungle I used to allow two days for a five-to-six-
mile circuit from the mine where I worked."

The Major stared at Hamish. "Hunting, were you?"

"Yes. Orchids."

"Good God! What on earth for?"

"Something I started when I gave up stamps. A couple of
years ago I identified a new species. The Kew Botanics
named it after me."

"Really?" At school the Major had been taught that a
gentleman doesn't brag. "I think we might give ourselves a
nip before we start to eat tinned rations."

The whisky was supposedly medicinal. Hamish produced

the flask from his backpack and turned to find the Major holding out his curious aluminum folding cup, with a top half that collapsed into the bottom. Next door the mumbling had ceased.

"What about them?"

The Major shook his head. "Don't believe in alcohol for O.R.'s. All it does is slow them down. I'm having a duty guard tonight. Rota. We'll all take turns."

"Doing what?"

"Watching that road down through the rubber. And listening. The Japs are bound to come by lorry. We're high here, which means gear changes at least a mile below us will be audible. If it should be your man Ho coming back I prefer to meet him outside, with our tommy gun trained on his car."

"But if it's the Japs?"

"We fade. Fast."

Hamish had no criticism of the strategy. The Major sat on the floor, tailor fashion, to work out his duty rota, which was basically democratic; two hours each for both officers and other ranks.

"I'll put Kneale on from twenty-one hundred hours to twenty-three hundred. You take over until one in the morning. Then Hudson after you. I'll do the three to five. After that, if it's as cold as last night, we'll all be awake. Understood?"

"Yes."

"The sentry will have our tommy gun. I'll explain things to the men while you get those tins open."

*

An icy wind came sweeping down the funnel of the narrow street between two blocks of four-story tenements, catching the small boy away from all possible shelter, prodding at him, chilling his bare knees and pushing up his shorts to freeze his backside. The hand-knitted sweater, already too small and stretched across his chest, was little more than a woollen net scarcely even filtering the blast. He wanted to run towards the steamy shop that would smell of new baking, with the floury morning baps waiting, already packaged, on the long counter, but his muscles refused to respond, as though the joints they operated had seized up, like frozen points on a railway siding. He could hear his mother's voice from somewhere behind, as though the wind had made a record of it for endless repetition: "Hamish! Yer no tae dawdle! Hurry up wi' they baps. I've the tea masked. And yer faither's up. He'll pit the fear o' Gawd in ye if yer no back quick."

Rain woke him, night rain in no way like those daytime downpours under the Sun's discipline, but uncontrolled, vicious, arriving with its own wind to assault a house on two fronts. The rain's intent seemed to be to drown the world. You lay listening to it, fears of blackness animated by a directed malevolence. In these night frenzies at Sungei Dema, usually with thunder bouncing from one hill peak to another, he had reached out for the girl beside him, finding her shivering under the sheet and welcoming.

Not Lali, though. If Lali had fears they were layered away under an assurance worn for so long it was completely convincing. When he woke beside her it was to find that she had reached down for a blanket and was cocooned away in it, isolated in a security arranged for herself. The shivering girl was Hasmah.

He had no memory of first meetings, couldn't recall an introduction to Big John, though it must have been at the club in K.L. when he was down for a boozy weekend from his first job at the Larek mine. He had certainly met Ruth at the club also, though he couldn't fix a sense of occasion to that, either, only the feeling that it had been at one of those dances at which he didn't dance. Yet Hasmah, up on that platform at the Ronggeng, swaying her body in the white light from acetylene flares, came up in his mind like a new print made from an unfaded negative.

"A whore, of course," Hans Ingold had said. "But a young one."

It had been so easy to arrange. The girl, coming to him on bare feet down the long central passage in Ingold's house, then standing in the doorway in that sarong too bright for virtue, had been made shy by the sound of laughter coming from the other bedroom. He had an unblemished print, too, of her body, still almost unformed, the small breasts that disappeared when she lay on her back. He remembered her crying piteously — not that night but months later, after he had brought her to Sungei Dema — something that she had never done before. It hadn't been a black night, either, but moon bright; Hasmah had been lying on her stomach, her head protected by both arms up over it, and he could only make out one word, "sejuk," cold. He had known she didn't want him to touch her, and he hadn't.

The ending had been hers, reached with a remoteness that must always have been there, though he hadn't wanted to admit it. The girl had brought him his papaya and early tea and, standing by the bed, had said, "I would go home now," expressed as a wish; he had thought he'd talked her out of it. But one morning three days later, she stood by the bed with the tray again and said exactly the same words: "I would go home now." Finally there was nothing to be done but to drive her to Jerantut and put her on the train for Kota Bahru. All the way, on a road that seemed to have more long straights in it than any other in Malaya, she had sat with her most important piece of luggage, a woven basket, on her knees, filling the car with a high-pitched bird chatter that was a sound of joy. He knew then that the tenderness he felt, perhaps moving towards a love, had been a waste. He didn't risk waste again. Ruth said that he got tired of his women easily. What she couldn't know was that they were all glad to go — even Lali, who was leaving a profitable arrangement.

The din of the rain on the rusting, corrugated-iron roof stopped as though responding to a conductor's baton. Dripping noises began, like a dozen taps with failing washers. Next door the two men started moving about shifting their gear, Kneale's methodical swearing a personal identification signal. Hamish considered sitting up to check whether his bedroll was escaping the water from reservoirs of ceiling sags, but decided not to bother. The Major's gear would be all right; before going off to his sentry duty he had stowed everything neatly against the wall with the least mould growing out of it, a procedure conducted with a maximum of boot noise and much heavy breathing, banishing the hope of sleep from those who were supposed to have earned it by two-hour spells of gun toting.

It was cold, Hamish's sleeping bag refusing to store and retain his body's warmth but offering instead a clammy damp. He had a hangover mouth — nothing to do with the nip of whisky, but something he had been waking with recently — as though the bile of a day's distaste for the military life had collected there to be spat out, leaving him in moderate shape to face up to more of the same. Kneale and Hudson, settled again, had decided to greet the pre-dawn by talking, but respected the Lieutenant's sleep by keeping their voices low.

They seemed to get on all right — Kneale, the garage mechanic now Technician Sergeant, and Hudson an ex-schoolteacher Corporal with political ambitions, who saw himself as part of the coming socialist takeover in post-war Britain. With both, Hamish was just slightly uneasy, perhaps because he felt he ought to be part of their lot and not the Major's. This was something the Major felt, too, finding it necessary more than once to point out to his commissioned guide that even on a small party of this kind it was important to maintain a certain distance between the command structure and the others. The personal views of the others were also subject to wartime censorship, as was made quite plain the first week after the Major took over as head of Operation Spearpoint. He firmly set the intellectual and moral tone of their mission: "We'll have no more of that Commie talk, Hudson! Understood?"

It seemed to Hamish that prohibitions of this kind only serve to drive subversion underground, so that the mumbling in the next room could now be Hudson expounding revolutionary tactics, how in any mass uprising of the proletariat it was the duty of the soldiery to shoot all their officers, even middle-aged temporary Lieutenants.

Hamish broke his rule of no cigarettes before six in the morning, and lit one. The men next door must have seen the lighter glow, for the talk stopped; the moment or two of silence that followed was broken by the sound of their own matches being struck. Then, with the warning of a three-round burst from a tommy gun, the war found them.

TWO

Hamish tripped over the surfaced root of a rubber tree and fell into a clump of undergrowth layered with thorns. Losing his .38 revolver, he groped for it on his hands and knees; the gun was his military identity. The light reaching him was leaf-filtered red from a huge fire down on the road. The tommy-gun duel battered his eardrums. He scarcely heard the new explosion but looked up at its flash, a whitening of the red. What came next could have been the grand finale at a fireworks display, everything left over thrown on the bonfire, with a couple of overlooked rockets taking off to burst high above the plantation, showering it with miniature incendiaries.

His fingers were bloody from thorn stabs, sticky on the barrel of the revolver. He was going to push himself up when a stream of bullets from a tommy gun across the road came sited high. He went on crouching. Fragments of shattered branches fell near. As though both sides had signalled an armistice, the gun yattering stopped, but echoes of the noise kept circling under his skull, seeming to isolate him from the new silence. What he heard first was a voice from somewhere below — not loud, not an order, but a long word or a phrase repeated on a diminishing note of urgency.

"Tasketekure! Tasketekure!"

Unless he stood up to look over the undergrowth, he couldn't see into the gulley. Very carefully, still on all fours, he began to push his way through the scrub. The voice went on calling, with a sudden surge in strength. The words weren't Cantonese or Malay or Tamil. The man down there had to be a Jap.

They used tricks, decoys even, cries and lamentations as from a wounded man, or voices calling, "Help me, Johnny. I'm over here, help me!" But their falseness was always detectable, as was clearly evident on recordings played during the Ceylon training course. Hamish was sure that the man beneath him had been left alone.

Firing started up again, this time from rifles; single shots with space between them, like a probe, from across the road. There was no answer from the rubber on this side. Hamish pushed up from his stomach and began crawling forward, digging elbows into the hard ground, using one hand to part the scrub, the other to hold his gun. The flames were dying down, but there was replacement light from the first grey of dawn. The wind that came with sunrise moved in swirls over the rubber forest, re-directing a column of thick, oily smoke towards where he lay, so that he had to drop his head onto his arms and breath close to the earth to keep from coughing as the man below was doing: a whooping tubercular, sound. Then, after the spasm, came the lament again, seeming hopeless now, something private, a protest with no audience in mind.

"Tasketekure!"

There was more coughing and, as though provoked by it, a tommy gun started up. When there was a reply, Hamish realized that the action had now moved away, to farther along the road and on both sides of it. He put down his revolver, pulled himself forward onto the gun, and, with both hands carefully parted the undergrowth ahead. As he did so, he heard singing, distinct words to what could only be a marching tune.

Wind had driven the smoke away. The bank in front of him dropped on an easy gradient, the heavy-trunked old rubber trees climbing it, their interlocked branches an awning against increasing light. It was the singing that pinpointed the man. He seemed to be lying on his back somewhere below road level, cushioned on a thick mattress of rotting leaves. It was a moment before Hamish made out his arms, outstretched on both sides of his body. There was some movement, as though the man was clawing at the leaves with his hands. The droned song went on. He looked utterly alone, indifferent to the gunfire now distancing itself from him, as self-absorbed as a fed baby lying in a pram. The word came again, erupting through the humming.

"Tasketekura!"

Firing wavered and stopped. Hamish heard what he thought was a chuckle, then a rustling of leaves. The man's shout, amplified by rocks, travelled under the aisles of trees.

"Tennoheika Banzai!"

He was sitting up, a faint light on his shaved head. His arm was raised high, as though pointing to some gap in the branches above. He screamed — a piercing, animal sound of pain — and fell back again, arms stretched out as before. There was a low whimpering.

Hamish had not seen the man's legs move, even when he was jerking himself up into the sitting position. They now seemed to be thrust out, rigid, while he twisted his body from the waist. The whimpering gave way to mumbled words kept low and private, covered by more rifle fire farther down the road. When the guns stopped, the man was lying on his back making no sound at all.

The sound was coming from somewhere else, a shuffling of dead leaves. In the gloom, a figure became visible for a few moments, disappeared, then showed up again in an area where bullet-shattered branches let in some light. He was plodding slowly forward, a soldier carrying a tommy gun. He came to stand beside the man lying on the leaves. No recognition signal passed between them. It seemed a long time before the soldier hitched the tommy gun over one shoulder and squatted down. A mumble of words seemed to come from the new arrival, the man on the ground remained unmoving.

"Tennoheika Banzai!"

The shriek had Hamish's heart thumping. The soldier pushed himself up and stood looking down, as though he couldn't believe that sound had come from the prone man. Slowly he unslung the tommy gun, carefully selecting a point on the wounded man's chest with the gun muzzle. He pulled the trigger. There were two bangs. The body seemed to rise to meet them, then was still again.

Hamish groped for the revolver. He was going to kill. He

wanted to. The soldier had put down the tommy gun. Leaning on one knee he was searching through the dead man's pockets. Hamish slid his body forward, needing to be clear of the scrub when he fired. Earth crumbled away in front of him; lumps of clay rolled down the slope. Hamish pulled the trigger once, then a second time. The soldier, rising with the tommy gun in his hands, swung around, then up. Flame spat from the gun's muzzle

*

Someone was calling him. He knew the voice but couldn't identify it. Nausea pushed through darkness, and from it he seemed to become conscious of light. He was lying on something soft and the light came from one side but he was able to move his head to put the light above him. The dull, barely opaque screen across his field of vision slowly dissolved, allowing first form, then colour, through. He was looking straight up at a thatch of leaves, like a crumbling roof through which sunlight filtered. He tried opening his mouth but one side of it seemed frozen, lips resisting the feeble bid his muscles made to force his tongue through. He finally managed to do it, feeling the inbalance of the opening; one side of his mouth might have been stitched up. His tongue brought back with it a taste of salt.

The voice that had reached him through the dark, calling his name, came again. He lay still, knowing that his throat wouldn't allow him to answer. As if a dental anaesthetic was wearing off, he was suddenly left with pain under the frozen half of his face, pain that came first in pulses from the quick beating of his heart, then unbroken and increasing. Again he tried moving his head to the side, away from the light, digging his hands into the soft leaves as he did so. He saw the bank he had rolled down.

The Jap soldier had left him for dead. He had a sense of achievement in having forced his mind to arrange that thought in a form that could be flashed on the screen of consciousness. With pain as a whip, he was coming back into a control of sorts. He began to raise his left arm, bringing it slowly up to the frozen side of his face, feeling a roughness

as fingers touched skin. Something crumbled. He brought
his hand across his body and looked at it. The crumbling
was dried blood. Panic surged up. A bullet track had laid
open a section of his skull. He had looked bad enough, rolling down to the bottom of that bank, for the Jap to leave
him without wasting another bullet.

He heard flies. His hand brought up to his face had disturbed them, but they were back, the air humming as they
settled. He brought up his hand again. The flies rose, but
stayed near. He set his jaws rigid, trying to keep his head
in one piece, pain flaring as he dug his elbows into the
leaves, forcing himself up, holding his body a few feet off
the ground. The flies whined in front of his face.

The warrior whose last shout had been for his Emperor
was still lying on his back, arms thrown out. A shaft of sunlight from the road reached his face and down to the dark
stain on his khaki shirt. His eyes weren't the narrow slits of
the propaganda caricatures; they were almost wide now, as
though surprised at being dead. It wasn't a young face, it
was formed by living, perhaps forty years of it. The savage
lines of the killer samurai, the turned-down mouth, weren't
there. Hamish might almost have been looking at himself
in another uniform.

The dead man was beginning to stink. A fly moved up
onto one of his eyeballs.

"Hamish! Hamish!"

The Major. He was coming down the road. There were
others with him, talking. Someone laughed. The search
didn't sound serious.

Hamish called out, a sound scraped over a parched throat.

*

They lifted him out of the car and laid him beside the
road. He could see that the car was a big one, American, a
Cadillac. It had been heavily loaded. They were lifting out
the radio and its dynamo now, more careful with it than
they had been with him. The thought was half-amusing. He
might have smiled if the emergency field dressing strapped
to one side of his head had permitted. The Major was at the

back of the car supervising operations. A man trained for work behind the enemy lines should have learned not to bellow.

The light was very bright and the sun very hot. Hamish closed his eyes again.

"We'll get this gear out of sight into the jungle pronto," the Major said. "A Jap convoy might come along."

"That would be inconvenient," another voice said.

Hamish was certain he recognized it. A moment later, when feet came to a halt on the tarmac beside him, he opened his eyes. The man looking down was Chinese. Under a cap with three stars above the projecting peak, the half-shadowed face looked much thinner.

"Hello," Hamish said.

It seemed some time before Cheng Lee Kwa asked, "How long have you been conscious?"

"Minutes, I think. But I came to once in the car. And almost came to when you were fixing me up. It was you?"

Cheng nodded.

"Any chips off my skull?"

"I didn't find any. You'll have a sore head for some days. Then a scar two inches long above one ear. The hair will never grow on it."

"I'm not so pretty that it matters."

Cheng didn't smile. He looked as though he had given up the practice for the duration. "Can you walk?" he asked.

"Of course he can't walk!" It was the Major.

"Help me to sit up first," Hamish said.

"We'll contrive some kind of stretcher," the Major announced. "First we'll need two poles — "

"A stretcher in the jungle is impossible. Our wounded walk. Much worse cases than this."

Cheng sounded like a bored surgeon near the end of his round of a ward that didn't have a single patient in it offering an interesting challenge to his skills.

"Now look here, Mr. Cheng — "

"*Colonel* Cheng. My rank in the Army of the Malaysian Communist Party will be recognized by your command in Ceylon, Major. That is, if negotiations between us are to be successful."

"Negotiations? Dammit, we're about to supply you with everything you need."

"Something your countrymen have long experience in doing."

"What the hell do you mean by that?"

"I mean supplying others, who can then do the fighting for them."

"I won't stand here to listen to that kind of talk!"

"It's no place to be standing to talk at all."

"I want to know what's behind this. Your attitude?"

"Very well, Major, I'll tell you. But for those shots from your tommy gun warning the Japs of our ambush, we would have captured the truck. Instead of seeing it blown up. On that truck were ammunition and grenades. We need grenades especially. All lost now. Also, the traitor Ho, instead of escaping into the rubber, would be dead. As well as his car we would have had the truck to bring my men to this point. Now they are having to make a long trek on foot, at risk from Japanese hunting parties all the way. Do you wonder I am not so pleased with our first contact?"

If there had been any Japs within a half-mile radius, they would have heard the Major then. "And how was I supposed to know you'd set up your bloody ambush, eh? Tell me that!"

"Admittedly, you could not. I thought it possible you might have a sentry posted at the house. That wouldn't have mattered. But I could scarcely foresee that your idea of sentry duty would take you a mile down the road from the house in a pre-dawn stroll."

Hamish opened his eyes. "Shut up! Both of you! I asked to be helped to sit."

It was the Major who responded, reaching down to grip Hamish under the arms, then towing him across tarmac to prop him up against a back wheel of the Cadillac. He was no longer dizzy, just felt it strange to have his heart beating at one side of his skull. In a little he would be obliged to try out his legs, but was ready to postpone the moment until the unloading — which the Major was back to supervising — was over. Meanwhile Cheng searched in the dashboard compartment, presumably for Ho's gun. A Jap agent, Ho would probably have been allowed to carry one as protection against the threat of the vengeance squads.

The angle at which the car was parked put Hamish in the shade and he kept his eyes open, staring at a view he knew well enough. They were somewhere below the Gap, but not far below it, on a hairpin bend where a solid buttress of jungle came thrusting down to meet the road at a corner, after which was a sheer drop of at least five hundred feet. The Cadillac, stripped of anything useful in a jungle camp, would almost certainly soon be making a dive onto the rocks at the foot of the cliff. Ho's pride and joy, a status symbol allowed the new order's successful and happy collaborator. It would be the car first, the man later. Wherever Ho was now, he would be running scared. The vengeance squads got a high percentage of the people they went after. Rumours of just how effective these guerilla assassins were had reached Ceylon.

Six men who might be assigned this type of work on occasion were now sitting in a row on a stone parapet edging the road, seemingly ordinary enough Chinese youths, unsinister even with ammo belts slung across sweat-dark shirts. But there was one who was different, in middle age, bareheaded, slouched, with a cigarette hanging out of his mouth and from which he inhaled and exhaled without bothering to lift a hand to move it. He had a face that might have been carved teak, the sculptor's chisel slipping to produce gouged lines. I wouldn't like him after me, Hamish thought.

Two more Chinese appeared to be stripping the engine, banging away. They brought the head count up to an unlucky thirteen, all of whom must have been in, or hanging onto the outside of, the Cadillac as it ground up the steep gradients. If there was another group coming on foot it meant that Cheng certainly hadn't wanted to risk being outgunned at the ambush site. As a reception party for the new arrivals from Ceylon, it was impressive if not particularly friendly. It looked as though the news of a landing from a submarine must have been passed on directly to Cheng from Wa Ting in Selangor, bypassing Ho on his rubber estate near Kuala Lumpur.

All of which, Hamish thought, makes my insistence on contacting Ho something that the Major is going to enjoy rubbing my nose in when he thinks I'm fit enough not to just die quietly of shame. Ho used to say he was my Chinese brother. In this country now, maybe you don't risk trusting brothers too much. But in spite of what he tried to do to us I still hate to think of his being hunted, waking at night to the sound of a supposedly secret hideout being broken into, knowing then for sure that so-called Japanese protection wasn't worth two cents, old British colonial coinage. His family was probably the price of his sellout, all those kids to be looked after in wild times. Not an argument, though, you could use on old teak-face over there as he came at you with a knife for one of the silent jobs. Why am I thinking of poor little Ho right now? That bullet must have jarred my brain.

Hamish stared at the view. He had never really been able to look at it when driving this road from Sungei Dema to the bright lights of Kuala Lumpur. It was too risky; you watched for the bend and the one after it, and with a rapt attention to the footbrake. There had sometimes been a smell of rubber burning. He had never even stopped to have a cigarette in a parking area while gazing out over western Malaya, spread out beneath him to the sea, usually with a heat haze over the Malacca Straits but sometimes, just before sunset, the sky swept clean by winds. Then even a quick glance created a feeling that horizons were limitless, just your sight inadequate. Nothing could ever make him really feel a hunted fugitive in this country in which he had searched for orchids and slept with Hasmah. She would be nearing thirty by this time, probably getting plump if she wasn't already fat, a red hibiscus flower over one ear, advertising her continuing willingness, already presiding over a slumped face.

Hamish heard the plane before the tired men sitting along the parapet did. He shouted the one word that would jerk them alert: "Jap." The aircraft came over a jungle-coated crest and at once started to drop on them, the wind whine of its descent louder than the noise of its single engine. There was no panic reaction from the guerillas; none of them took cover; they had met this visitor before. Teak-face picked up his tommy gun, aiming it up, but he didn't fire; instead he waited until the machine, caught in the upward thrust of a thermal, presented its underbelly; then he pulled the trigger. The thermal took its load up out of easy range. Lucky for the pilot, Hamish thought. One of the many things you could say about the Japs was that timidity didn't seem to be a national characteristic, their apparent complete lack of it making them foolhardy a lot of the time, like now. An unarmed recce plane was not called on to dive the enemy.

The goggled pilot looked back at them from his open cockpit. In spite of its fried-egg markings the machine appeared to Hamish very much like one of the Tiger Moths used by the K.L. flying club, quite possibly overlooked in the sudden evacuation, like a lot of other things.

"Will he have a radio?" the Major yelled.

"Yes," Cheng replied, no longer looking up.

"Where's the nearest Jap unit likely to be?"

"They sometimes have a company at the Gap resthouse."

"But you said that was only a couple of miles up the road?"

"There's enough time. Even Japs don't risk death on these bends. They've lost a good many lorries along here. As well as the ones we've blown up."

*

Thirteen men, plus radio, plus hand-crank dynamo, plus an already opened case of medical supplies, left a trail behind them through primary jungle that might have been made by a herd of elephants on the move to new feeding grounds. The Major, up front and still apparently in competition with Cheng for seniority, protested about this in a manner that was heard down most of the column. Whatever Cheng said in answer didn't reach as far back as Hamish, who was beginning to have some doubts himself about this heavy-footed approach to a secret stronghold. And their rest halts seemed a shade too casually long for his liking, though he needed every minute of them, lying flat on his back to ease the aggressive thumping in his head.

During one of these breaks, Cheng came back down the line and stood for some time in front of Hamish, who had his eyes half-shuttered but could still see the M.C.P. Colonel perfectly well. In khaki shirt and long trousers soaked with sweat, the guerilla leader looked like a man who has earned high rank the hard way. Not yet seen with his cap off, there was no way of knowing whether the smartest corporation lawyer in K.L. now had his head shaven as a prophylactic against lice but, even with bare bone up there, he was going to look like one of the world's natural leaders — which in some way was just a shade frightening, as though his present role might only be chapter three or four in a long story that was going to see the action intensifying. As a mine engineer in the tropics, you didn't often run up against men of destiny, just tribal chiefs like Big John, and somehow the experience was a shade unnerving, even when you had played bad golf with the man.

Why the long stare at me? Hamish wondered. Do they shoot their wounded, too?

He opened his eyes wide. Cheng, still staring, rationed his words. "All right?"

"No. But I'm still walking."

"There's a long way to go."

"I'll make it. How's the Major?"

"Hot."

"He's going to be cross when the Japs telescope into us from behind."

"Japs respect the jungle. They won't come in with one company. They wait for reinforcements."

"Which gives us time to dig a concealed pit in the middle of this trail? Filled with poisonous snakes?"

"No pit," Cheng said, and went on down the line of resting men.

There was a break every hour while they were in the thick stuff. The only loud continuous sound while they moved was the whack of parangs cutting a path and the wheezing from the men carrying the loads. Hamish joined them in that, though he was only carrying himself. Like a spy from the enemy, an elderly monkey kept following the party; he could be heard crackling in branches overhead, but was seen only when he had guessed successfully at the route they would be taking and chose to reveal himself perched in a tangle of vine, contentedly picking at his teeth with a twig. He was an old gentleman with many seasons behind him who really didn't give a damn about anyone's war but was still curious. Occasionally a bird took off, squawking from the top branches of the jungle roof, and huge mosquitoes that must normally feed on vegetation came in hordes for a change to a blood diet.

On a bank, after passage through ankle-deep mud, Hamish felt the thrust of leeches working their way through the eyelets of his boots but he couldn't stop to do anything about it. He talked to himself a good deal. With teak-face right behind, there didn't seem anyone but himself to talk to, and it took his mind off pain. If they ever try to turn this country into a tourist paradise, he thought, I could do the come-ons for back-to-nature tours like this one: "If you think you really work up a sweat on the squash court, a new experience awaits you on one of our jungle treks." Not snappy enough for a brochure. I need the stimulus of a massive saline intake. The Major has the salt pills in his pack, damn him. I wonder what he's going to be like when he really develops prickly heat? Irritable. Isn't it funny how you know when you're not going to die? I'm not going to die as the result of this hike. I know that. Others may, but I won't.

I'm delirious, he thought. Though it's not quite that, just a partial amnesia helping to improve my survival chances. Retrospective vision is hazed, but the haze clears the moment I see Cheng staring in my direction. I'm ready to sting if he comes close. If that man decides at any point to write me off, I'm finished. Maybe the Major's beginning to feel this, too. The bellowing has stopped.

*

The fourth rest break, like the others, went on for so long that even Hamish wanted it to end, tired as he was of lying on a bank, gasping like a landed cod, left to interpret the

sound of mountain wind over the top of jungle as the rustling feet of a Jap encirclement. Teak-face didn't appear to
like the waiting much, either; his extinct cigarette butt
looked in danger of being swallowed as he sat bent over, head
slumped towards his crotch, inhaling his own smell.

The monkey had left them. At his time of life gun battles
weren't things he stayed around to watch.

Suddenly they came to a stream, the jungle having broken
to allow sunlight down to it, the clearness of its water a
surprise after the black slime of bogs. It ran fast but shallow
over what looked like granite worn to a smoothness almost
suggesting a drain, with the jungle dyked back by more of
the rock. There were some cracks from the pressure of fat
roots, but none of these had broken through. Cheng, the
Major, and two of the guerillas were already wading up the
flow, on a water path that flushed away all traces of its use.

Hamish found fighting his way up the stream exhausting,
the water sometimes up to his calves. He was very slow, but
so were the load carriers behind, splashing about, shouting,
though this was almost covered by the roar of a cataract. He
didn't see it until he was around the angle of an arm of
jungle the water was taking a few hundred years to undermine; then it was part of a bluff whose rock defeated both
trees and scrub, a light-coloured stone shining in the sunlight and, almost central to it, the cascade whipped to foam
by boulders pushing through its drop of at least a hundred
feet.

The leaders of the party were waiting for the rest of the
men by a pool at the foot of the waterfall. Their interest
seemed to be focussed on the pool. Ten minutes later
Hamish, dragging himself out of the stream, turned his head
and saw why.

The pool was deep, in violent, frothed movement, but the
lip over which the water escaped was shallow, holding the
bodies prisoners. There were four of them, tumbled, collid-
ing, pushing towards the outflow, sucked away from it, a
stiff arm thrust up, then withdrawn and replaced by a
bleached face. Long strips of unwound leg puttees wove in
and out amongst the tossed corpses. Three of the men were
Jap soldiers. Hamish couldn't be sure about the fourth.

THREE

The Major sat bent forward on the edge of the bamboo sleeping platform, his feet on an earth floor, one arm buttressing his chin as he stared out through the open door of the hut. Seen from behind, he might almost have been a high-powered salesman suddenly conscious of a loss of power. Hamish reached for a packet of Co-Prosperity cigarettes. He was trying to ration himself to ten a day, certain that any analysis of what they were made of would show bullock dung dipped in the nicotine spray generally used to kill pests on tomato plants. They were giving him a cough that hurt his head. He lit one and began to cough. This disturbed the Major's reverie. He turned his head.

"I suppose it's any time now?"

Hamish, unable to speak, nodded.

"I keep wondering what kind of a trial he had? Not much. From what I can see it didn't take more than twenty minutes."

"It wasn't exactly a trial," Hamish said. "The man had confessed."

"Under torture?"

"Pressure probably. That his family wouldn't be touched if he told everything."

"Irregulars like these fight a dirty war."

"As against our clean one?"

"Don't try to be clever! You know perfectly well what I mean."

"Aren't you forgetting one thing, Major? The biggest threat to any guerilla unit is infiltration by the enemy. You have to stamp out even the risk of it. Which is what Cheng is doing."

"Don't you think I see that? It's still a dirty kind of war."

In a previous incarnation he had probably been on a horse at Balaclava, finding bullets rather dirty, charging with a drawn sabre instead. Hamish inhaled and coughed. From the parade ground beyond came voices. The clearing had been made to suggest, from the air, an abandoned Sakai settlement, with a ruined longhouse as its centrepiece. Nothing was ever left out there that would indicate current occupation; even washing had to be hung under the trees. The huts circling the open area were all back in deep shade, making them damp, with mosquitoes active all day. The bamboo platforms were infested with little mites that came out, bit, then nipped back into shelter again. They kept the Major from sleeping, and he thrashed about on creaking poles.

"You know Cantonese," the Major said in a tone that was practically an accusation. "You were sunbathing out there yesterday. You must have heard what the men were saying."

"They're not a chatty crowd. I didn't hear much."

"You know I want to be told *anything* you hear. I'll be the judge of whether or not it's important."

Not Balaclava. A schoolmaster in one of those institutions where they beat the boys who ask for more soup. Hamish went into a spasm of coughing that felt as though it could be rupturing the scabs forming above his ear. The Major waited until the convulsion was over.

"Cheng didn't talk to you separately yesterday?"

"No."

"I think we were entitled to a more complete explanation than the one we got."

"It seemed pretty complete to me. The guerilla we saw dead in the pool had sold out to the Japs. Almost a classic case of forty pieces of silver. The man they have just tried was his accomplice in the deal. They were both cooks. Which is why the cuisine here has fallen off so badly in the last twenty-four hours."

"Under the circumstances, your flippancy is disgusting!"

"Sorry. Weak characters use it to help them face up to a far from ideal world."

Hamish worked his way to the edge of the bed platform, walking barefoot to a jar in a corner, using a dipper to pour water from it into a porcelain cup. He stood drinking with his back to the Major. He wasn't sure whether the water came from above or below the campsite. If below, it would be teeming with a fine assortment of microscopic invitations to disease. He had a re-fill and drank that, too. Temperature in the shade was high, but the humidity higher. He felt a buildup of sweat lining the ducts leading to the pores on his skin. He turned to find that the Major had abandoned his "thinker in bush-shorts" pose to go to the opening where he stood staring over the parade ground.

"There's a Gestapo operating in this camp," he announced.

Hamish had no comment.

"Everyone's watching each other. That cook had been suspect for a long time. Then at the right moment, pounce! They even let him get quite near the camp, showing the way to those Jap guides."

"How would you have dealt with the situation?"

The Major's answer was to say sharply: "They're starting!"

Hamish climbed back onto the bed platform. Living close to this man left him with a perpetual lust for snatched sleep.

"If the second cook confessed under torture," the Major said, "I don't see that there's any real evidence against the man."

Hamish stared at the attap thatching. "Circumstantial, but real enough."

"The second cook may have been afraid of the traitor."

"He's had his chance to say so. What's in your mind, Major? The establishing of standard British justice in the middle of the Malayan jungle in the middle of a war?"

"What would be wrong with that?"

"Nothing. Except it won't work. If I were in Cheng's place I'd be doing what he's doing. There's no alternative. You believe in morale and discipline. That's what Cheng is defending. In the only way he can."

"*You* are defending a summary execution!"

"Call it what you like. Wars are a wildly abnormal state. During which justice becomes wildly abnormal."

"Certain standards do *not* alter."

"They get put in cold storage for the duration."

The Major stared out over the parade ground. It was some time before he continued. "They're bringing him out now. Aren't you coming to watch rough justice, Hamish?"

"No."

"I wasn't sure I knew who the second cook was, but I recognize him now. He brought us our food a few times. A cheerful fellow. His smile made quite a change in this place. They've got him up against one of the posts of the long-house. They're not tying him. He's just standing there. They're not using tommy guns. Three rifles. The execution-ers are standing much closer than you'd expect with a firing party. I can't see Cheng. Maybe he isn't coming. If you'd ordered this killing would you have stayed away from it?"

Hamish didn't say anything.

There were two shots, one on top of the other; then seconds later, a third. All their echoes bounced back from the bluff above the parade ground. A half-minute's silence was followed by a flaring of orders to start the tidy-up.

*

Hamish followed a path that led up from the camp latrines. Flies came with him, fascinated by his eyes. Not many guerillas walked this way, or often; and, since the track had been cut, ferns had grown out over it, trying to claim it back. His feet were on rock in places and yet the jungle trees had found soil in the clefts, wedging themselves down into them, stunted in comparison with the deep forest giants but still in contest with vine and scrub to get leaves up into sunlight. An early morning breeze was at work but it wasn't potent enough to penetrate the greenish gloom through which he moved.

The path became steep; then, reaching the rock face of

the bluff, became almost a staircase, with steps that had been chiseled out, but there was still no view, screened as it was by the tops of the hardwoods. It became cooler, giving him that old sense of another tropical day offering a clean start that would nevertheless soon be polluted by heat. It was cold in the mountains, before the mists began to steam away and down in the camp huts that never got sunlight men woke coughing, clutching coverings about them, trying to wrap themselves in the luxury of a last sleep. Though in some places he was having to cling onto vines to pull himself up, he hadn't begun to sweat, and he climbed with the feeling that a surprise was waiting for him, possibly even a pleasant one. Suddenly, and almost directly above, a golden oriole made that into a promise. The flies had gone.

Hamish had never heard the bird in the jungle before; it seemed to prefer to put on its performances for man. This one might have been waiting for him. Though Hamish couldn't see the rising sun, the bird did, singing in notes that were more silver than gold, like the thinly worked Kelantan silver, which looks fragile but isn't. He stopped for a moment to listen, and the bird, as though keeping an eye on him, tried for a new arpeggio it seemed improbable it would be able to peak out, but it did. Hamish wanted to applaud.

The surprise was a totally uninterrupted view, rarely offered in the jungle, from a balcony of rock sticking out of the cliff face. He looked at his watch to find that the sun, already breaking up the mists, had been at work for longer than he had thought, and between the ledge and Fraser's Hill there were only patches of it left, steaming away at the edges, their weakening mass crumpled by the new wind. There were no houses to be seen at the hill resort not two miles away, the clearings for lawns and English flower gardens up there hidden by climbing rain forest. The scarring for the precipitous final road to them was also invisible. The road he could see was the one dropping from the Gap and gouging the sides of ravines with the gradients that had once tested his car brakes going down and his lowest gear going up. Climbing it were three lorries.

"Would you like to use this?" Cheng asked.

He was holding out a brass-bound, collapsible telescope that looked as though it might have belonged to Ruth Gourlay's slave-running ancestor.

"I hope I didn't startle you?" He sounded almost disappointed.

"I nearly fell off."

The man had certainly forgotten how to smile, but then he hadn't been too blithe about living as a lawyer looking after Chinese tin interests under assorted colonial laws. Hamish took the telescope. After a moment of focussing, the magnified picture told him that the lorries were full of Jap soldiers. He handed the instrument back and Cheng used it until the trucks had disappeared. He didn't seem to be in any way disturbed.

"Did you come up here in the dark?" Hamish asked.

"No. I slept in the cave. I do sometimes."

Its entrance was behind them, not very large, and uninviting. Hamish avoided caves in Malaya, largely because he didn't want to find himself challenging snakes for squatters' rights.

"It can't be very comfortable?"

"It's all right. I have a sleeping bag I leave here."

"The O.P. is manned all the time?"

"O.P.?"

"Sorry. Even us temporary soldiers start picking up the jargon. Observation point."

"I must learn it, if we are to be in communication with Ceylon. No, this place is not manned permanently. There would be no point. We can see movement on the road, yes, but not what happens if they go into the jungle. Or even whether they intend to, like those three lorry loads."

"Japs coming for us?" Hamish asked.

"I doubt it. But if they are we'll know soon enough. I have men out."

Cheng turned to the cave, bending nearly double to get in. He came out again with a satchel.

"Would you like some breakfast? They always give me two rice balls when I'm to be up here all night. I only eat one."

Stern asceticism.

"Yes, thanks," Hamish said. The rice ball had some of yesterday's curried sauce worked through it, replacement cooks able on short notice to come up with that Chinese flair for making even the apparently unpalatable tasty. Hamish remembered a banquet in his early days at which he had been expected to use chopsticks to dip still-active slugs into what looked like pea soup. Struggling to overcome absurd Western prejudice, he had popped them into his mouth. They had been delicious.

Cheng, his rice ball finished, found a leaf on a plant projecting from the cliff face and used it to wipe his hands. At home he would probably wash them eight times a day. He dug into the satchel for a packet of cigarettes, holding it out when found. They were Lucky Strikes. Even the least self-indulgent of the Big Chiefs allow themselves the little extra here and there, if only to show that they are human like the rest of us. Hamish inhaled slowly, and as he did the view improved, the colours becoming sharper, and it wasn't only from the rising sun.

"How do you get on with your Major?" Cheng asked.

"When he keeps me awake with his snores I hate him."

"And at other times?"

"We could never have a deep friendship."

"Why was he put in charge of this party?"

"It's a question I've asked myself often. And I mean to ask brass in Ceylon when I get back there, even if it sees me stripped of my present rank at a swank parade."

"What is a swank parade?"

"It is a British Army military performance attended by ladies wearing tea gowns and picture hats. With a band playing."

"This is still done?"

"I expect so. In places a few thousand miles from any fighting. We have quite a lot of these left at various spots around the world."

"I think you people are mad."

"Count me out of that. I'm as sane as you are."

"We are not having the British back."

"What? Who's we? The M.C.P.?"

"Yes."

"You think you're going to rule Malaya after this?"

"Yes."

"I don't."

"Britain will be too weak to resist us."

"I'm not thinking of Britain. I'm thinking of the two other races symbolized on that three-star cap badge of yours. Correct me if I'm wrong but don't those stars stand for the three main races in this country — Malays, Tamils, and Chinese?"

"They do. What of it?"

"I don't see any Tamils or Malays in your camp. And how many have you got enrolled in your M.C.P. in other units?"

"If there are not many yet that will come. We are the spearhead of the resistance. Against the Japs. And when the time comes, against the British."

"Meanwhile you grab everything you can get from us."

"Yes. Wouldn't you?"

"Why admit that to me? I could add a personal postscript to the first message our boys get out on that radio to Ceylon."

"But you won't. Because when the Japs are gone you are one who will help us."

"Balls to that!"

Cheng stubbed out his cigarette before throwing the butt towards the jungle beneath them. Hamish felt the swelling of an irritation that wasn't far off anger.

"There's one thing you Chinese forget. It's that none of you has a better right to be in this country than we do. Not as good, in fact. Because we were here first. Was it your father or grandfather who came from China?"

"Grandfather."

"And that's about as far back as any of you can go. Except for a handful of traders who used to operate in the Malay towns along the coast. You know perfectly well what I'm getting at, Cheng. Chinese came pouring into this country after it was opened up by us."

"So?"

"Sheer force of numbers now doesn't justify a takeover."

"We think it does."

"The Malays and the Tamils won't."

"The Tamils are nothing. The Malays we will deal with."

"Look, even if I have no message out to Ceylon about what the M.C.P. really stands for, the Major *will* have. His first impression of your lot as potential allies isn't very good. He thinks you're high-handed opportunists whose allegiance is likely to be to Moscow after this war, not to us. He may send these views back to base."

"Then we'll see that he has no opportunity to do so."

"You'll keep him from using the radio?"

"No. He'll use it. For identification. But under supervision."

"Translated, that means M.C.P. censorship?"

Cheng shrugged. He took another Lucky Strike, considered not offering the pack to Hamish, then decided to be civil. "I do not get on with that man," he announced.

"It's mutual. You both got off to a bad start."

"What do you mean?"

"That seniority struggle. And hard on its heels you took charge of the radio without a formal handover. There should have been a ceremony. Perhaps at sunset with a drummer or a flute solo. You have no sense of ritual, Cheng. The British Empire has survived for hundreds of years on very little else."

"It will no longer survive."

"All right. But in the meantime you've locked up medical supplies that the Major thinks he should have been allowed to hand out himself."

"Like a missionary to the heathen?"

Hamish laughed. "Well, why not? After all, it's been a rough trip to get here. You ought to have appreciated that."

"Thanks for the good advice."

"You can have it at anytime for a couple of Lucky Strikes A whole pack and I offer a short course on how to get on with the Major."

"That won't be necessary."

They went down the precipitous path together, Hamish

with the feeling he remembered from eighteen holes on the Kuala Lumpur golf course: that the contact couldn't be said to have done much to cement a relationship. If the O.P. wasn't permanently manned there didn't seem much point in having it, except perhaps as an escape from the claustrophobia induced by the tree-hung camp. Maybe Cheng went up there to brood on a Marxist Malaya, like Hitler in his mountain eyrie working on overall plans for a Nazi Europe.

They heard what was happening at the camp before they could see it: the bellowing of a physical training instructor stretching his lungs to maximum. The voice was teak-face's. He had the kind of personality that results in a near hundred-percent turnout, the parade ground covered with guerillas leaping to clap hands over their heads and then landing with feet wide apart — a stance from which they went into a curious back roll Hamish couldn't remember from any of his school torture sessions.

It was the back roll that was causing the Major some problems. The movement was not in his repertoire either and, in a half-bid to execute it, he lost the timing completely and suddenly gave up. Huge and barrel-chested, wearing only his shorts, he stood slightly swaying behind all those modestly built Chinese, looking like Goliath come to the temple after a heavy night on the town.

To get to his hut, Hamish had to skirt the area of action, and by the time he reached it the Major was already established inside, sitting on the edge of the sleeping platform, ready to hurl an accusation.

"You were with Cheng!"

"Yes. We met at the latrines. Not a time you chat much."

FOUR

It was strange to be woken in the night by a sound that wasn't from inside the hut. Moonlight reached almost to the sleeping platform. The Major's space on it was empty, his bedroll folded. The noise came again, an order shouted. It sounded like teak-face. Hamish pushed himself forward to slip into the clogs he had taken to wearing in camp to save his boots.

The party assembling on the square looked too large and too heavily equipped to be a vengeance group. In the shadow of the ruined longhouse, moving bodies blurred into each other, but there were at least twenty-five men. Some seemed to be going as porters, with heavy backpacks but no visible guns. To get a better view, Hamish left the hut, walking along the edge of the parade ground, then standing clear of tree shadow. If he was seen, no one took any notice. It was much the same in daytime. Walking about the camp, he came near to feeling he was an unseen presence, like a ghost well known for its hauntings but totally ignored by rational minds refusing to believe in what could not be scientifically proven.

There was certainly no mixing with the guerillas. Meals were delivered to the British officers' hut almost as though it was an isolation ward, camp orderlies on this duty streamlining Chinese politeness to a point where it nearly disappeared. No one ever dropped in for a chat about the war, and if the Major had dreamed of presiding over a jungle officers' mess made up of irregulars being wooed back to the British Crown, any hope of that must by now have withered.

It was obvious that Cheng had issued orders to his men about keeping contacts with the British men to a strict minimum; maybe this came partly from the new convert's urgent need to defend his faith. As a pretty successful exploiter himself of capitalism in the old life, Cheng knew the particular temptations the system offered, and this made him nervous that a few advocates of free enterprise at large in his unit of shriven Marxists could pose a real threat to the teachings of dialectical materialism.

To Hamish all this had been a surprise, almost a shock. He saw now that he had been expecting to find in the guerillas a necessarily tightened-up version of the usual Chinese approach to living, a kind of merry self-interest. From his contacts with the race he would never have believed any of them capable of subduing their natural ebullience with the dictates of harsh dogma. But it had happened here. Laughter was apparently only permissible when its source was some anti-imperialist joke put out from the platform at one of the concerts. These weekly affairs, presented as entertainments, were dedicated to a Marxist uplift drearier than most other kinds of uplift, its hymns grim chants about the marching feet of the proletariat about to take over the world. What he missed most in camp was the complete absence of Chinese chatter, the excess of noisy talk, regardless of circumstances, that had seemed like the identity stamp of race. But here the chatter had been dissolved under regulations about which no comment was permitted, and which made even casual talk suspect, thus suffocating it.

You couldn't criticize the discipline resulting from all this. Besides, up against Japanese ruthlessness, the guerillas had to be efficient. But the feeling remained that in coming back to camp these men should have been able to look forward to something more than a period in an indoctrination unit. What Hamish saw made him wonder what the desertion rate was likely to be.

A cloud from the South China Sea, delayed by one of the peaks above the camp, broke free from it to hide the moon. Teak-face used the sudden darkness for a testing of flashlights. Not every man had one, for batteries were hard to come by. Hamish made out only four answering glows, which meant that most of the men on the party would be groping through the jungle, not able to see where they were putting their feet. As the moonligh returned, still thinned by cloud-edging, a figure hurried across the parade ground from one of the huts. Tall for a Chinese, it was certainly Cheng, the bump of a pack on his back meaning he was going with the party, not just out to give his men a pep talk.

They didn't move off until the moonlight was bright again, the single-file column coming quite close to where Hamish stood, the commander in front, teak-face having dropped back to near the rear to ginger up any laggards. One by one they went into the forest wall like divers into a huge, overhanging wave. In so far as Hamish could see, not one of them had looked at him.

*

"They want us to supply everything they need for their damned Commie revolution," the Major announced.

Hamish, agreeing with the assessment, didn't say anything.

"I can't even begin to get an assurance out of Cheng for their cooperation when we invade this country. We could find ourselves fighting Chinks as well as Japs. I said that to Cheng. No comeback. He just looked at me. What do you make of him? Think he'd betray us?"

"Depends on what you mean by betrayal."

"You know damn well what I mean. Sell us down the river. Go over to the Japs just before we make our assault landing."

"No. He won't do that. He hates the Japs more than us."

The Major brooded, sitting on the edge of the sleeping platform, wearing only a towel; he was just back from a sunrise bath in the icy stream where the accepted technique was to stand up to your calves in the flow, pouring dippers of water over the rest of you. He always rounded things off with total immersion, which would normally have left him with goose bumps still visible, but anger at the way he had been obliged to spend half the night must have warmed him up again immediately.

"Any idea where Cheng was going with his party?"

"No," Hamish said.

"What's your guess?"

"Could be a tipoff that a Jap convoy is planning to use the Gap road. They seem to have a good intelligence network in the towns."

"Not surprising. I can see the way they'd recruit spies. Ask a chap to work for them and if he said no, cut his throat. One way to bring in the volunteers."

For a moment Hamish thought the Major had made a blackish joke, but he seemed quite serious, getting rid of the towel in favour of a pair of shorts. Then he mounted the platform, found his pipe and tobacco, and settled with his feet back on the earth floor. He smoked rarely, but when he did he took the drug seriously, sending up volumes of smoke and apparently inhaling, for coughing was as much a part of the process as the sneeze is to snuff. Through a haze he suddenly said: "Didn't use the code."

"What?"

"Talked in clear to Ceylon. No point in not, since the Japs know we brought the set in. Thanks to your friend Mr. Ho. Not sure what Ceylon made of it, though. The static was terrible. Only got about one word in three of the signal back to us. You'd think the back room boffins would have invented a field wireless that worked properly, even long distance. I mean, war's supposed to bring out man's inventiveness and all that. But that damn set sounded like it had banshees sitting inside it."

"Who were you talking to in Ceylon?"

"I haven't the foggiest. Didn't identify himself, or themselves, code or any other way. Which made me wonder. Did they think we were captured by Japs and being forced to make contact? With Cheng standing there watching the whole thing it felt a bit like that anyway. It sounded as if they were suspicious of him."

"He talked to them?"

"Tried to. No idea how much they got at the other end. What did come through didn't sound as though they were welcoming him into the Allied fold. Direct communications are all very well but, if everyone is suspicious of everyone else, I don't see how that gets us much further forward. We'll try with the code tomorrow. Which means I'll have to mug it up. Hate the damn things. Always have. Aunt Flora is well and sends you greetings. What's that translate to, eh?"

Hamish replied, "We are short of small arms ammo of all types."

"Memorized the whole book have you?"

"Nothing like. Is there any way you could have a go at the set while Cheng's out of camp?"

"Not unless I want to stop a bullet. He's left three armed men guarding the hut, two inside, one out as sentry."

"Does Kneale have access when he wants?"

"Only when the man he's training as operator is with him. That's an ex-schoolteacher from Singapore. Knows English well. Very much under Cheng's thumb. I couldn't get anywhere with the man."

Hamish came near to feeling sorry for the Major. So much of the boom had gone out of him, as though he was beginning to realize that his own false start with Cheng had doomed the mission almost to the point where it might as well be aborted. Only you can't just abort an operation when you are plunked down in the middle of jungle surrounded by an active enemy plus being ten weeks away from your submarine rendezvous date. For some time now the Major had said nothing about the plan, agreed on in Ceylon, that he was to remain in Malaya preparing the ground for the arrival of the British expeditionary force that was going to drive the Japs into the South China Sea. The scenario had been that Hamish, with Kneale and Hudson, were to work their way back to the west coast to catch the submarine out. Not very long ago the thought of leaving the Major on his own to the tender mercies of the guerilla leader wouldn't have disturbed Hamish too much, but it was beginning to. There was in this man the thing you can sometimes detect in people you don't know very well: a potential for martyrdom that is really just dressed up stubbornness, with duty sanctified into a religion. As a bad soldier himself, Hamish was quite ready to admit that this could well be the only way to win wars, for certainly if you were caught in one, and took time out for anything like gaining perspective on it, you either got shot or saved yourself by making a beeline for neutral territory in which to sit it out.

"Must get some shut eye," the Major said. "Bloody awful night."

It was almost a relief when the snoring began. Hamish left the hut quietly, as one might a nursery.

*

He was up on the ledge when the explosions started. He felt an intruder, almost a burglar, while he was in Cheng's cave, reaching over the folded bedroll to the rock shelf on which the brass-bound telescope lay together with a tin box holding a packet of Lucky Strikes with nine left in it. British matches were wrapped in oil cloth for protection against damp. He took one of the cigarettes, certain that Cheng would remember precisely how many he had left in the pack, used one of the matches, possibly also counted, then went out to sit in a kind of rock-hewn throne, the view from it offering a Devil's choice of at least three Malayan sultanates. He had almost finished the cigarette when there was a flash, bright white even against sunlight, followed by the thump of a land mine going off, then another, then a third.

He went back into the cave for the telescope but, before it was focussed, the battle had switched to grenades, the noise of these exploding amongst trees like distant whip cracks. Automatic fire reached him in indulations of different intensity, as though heat thermals were interfering with the sound waves. He couldn't see anything at all beyond a drift of dust from the land-mine eruptions — the action taking place on a stretch of road hidden by jungle — but he could hear the violence, his imagination providing the visuals. There were four more big explosions and afterwards twin columns of black, oily smoke slowly appeared, rising straight up before being caught by some stray breeze that pulled them down from the peaks and bent them over towards Kuala Lumpur as though in an appeal for help.

A spotter plane did come, but not for at least half an hour; it was a single-engined job making a noise like a motorbike, circling a point in the mountains in a kind of futile pinpointing and then giving up and flying off home again. As the sun grew hotter, Hamish left the rock chair for the shade of a straggle of scrub growth; stretched out in it, but not to sleep, he let the hours slide away from him in a luxury of self-indulgence, almost conscious of each minute's pushing the war towards its inevitable finish without his ineffective assistance.

It was half-past three when he stood up. He had missed the main meal of the day but felt rested and not hungry. He slowly made his way down the steep drop, his arms and legs still under the influence of lethargy. The flies found him when he was fifty yards from the latrines and convoyed him to the camp, which seemed empty, no one moving on the parade ground, as though Cheng's absence permitted a stretched-out siesta hour. In his role as camp ghost, Hamish usually skirted the parade ground, staying in tree shadow, but now he walked straight across, past the ruined longhouse, and had almost reached his hut when there was a crackling of trampled undergrowth and men's voices. He stood waiting.

Cheng came out of the rain forest first, the uniform he had devised for himself black with sweat and the cap with its three stars gone. He was followed, at some distance, by a straggle of guerillas, then two men supporting a third, then one man supporting another. At the very end of the column was teak-face and, just in front of him, a boy in a torn white shirt and khaki shorts, his legs bare and bleeding. The boy's black head was bent, but he raised it suddenly to look around the camp, then to stare at Hamish. It was Angus Gourlay.

PART
FIVE

Ruth

ONE

It was always the same when the jungle took him, a travel-
ler's palm he had bumped trembling for a moment, then
in the windlessness denying it had ever waved a frond.
She only heard him for what seemed seconds, though it was
probably minutes, before the aggressive, daytime, insect
hum of the rain forest denied her this evidence as well. It
was like a death rehearsal each time, the sudden disappearance, the voice gone of which there might soon be no record except in her mind.

At these times she did what she had done before: turned
back towards the hut, passing the garden where the weeds
almost shouted for her to stop; but she was not looking at
them, or at the rows of vegetables — the successful pump-
kins, corn, and sweet potatoes, the eggplants and the ram-
pant cucumbers. The failures lined up for inspection, too,
delicacies that were to have been her special interest in a
jungle clearing — celery, the small white turnips, the radishes, all suffering from tropical elephantiasis, huge, gross,
the radishes especially, swollen to the size of tennis balls
and wooden to the knife. She passed the banana palms, a big
clump planted by the Sakais who had been here but had not
stayed long enough for their crops to use up the natural
nutrients in the soil, so that secondary growth soon shaded
the ground, protecting it from the sun's bleaching. Big John
had cut down the scrub and had even done some digging
before they knew for certain they would be coming to the
hide.

She wouldn't remember with nostalgia this hut in which

she had sat out a war. The Sakais had left behind one of their least pretentious housing units: two rooms and a three-foot-wide porch, the whole mounted on poles pushing it eight feet above the ground. It was floored with fat, round bamboos set with half-inch gaps between each, which made for good drainage if the roof leaked or if there were domestic accidents. At the time of the Gourlay takeover, most of the attap roof had gone, and what was left was stripped and replaced by tarred felt that gave off a strong smell when the sun warmed it up, but had the advantage of not harbouring the usual huge assortment of crawling insects, including four-inch centipedes. Access to the porch had been provided by a bamboo pole ladder, but Ruth had insisted on wooden steps and a wooden floor in the eight-by-six living area, though she accepted the poles where they slept. The four window openings now had fitted shutters that could be dropped quickly in a sudden sumatra; in the daytime these were held up on long poles and helped to provide shade.

The ritual Ruth established each time John went back to the mine, or into the jungle with his gun to hunt for the pot, was music, and it always started with the same music, a worn record of Kirsten Flagstad singing Isolde's "Liebestod." In spite of Ruth's necessary lie that Wagner had been a Norwegian, John was for some reason suspicious, as though even to musically deaf ears the Teutonic undertones were audible and he wasn't going to have German music anywhere near him. For her the record opened a door into the past where increasingly she lived, there not being much alternative. It was John's past, too, she conjured up, even though he might no longer care to acknowledge parts of it.

The gramophone had its own shelf in the hut's living room but it was more often on the porch, where Ruth sat with her legs thrust out and her back against a wall, ready to crank the handle when a weakening mainspring demanded as much. A supply of steel needles found protection against jungle damp in a greased paper from an emptied butter tin. The soundbox was temperamental, sometimes for no understandable mechanical reason rejecting Miss Flagstad's high notes, sending out instead shrieks from a torture chamber. On other playings it allowed the singer full range. Listening was a gamble.

Ruth changed the needle and, while violins were still toying with the central theme, felt certain that this was going to be one of the machine's better days, allowing her to close her eyes while she let that big voice challenge the vast indifference of the rain forest with the rising and falling pulse of love.

In the tropics a recollection of snow to someone who has once been used to it whips up a nostalgia for that sense of purging that comes with the first serious snowfall — dirty old cities, their sins temporarily forgiven, allowed to wear white until the next thaw. It was from snow and listening to *Tristan and Isolde* — or rather the postscript to snow, hard frost and hard stars — that she had come up the steps of a Boston brownstone to John Gourlay. He had been a stranger, standing all alone over a floor hot-air vent just beyond the arch from the hall to the living room; very tall, his face looked both young and worn at the same time, as though from a slight excess of living. They'd stared at each other, unsmiling, until he'd said, "Hello."

Aunt Maud had arrived, bustling, before Ruth could say anything, her skirts with that special crackle they seemed to keep for company. She was carrying a tray laden with coffee things and a chocolate cake, but made her announcement before she laid it down.

"This is your cousin John."

"Hello," Ruth said then. "I didn't know I had a cousin John."

He still hadn't smiled, his voice serious. "You have to go a long way back for the link. To Scotland. About a hundred years ago."

"A link's a link," Aunt Maud said. "He's our cousin. From Malaya."

"Where?"

"You haven't heard of it?" he asked.

"I don't really know. I've always been terrible with geography."

"Singapore mean anything?"

"Yes, of course, I know where that is. Well, sort of."

"I'm a few hundred miles to the north."

"He lives in the jungle surrounded by tigers," Aunt Maud said. "And he's staying here."

John smiled, but his smile didn't quite take away the slightly worn look.

"That's very kind of you. But I've got this hotel room. All my things are in it."

"Then you can just fetch them out again. No kinsman of ours is going to come to Boston and stay in a hotel. I just won't hear of it. So there. How do you like your coffee?"

He had come off the hot-air ventilator, but only just. He liked his coffee strong, with a touch of cream. When herded to a chair, he chose one that was too low, and sat with his knees sticking up like twin peaks.

"Emmeline's already fixing up the guest room," Aunt Maud announced. "That's the coloured girl who opened the door to you. I call her a girl, but she's been here twenty-three years. A good while before Ruth was born. I like a stable house with things that don't change too much. Ruth's mother's dead. She was married to something of a no-good. It happens in all families. He's dead now, too. I didn't weep. Ruth's at Vassar. Did she tell you?"

"I haven't had time to tell him anything."

"Oh. Well, there will be a lot of time later. Would you like to telephone right now, Cousin John? To the hotel?"

"Aunt Maud, maybe he doesn't want to stay with us? Maybe he wants to be free?"

"There's no point in being free in Boston. This isn't New York. We have standards. Ruth, why didn't you ask Harold in when he brought you home from that concert, or opera or whatever it was?"

"His mother's waiting up for him."

"Oh. Now there's a steady boy. Do you like music, too, Cousin John?"

"Not really. You don't hear much where we are. I suppose I've never got used to it."

Even as a ghost, Aunt Maud never lost definition, nor her voice its crackle. That is one kind of immortality even if it only lasts a generation. Big John had phoned the hotel and then went back to it, arriving at his cousin's for the second time, but now with his suitcases in the hotel's huge Daimler limousine imported from Europe. Aunt Maud had watched from the front windows, ready to challenge him the moment he came down from settling in and washing his hands.

"Cousin John, do you have an automobile out there in Malaya?"

"Not yet."

"Well, don't get one. If this craze goes on they'll just be the ruin of America. And there isn't one thing you can't do taking streetcars."

"You quite like an electric brougham," Ruth said.

"No, I don't. I ride in one sometimes, but I still don't like it. It's far too fast. If you're passing shops, you can't see what's in the windows. Cousin John, what do you like for breakfast? You can have English bacon and eggs if you want."

"How about Scotch porridge?"

"That, too, I guess. Though I'd have to instruct Emmeline...."

Kirsten Flagstad had stopped but the record went on with a scraping noise in the special groove, which meant that you were wasting the needle. Ruth reached out and lifted the arm up.

Three members of a tribe of grey monkeys who lived within neighborhood range had come over for an exercise session in one of the trees edging the clearing. She wondered once again whether it was the singing that had attracted them. They began making a loud enough noise of their own, screeching; the smallest and probably the youngest went in for wild leaps and drops, reaching out to catch a vine when only feet from smashing into the ground.

John had shot one on a day when he could get nothing else, bringing it back saying that monkey meat was quite good; he'd eaten it a few times. She had looked at the little hands, one of them clenched, and told him to take it away and bury it.

*

Probably one of the reasons why I've never wanted to go back with John to the mine is that I couldn't bear to see my gardens. I've never asked him about them and he has never volunteered anything, or not much, as though all he noticed was the emptiness of the looted house. He said he had never realized what a weird shape our living room was until he saw it stripped of everything except my Boston tallboy which, for some reason, has been left. Maybe the looters saw the powder on the floor underneath and thought the thing would just crumble if they tried moving it. I wonder what's happened to my elephant table? Burned most likely, too big to move far. The one thing John did tell me about the garden was that there had been a huge bonfire in the middle of the canna bed nearest the house. He said he made out a charred piece of our camphor-wood wardrobe in it, and picture frames.

Maybe I had too much of my treasure in this world and had to learn to live without it. Oh, you pious bitch, you, Ruth Gourlay! I'm damned mad that most of my best things got burned up, but at the same time part of me says that it doesn't matter two cents.

I'm developing a real feeling for the sweet potato, somehow highly moral as plants go, and that's saying a lot for a plant in the tropics. There isn't a growing thing that knows better how to adapt itself to a sudden crisis. We were eating from these, roots and leaves, long before anything else was ready except the bananas. Bananas breed like rabbits. Maybe that's why I never allowed any in the kept areas at Sungei Dema. I didn't want to be reminded all the time of that terrible fecundity. I can see now that I kept those mowers going on blue jungle grass because I needed an open field of fire against any threats of assault from the jungle, the things I had expelled trying to sneak back again.

It could be that gardeners play a kind of theological game. Out into the enduring dark goes anything that gets the weed rating, while we welcome the bright lily to everlasting joy in a heaven with perpetually tidy edges to its borders.

I can remember when I read Thoreau's *Walden* that I could not take all that breathing with leaves and nature's heavy heartbeats and whatnot, and yet I'm getting a bit like it, maybe as part of a frenzied attempt to keep my body and mind occupied. Though it's not really all that easy to fantasize about a clearing in the jungle. Nature isn't slow enough in this heat for you to work up a thing about watching the little green shoots pushing their way slowly out through the dirt. Here you go to sleep leaving a patch of bare ground and next morning there's something a foot high there, already looking threatening.

I have never got over missing snow. In Omaha, sometime around three in the morning, I once got out of an overheated Pullman car to walk almost alone on the platform, breathing the air that cuts you as you take it in. There had been plenty of snow in the Rockies, but picture-postcard stuff — looked at, not felt. In Omaha I suddenly seemed to be inhaling America again, even if that freshness was just slightly tinged with coal smoke from the engine. My car porter shouted his "all aboard" as a special threat to me while he pretended to pick up his little stepping stool to take it up into the vestibule. When I got to him it was to be told that I shouldn't be walking by myself on station platforms at this time of night, even in the Midwest. Ever since San Francisco, he had called me Miss in spite of evidence to the contrary. Roy was in the berth above, my four-year-old who had stared at that bunk as it was being made up the first time, and then shouted: "I won't sleep on a shelf!" The porter had said: "That's where you're going to sleep, son," and had thrown him up.

There'd been dawn light edging the green blinds on my lower-berth windows when I woke. I'd raised one of them. We must have been moving into eastern Iowa, flat lands, or if not exactly flat, rolling in long, low almost imperceptible mounds, corn country sheeted white now, the clumps of farm houses and big barns and the shelter belts of trees all looking as though they had been excused work by snow. I'd been a stranger visiting from a place where nature's tempo doesn't allow for any rest at all, and suddenly I found myself hating what I had left in Malaya, a sun that never wanes to make seasons. Though this wasn't my part of the

States, under snow it had become the home I had earlier lost. Sitting bolt upright on that berth, my back propped by pillows, I wept for what I had been missing without really knowing it, wishing — in spite of Roy in that bunk above me, in spite of John fighting in the war in Europe from which he might not return — that I had never come back that night in Boston to a tall man standing over a hot-air grille, had never heard of him, had been left immune, free to stay in my own place from which a world beyond America was something you didn't think about too much. This has been my only real heresy from love, but it has recurred.

I seem to sit out wars — the first one in Boston, this one here — but there are parallels between the two situations, wildly different though they may seem. Boston, even back then, was suddenly subject to change, as though that war across the Atlantic was taking from us more than young men; something else was being sucked out of America that wouldn't be returned: our immunity. Before Pearl Harbour, Fay said something about how wonderful it must be to be an American knowing that whatever happened Hitler could never really reach your world. It wasn't very perceptive of her, and my protests seemed to embarrass her more than anything else, making her want to shut down the subject. I couldn't really explain that in 1917, living in Aunt Maud's house, I had an almost continuing sense of being on the edge of a change that was going to do more than put cracks in the solid-seeming things that had endured for long enough; it was going to bring some of them tumbling down. It had happened then, and now it's happening again. And back in that brownstone flanked by others as immaculately respectable, we felt the first small tremors domestically: the home wounded by Emmeline's death, and the hopelessness of trying to find anyone else who could ever begin to fill her role. I can hear Aunt Maud, suddenly much older, with the whip crack gone from her voice, saying, "It seems people don't know how to find their place anymore, and fit into it."

I wonder what keeps me from making the same protest now? There is a much bigger crumbling around me than Aunt Maud could ever have imagined, but in a funny sort of way it's almost as if I had been innoculated against the shock. Or at least semi-prepared for it, perhaps because during all these years of making my contribution to the Gourlay dynasty I have had the secret feeling that it couldn't and wouldn't last.

It was a feeling that used to hit me particularly when we were being social, not so much in our own home as away from it. We would go down for one of those weekends in Kuala Lumpur: golf for John in the afternoon; Saturday sundowners at the Dog, the bar packed with the men, the women in wicker chairs all along those verandahs looking out over the grass of the padang towards that mock-Moorish administration building. And suddenly it all seemed just a performance on which the curtain could drop anytime. Everyone, including me, maybe even especially me, was hard at it, acting out parts without good lines, and some of the drunks with no lines at all. Hamish got pie-eyed on those evenings, as though away from his Lalis and his orchids he could only blunder about putting on a caricature of the Scot who has made it about a third of the way up his particular ladder and is liable to stick there until the end. I can remember thinking before John hired him what an unattractive little man he was, and I was really quite angry when I heard he would soon be walking the sacred turf of Sungei Dema with the right to be there.

I'm not imagining the feeling that things couldn't last. It has been with me all my time in Malaya, and probably accounts for my reputation as an organizer. I'm not an organizer at all and in any setting that was a continuation of the one I was born to I'd have probably just gone on living in terms of house and garden, garden and house. Out here I've had to operate domesticity on such a large scale that it almost ceased to be that, though sometimes my roles in things like the village clinic have seemed basically fraudulent to me, just necessary as time-eaters.

K.L. gossip had shallower roots than most gossip; you can't really get deeply interested in the affairs of transients, which is what nearly all the women on those verandahs were. I can't remember meeting a single one who regarded Malaya as her real home. Home was a kind of fantasy, some place in England, with their real social backgrounds upped a few notches, often a lot more than a few, to give credibility to their current roles as memsahibs. A big part of the game on those verandahs was de-notching the woman opposite you, establishing her real "home" level. They were trained experts at it. The fact that none of them had the expereince of the States to put me firmly in my compartment was an irritation to them; the best they could do was classify me as a total outsider. Also, married into a tribe some of whose members lived permanently in Malaya, I was totally without that dream of a twelve-room thatched cottage down an English lane, which made their oddness rub off on me. And, though I never really heard even echoes of this, there must have been talk about the Gourlay Chinese blood.

The curious thing is that John, who positively loves bragging about Josephina, would move in to knock the head off anyone who called him a Eurasian. I honestly believe that in his lifetime no one ever has, and he is totally unconcerned about this streak in his bloodlines. I'm not so sure that Roy is as unconcerned about it. I probably made a big mistake in never talking to him about his ancestress, somehow avoiding the subject, not as taboo, but as something left for John to deal with. And, of course, John didn't really deal with it at all, just made a kind of conversational feature of the pragmatic Gourlays who started themselves off as a local institution via a dusky-skinned bride with money bags behind her.

I don't think thoughts of Josephina worried the other children at all, though I can't really be certain of that. When your young have grown up, all the things you felt sure about concerning them seem to slide away and you're left with a big "I don't know." I was probably closer to Roy than to any of them, but some time in his teens he closed a door that never really got opened again. And when he used to come home from school in Sumatra and make what was very nearly a beeline down to see Hamish, I went through a period of almost outrage that my boy was being indoctrinated by a man whose values I saw as pretty close to the disreputable. I needn't have worried. Roy closed that door, too, in his own time, almost as though he had taken what was useful from the relationship, then had no further need of it. Before he married Fay I had the feeling sometimes that Roy saw his father as a bully. I don't know what he saw me as. The complement of his father, perhaps? And, God knows, that's what I always have been.

*

The radio had its own small hut at the edge of the clearing, one built like a temple to house the voice that came to them not through a speaker but earphones, and sometimes spirit faint, unbelievable as human, sounding instead like a huge sea sighing between them and its source. Twice a week they listened; occasionally, in an outbreak of indiscipline, three times, but always only to the news, the temptation of other programmes put firmly behind them. The voice was from All-India Radio, was British, and therefore the unchallengeable truth. John, who had scant faith in Old Country governments after what any of them could do to damage the price of tin, nonetheless accepted certain British institutions as unassailable towers of virtue, and broadcasting had become one of these. The standards that applied in Britain would have been translated to the largest colony and words from such a source could be taken as gospel. He dismissed Ruth's suggestion that the Allies might not only have heard of propaganda but could actually be using it. "*Not* in the news," he said.

He wrote down everything that seemed relevant to their part of the world, but it was depressing how little of this there seemed to be, not a hint yet of anything that could be interpreted as a plan for the re-invasion of Malaya, a campaign to recapture Burma almost certainly having to come first. John had a theory that Burma could be left for the time being, the effort concentrated instead on taking the Isthmus of Kra in lower Siam, and using this as a base from which to strangle Jap supply lines north, then turning our forces south to penetrate Malaya, preferably coming down the east coast to make Sungei Dema a strong point. Ruth knew that with someone else he would have enjoyed discussing strategy but had decided long ago that their intimacy wasn't of the kind that probed to all quarters of their respective minds, so he contented himself with drawing maps on which large arrows pointed this way and that.

The radio was powered by a car battery, with a reserve up on a shelf to keep it from the damp. In spite of that reserve and strict rationing of the set's use, somewhere up ahead, and perhaps not too far ahead, was the day when that thin wheeze of a voice wouldn't reach them through the hiss of an aerial sea. Then the clearing would become the prison it hadn't yet become, the only news of the war reduced to wild, Jap-fomented stories of endless Allied defeats, and relayed by a credulous Hang who was coming to believe them in spite of what John told him of the "truth."

The set in its shrine was a terrible temptation on the days when John was away for hours. She had never offered to go with him, even on the hunting expeditions, knowing that he needed the time away from her and away from the play-acting of their imitation life in hiding, the pretence at domesticity, the dozens of little ways they both found to water down the thick intensity of an hour-by-hour relationship that was, for her at least, totally unrelieved by any other human contact. The temptation of the radio was the temptation of another voice, *any* voice. The set seemed to send out a continuous signal to her from its roofed shed as might a whisky bottle on a shelf to a would-be reformed alcoholic. She set herself tasks to keep the devil's voice at bay, two rows of sweet potatoes to be weeded before she even considered going over to put on those earphones and turn knobs. As the thirst became almost ungovernable, she told herself that, even if she gave way to sin and groped with dials for that voice, probably all she would get would be hobgoblins shrieking with glee at her failure. And the battery would be wasting.

When John was away from camp, and with the first hours of solitude behind her, she began to long for him again. It was still, in spite of the years in his bed, her pregnancies, the angers between them, a feeling that had kept its connection with that first shock of love. There were times when she resisted an invasion of emotional privacy, almost ready to classify it as an absurdity, habit put on a pedestal. And yet it wasn't habit. For her feeling hadn't rusted; it lost lustre sometimes, even seemed gone, as it did after one of his Malay women, but its return was almost humiliatingly inevitable. She would come out onto the shadowed verandah at Estate House to find him sitting in one of the big chairs, humped over, apparently desolate in his isolation, and an anger so carefully maintained would suddenly drain away in a terrible panic that he was weeping.

Once he had tried to explain with a great many words and some surprising flights of fancy, which nonetheless all boiled down to a simple statement of physiological fact. It wasn't at all that he was bored with her body, just that every now and then he became interested in another body as well. She remembered being surprisingly smitten by an almost uncontrollable desire to laugh, but for the sake of her own prestige had suppressed this, had offered her body again instead of her mockery, and it had been good, better, she hoped, than with any of his whores.

Almost as though it was the only surprise left to them in this pattern, he never came out from the jungle wall in the same place, and this time she didn't really see him emerge at all, his big frame almost part of an extending shadow until he was actually walking the path between the vegetables and a row of cannas she had brought from Sungei Dema but which had stubbornly refused to flower. She put down the chunkle and went towards him. He looked more than tired.

"The Japs know we're here, Ruth."

TWO

After what he had told her, she lay awake in the dark, though he slept. There was a wind, but it didn't really penetrate with any strength down into the clearing. Little eddies of it broke from the main flow, like visiting animals on small missions of malice, rattling pots left in the under-house cooking area, banging a loose board on the radio shack, and finally, as though bored with everything else, mounting a minor attack on the little house itself, a flurry of warm air lifting one side of the white netting to make a passage for mosquitoes.

Like John, she slept naked. The mosquitoes stopped their whining as they settled on her legs. She whacked at them and they whined again, coming nearer her face. John stirred and began a mumbling to which he was prone in sleep, not actual words, but sound that seemed to come to the very brink of sense, then withdraw from it. She had once told him that under anaesthetic he would reveal the horrid truth about himself, and he hadn't been amused, which immediately had her wondering what he had still managed to keep hidden after all their years together.

Now he might be interrogating someone, probably Hang, and with suitable pauses for the replies. He had come back from that day's contact with his mine foreman disturbed by much more than the idea of the Japs about to start an active search for the stay-behind Gourlays. What really troubled him were the clear signs that Hang, who had almost been a symbol of John's continuing control of Sungei Dema, was moving towards a kind of defection. It wasn't that the man was able to betray them, leading the Japs to their hide. He couldn't do that; the hide he knew the way to wasn't the one they were using.

The false camp had been Hamish's idea, insurance against what might be happening now: the Japs' picking up a rumour that the Gourlays, though deposed, hadn't fled their kingdom. The site chosen was more than half a mile nearer Sungei Dema than the Sakai clearing and there was no hut, just a huge, ex-army bell tent that had been roughly floored with planks, everything inside and around about arranged to suggest that the decision to stay behind had been a sudden one, inadequately prepared. Under sagging canvas they had left cases of tinned food, one of John's old guns, a short-wave radio and battery; and outside were pointers to occupations for some time, including the heaped ash of wood fires. The Japs, finding the place, could be expected to believe that the two who had used it were now victims of the jungle.

It was maddening the way mosquitoes always rejected Gourlay blood when hers was available. She sat up to slap them and the bamboo creaked.

"What's the matter?" John asked.

"I'm being bitten. And you've been talking in your sleep again."

"Oh."

The news always seemed to make him uneasy.

"To Hang, I expect. From the tone of your voice."

"The tone of my voice? What's that mean?"

"Just that I'm sure it wasn't one of your Malay women."

There was more bamboo creaking as he rolled over on his back. She could see his shape and the position of his head on the hard pillow. He seemed to be staring up at the faintly white ceiling of their net tent. The wind flurries came and went and Ruth whacked at mosquitoes coming in to land, but otherwise there was silence. It went on for a long time, a reproof to her for having re-opened what ought to have become a taboo subject. In their present circumstances his Malay women were irrelevant and should have been dismissed from her mind, which they hadn't been. After her earlier, sympathetic understanding of his worries about Hang, he was at a total loss to account for this new middle-of-the-night mood, though it was just like a woman to move to the attack when her man was still half-groggy with sleep. She could feel his resentment building up, though he was determinedly capping the pressure with silence while he organized his defences. Before the Japs came he'd had a fairly simple formula for bringing one of these surprise flare-ups under control: the offer of a distraction from their usual patterns, perhaps a weekend up at Frazer's Hill where they could wear sweaters in the evening and toast their feet in front of a log fire. Or there was the alternative of a longer trip to the Cameron Highlands and, if the stress situation looked as if it might become chronic, a husband could always suggest Australia, that mecca for discontented Southeast Asia wives.

Ruth wasn't discontented and never had been. She would ten times rather be with him now in this jungle hut than safe in Sydney with Fay, two women getting up each morning determined not to talk about their men still in Malaya.

"I think you're worrying too much about Hang," she said, her tone calm.

"Oh?"

He remained aggrieved, silent for at least a minute before he said, "He's changed a lot. Secretive in a way he never was."

"John, he's afraid of the Japs. Like everyone else. And they've interrogated him twice."

"I keep thinking about what could happen if they interrogate him again."

"Well, supposing he does talk? And takes the Japs to the tent site. Hang doesn't know that we don't live there. Hamish would never allow him to get even a hint that we were pushing on beyond it. And I'm sure he didn't. So at the tent site the Japs would simply find what we meant them to. They're not going to start looking for our bones in the jungle."

"No," John said. "Especially if they have Hang's confession that he saw me only a day or two earlier."

"Why have you completely lost faith in the man?"

"I don't know. Perhaps because of the position he's in. Living on there in the empty village. And the Japs keep coming back to see him. Supposedly on inspections of the mine, but it's flooded. No use to them. They've got all the tin they could possibly need. And there's a new commandant in Kuantan now. A Captain Oiishi, who seems fascinated by Sungei Dema. He's been all over it. They've even been digging in parts of your garden."

"For gold bars we buried along with the family silver?"

"Whatever they think they're doing has got Hang more than just jumpy. They come back at night sometimes. He sees car lights making either for our house or for Roy and Fay's. It must be weird to see the houses from the village when they are suddenly lit up again by pressure lamps. He told me that one night the Japs were there for hours and seemed to be having some kind of party. Two carloads of them. When this sort of thing happens he has no one to talk to except that half-mad old woman who is supposed to cook for him."

"I don't think you should see Hang again."

"Ruth, I've got to go back to the mine!"

"All right, do it. But don't contact Hang when you do. He's not giving us any real information now. Just rumours. And they don't do us any good. If the Japs are baiting a trap with Hang, and you don't meet him, you won't run into it."

She might then have added a question about what would happen to her if the Japs caught him. They hadn't even skirted the edges of discussing this, as though it was something he refused to consider. She considered it, but in silence, particularly when he was away from the camp — and not just during his visits back to Sungei Dema, but also when he was hunting, when the risk wasn't from the enemy but from any of a hundred things that could happen to a man alone in the rain forest.

She knew that if he didn't come back from half a day away with his gun and she went looking for him within the radius of the one mile he said he always kept to, her chances of finding him weren't even one in a thousand. The thick undergrowth beneath the tall hardwoods was padding to your cries; it threw them back at you, already half-muffled. She had thought, too, about what she could do if she did find him in the jungle — perhaps with a broken leg, or un- conscious — and had decided on a form of stretcher she could make: two poles with a blanket nailed from one to the other, something she could drag with his heavy body on it. It might take her days to get him back but she would do it in the end. To have a plan ready to put into operation, even as rough a one as this, was a form of reassurance. And after an accident, if he was still conscious, he could signal with his rifle, though the ridged ground baffled this sound, too. More than once he had shot a game gird quite near the camp and she hadn't heard the noise.

The restraints between them, the matters never raised, had their own function in an emergency living. They were encircled by as many possibilities of what might happen as there were tree trunks in the fringe surrounding the clear- ing. Serious illness was one of them. The scheme they had embarked on contained elements of such sheer folly that it was best never to look at these, and on the whole she didn't.

Now with John admitting his own uncertainties, really for the first time since they had left Estate House, it was as though a valve had been opened on her own carefully hoarded confidence, allowing it to flow away. She lay beside her man gone silent realizing that it was the nights, when you woke in them, that were almost unendurable. In a way this was contributed to by your dreams, which were always of the old life, the norm, and you came awake, chilled by the pre-dawn wind, to an abnormal situation that for min- utes, hours even, appeared unendurable. The days were not nightmare-haunted. The routine available was purposefully kept crowded, loaded with a flurry of half-unnecessary do- mestic jungle bustle from which you moved on to fill more time in your garden. The play-acting under sun was con- tinuous and sometimes almost enjoyable. It was the dark's coming that put lead on your spirits, the need to eat your evening meal under the last flare of sunset, for afterwards there would be no proper light. The batteries in torches, the two pressure lamps, and the candles were all hoarded for the emergency that it was hoped wouldn't happen. You can't read by a campfire and the books she had brought were mostly unopened.

She could play her records but after twenty minutes of Mozart John would go creaking down the steps from their strip of verandah, apparently to urinate, but staying away for so long that she would end by lifting the arm off the record to ask whether he was all right. From a distance the answer would come that he was fine, and she was to go on enjoying the music, which was as good as a guarantee that she wouldn't.

"Maybe we should move," he said. He'd been thinking too. "Get out of here."

"*What?* John, you can't mean that?" When he said nothing she added: "The idea's impossible!"

"No, it's not. The Sakais do it all the time."

"Well, I'm not a Sakai!"

Again he went quiet.

"John! We will just not talk about moving from here! How would we eat for one thing? I've got this garden going."

He took time to consider that. She snatched his conclusion from him.

"Don't tell me the Sakais make a new garden every year!"

"Well, they do."

"Oh, God!" A moment later she added: "And that's a prayer for patience."

"You and your prayers," he said.

"It could have been my prayers that kept me from packing two suitcases and going back to Boston. Ending the experiment of this marriage."

"Experiment? You've got a son in his thirties."

"So what? The experiment goes on until one party drops out! Look, I know my name's Ruth, but I think I've stretched that 'whither thou goest I will go' thing just about as far as it can be stretched. And that means that Grannie Gourlay is not setting off into unknown jungle behind her man with a minimal survival pack strapped to her back. I'm staying here, *right* here. And that means that you damn well better, too."

"All right," he said.

She wished she could see his face, but moonlight was reaching them third-hand, filtered by the tops of trees and then through a propped-out shutter. He was on his back still and, maddeningly, would soon be asleep again, having resolved an argument by suddenly giving in to her, thus sponging the matter from his brain. Too often she had won too easily, like this, which left her with the nagging worry that she might be wrong, while he remained composed in spite of his certainty that she *was* wrong. Hamish had once said that the Gourlays all had the great gift of owning themselves completely. As was true of many of the man's pronouncements that had rather irritated her at the time, it was only later on that she appreciated just how shrewd he was.

"John! Don't go to sleep!" Her voice was loud. He said nothing.

"If you don't see Hang again, I'm sure everything will be all right. Don't you agree?"

"No."

"Why not?"

"What's Hang going to think when I don't show up?"

"Does it matter what he thinks?"

"It could. He might put two and two together and decide we weren't at the tent camp. And never had been."

"Why?"

"Because half the stuff he carried to the tent site isn't there now."

"So he'd realize the tent site was just a staging post?"

"Yes," he said.

"He still wouldn't have any idea where we are."

"No. But he could make an intelligent guess as to how much farther into the jungle we went."

"To tell the Japs?"

"Could be. If I don't meet him he'll think one of two things: that I've stopped trusting him, or that something has happened to us. Either way he's going to start thinking about his own skin."

"How do you mean?"

"If we're dead there's no point in protecting us. He might as well lead the Japs to the tent site and get some kudos from that. And if he thinks I've stopped trusting him he's going to get angry, isn't he? I know him well enough. From anger he could do anything."

"John, you had complete faith in this man! You wouldn't listen when Hamish begged you not to use him."

"We had to use someone to get that stuff at least as far as the tent site. And I had no idea then what the Jap occupation was going to do to people, especially the Chinese."

After a moment Ruth asked, "If we stay here you're going to go on seeing Hang?"

"Yes."

She was certain that he was waiting for her to ask what plans he had made for them if she agreed to leave the Sakai clearing. She wasn't going to ask that. She was damned if she would.

*

The clearing was on a gradient that climbed quite steeply at its north end, which helped to counteract the feeling of living at the bottom of a well, but there was still no view from any part of it. The sense of imprisonment became acute sometimes, especially during the middle of the day when there was no hope of a breeze. It was then that it seemed to Ruth the rows of her plants went limp, leaves drooping, even the sweet potatoes for a time discouraged, all doing what she was — gasping for breath. During those hours when it was senseless to move, John usually lay on the hard-packed ground under the hut, nothing but a straw mat under him and, as she kept pointing out, at risk from snakes. She was above, on the narrow verandah where there was a chance some fluke movement of air would reach her body through the gaps between the bamboo poles. She wore nothing but an old yellow cotton sarong bought from a village bazaar; it was loose, a protection against insects, but her breasts were bare, their undersides sweat traps. By her was a basin of water and every now and then she wrung out a cloth to sponge herself

Though he was really just beneath, John and she never talked at these times, the physical effort of uttering words too much for them. She didn't sleep, though she occasionally experienced a trance-like state that hazed the present. If she let the sweat run, lying perfectly still, she was able to make journeys to coolness, even to snow.

Sometimes she made a conscious effort to think about her children — a kind of echo of that semi-religious duty of the letters to them on Sunday afternoons. Here, with the ritual of pen to paper denied her, and being cut off from Estate House and its nurtured associations with family, she was reminded of the king in *Hamlet,* on his knees in that gesture to prayer but lamenting that, though his words went up, his thoughts remained below. Hers refused to travel, staying stubbornly in a Sakai clearing, trapped by things like the possibility that her jungle cookery, largely based on a use of curry powder to disguise too pungent game, was almost certainly responsible for the loose bowels John had been complaining about for a week.

It was the impossibility of in any way sharing her childrens' current experience in living, whatever these might be, or of their even beginning to imagine hers, that seemed to push them into a remoteness much beyond the usual remoteness imposed on their adulthood. Even her sometimes sharp concern for Roy, possibly caught in Malaya, too, was something that didn't last long, quickly over-ridden by other pressures; fear for what might be happening to him was almost suppressed by fears that loomed much closer.

She had never laid claim to an intuitive understanding of how things were with any of her children when they were away from her, not once able to issue to a rapt audience of club verandah mothers a claim that, for example, when Roy had broken his leg at school over in Sumatra she had known a week before she got the letter. It could have been that all her potential for paranormal communication with another person had been used up keeping track of John, for it hadn't been the smell of cheap scent that had repeatedly betrayed him; she had known what was happening as surely as if he had sent off a telegram of announcement immediately after an illicit orgasm.

What had angered her so often was not the challenge to their love, but the challenge to her ability to give him pleasure, maddening because she knew that they had often been good together, even very good sometimes. She couldn't really begin to understand his curiosity about other bodies and how they might react to his body. It seemed possible that if she hadn't met John she might have worn all her life the label of a New England spinster dedicated to good works as a kill-time. But she *had* met John, and she had reacted, and so had he, and he still did, but this didn't put an end to his Malay girls. She knew that they had nearly all been Malay because once, with too much whisky in him, he had said that Chinese girls were highly professional but gave you nothing, whatever that meant. She had wondered about it quite often, but still hadn't come up with a satisfying answer and the one time she had raised the subject again, John had put on the Presbyterian expression he kept for funerals and had clamped his mouth shut.

God alone knew why she loved him, and went on with the process after all these years; there was no logical explanation at all, just as there was no conceivably logical explanation for someone with her background ending up in a hole in the Malayan jungle growing her own sweet potatoes and never getting her fingernails really clean. Accidents, accidents, and yet if he went into that wall of trees and never came out again, it wouldn't just be the desolation of her having been left alone, but an end to the core of her life, which was still John in her heart and mind as it had been from the time, after that first meeting in Aunt Maud's house, he started sending her postcards from Europe.

He hadn't seemed to think a lot of Europe. She could even remember the words printed carefully on the reverse of the picture of Chartres Cathedral: "Came to a service in this church, but didn't stay. Hope the weather is fine with you. Rainy here." And reading that inspirational message, she had been sick with longing for his presence, his arms around her as she had yet to experience them; she was ready to take the tigers if it meant she could share a house with him.

The snakes had been more of a problem than the tigers, which she had never actually seen, though the dogs screamed when any of the big cats were around. He had taken a ship back, not to New York, but directly to Boston, following a line that ran from Scotland, where he had been visiting roots that did little for him, to the dock where she had been waiting, trying not to look too eager and then, suddenly, with a wild joy, seeing the eagerness in him.

It didn't seem a hundred years ago, or ten, or thirty, or anything; it was just there, like their honeymoon was just there: the out-of-season hotel Aunt Maud had used twenty years earlier and thought would be just right, with the fall colours lovely. It had rained, a heavy autumnal rain making its last serious assault on Vermont before giving way to snow, and the dye used to tint the leaves that year had been of poor quality, leaving them streaky and pale. Nothing she had been looking forward to happened. They went self-consciously to bed — no pleasure for her and, she was pretty sure, none for him either — took long walks under dripping trees making what she would now classify as tea party conversation, coming back damp to keep their voices down in a dining room given over to the elderly taking advantage of the cheaper rates. When she had just about decided that if this was marriage it was awful, he suddenly had said, "Let's get to hell out of here."

They had gone to New York.

THREE

It was one of those dreams that don't just dissolve as you wake, but hang on as vague discomfort in the mind unless exorcized by remembered fact. In the dream, Ruth could leave neither Fay nor that ghost of her own yesterday's self walking down a seemingly endless corridor in the E. & O. Hotel in Penang. She'd had to take the two of them somewhere, if only into the dining room.

It had been a long thin room in an almost absurdly long, thin hotel in which nearly every window's view featured a blue-green sea seen through palms. A table for two pushed in against its own window had been unoccupied during all their meals, set and ready, but apparently for no one present. When story hunting on the island, Somerset Maugham and his male companion always sat there. Their waiter, a Goanese who looked as though he might be addicted to fetishes, told them this solemnly at their third dinner. Fay, starting on her soup, had said: "You'd think God came often for weekends."

Ruth could remember very clearly her reaction; mild shock, a kind of mental holding of her breath before she decided that the Almighty had no need to be defended against one of Fay's quiet, if odd, little jokes. She'd said nothing.

Fay had looked up suddenly. "Sorry."

They had both laughed.

I miss her more than any of my children, Ruth thought.

The escape to Penang for a whole week had come suddenly just days after Fay had been told in K.L. that she was pregnant again. They had been sitting by the pool at the Pink House, Ruth feeling what she could see now was a kind of granny's pleasure that, though Fay had taken her time about producing another Gourlay, she had got around to it in the end. After a second child the third would come more easily, a second pregnancy in many ways the hardest to face up to; you have lost that first frenzy of love with its intense biological urge to produce its symbol in living flesh and blood, and are instead inclined to remember with a certain acuteness the pain and stress involved. And that first frenzy of love hadn't ever been particularly obvious as something glowing between Fay and Roy. Certainly they had been living together for three months in Europe and America before they'd showed up at Sungei Dema but, even allowing for that, Ruth had expected to see more than she did — particularly, perhaps a transformation in Roy from a young man about Southeast Asia into a caring husband. For all she knew, then and now, he might actually have been caring enough, and Fay responsive enough, but if so it was behind a curtain hung in front of their marriage and with no areas on it that were in any way even faintly transparent, but firmly printed with a tidy, moderately attractive pattern. Even when they had disputes, all Ruth ever saw of these were the controlled postscripts; usually Fay gone quiet and Roy with what must be an almost maddening capacity to match and even surpass her quietness. It had seemed to Ruth sometimes that, compared to the Pink House, the old wooden bungalow on top of the hill simply pulsed with life and, of course, whenever silence threatened up there she just put on a record with a new needle until John came home, bringing his own noise.

Wearing shoes with crepe soles that would have made anybody else's feet too hot in this climate, the quiet, caring husband had come along the concrete slabs edging the pool, his eyes appropriately on the wife he had quite recently made pregnant. Looking up at her son as he stood beside Fay's chair, Ruth felt a shock that was almost physical. His eyes and his expression revealed satisfaction, just that, nothing more. For a moment she couldn't believe it.

The hand he put on his wife's shoulder was the hand of a man who has passed a crucial virility test just when he was beginning to have doubts about his potency.

A kind of black rage, that was partly against herself, came slowly over Ruth, never challenging her control, and her voice was quiet when she spoke. "Fay and I are going to Penang for a week. We both need a change."

Roy stared. "What do you need a change from?"

"Sungei Dema."

Fay was astonished, too. Then her expression altered, as though the understanding between them, usually real enough, had suddenly been vastly strengthened. "I think it's a lovely idea," she said.

Roy's protest was loud. "But what about Angus?"

"Your son has his father, his grandfather, and a highly competent amah. We're not going to Europe. Only to Penang."

He stared down at his wife. "Fay, you really want to do this?"

"Yes. I've said so."

They had taken the new Fiat touring car, which John always used with its black hood up, but Ruth had this lowered so that they drove in hard sunshine to the ferry at Jerantut and then up over the main range through a sudden shower that soaked them and left them chilled; then they drove down to the heat again and turned north at Kuala Kubu. They left the car at Butterworth and went over on the ferry. Their intention was to be massively inactive, nourishing their spirits with a view of water — one of the things Sungei Dema didn't have — but on their second night they met, in the hotel bar, a rancher from north of Casper, Wyoming, who ran uncounted head of cattle on a ranch the size of Rhode Island. His wife had just divorced him in Reno on the grounds of his devotion to cattle and even after alimony he was still rich enough to be able to take off suddenly to see if the world offered anything that Wyoming didn't. Sipping drinks out on Asia's longest hotel terrace, he allowed that in one or two places the world just might do that, though mostly it was terrible cattle country. The rancher had rented a car and kept taking Fay to the north coast beaches to swim while Ruth sat under a palm thatch umbrella reading Somerset Maugham.

On their sixth night, after the rancher had brought Fay back from a Chinese opera, Ruth said: "Wyoming sounds as though it might be a real change from Sungei Dema. Or have you grown sentimental about us?"

Fay said: "I think I've grown sentimental about you."

Dear Fay. Where was she now? Near Sydney? When she had time from the children, and from doing all the house-work and the shopping, would she be thinking about us, maybe?

"John? Are you awake?"

"Why?"

"What sort of provision did you arrange for Fay? Or did Roy?"

"Eh? What?"

"Money! In Australia."

"I don't know what Roy did."

"It never occurred to you there's a good chance he did nothing?"

"Mary Jane's out there. She'll look after Fay. But I'm sure Roy fixed up something."

"When did you last send Mary Jane any money?"

"I sent her a thousand pounds the month before the Japs invaded."

"Which could be all that the four of them have to live on for years."

"The war isn't going to last that long. And it's still a helluva lot of money, Ruth. And they could get credit."

"What on?"

"My name. The mine. We're a company. Even if the mine is flooded, the tin's there."

"In Japanese-occupied territory."

"Oh, to hell with that! I've told you, the war isn't going to go on and on."

He began heaving around.

"What's the matter?"

"I've got to pee."

Whenever he went out from under the net, he let the mosquitoes in. From the ladder came a shout: "What the hell?..." A moment later: "Fay! There's a fire. It's —"

He didn't finish. From the poles on the verandah, and still on her knees from having crawled out under the net, she saw the fire, a red glow in the sky from what could only be Sungei Dema. John was at the foot of the ladder looking up towards colour made sharply lurid by the black, serrated edging of jungle trees.

She knew it was Estate House. There was nothing else at the mine that could make such a huge bonfire. She could see her home burning, the flames leaping up from it like a volcano erupting there on the crest of its rounded hill, and probably running out from that centre crater into the neglected, tall, dry grass of what had been her lawns. She thought of the house as it had been when she first came to Sungei Dema: dark inside in spite of the open grounds surrounding it; the sprawling, verandah-shadowed bungalow of a widower whose son hadn't taken to breeding fast enough to please him, a delay that had risked the Gourlay line. She thought of the rooms they had added when the old man had died and the place was really hers: putting in new windows, pulling down partitions, choosing hardwoods that would be resistant to ants, buying furniture for those new rooms, having more furniture made, and quietly getting rid of the most hideous of the family heirlooms.

She should have felt that a huge part of her life was being burned away there on that hill, but she didn't. Wars took your houses. You could be thankful for the rings still left on your fingers and the strength still lasting in your body. It was John, rigid at the foot of the ladder, one hand out to hold onto it, who was smitten. Her heart wept for him, but there was nothing she could say.

*

She was weeding with a long hoe between the six-foot-tall rows of the new corn crop when he came down the steps from their hut, bending almost double to avoid the roof overhang, then straightening to show the survival pack already on his back. Fronds and the fattening ears of corn half-hid her, but he knew where she was all right. The hoe rang on one stone, then another. He went into the hut, still without turning his head, reaching up for something in the hanging cupboard, though she couldn't see what it was. He could take what he liked with him on this folly he was persisting in against all reason, against half a dozen arguments that all made sense separately and, together, added up to the improbability of his return. She had tried being quietly reasonable but he had simply withdrawn into the defensive silence he had used so damned effectively over the years, his only real cunning against her, but all he needed, as he had proven so often. Then, much louder, she had asked what he expected her to do if the Japs caught him? Was she to sit here waiting, opening tins of corned beef until these ran out some ten years before the triumphal return of the British Army? She had shouted that the Japs had set fire to Estate House for one reason, and one reason only: to flush him out of hiding, just as it was about to do. She hadn't said, however, that if he didn't go back to Sungei Dema she would be willing to play the Sakai wife, going into the jungle with him to find a new hide, taking only what they could carry. But if he had been waiting for her to say that, he could go on waiting.

She was aware then, hoe in hand, of the almost absurd symbolism of what she was doing; tilling the garden of the small shelter they had made for themselves, a shelter he was deliberately putting at risk by folly, against a surrounding malevolence. He had done the heavy digging for this garden, or most of it, but the rest was hers. They ate from the work of her callous-studded hands. Sometimes, when she was putting on what grease she could spare to reduce her skin's cracking, her hands shouted her age at her. She could leave the mirror hanging in shadow, never taking it out into hard light for what it had to tell, but her hands were always visible to her, becoming veined and brown-speckled on their backs. Grave marks, Aunt Maud had called those patches, not seeming to mind, probably thinking of a funeral with plume-decorated horses pulling the hearse and the usual hymns about immortality.

It isn't immortality I have ever asked of God, just His help. He isn't giving it to me now, is He? Dear God, stop that stubborn, stupid man from going to Sungei Dema!

Still in the hut, John was straightening the small pack on his back he always wore in the jungle, working it up to the right position between his shoulder blades. Ruth knew exactly what was in it: two tins of meat; hardtack biscuits they never used in camp, where she made corn bread on a griddle; a medical kit containing a field dressing and a small packet from their supply of sulfa powder; a water bottle; tablets for disinfecting jungle water if he had to use it; and a clean pair of socks. He also carried spare ammunition for his gun though he said he normally took this out when he left the .22 rifle at the edge of the jungle fringing Sungei Dema; he always went unarmed to his rendezvous with Hang. He had a stubborn faith, surviving even against the atrocity stories reaching them via Hang, that the old-fashioned codes of warfare were still being observed, that if, on capture, you were empty-handed you couldn't be branded a guerilla. Ruth would not believe this, saying that if the Japs caught you they could label you in any way that suited them before they shot you or cut off your head. The argument had ended with another Gourlay pronouncement: "Even the Japs have to consider world opinion after this war."

Through the corn silk that hung unmoving in the windless, rising heat she could see that he was ready to leave, but he went on loitering in the shade of the hut, as though there was something still left to be said between them and he was hoping that she would come out from half-hiding so that he could say it. As clearly as though she could read his mind, she knew that if she didn't go to him he would leave the camp without another word. She used the hoe again. Sweat rolled down her forehead. The band she usually wore below her hairline to keep the stinging drops from her eyes was hanging on a line near to where he was standing. She had the excuse to go towards him. She didn't use it.

He came down the path through the middle of the vegetable patch, not really moving much faster than the pace the jungle ahead would hold him to once he was in it. If he looked down the row where she was as he passed it, she didn't see him, for her head was bent over her work. When she did look up he was beyond their cultivated area, walking with his rifle slung from one shoulder, his back to her, through a section they had cleared but which the forest was continually contesting. She stared at him through the corn, thinking suddenly how often in their time together she had seen his back going away from her like this. She thought, too — and with a hope that it was the same for him — how you never see those you really love as getting old; in your eyes they are protected by a superimposed print of what they were once.

At the edge of the jungle he stopped but didn't turn. His arm came up in a signal to the woman he knew was watching, his palm open towards the wall of forest. They were ending another clash his way, by John's doing what he wanted. She had been going to call out to him, but didn't.

FOUR

I get scared at night when I'm not sleeping, threatened by a whole parade of little things that add up to something like a lump I've swallowed and can't digest. But fear comes from wanting to live. It's in the middle of the day in this damned well of jungle that you haul yourself up on the poles of this porch and lie down to hear your own exhausted heart thumping away with a threat in each beat. And you're old and alone, and what you feel isn't fear at all, for yourself or anyone else, just a sense of having overspent your credit, waiting for the creditor death.

Oh, God, I'm being dramatic, which means I don't really feel that way at all; just looking at myself pretending to feel that way. My heart's thumping all right, but it's not from a body worn out by what I've made it do, it's from fear. Not the little nighttime ones, but the big one, John. Oh, Christ, John! Don't start weeping. What good does it do? And he'll play safe. That's the way he'll react to the way we parted, so that he'll come back out of the jungle, sweaty but calm, wanting to know what's cooking for supper. He won't have to say he wonders what all the fuss was about, but the question will be evident in the way he looks at me with what he considers his quiet smile. Which is when I could get up from what I'm doing and kick him.

The damn formulas of marriage, tried and tested and normally to be relied on. It's only love that makes them endurable; nothing else could.

It's hotter today than it's ever been down in this hole. I swear it's hotter. Unless I've got a fever. I had my quinine yesterday and so did John. That's one thing we never forget, or at least he doesn't. What will happen when we run out of our supply? We'll get malaria, that's what will happen. John will say that the Sakais get it and then get better. I remember Hamish that time with a rigor on. He was between women, with no one to look after him but his old cook. John asked me to go down and there he was, not able to speak through chattering teeth, but still perfectly conscious, looking up at me doing my duty as lady of the manor. The amateur nurse had no treatment for his condition that he couldn't administer himself when those terrible vibrations had eased off, but I went out into that dirty kitchen to rage at the cook for not cleaning the pans properly and to make quantites of lime juice. About two gallons of the stuff. He said afterwards that he drank it all and it washed the virus away.

Why am I thinking about that? Oh, Sakais. I should have said I'd go. With a pack on my back, mostly full of our quinine supply. When John gets back will I say I'll go? Will I?

Would it really have been so awful to have been with Fay down in Australia, waiting for our men? Would I have spent most of my time feeling guilty from what I saw — though no one else would — as running away? They have big gardens outside Sydney; I could have dug there, working on my fantasy of John in my spare time, building it up, so that when the real man arrived after his jungle experience, not one piece of him would fit the fantasy and we'd probably have to divorce, to the slight distress of our adult children, who would think it somewhat unseemly.

My brain is melting and seeping out through pores with the sweat. These great trees are in a conspiracy to keep any oxygen from reaching me. The little breezes are our allies, sneaking past an encirclement of hardwoods. But at this time of day the breezes never manage to reach camp. They are always defeated by trees in alliance with full sun. The jungle's strategy against us is slow suffocation; and not just us, but everything we've brought, the things we've made grow that shouldn't be growing in this place. And the forest's malice isn't just directed at me for what I have done *here.* The catalogue of my crimes against it is long. At Sungei Dema I cleared that huge area and kept it clear over the years, getting up most mornings to more of the war, walking in triumph on mown grass at whose edges the advancing roots of trees were continually being amputated. These cousins of those trees hate me. Sometimes I'm sure I can see them move, inching in.

John says that when you start getting heat hallucinations, you ought to eat something — not much, just a few bites, the process putting you back inside your usual rational self. The trouble with this recipe is that you have to be sure you have a usual rational self to get back into, and I'm not sure I do. A rational me would have taken damn good care to see that I didn't end up where I am right now. And it wouldn't have let me fall in love with a big man standing on a hot-air vent. It would have defined what I felt then as simple sexual attraction, something to be worked off in a semester back at college by early morning sessions in the gym. But I didn't go back to college, as You know perfectly well, God Almighty.

It's hard in this place to believe that I'm still under His eye. It wasn't always easy at Sungei Dema either, with no fixed place in which to say the prayers John thought were merely my talking to myself. Maybe people of my kind need something like a cathedral in which to forget that small monkeys have tiny hands. Aunt Maud wasn't up against this problem at all, though. She didn't have a cathedral, just the Episcopal church two blocks over where they were particularly proud of their new organ. Her God was interested enough, up to a point, in the rest of the world, but He still managed to focus His main attention right down on New England. It wouldn't really have surprised her to learn that in the jungle He doesn't seem so readily available. She might even have said that sensible people didn't plan on living in parts of the world where He can't get to you easily. I can remember her announcing once that the Good Lord never sends us more than we can bear. Maybe, in her last five minutes, if she had been conscious, she would have endorsed that.

I miss her much as I miss America, and I guess I always

have. In America we have tornadoes and earthquakes and floods and terrible droughts sometimes, but we don't have this kind of jungle. And the things we do have include the continuity of a short history. You don't get lost in our history, or really frightened, even by things like the Civil War; and a very little attention brings it all into range. It's a manageable step from the Pilgrim Fathers and the First Thanksgiving to standing in school assembly every morning to say the creed: "I pledge allegiance to the Flag, and to the United States of America, and to the Republic for which it stands, one Nation, under God, indivisible, . . ." The schoolgirl believed that creed, and the young adult, clutching at sophistication with two hands, or what I thought was sophistication, went on believing it. That was my generation, I suppose. We went bright-eyed through our days and to our fate. What I read of the cynicism after World War I shocked me because I had been sure that the good was always available if you reached out for it, and, more important, that it was definable, a positive with firm edges.

You lie on your back but the sweat out of your hair still gets in your eyes to make them sting. I haven't been crying. I'm not crying for anyone, not for John, nor for my children, now a few hundred light years away. I'm not going to think about anyone either. Even though it's still far too hot, I'm getting off these poles to do something. There's plenty waiting to be done. I must have a meal ready for John when he gets back. There's nothing to cook, though. He was going hunting today, for pheasant or blue partridge, since I don't mind so much the gutting and preparing of them but can't bear to do it with those mouse-deer he brought in, even though he says the meat is so delicate. I think if we ever get out of this I'm going to become a vegetarian.

If I know him at all he won't come back until nearly sunset, stretching out his absence to a maximum as a way of getting back at me. And then arriving as sweet as the fresh milk we never taste. I won't show my relief when he comes out of the forest. He hasn't any right to it.

*

Ruth put on a kimono to go to her bath, a kind of modesty, as though one of the visiting monkeys might be watching. She remembered buying the thing years before in Yokohama during a half-day stopover of the *Tenyo Maru* en route to San Francisco via Hawaii. John had been with her that time. He always booked on Japanese ships when he could because he liked the politeness, though the food was terrible. It pleased him to come back from a trip ashore and to be met at the top of the gangway by a smiling ship's officer expressing joy that you had honourably and safely returned. John loathed all P. & O. liners, where the food was terrible, too, and all the best cabins were taken up by colonial civil servants who wouldn't dream of playing shuffleboard with anyone who couldn't match their rank. In the dining saloons of the old *Mooldera* or *Rawalpindi*, tin miners who had the impudence to travel first class, instead of down in second with the missionaries where they belonged, found themselves assigned places near the continually swinging doors to the galleys, about as far from the Captain's table as the High Church Anglican believes a non-conformist is from God.

The P. & O. was one of perhaps half a dozen topics on which John could speak for up to fifteen minutes without visibly pausing for breath, and in a very loud voice. Though he had never admitted as much, Ruth was sure that at a tender age he must have been subjected to some soul-searing experience on board one of their ships. It was just as well the Japanese had expanded their passenger services throughout the world, because he wouldn't travel on what he called the frog boats, either; the food might be all right if you liked sauces, but everyone spent all day eating it, and no one talked anything but French, which he considered a dead language.

It could be that the service and politeness — with English spoken, however haltingly — that John had received from the employees of the N.Y.K. Line or their rivals, the Toyo Kissen Kaisha, had deepened his sense of outrage at this war. For years before Pearl Harbour, Ruth had been aware of how he continually made excuses for the Japanese, half-backing up their argument about the need for more living space, and tending to discount as wild exaggerations the atrocity stories coming out of an invaded China. But then they had sunk the *Prince of Wales* and had bombed Pearl Harbour. For John, it had almost been a personal affront, and his rage had held the note of a man somehow betrayed.

Recently, though, there had been a change again, a noticeable tendency to discount the new crop of atrocity stories, this time set in Malaya, that came to them through Hang. It was as though, fugitive in hiding though he might be, he was again beginning to remember those good days on Japanese liners, the cheerful attention of stewards and ship's officers willing to break through formality by showing photographs of their families. The attack on Malaya and the occupation remained an outrage but, once the Japs were whipped and shown their place in the world, it ought to be possible before too long to forgive and forget.

Now they had slapped him in the face again by burning down Estate House. No need to do that, no point in it, just malice. A red sky to the east had advertised that malice and brought John back to a rage from shock. There had been no shock for her; it was almost as if she had been expecting this to happen. For all his apparent calm in refuting her arguments against his going back to Sungei Dema at once, or his total silence over some of them, he had left with that fury still smouldering, making him careless.

She wouldn't think about that. She pulled the kimono tightly about her body and started to walk towards the point of her daily penetration of the jungle, a path leading twenty yards into it to the stream. The kimono was thin, cheap cotton, a blue print on white, and nearly rubbed into holes by the Chinese washerwoman at Sungei Dema; it was so shabby that even John had noticed and brought her a new one, patterned with magenta paeony blossoms, back from Singapore. She had decided that she looked like a tired whore in it. The paeonies had now gone as loot or fuel to a bonfire, while these faded blue flowers were surviving.

The path into the jungle was a tunnel. Fat roots, like dormant snakes, writhed across a track John kept clear by constant hacking with a parang; more than once fecal traces beside it told them that a black panther, or a leopard, had at night used this route to water. John said that in daylight they were perfectly safe but, if she was nervous, she should sing in the tunnel; the sound of a human voice was a guaranteed insurance against animal intrusion, even from one of the big cats. The thought of snakes worried her. John had killed an eight-foot hamadryad at the top of the clearing during their first week in camp, but she had never been challenged on the path, though there were sometimes long rustlings in the flanking undergrowth.

The Sakais had chosen this site for its water, the stream coming fast and clear down a steep gradient. Where they had used it, the flow had cut through soft rock, with no traces of leech-bearing mud; their path led straight onto a broad, flat stone beside a two foot-deep pool alive with bubbles. On that stone Ruth felt safe, as if swirling water on three sides, and its noise, established a neutral zone against the surrounding forest. There was more light here, too, the branches of the trees flanking the stream only loosely meshed, filtering sun to a greenish glow. Towards the end of the day, this spot was much cooler than the campsite, as though the steep stream had some private access to oxygen and brought an extra ration down its course.

Her bath was a rationed luxury, like the soap she took to it only twice a week. John and she used the path to the stream for washing themselves when they woke in the morning and again before sunset, but throughout the day the temptation of that coolness could be even stronger than the devil's voice urging her to switch on the radio. She would stop in the midst of weeding, wet with perspiration, telling herself that in this life disciplines were an idiotic affectation and that she should shake off the last traces of a Puritan ancestry, or whatever it was, and rush down to pour cold water over herself whenever she felt like it. But the disciplines held and the weeding got done, as did the cooking. She even managed to bake twice a week, adapting her recipe for corn bread to a griddle greased with animal fat and put over a fire of green jungle wood from which the sap hissed.

There was something sacred about that bread and the effort needed to produce it. The end product was not very good, but it was evidence of the human animal's uniqueness, a result of staged labour entirely from her hands — the seed planted by her, the ears harvested, the kernels first crunched up on a hallowed stone, then put through a coffee grinder.

She wouldn't let John do anything about their bread; it was her task. He cooked sometimes, after cleaning game. Crouched over a smoking fire, wearing nothing but boots and very dirty shorts, he still looked less like a reversion to primitive man than a business executive weekending in his own garden and demonstrating he could manage a barbecue just as well as his corner of an oil company. The meat always got burned, which he said was the way he preferred it.

After bathing, Ruth sat on the rock like the Copenhagen mermaid except that she had feet that had to be dried, then thrust into the lace-up boots John insisted she always wear about the camp against the snake and scorpion threat. These were of soft kid, a bore to have to do up, but they gave ankle protection and, after his lecture on what they *couldn't* do about snake bite here, she had trained herself to a boots-first rule.

She had put on the kimono and was rinsing the towel when she thought she heard a shout. She straightened and stood listening, waiting for John to call again. What she heard was one word repeated twice.

"Kochi! Kochi!"

Not John!

"KOCHI!"

Japs! She didn't look up the path. Beyond the shallow of the side pool, the stream had gouged a depth that brought it up to John's waist. The water covered her breasts. Her feet slithered on pebbles, the current's strong hands on her ankles. The towel tugged away from her, sodden and heavy, but she wouldn't let it go.

There was a hole in the bank from a recent cave in, like the entrance to an animal's burrow but clawed open by water and still clear of leaf and vine tangle. The huge root of a hardwood, exposed and almost polished by the flow

formed a front ledge. She was squirming up on this, clutching for a hold with one hand, the other still clinging to the
towel, when the first shot was fired.

*

She was unaware of how much time was passing, as though
what was happening at the campsite was sealed inside a capsule around which time flowed, leaving the capsule itself
undisturbed. She didn't know how far she had come into
the jungle from the stream. It might only be yards. The
noise they were making at the clearing reached her, along
with a smell of smoke. More than once there had been voices
coming from the stream bank, but no sounds indicating
that they had crossed the water and were hunting for her on
this side. They didn't want to kill her. They could easily
have done it as she hauled herself up into that hole on the
bank. There had only been two shots, with shouting in between, and a word in English. "Stop!"
    She hadn't stopped, hadn't seen them, never looking back.
She had gone on crawling, torn at by thorns, still with that
towel towed behind, often snagging, yanked at, as though it
were important as extra protection for her body, a second
covering to pull over the worn and ripped kimono. Perhaps
the kimono had stopped their putting a bullet in her back.
Bought in Yokohama. Made in Japan.
    The green light was becoming duller, she thought, regis-
tering the day's ending. Then rain and thunder came in a
drumming assault on the leaf thatch. She made a tent of
the towel, her body a parcel under sodden cloth, knees
drawn up, arms hugging them. She began to shiver. She
watched a scurry of ants big enough to be the menacing war-
riors often seen in her gardens at Sungei Dema, armies of
them, as purposeful as Nazis marching on Moscow. This
was just a small rabble that might have been in disorganized
retreat from a lost battle. She wondered whether ants could
be afraid of thunder.
    She now had no sensation of fear, her terror had been lost
somewhere along the crawl to this hollow. It was like waking from an operation and feeling no pain but knowing that

the drugs would lose their effect and, even before they did, you would find yourself fighting the fear that comes not from the arrival of pain itself, but from uncertainty about what its limits are likely to be, whether those limits will be beyond bearing.

Rain on the jungle roof obliterated the sound of the stream and noise from the campsite. Lightning, until now invisible, pierced the leaf layers as a sustained white flash. Thunder erupted directly over the tree pillars surrounding the hollow. Immunity from feeling was breached.

The Japs had caught John! Why hadn't she thought of this before? They had forced him to give away the position of the campsite. There was no other way they could have got here so quickly. They had come on a compass bearing and would leave it on another, when their work was done.

Leaving her! That was all they had to do. They had burned the camp, she knew that, she could smell it. No food, no shelter, nothing. A woman wearing a kimono with a towel for a tent. The taste in her mouth came from deep in her throat, like a vomit. Thunder crashed down, its postscript of grumbling going on for a long time.

She couldn't stay here. It would be the beginning of a wait for a completely private death, the kind some animals seek, alone in a hollow. She would go back to the campsite, even if the Japs were still there. What else could she do? They had John. There must be some kindness left in them, some kinship with those Japanese on the ships, showing the photographs of their wives and families. They would let her be with John. There had never been any alternative for her but to give herself up if he was captured, the one possibility he wouldn't talk about.

The rain came to one of its sudden, disciplined stops. She took a long breath, then listened. The dripping from the trees covered all other sounds for some time, but finally she heard the noise of the stream, a beacon.

*

She stood at the edge of the campsite. The Japs had gone. There was no need for them to stay. She remembered pictures of Tokyo after the huge earthquake, when nothing was left but smoking ruins. Here there were smoking ruins and a stink. The only thing that still stood was the little hut for the radio set. The door was torn off but its roof was intact. She could see no sense in this. Why was this roof all right while the roof of the Sakai hut in which she and John had lived was flat on the ground, its felting still smoldering. It had been the core of a bonfire onto which everything else had been thrown, including corn stalks and blackened sweet potato plants. The ground where these plants had been growing was left raw from a frenzy of hacking with the instruments she had used to cultivate it. The tools themselves had disappeared, too, along with all traces of pots and cooking utensils. The gramophone had been carefully carried away from the hut, set on the ground well clear of the fire, but an axe had been put throught it. A record was still on the turntable but had been split in half, its paper label projecting out over the wound in the machine. She bent over to read: J. S. Bach. Prelude in E minor.

She walked slowly to the radio hut. The set had been pulled out and given the axe treatment, a butchery of wires and glass tubes. They had left the battery intact under a bench in the hut, as though to mock her with its present uselessness. On the bench where the set had been was a neatly folded pile of clothes. They were her clothes: a shirt, trousers, a cashmere cardigan bought in Singapore and once kept for best. There were shoes, too, at the back, and socks — a little pile of what she might need. On top was a note. She had to take the paper out into the open in order to read it.

Lady,
  Husband now safely capture by Imperial Japanese Forces. He speak to say you come also to him. This he makes as order to dutiful wife. To do as instructed come to Sungei Dema concrete house for waiting in safety Japanese soldier coming. Useless for hiding in jungle is now this place. To stay is to die soon. Have faith in dear mercy of famous Japanese warrior code Bushido as husband now experiences.
                              Signed: Captain Hinomaru Oiishi,
                              Imperial Japanese Army.

It began to rain. She turned into the only shelter available, standing to stare at the pile of clothes. She remembered Aunt Maud saying that the Good Lord never sends us more than we can bear. She put her hands up to her face and pressed her fingers hard against her lips.

FIVE

A sound woke her. She couldn't believe she had slept, her body twisted, partially under the bench. But it was light. An animal was out there, moving amongst the ruins, looking for food. A boot crunched.

A Jap!

The man was shadow filling in the doorway. "Ruth?" he said.

She screamed, unable to keep the sound back, feeling it tear up her throat to break free, not her at all, an identity escaping, like one of those devils cast out in the Bible. She wanted to deny the scream but couldn't. She didn't know the other voice that had said her name, not until he said it again.

"Ruth! Are you? . . ."

He couldn't see her in the near dark made by his body blocking the light. She pushed out one leg and then was freed to name him.

"Hamish!"

He was down beside her. "Ruth, are you hurt?"

"No. I'm all right. I'm fine. You could say I'm fine. . . . Oh, Hamish!"

He caught her arms, pulling her up against him, holding her.

"They left my clothes," she said. "To come to them. And a compass."

"What?"

"The Japs. They've got John. Yesterday. He would go, you see. He would go. Hamish, where did you? . . ."

"Don't try to talk. When did you last eat?"

"I'm not hungry. Not at all. But it must have been yesterday. That's right. Before I went to my bath."

"Come outside. The bottom of that kimono's wet. The sun's up. I'm going to give you some whisky."

He was talking as if to a child. He thought she had no control of herself. But she had. After the scream, she was calm. The devil of terror had gone, after staying with her all night.

"I don't need to be helped," she said. "I'm all right. Just stiff from being cooped up in here. I couldn't stretch out properly. I didn't want to push my legs outside. I was thinking about snakes. John says they come into the clearing because the ground stays warmer here than in the jungle. So we get them at night sometimes. It's like that at Sungei Dema, too."

He was standing again, but back from the opening.

"Ruth!"

He wanted to check her flow of words. He didn't realize what a relief they were. It felt as though she had talked to no one but herself for weeks. She took a deep breath, then spoke very slowly and distinctly, her voice sounding remote from the question it was asking.

"Where have you come from, Hamish?"

"I spent last night at the tent site. I'm with a small party. I left them there."

"And before that?"

"I've been with the guerillas."

"Oh?" She wished he wouldn't stare at her. "You've been there all the time? Since the Japs came?"

"No. I got away to Ceylon. I came back to Malaya a couple of months ago. By submarine."

She pulled herself up by the frame of the door. He didn't try to help her.

"Help me off with this back pack, will you? The whisky's in there."

She was glad he had asked her to do something. He turned around so she could take the pack when he had loosened the webbing holding it to his shoulders. She lowered the heavy weight to the ground, as though its contents were precious to both of them and then, straightening, felt dizzy. He caught her as she swayed. Holding her arm tight he led her to the door that had been torn off the radio hut, making her sit on that.

"This was my garden," she said. "Look at it now. They've got John. There's a note in there. By the clothes they left me. But I've told you. Go in and read it."

He went into the hut. She sat hunched over, staring at the bonfire from which thin little columns of steam still rose in spite of the rain in the night. Beyond the bonfire, against the green wall of the jungle, she tried to picture where John would be this morning as a prisoner. Kuantan, perhaps, in a police station cell. She remembered the building, small and tidy, painted white, the Malay sergeant cultivating flowers in pots outside that made it look more like an inn than a zinc-roofed symbol of the law. The sergeant would either be serving the Japs now, or dead. If they had taken John to the police station, she hoped the sergeant would still be there. She remembered him well. The man would be as kind as his new masters allowed him to be. Did you get food when you were a prisoner of the Japs, or did they starve you to make you talk? But John had talked. He must have done since they had come straight to the clearing.

Hamish came out of the hut. "He'll be all right," he said. "They'll send him to a civilian camp. Probably in Singapore."

"Unless they caught him with his gun. He took it with him."

It was a moment before Hamish said, "Even then."

"I'm going to him. Like the note tells me to."

Hamish didn't answer. He opened a back flap on the pack and drew out a flask.

"Funny sort of breakfast," he said. "I used to do this on hangover mornings in K.L."

She took the flask, unscrewed the cap, then sipped. She felt the warmth of the whisky in her throat and was grateful. The night had been cold.

"We've been teetotal," she said. "Harder for John than

for me. He had ideas about making a banana rum, but I wouldn't let him try. We needed our wits about us all the time. The temptation would have been to lose them. You think I'm talking too much, don't you?"

He said nothing, digging into the pack. It was better to have him bent over doing that than staring at her, as though he couldn't quite believe what he saw. She was looking awful, of course. Her hair had gone lank from those soapless washes in hard stream water. She never looked in the mirror as she combed it, but her fingers told her it was like dried-out corn silk. He must have noticed her hands, too. They looked as though they would never recover from years spent scrubbing floors. Bent over that big pack, he might only be pretending to hunt for something lost in it, needing time to come to accept that the woman sitting on a torn-off door was the Ruth Gourlay he had once known, sure of herself most of the time, ready to bully him when she thought he needed it.

She knew suddenly that he had come to the clearing expecting to find no traces that anyone had lived here recently, John and she either dead or long since captured. His shock at seeing her curled up inside the little hut had been even greater than hers at seeing him. Whatever he was in Malaya to do, part of his duty as he would see it was to come here to establish what had happened to Ruth and John Gourlay, and the last thing he had been expecting was to be landed with her alone to look after. Well, he wasn't going to have to do that.

"Got it," he said, pulling something out of the haversack.

He was squatting down, sitting on his heels like a Tamil, thigh muscles able to push him straight to his feet while his hands were occupied. His body, like an animal's, had stayed young not from any specific training but from constant use. Except for malaria she couldn't remember his ever being ill. He said that when you had had a hungry boyhood you could adapt to anything afterwards, and that he had adapted to Malaya. He only drank when he went down to K.L. every month or six weeks. Being social meant that you got drunk. He had been an awkward guest at Estate

House dinner parties, long silences punctuated by his suddenly launching forth on a long story that had little relevance to the general talk. This abrupt thrusting forward of his own identity only served to underline his complete indifference to visitors to Sungei Dema, almost as though he was determined to let them see that they were aliens at the mine and the sooner they moved on the better. Here, in a burned-out clearing that was like a setting for madness, he was establishing a weird kind of norm for her, giving her back strength and doing it by silence. What he offered wasn't a kindness that would have taxed her by requiring gratitude in return.

The pack contained some kind of emergency ration. He began handing her things to eat. She put them in her mouth and chewed, tasting nothing. She felt it was urgent he understand that what he was doing for her now had nothing to do with assuming responsibility for her. She swallowed something dry that stuck in her throat and, though she wasn't choking, she took the flask when he passed it over again, having more than a sip this time.

"I'm going to John," she said. "After this. When I've dressed in those clothes the Japs left me."

"No, you're not." He wasn't looking at her.

"How will you stop me?"

"I won't. Angus will."

PART
SIX

ONE

October 12 At Sea.

It has been a pretty hairy two days. With route-to-rendezvous left up to me, I decided to keep *Romulus* hugging the Sumatra coast as near as depth allowed, then to cross the Straits to Malaya when we were dead opposite said R.V. at Pulau Klang. What I didn't know, and H.Q. at Trinco couldn't have known either, was that the Japs appear to have given up using Malacca as their destroyer patrol base, moving this across water to the big bay just south of Panipahan on Sumatra. This meant we were practically sailing into it before coming about N.E. for a night surface crossing to rendezvous. Radar had spotted a plane coming up from due south and I had ordered a crash dive just as the straight line of a moonlit horizon was broken by black ship hulls. We were lucky in that before the dive we were under cloud and they hadn't spotted us; apparently they were out on a routine patrol. Their asdic must have told them about us; we were depth-charged, but never at anything like range; all we got was a bang on the hull like someone badly wanting in. That was 2200 hours on the 10th. Just after 1200 hours yesterday, we surfaced about forty miles off the Malayan coast and twenty north of R.V. point, again having to dive from a Jap destroyer patrol, charging down from the north this time. Heat haze hid us and though, when we were on the shallow bottom, their asdic must have pinged loud and clear we didn't even rate one depth charge. Probably assessed as a wreck. We hope they go on doing that. However, one thing is pretty clear. The Japs are as jumpy as hell in this area. They must know that small-party infiltrations into Malaya from subs are going on, and have orders to stop us.

Yesterday we were depth-charged again when two hundred down and cruising at four knots. A sudden attack, no warning. It turned into a lot more than someone's banging on the hull, left us feeling the rivets were about to start popping. We were in the wider and deeper waters between Penang and Medan, with at least four destroyers up there operating a grid pattern of depth-charging that was probably something we taught them in joint exercises just after World War I. They didn't seem to have learned the lesson too well; only three of the misses rated near. But these were nasty enough. Moments when you know that you didn't give the business of becoming a submariner deep enough thought. With all the activity in these waters it looks to me as though the Japs are expecting some kind of sea-bourne assault on Malaya at any time. If they do, it shows their espionage infiltration into British High Command India must be absolutely nil. Concentrations for something like that would take months of buildup, and there are damn all signs of anything remotely like that starting to happen.

Not a statement a Wavy Navy sub commander should be putting in his journal. He shouldn't be keeping a journal, full stop. I wonder if you appreciate, Sally, that in doing this mainly for you I'm running the risk of having His Majesty's Lords of Admiralty hang me up by the ears. And don't say, when you read this, that the risk to you as a W.A.A.F. was just as great. It wasn't. Compared with ours, your Air Force discipline is bloody slack, especially for the girls. Anyway, risks aside, I still think it's the only sensible way to maintain a relation like ours in wartime or, what I really mean is, to give it a chance to survive the war. Letters in which all the censor lets you say is I love you over and over are a bit off key for two people living pretty active and very separate lives. Forgive my saying this, but they're particularly inappropriate for a girl like you to write just before she goes out to dinner with some six-foot-two U.S. bomber pilot fresh from Texas training. No, the journal's the thing. We'll make a small ceremony of our handing them to each other for a good long read to fill in the missing years — that is, of course, if the old glow starts up when and if we do meet again. If it doesn't we've still got these journals to hand to someone else.

The old glow hits me at weird times, rarely when appropriate, as, say, when we're running along on the surface over a moon-white sea with a star-spangled wake of phosphorescence stretched out for a mile behind us like a visual call sign to the Japs. I know that's when I should be thinking of you, but it's usually when Service Food, particularly the food on this ship, starts up my peptic ulcer and, to be quite honest, that's when I tend to belch into the night from the conning tower. Also, from evidence available of inner reaction to those moments when the next depth charge could really rip open our hull, I don't think that my last thoughts, if it has to come to that so soon, will be of you, love. They'll be of Dick. Wondering why the sodding hell he ever allowed himself to be sealed away in a tin cylinder lying on the bottom of the ocean.

But if you ever see this, it hasn't come to that, has it? Which makes my candour unnecessary. I still think it's right, in a journal written with the idea of being read only by the loved one. And it's my hope that you're being just as honest, so that I won't find myself wrapped up in trying to work out, from between your lines, whether or not you ever did go down to a barbed-wire barricaded Brighton with that beautiful fellow from Texas.

When does the old glow most often hit me? I hate to say this, particularly as a Lieutenant Commander on active service, but the answer is usually during lustful dreams. And I'm not always fully asleep then, either. There is something deeply sensuous about the bump-bump of a sub's engines when you are lying in a narrower-than-coffin bunk in the broom-cupboard-sized Commanding Officer's cabin. So now you know what kind of a beast I am in my private moments, if you didn't already from past experience. At my school we were taught that the decent chap sublimates lust by beautiful thoughts. Or rugger. Or both. None of us believed it for one moment.

Another time the glow tends to hit me is when I'm in the company of those who bore the underpants off me, almost invariably those of superior rank; the tendency towards being boring increases as the rank does. In spite of the open arms with which us Reserve temporaries were apparently welcomed into the Senior Service there is a game the Regulars play with us that could be called "I say, Willie, do you remember that night with Pongo in the Seychelles in '36?" The point of the game being that I have never been in the Seychelles and Pongo is now the kind of Captain who would cut me dead at a reunion dinner. Maybe I joined this branch because in a sub, especially in one as small as *Romulus,* the percentage of Regulars on board is certain to be low. On this ship they are entirely confined to Ratings, except for our sub-Lieutenant Haskins, who intends to survive this war, stay on in the Service, and end up as a sea lord sagging to one side from all the medals worn over that part of his chest. He'll do it, too, if he doesn't have a heart attack too early; he never puts a foot wrong. And he's keen. God, he's keen.

I was talking about the glow lit between us, Sally my love. Sally who is in all probability not at this moment disciplining herself to the kind of total faithfulness that I tried so hard to groom her to accept as something we Paresons absolutely demand in our women. And I believe, that quite aside from the Americans, the Old Country is now stiff with Poles clicking their heels and exuding total maleness, or something. I have a feeling the heel clicking might get you. Why did I have to start glowing for someone who looks like you do when what I really need is a plain, sensible girl of the right background who would bring me a plump parcel of money and think it tremendously jolly to spend her postwar life dedicated not only to me but to that bloody great house I've inherited? She'd be ready as well to produce a minimum of four new Paresons to carry on the line — preferably six, which would give us a margin for accidents. I can't see your producing six Paresons. More likely you'd baulk at the first. And you've no money, either, which would be needed to fix an acre and a half of eighteenth-century roofs.

But I glow for you. It's on me now, here in my marine broom cupboard.

*

October 14 At Sea.

It is thirty-seven hours after rendezvous time. I feel bloody about that. In operations of this kind no one expects to keep to schedules, but even allowing for the fact that the men we're picking up must have seen the destroyer patrols rushing up and down past their island, not to mention air sorties by those low-flying Jap seaplanes with bombs pinned under their wings, there comes a time, if you're waiting under palm trees behind a beach, when you really begin to wonder if the pickup has been called off. And with no notification. Not that there is any way that this lot could be notified, since they won't have their radio now. I can see them, getting eyestrain peering out over a night sea before moonrise, looking for the darker shape of a surfacing *Romulus,* and with more than a tiny pea of a thought that we aren't coming swelling into something near hatred.

It would be a lot easier for me if I hadn't landed this party in Malaya, didn't know any of them, particularly didn't know Hamish. He sat in this cabin with me two nights after we left Trinco, using the folding seat while I was up on the bunk. The bottle of whisky he had brought on board passed between us, but mostly it stayed with him, Hamish a refugee from the company of his C.O. He said that a submarine was no place for him to be in with his Major, that it was bad enough in the open air. Before that we had identified each other as what we both are, service temporaries living through a war on the hope of seeing the day when we can hand in our uniforms and say thanks very much for any medals we may have accidentally earned, but we don't really have any use for them now, either.

I have to decide within the next half-hour whether it's tonight that I take *Romulus* out of our mangrove estuary here on Sumatra for the run across the Straits to Klang. The moon is just a new sliver, which means that on the surface we'd spot destroyer searchlights long before they picked us up, and the Japs go in for a lot of lighting. But it's the seaplanes that worry me most. I've no clue where they're based, but they can come out from behind a promontory or island with practically nil warning, and at only a hundred feet above water, the pilot throwing out float flares that will be illuminating the sea nicely for his rapid about-face return flight. Which could make us a sitting target off Klang island. Even if there was time to dive, we have only about ten fathoms to dive in off R.V. point. Malay's west coast is no area for effective sub operations, as Navy H.Q. at Trinco has pointed out to Southeast Asia Command more than once, only to be told to shut up. The Senior Service in these parts doesn't seem to be getting the respect it's used to, maybe because military brass see our record of effectiveness as somewhat wanting.

So that's my problem as we sit here with all hatches open. Below decks the ship's giving off an oil reek that could be her plates sweating the stuff. I take *Romulus* over to Klang and we get split open by Jap bombs and I'm that part-time sailor who lost his ship when any half-fool Regular would have known automatically that the odds didn't allow him to expose her to that risk. If I don't go, I'm a gutless Wavy Navy number who skipped the action and came running home to base with excuses. Over the last few days, too, I've had a strong feeling that nineteen-year-old sub-Lieutenant Haskins is logging every order I issue as a reference for what *not* to do when he gets his first command. I know he thinks I'm on too easy terms with the Ratings, that unless they feel that their Old Man is at least half a bastard discipline gets slack. I don't think I'd care for Haskins's kind of Navy much, not that I really care for this one all that much either. One of my troubles is that I have never really loved ships, particularly submarines. I don't believe they have identities to which you can respond with affection, which is another reason why I could never be part of the Great Tradition.

*

October 15 At Sea.

Operation Klang has gone like one of those beautiful

dreams I can't remember having had since I was about ten: as though all the good fairies no one told me had been gathered around my cradle on Day One had met up for a reunion and organized everything. I had that sensation of events taken largely out of my hands, steered by a higher authority that knew exactly what it was doing. It's a lovely feeling, and I wish I could have it often.

First we surfaced halfway over into one of those tropical upheavals they call a sumatra in these parts: wind, thunder, lightning, and rain; the kind of weather conditions that low-flying seaplanes really don't like. And just as we might have prayed it would, the storm lasted much longer than they usually do. The finger on the radar screen kept flicking over a clean disc, with never a hint on its pure surface of the kind of blip we very much didn't want. The two problems we had coming in to Klang Island were, one, quite a heavy sea running and, two, identifying the exact position of a beach I had last seen under hazy moonlight. Lightning came to our rescue from its nest in a solid lump of black cloud, a bolt forked at the end like an eagle's claw. Though we were then opposite mangrove, I recognized a bluff of rock pushing up through the swampy stuff and then our stretch of sand just beyond. We moved the ship down on reversed props. I did the flashlight signalling from the conning tower myself and in about five minutes there was an answering flash from the palms. After that the code word.

I assigned Haskins as C.O. the rubber boat with one Rating to work the outboard, knowing that I could count on our sub-Lieutenant to do the correct thing, whatever that is, on the lifting of military bods from behind the enemy lines. Also, he was the man in our command group I could most easily afford to lose if suddenly we had to abandon the mission in a crash dive. But the power was working for Haskins, too. It allowed him to beach the rubber boat, lead her up — with more flashing of light than I cared for — then put to sea again.

I went down onto the whaleback to help my passengers aboard. *Romulus* was heaving about. There was a lot of spray, and some solid wet, but we managed to haul them all

up over slubbery plates. I was surprised by one "thank you,"
a woman's voice, and American. The boy who came after
her said nothing.

*

October 17 At Sea.

The charmed life of *Romulus* continues. It is almost
weird. I'm not really sure why I decided to do what is the
last thing one is supposed to do with subs: expose them to
maximum risk from attack by staying in shallow water. I
certainly didn't have any very deep water in the Straits of
Malacca as an alternative, but to more or less hug the Malayan coast as we did, with an average of fifteen to twenty
fathoms in which to manouevre, was asking for death if attacked. My instinct said we were less at risk doing this than
we would be out in the main channel where the Japs would
expect us to be on a return run to base in Ceylon. I had, as
well, a feeling that they would learn about our pickup soon
after it happened and be hunting for us. It might even be
that they had deliberately allowed the pickup in order to
pinpoint *Romulus* and destroy her as we tried to escape
from the shallows of the Straits into the depths of the An-
daman Sea. So I hugged the coast. The one time we surfaced,
skirting the Sembilan Islands, there was depth charging going on just over the horizon to port of us.

Like most sailors in these waters, I'm chronically suspicious of our charts, but so far we have not been let down and
a relatively deep anchorage promised in the sheltered bay of
a small island just north of the Malaya-Siam border turned
out to be there all right, offering just what is needed — a
rest before we start our night surface run for deep water and
ultimately a passage through the Sombrero Channel between the Nicobars. Though we ought to be well clear of
any threat from seaplanes, I'm being very prudent; we're taking our rest at five fathoms in shadowed water, lying on a
sandy bottom, and with most on board in their bunks, those
that have them. Five passengers make *Romulus* feel pretty
crowded, especially when the air circulating isn't fresh. I
gave the wardroom to Mrs. Gourlay and her grandson, the

sofa for her, the boy sleeping on the deck under the table. Hamish is in here with me in the sleeping bag he took ashore at Klang. The thing's been subjected to pretty intensive use since, which makes it pretty smelly. I think being in a submarine gives him claustrophobia he has to fight all the time. I've had the feeling myself, though it's not chronic.

Mrs. Gourlay I've scarcely talked to. She stays in the wardroom with the curtain drawn over the door, as though she feels her duty now is to keep out of everyone's way. The boy stays with her. I don't know whether she is making him do that, or he wants to. I was expecting to have to put parts of the ship out of bounds to him, but there's no question of that. There wasn't a peep out of them when twice, while running on the surface north of Penang Island, we had to go into crash dives away from aircraft appearing on the radar. The drill for them was to stay in the wardroom and they did just that. When passing the curtain, I've yet to hear either of those two talking to each other.

I think all the party are suffering from the kind of mental exhaustion from sustained stress that takes a lot longer to get over than physical fatigue. Apparently Hudson and Kneale spend most of their time sleeping, not eating much. One of the Ratings living aft with them said the two just lie there like a couple of stiffs ready for their weighted sacks. I got it from Hamish, politely answering my questions, that their trip across Malaya was rugged. Three times they thought they had been betrayed to the Japs, often having to hide from patrols. Once, needing to use a bridge over a swollen river, Hamish killed the Jap sentry guarding it. He had to do the job at almost point-blank range, sneaking up behind the man. Nothing impersonal about that kind of killing. Something you remember. I think he's remembering it.

The boy's story is decidedly patchy. I get the feeling that Hamish is operating as censor there, that there is considerably more to it than he is prepared to tell me or anyone. I asked how the boy got off Singapore Island after the surrender and Hamish said he managed that the way the Gourlay males manage most things, by using someone else, in his case a P.O.W. on the run. Later it was some portrait painter still in his house on the Malayan coast and finally the British mistress of a Jap General who took the boy in and saw that he got three square meals and two clean shirts a day. For all her trouble, she got the bullets when the General's car was attacked by guerillas, pushing the boy down on the floor while she stayed up as target. The only damage to him were thorn scratches from a jungle trek later.

Hamish sounds as though recent experience has dried him out emotionally. I've had mild attacks of the condition myself, but you get over them. Meanwhile, though, he has opted out, at least for the duration of this voyage. All he seems to want to do is lie on top of that smelly bedroll with his eyes shut, though I don't think he's doing much sleeping. I think when they get him back to base on Ceylon he's going to be pretty bloody-minded at question and answer sessions with the red tabs, not giving two damns when they threaten him with a course at one of these new psychiatric reconditioning units.

*

October 20 At Sea.

Last night, at 2300 hours, we were precisely five hundred and seven nautical miles from the nearest point on the coast of Malaya. The 2100 hours since then have put us well out into the Indian Ocean, with less than eight hundred still to go to base at Trinco. If tension on the *Romulus* hasn't exactly switched off, it has eased quite a few notches, most of us in the mildly euphoric state that comes immediately after the removal of stress. A kind of joy.

I was already feeling this last night while we were still on the wrong side of the passage through the Nicobar Islands and within the possible range of Jap fighter bombers based on Trang airfield in the Kra Isthmus. I think what started to give me back the confidence the commanding officer is supposed to feel all the time, but doesn't, was the knowledge of the depth of water under us. You wouldn't think that a submariner would be much cheered by the fact that if anything goes wrong with his ship it will sink ten thousand feet before hitting bottom, but the real bogey to subs, as also to whales, are the shallow seas in which we can't do properly the thing for which we were built: dive. On the approach to the Sombrero Channel through the Nicobars, I had seven teen hundred fathoms under me. I could only use a mod erate number of those fathoms at the top of a sea hole but it is still a good feeling to know that you have all that room in which to manoeuvre. Also, depth charges had all that vast space in which to miss us and get lost.

Romulus was running on the surface, ten knots steady, only a new moon but very bright supported by gleaming, fat stars. Little Nicobar was almost dead ahead, a dark lump on the horizon, like a ship in wartime blackout. There was the possibility of a Jap destroyer somewhere in the area, but we know they weren't using the islands as even a subsidiary base, because all the anchorages were too exposed to attack. Also, if they were still looking for us the natural place for them to be doing this was in the Great Channel much farther to the south. So my confidence was okay and getting better all the time.

I was taking the watch, up on the conning tower alone, the only real niggle of discomfort brought on by a feeling that this was the kind of night that put too high a shine on our wake, the V stretching back for a couple of miles. Phosphorescence was particularly pretty up at the sub's blunt bows; the glittering waves were being folded back in neat, smooth ridges. A N.W. wind earlier had dropped to be replaced by sporadic breezes coming scudding in speckled patches across a flattened out sea. When they reached me I could smell the land in them. The Nicobarese are great fishermen, but there were none of their boats where you would expect to see them, as though war made them furtive, as it does us all.

Mrs. Gourlay's voice was a complete surprise. I hadn't heard her on the ladder.

"Is this place as sacred as the bridge on a ship?"

I told her it was more so since you had to be specially trained to get off it fast in a crash dive, but that I'd make an exception in her case. I helped her up through the hatch.

She went and stood with her hands on the rail, looking towards the Nicobars, breathing deeply for about a minute before she asked whether I had a special feeling for subs. When I said no, she said that coming up from below was like coming up from a tomb, and she wasn't being rude about the hospitality she had received on board. I said to get the real feeling of coming out of a tomb you needed to have been depth-charged for a couple of hours before being able to open that hatch into fresh air.

We then had quite a spell of what couldn't be called companionable silence in that she mightn't have been there at all and when she did speak, though it was a simple enough question, it somehow sounded forced.

"Have you been in this part of the world for long, Commander?"

I didn't think it was an invitation for me to give a potted history of my war so all I said was that I had been based on Trinco since before Pearl Harbour. She turned her head to me suddenly as though she had heard what she had hoped to. Probably I should have been ready for her next question. Hamish had warned me she might ask it. But I wasn't.

"Commander, can you remember, was the *Ming Kai* one of the refugee ships from Singapore that the Japs sank?"

I think I came up with my answer fast enough, but it was pretty horrible being stared at in the moonlight as I produced it. I said I couldn't recall a ship of that name being lost.

I don't know what she saw in my face, but she didn't challenge the lie, turning her head to look at Little Nicobar. She was still looking at the island when she said, "I suppose if there were survivors of those ships the Japs would have them in camps somewhere?"

I rose to that, like a bloody fool. I said I'd heard of camps in Java for those survivors. She looked at me again. I knew she had nailed my lie.

Maybe another woman would have wept. Maybe she is too tired for tears, I don't know. All I know is that I've betrayed Hamish by letting out something he was keeping from her. His idea was to tell her in Ceylon, after she'd had

a rest. He would have to tell her by then to stop her en-
quiries to Australia.

I haven't told Hamish about this. I'll do it tomorrow.
He'll curse me.

Mrs. Gourlay stayed up top for at least another half-hour.
It felt a lot longer. She began talking again, and I had the
feeling it was for my sake, neutral stuff about how she could
never see tropical seas as a setting for violence. You could
imagine war in the cold Atlantic or the Med, but somehow
never in these waters. Maybe it wasn't neutral sutff, maybe
it stemmed from what was in her heart, but her voice was
steady, controlled. She said she had missed the sea while
living at the Gourlay mine.

After that, I think she was waiting for me to say something that would put some kind of cover on what had passed
between us, but I couldn't. So she decided to do it herself,
starting up on a new tack, about how Hamish was sure that
when the Japs were thrown out of Malaya there would be
fighting in the country between the guerillas and the British.
This seemed to give me my cue. I asked if she would be going back.

"For some of the Gourlays there's only one place to live,"
she said. "Malaya. It's that way for my husband and my eldest son. And now my grandson, too. He didn't miss the *Ming
Kai* by accident. He meant to." She turned towards the
hatch. "Yes, I'll be going back. Could I have your hand
again, Commander? To help me onto the first rungs of that
iron ladder?"